Locus Solus

Locus Solus

MARK AMERIKA

COUNTERPATH DENVER 2014

Counterpath
Denver, Colorado
www.counterpathpress.org

Library of Congress Cataloging-in-Publication Data

Amerika, Mark.
Locus Solus / Mark Amerika.
pages cm
Includes bibliographical references and index.
ISBN 978-1-933996-48-6 (pbk. : alk. paper)
1. Literature, Experimental. I. Roussel, Raymond, 1877–1933. Locus solus. II. Title.
PS3551.M37L63 2014
813'.6—dc23 2014034095

Contents

All language is but a poor translation. —Franz Kafka[1]

What must be translated of that which is translatable can only be the untranslatable. —Jacques Derrida[2]

1. Starting with a Kafka quote seems most appropriate to me in that it captures something unique about the writing process I immersed myself in while composing [translating / performing] this work. Was it not also Kafka who once wrote that "[art's] capacity lies in finding in the dark void a place where the beam of light can be intensely caught, without this having been perceptible before"? This work is not so much a novel as it is an experimental work of *process art*, something I'm quite comfortable with, especially given the ways that much of my practice relates to *duration*. The artist Tony Conrad, whose work also experiments with duration, has written: "Phenomenologically, duration is the inverse of memory: duration bespeaks continuing presence."

2. Derrida appears everywhere in my mistranslations, remixes, novels, hypertexts, sound experiments, etc. In fact, a Derridean filter was what initially launched my stylistic tendencies in *GRAMMATRON* [http://www.grammatron.com], although I put it to good use in some of my earlier work as well. One concept that Derrida explores and that crossed my mind while immersing myself in the auto-translation / remix process with *Locus Solus*, is *chora*. According to Derrida, chora "receives everything or gives place to everything." He continues:

> Since it is absolutely blank, everything that is printed on it is automatically effaced. It remains foreign to the imprint it receives; so in as sense, it does not receive anything—it does not receive what it receives nor does it give what it gives. Everything inscribed erases itself immediately, while remaining in it.

As an artist who uses theory as primary source material for his various remix performances, I read the Derrida quote above and try to relate it to the process of auto-translating / remixing Roussel. For example, it's impossible for me to read Derrida's riff on chora and not think about Mallarmé, especially his *Un coup de dés jamais n'abolira le hasard*. As part of the auto-translation process, I intentionally open myself up to a chance throw of the verbal dice and specifically open myself up to how Roussel's text, however I receive it, subsequently triggers my marks on to the blank white page or, in this case, the more fluid screenal interface that appears as a virtual slate whose hexadecimal configuration reads #ffffff. (For more on the use of Mallarmé as source material for my artwork, see my interactive tablet application, *Crapshoot*).

Whereas the name *Locus Solus* can be translated as solitary or unique place, looking back on the four-month performance translating the work, a Mallarméan echo reverberates in the background, reminding me that "nothing will have taken place but the place," that is to say, *the always already unique place for writing itself to take place*. This "place" reverberates throughout my auto-translation as a site of remixological inhabitation. The experience of auto-translating / remixing Roussel never felt solitary in the conventional sense of that term. Even though I had no idea where I—or the story—was going, I never felt isolated. If anything, the auto-translation / remix process felt undeniably *social* in nature. Within a short period of time, the overriding sensibility could be described as *inter-* or *trans-subjective*.

It would be impossible for me to broach the dual subjects of Derridean chora and Mallarméan place without being reminded of the concept *choragraphy*, which was first introduced to me by my former undergraduate professor at the University of Florida, Gregory Ulmer:

> Choragraphy is a practice, using image categories, to reason with the Internet as a dynamic whole (the same relationship rhetoric and conceptual topics have with the library as a whole). Chora is to electracy what topic is to literacy—the organizing "space" and practice through which rhetoric relates living memory to artificial memory. It is the relation of region to place. Literate topics include collections of interrelated commonplaces plus operating procedures for generating a text on that topic. Choras gather multiple topics associated with a geographical region into a scene whose coherence is provided by an atmosphere or *Stimmung*. This atmosphere or mood is an emergent quality resulting in an unforeseeable way from the combination of topics interfering and interacting with one another.

For me, this unique place or "scene of coherence" is not solitary in the conventional sense of an imaginary enclosure for an isolated figure, the lone writer, to tap into their genius as a way to express their inspired vision. Rather, I assume this *Stimmung* will have taken place as an artificially created mood, one where an unconscious, remixological apparatus that has any number of useful filtering effects at its disposal, and that intersubjectively jams (with) the transmission process itself, makes its writerly presence felt. Therefore, when I use the term *auto-translation*, I am not just referring to the online programs I used to serve up mangled English renderings of Roussel's original text in French. My goal was never to faithfully weave together a narrative out of whatever words the auto-translation program gave me, but to track my own performance as an artist living in the world, someone who operates in simultaneous and continuous auto-affect mode, remixing whatever experiential data I happen to be circulating in, something I discuss more fully in *remixthebook* and in the opening "Spontaneous Theories" section of *META/DATA: A Digital Poetics*.

It should also be noted that Ulmer was working on his book *Applied Grammatology* when I was taking avant-garde theory courses taught by him in the early 1980s and that he also supervised my undergraduate honors thesis. Those classes were unique places of *choragraphical practice* before I even knew what everyone was up to.

1

Pullulation[3]

Her invitation was to a large property that goes by the name Locus Solus[4]

3. I'm trying to remember where this word came from and why I decided to start the translation with it. It's certainly nowhere to be found in Roussel's *Locus Solus*, at least as far as I know (and let's keep in mind that I really don't know much of anything about Roussel's original text since I do not speak, read, or write in French nor have I ever read any translation of Roussel's work). It must have something to do with Marcel Duchamp, as in "Cops pullulate, Copley copulates," which is a direct puncept from Duchamp himself (and no, I'm not pointing to its original appearance in a specific text he wrote about his cross-dressing alter-ego, Rrose Sélavy). My guess is that the word itself is suggestive of germination, of sprouting up, and this appealed to me because I imagined that by starting with this one word, before even getting into the auto-translation and subsequent remix performance, I would, in a sense, be seeding another project that I would put *inside the green box*. I'm also attracted to the idea of a swarming text, a field teeming with text, a durational achievement that rapidly breeds text out of text out of text ad infinitum.

Now would be a good time to also note that the reason this entire project started, that is, the attempt to read and eventually auto-translate Roussel, was because the big project I am presently working on, *Inside the Green Box*, is a transmedia investigation of Duchamp's *La mariée mise à nu par ses célibataires, même (Le Grand Verre)* and Duchamp had clearly indicated that Roussel's work heavily influenced the creation of his *glass* (see below). In many ways, my own work is a *glas* of the glass by way of Roussel (and back again).

4. Already I have no idea where I'm going with this. Her, who? But the thought crosses my mind that she will not be the same "her" that Roussel has proposed. How could she be? I am a different [her] than [he] could ever be, writerly.

It's at Locus Solus that one of The Massive's[5] most accomplished ringleaders, a flickering avatar named Camera[6], is located year-round, surrounded by an array of followers who are passionately committed to the discovery of innovative uses of language across the media spectrum

The villa at Locus Solus contains fifteen luxuriously furnished rooms that are also media labs, connecting the various guests to different interfaces that continuously reveal The Massive in all its networked glory[7]

Like the avatar they have all come to see and be with, the visitors who pass through this storied property are known to devote their every waking and dreaming hour to the material difficulties raised during all phases of productive communication, and most feel obliged to articulate these struggles in creative artworks and theoretical assignments that often verge on the absurd

Camille's arrival was uneventful and at first she hid herself under the old oak trees just inside the entrance to the property

The shade provided by the stand of oaks enveloped one of the smaller edifices designated for more precise clusters of participants who could, if they wished and if necessary, gather for a quick meal

5. The concept of *The Massive* came quickly but as you will see, it did not last long. Still, I think there's quite a bit of potential to develop a more sci-fi angle to this remix, one that takes into account The Network or what others have variously called the matrix, cyberspace, or even the electrosphere. *This* cover version of *Locus Solus* is being played in virtual reality, no doubt.

6. Not everyone will be particularly pleased with the name Camera. The more obvious choice would be Cameron and, in fact, one of the online translation programs kept referring to the protagonist as Cameron. I chose Camera intuitively but I also like its near-anagrammatical relationship to Amerika [kamera+I] as well as the fact that I see the lead character as being a kind of obsessed film director (as well as inventor, intermedia installation artist, writer, scientist, alchemist, etc.). At heart, I could not help but imagine Camera as an overall freak, perhaps an alter-ego of an even freakier Roussel, and given the nature of the narrative and my role in translating it, as well as my own literary history of creating outsider personae, I embraced the idea of further corrupting the already-corrupt(ible).

7. Make no mistake about it: my initial lines of translation are really more pseudo-autobiographical in nature than any real desire to maintain an allegiance to what I imagine is the Roussel text whatever language it's written in. "The Massive in all its networked glory" as well as guest rooms that double as media labs feeds into my imaginary, utopian vision of a kind of Black Mountain College focused on new media forms of art and writing. I ride this angle for as long as the original and its auto-translation will let me.

After all of the invited participants had finally arrived and were congregating near the oaks, the master of ceremonies, appearing as if in auto-affective avatar mode, began to project his warm and persuasive voice, which Camille immediately found herself attracted to[8]

It was as if purity, clarity, and simplicity had merged into a vocal intonation that would rip her rigid preconditioning to shreds[9]

After the short welcoming speech, everyone started following the leader up a very steep, sloping driveway

The higher everyone walked, the more the gift of a coastal scene, off in the distance, was wonderfully revealed

The walk uphill continued and soon the group came upon a deep stone niche—containing a strange statue that seemed almost lava-like in its loose

8. I'll let others psychoanalyze why I chose the name Camille and why she's already magnetized to the semi-creepy protagonist we'll follow throughout this story (yes, the young French actress in my feature-length film, *Immobilité*, is named Camille and it's possible I saw her starring in this role too, but the idea of seeing one star in an auto-translation being transmitted over the Network would need to be investigated further). It's important to keep in mind, though, that I personally find it crucial for the networked artist of the early 21st century to resist the defeatist retreat back into the ready-to-be-psychoanalyzed 'self' per se while seeding new forms and tempos of life itself. Fortunately, for Roussel, he was pre-Freudian, so he too (like those of us who resist Freud), could let it all hang out without fearing the repercussions.

9. The phrase "rip her" indicates where this first chapter is going. It's much more psychosexual than any other chapter in my version of the book, even those later chapters that dip into necrophilia. This heightened state of pornosophy probably has something to do with why this book was started in the first place. Besides the fact that I wanted to remix Roussel as a way to further my reading of Duchamp's *Large Glass*, there is the banal reality of my own day to day existence and how it plays into the first chapter of this book. You see, I had been called for jury duty and, to my utter surprise, actually found myself selected for a four-day trial (this is in early February, 2013). The trial itself was a low-brow porno story featuring "white trash" characters whose lives were so different than my own that by the time I got home, I needed something more intense than a stiff drink (though that helped too). My response to the banality of the trial and the parade of in-your-face unreliable narrators who took the stand was to just start auto-translating Roussel's *Locus Solus*, line by line, for as long as I could before I was too exhausted to continue. As the translation developed, images of the trial would seep into my active remix process and I would attempt to deflect those images by focusing more intensely on the translation. Little did I know that *Locus Solus* itself would also introduce me to an alternative cast of oddball characters that I would at times feel as though I were creating out of thin air.

black formation but that, on closer inspection, revealed a smiling naked child with an arm stretched forward in a gesture of offering; but what was it offering?

A small dead plant merged with the slow-forming dilapidation that the child embodied and where the frozen gesture had taken root

Camera absentmindedly led the way as if the visitors were just ghost figures trailing his meditative thoughts, but he still had to answer their unanimous questions

"Think of it as *semen-contra* shot into the heart of Shangri-La," he said to no one in particular, pointing to the stone child as if magically conjuring it into the material world[10]

* * *

Camera was intimately aware of the presence of the nomadic travelers trailing him and imagined that their entire lives were being composed as works of art devoted to various and rhythmical expeditions that would eventually lead them to this transitory Shangri-La he was taking them to

Forever morphing current and future bibliographies, covering regions of thought still in formation and often self-cited by these utopian explorers, were circulating in The Massive even as the group continued its slightly strenuous climb up the sloping driveway

Whether this potentially life-affirming, fictional alter-world nestled within a hidden code secretly scripted inside The Massive's quantified lifestyle parameters was ever truly discoverable is not our concern, or so Camera suggested in quite different words than those just translated—and in his case, uttered among the deep breaths and grunts of the group as they continued their collective pace upward

"What you will soon find is that—" and here Camera hesitated, before moving on

"What you will find is that what matters is precisely the formal renderings contained in the fruits of your memory as you taste the enigmatic appearance of thought's imaginative potential—especially as it becomes revealed in your distant minds while wandering"

10. The term *semen-contra* immediately struck a chord, one that had less to do with the porno narrative I was listening to in the courtroom every day and more to do with what I imagined to be *Duchamp's reading of Roussel*, although by this time, I was not at all certain how or why.

After some not-so-silent steps signaling the sound of rubber soles digging into the pavement, Camera kept digressing

"There is always a next episode—and we are its phantom players"

"For now, anyway—no?"

Imagining a silent dismay weighing on the visitors psyche as their tiring bodies dragged along the artificial tarmac, Camera began telling the story of a Queendom where the matriarch had suffered a twenty year sentence of not being able to choose a husband[11]

The matrimonial delay caused the Queen to suffer from amenorrhea, which created a circulatory congestion that eventually coagulated in her brain, causing bouts of severe madness

The ensuing brain disorders coincided with serious nerve damage and, given the absolute power embodied by her role as Queen, led her to issue wildly absurd orders that she kept distributing with greater frequency and with stronger conviction

"A revolution is about to explode" she told her people

But literally nothing was happening and her people were, for the most part, getting bored with very little to do

The general impression of her being such a sweet and wealthy caretaker of her people was now giving way to the abrupt realization that everyone was developing deep migraines that none of her royal physicians could help assuage no matter how hard they tried

She insisted Her Queendom was becoming vulnerable to attack and prophesied that soon many innocent people would be killed and the crops they all depended on would be burnt to ashes

11. And thus begins the stories-within-stories, the digressions-within-digressions, and the plenitude of seemingly irrelevant meanderings into narrative space that only someone who had nothing but time on their hands would even consider composing. Already, by this time, the trial I am following during the day is disappearing (but still resonant in its own way). A few of the narrative tricks that I had employed in my own earlier novels, films, hypertexts, Internet art sites, etc., were clearly going to come in handy as I began auto-translating Roussel. I would even encourage a kind of *metafictional presence* throughout the text as if Roussel were an Amerika-pullulated precursor a la Borges and his essay-fiction "Kafka and His Precursors." Why not? He (Roussel) had clearly influenced many writers after they had read him, so I would let him influence me as I wrote him back into the 21st century.

"The scope of the ensuing terror and famine will soon become untenable" she insisted and everyone was still not sure where she was coming from

In fact, most of them were doped up on the budding plant life that filled their fields of dreams and these dystopian nightmares she kept pontificating on were becoming a real drag

"It's time for everyone to coalesce against a common enemy" she said and hoped that all of her subjects would empathize with the ferocious fears that crawled through her terror-stricken body

Eventually everyone gave up listening to her and started smoking more mushroom dung-packed Earth joints while uprooting tribal Memorials that were emblematic of their need to immortalize the crazy enthusiasm for life their people were once known for

They were not by any means freaked out about their future

Soon, announcements declaring the harvesting of even more happy outgrowths of the enriched topsoil—and the solemn duty to celebrate the freak tribe's continual fetishization of a shared audio-visual program focused on intersubjective performance art—were smeared on parchment plastered throughout the region

The experiments in ritual mushroom dung-packed Earth joint smoking, intersubjective performance art distributed through the telepathic networks of The Massive, and communal events in defiance of total tribal boredom, helped the group consolidate its shared sense of linkage

"Linkage," Camera repeated as they continued their ascent to the villa at the top of Locus Solus

More statues of smiling naked children were installed all throughout the property, each one gesturing an offering toward whosoever walked by

Camera kept telling his story about the mad Queen, the eventual merging of the freak tribe with other simpatico tribes, and the cultish group passions that speedily gained traction via the neurally networked performance artworks of the Superstoners whose streaming videos doubling as live autoportraiture were successfully repackaged as contagious media full of new chants that, when accompanied by electronic noise, transformed their freakish rants into intuitively generated forms of language poetry or what some simply referred to as grunt phraseology

"Intuitively generated grunt phraseology is an auto-affective way of performing your subliminal *lib*-idinals," Camera continued

"Think of it as if you were finally being programmed to become the medium you always wanted to play—and all you had to do is simply turn on the apparatus and let the language speak itself—so that you could then just simply *be* yourself"

And then he began switching up his delivery style and emptied his head of animated shards, suggesting that he too might have a swelling brain filled with a thick nocturnal fluid composed of 4/5's blood and 1/5 pure semen-contra

The immediate conspiracy of the scourge

This madness of sovereign entities worsening

A large procession of illuminative thoughts parading through her head as fervent prayers looking for their next publication outcome

Disruption of the elements

Time-tracked through the sameness of a damaged evening

The acute pain of an hourly disaster that exponentially grows with the sole intention of creating news

Morning fetish rooted in the arch of her foot pressed on his face

Another hesitant moment before finally licking the nitrate glow of her seminally cured flank of flesh

Alleviating the stink by sinking into her mound of molasses

Administered at the height of autobiographical delusion, the liquid plant life entering the blazing vein

Incontinent, and always late for dinner

Soiled in superstitions (but somehow still preventing the next crisis from happening)

Transforming a multitude of small arousals into a single assumption

Omnipotent unanimity

Camera wouldn't stop and everyone kept unconsciously following him up the path

Having been deprived of any meaning, there was still the taste of oblivion

The hooker hooked on her own cum-contra presses anonymous yellow stains into her rotting scrapbook of whoreticultural debris

Wearing out the niche by doing nothing but refusing to close her eyes

Smothered horizontally above the floor and below the platform, her stone feeling gave the colorful impression of nothing coming between us

On the horizon of his exceptional expression, a delicate cloud reflected the red twilight and lifted his mustache softly northward

The aggravated young woman was ecstatic as they found her gauzy remains

A sumptuous sculptress took advantage of the puppet she was dating and, when she was done, deprived him of one of his eyes

Close to the ground the word Ego dug into the snow where the maroon islander also started digging—his own grave

Two topics kept coming up and demanded articulation: green and blue

When asked, they all agreed that a plastic trilogy was better than the analysis of a childhood wound

Seven years later, the lucre of corporate identity became her new master, and everything was perfectly set up for an inopportune cyclone of spiritual destruction

The skillful excavation of many valuable things buried in the ash of the burnt down museum was itself a cleverly curated project whose documentation sold for millions at private auction

The collector of antique hardware and outmoded software was suddenly included in an international recall for all early 21st century artists who refused to update their file-sharing programs

The rapid exposure of an image capturing the decline of a precariously extended play version of something formerly known as "good health"[12]

12. This long riff, written in italics, was my response to having no idea where the story was going, at least the one being presented to me via the online auto-translation program. This was about the time I really thought of just giving up on the project. The porno trial was over, the defendant had been unanimously found not guilty (though *some* weird shit was definitely going on, the case presented by the prosecutor was very weak), and I had other, more pressing art and writing projects to attend to. But then I just said, "Fuck it," and began grabbing text samples and doing what I wanted with them. For example, the phrase "rapid exposure" at the tail end of this riff is a definite reference to Duchamp, and since the Duchamp-Roussel connection was why I started researching *Locus Solus* in the first place, I decided to go on. Duchamp had once said, in an interview, "it was fundamentally Roussel who was responsible for my glass . . . Roussel showed me the way," and so I hoped he would me too. Big mistake?

Camille started imagining what was still yet to come and fantasized that they were finally upon the villa's main building and that as soon as the group walked in they would be greeted with a drunken hello

Hanging from the chandelier would be this anomalous caricature of one of Camera's first visitors, Princess Hello, who had never left the grounds since she first arrived many years ago

Hello's extended pleasantries were starting to take on different meaning now that Camille was hearing that her first child had died so young

For so long Hello was into sharing and thought one could not succeed without giving—but now she felt confronted with many conspiracies as she slowly drifted toward needle-skipping dread

Hello, whether true Princess or not, would have made such a fine character, especially given how much of an impression she had made on Camera from the outset of their relationship

In the long run, it was her love gasoline[13] that would save her—that, and her desire for any hot fetish she could worship by seizing on to the pulsating organ as an object she would often use as a counterintuitive procedural device to prevail against any suggestion of legitimacy

An ancestor of the first inhabitants occupying The Massive, Hello's actions were manufactured out of the secret agenda safely kept in the family jewel box, and besides, she readily admitted that she could only quench her thirst by indulging herself in her brother's juices

Of course, by allowing events to teleport her to the distant alter-time, the constellations above were sending her even more greetings than Hello could have ever prayed for

It was this connection to the sidereal and her ongoing desire to reach an endpoint of total sacredness that fed into Camera's attraction to her as well his commitment to include her in the story he was telling

Confident in the supernatural power of the enveloping spirits representing his own illustrious ancestors, Camera continually dreamed of A More Beneficent Massiveness while holing up in his mysterious hideaway situated on the rich park grounds

13. More Duchampian green box notes make their way into the translation. It could not have been more literal.

Appearing before him was a flashback vision of a nude descendant[14] who visited him in his last dream

Who this descendent would eventually become while rendering itself into being was a mystery, but in a way that no longer mattered since it triggered more shards of impressions that came from the gastric secretions festering in the gut inside his head

Once again he began dictating random lines of unanswerable dialogue[15]

Never follow instructions

Melt the crown and transform it into banal seedwater

Camp in the honesty of an incredibly lonely night

Climb the heights of Mount Chaotic while resisting its suspicious soil

And then after pausing mid-rant, he would awaken and write

Night sunk in

Ink squall, squid pink

Chewy clitoral textures and thoughts of . . . is it Camille?

Where was she now?

Still walking and imagining what was soon to come but really having no idea, just applying her thought-fantasy to the rim of experiences circling the rumors that came before her

Camera's entire head was submerged in one thick rock-hard thought demarcated by flexures of trembling lust that telemorphically rendered his distorted face into a crackling crust of dried perforations

Hello? Was he sensing Camille dreaming him?

Who were these other figures and why were they intruding on his invitation to collaboratively expand their ability to venture forth?

"Facial craters," he would whisper low and under his breath

"Ruinous woes," would come the murky depth of a living reply walking beside him

14. The phrase "a flashback vision of a nude descendant" can only suggest what?

15. Random in the sense that the translator, the one who readwrites while remixing, is at a total loss for (and with these) words. To my mind, remixing is already

* * *

The program Camera had detailed in his mind before his guests had arrived would start early the next day when everyone was feeling rested and ready to start developing their formidable language skills using their bodies as readwrite instruments to measure the inventive scenes he would serially conduct for them

This meant that as they kept walking up the pathway they would need to continually tune up their instruments by engaging in dialogues which at times would sound more like monologues scratching at each other's egos[16]

Joel spoke first:

"My goal is to literally *become* the influencer, to use my virtual presence as a marketing platform, something that will be targeted at avant-garde sensibilities but with a practical metrosexual appeal that will enable me to *monetize* the difference"

Then Camille spoke:

"Yes, but I wonder how your ability to monetize the difference will actually lend itself to a *sterilization of sameness*"

Duke changed the subject and went next:

"Well, I am someone who practices magic, and have found a way to bellow two entirely different incantations in one simultaneous chant. Do you want to hear it?"

Then Monette kicked her small foot into the non-conversation by first not acknowledging what Duke or anyone had said and instead offered this:

---

translation and translation is remixing the already remixed. My relationship to *Locus Solus* is one of reading-writing-remixing the auto-translation as source material. The process of giving the novel a "close reading" is transformed into a sustained engagement with the text as *durational achievement.* All throughout the process of making my version of Roussel's work, the act of communication felt more akin to a Marina Abramovic performance art piece than, say, a playful take on the art of literary translation (though it may end up being that too).

16. Looking back on this chapter, after now having lived with the auto-translation for months, I can see how Roussel plays with the reader by introducing us to these caricatures of characters who, by the time we set off into the park and its elaborate art installations, really become less and less significant, almost disappearing, although I don't particularly miss them. In fact, as the writer of this work, I find it liberating to bring these personae into the story only to then force them all to follow my lead without ever really taking them seriously again. Fuck them!

"What's the value of revelation? I wonder because I often ignore what reveals itself to me. First, I think—*to win*. What does it take to win? But when the answer seems ready to present itself to me in some clear and manifest form that would indelibly indicate to me what I would need to do to instantiate the cumulative effects of my innate power, what do I do? I go back into hiding is what I do. I mutter some magical phrase to myself and dream of a life contained within cabalistic context"

"You retreat," said Cam, "which is what we do here too: this is a retreat for those who are looking for a way out—before they find their way *back in*"

"Not really," responded Monette, "I am more like a girl who has transformed into a bird, a dove who peacefully goes about her own business and can fly away whenever she wants"

Joel tried to get back into the conversation but then again he would also be dead in a month anyway so did it really matter?

The moment he would die was the same instant that Monette would immediately identify a new, heretofore unseen star shining in the sky

"One month from today, at 7:45 a.m., I can see it—gone, all gone"

Prompted to recognize the supernatural incident predicted by Joel, i.e. the hour of his own death, everyone assumed that it was he who had the magic powers, not the dullard Duke

"There are a thousand and one ways to transform the text into visual data," Camera was saying aloud but only to himself as the Thinkernaut crew, having reached a plateau, spread itself around the common meal area inside the main villa

By the next morning there would be seven of them ready to start the tour: Camera, Camille, Duke, Monette, Hello, Carmella and the pre-death Ghost of Joel

Carmella had been taking her time before she spoke a word but during the early morning session she finally spoke:

"I have a radical proposal"

All of her fellow researchers were ready to hear it

"The Ghost of Joel burns brightly before us, a site-specific art star flickering in the heavens"

All of the participants, including Joel, smiled widely, especially Hello, who then spoke:

"You know, I have his mobile," she said as she exhibited his phone to everyone, "and I was the beneficiary of his retirement account. Which was oddly rich given how young he was. He seemed to me to be so untouched. We barely knew him and then he was gone. I know you're thinking, 'Why Hello?' It must have something to do with the way we interfaced. Although it was really more about his expressive typeface. The way he used stories to create a design experience for me to fictionally lose myself in. Not to mention the way he punctuated himself. And his constant, some might say *addictive*, desire to text. To always text, even if it meant wearing a data prosthetic when he went to bed. Like I was saying, I have his mobile. This is a kind of living relic"

She showed everyone at the table her evidence and even Joel was impressed

"A royal archive and a zone of potential interrogation," Carmella said

This was all new to Camera, this group session that he had hoped would turn into a grope session but was now just hoping he could still run the show:

"Do you have the password?"

Carmella was not impressed with Hello's opening bid and said she had herself been given access to Joel's accumulated wealth and that she could prove it by entering the correct pin numbers and passcodes[17]

This undoubtedly surprised Hello but she didn't let on

Camera decided to try and get back on track

"Strict anonymity, a compelling brand, an almost divine provenance . . . these are the things that will help you transubstantiate the material into the virtual realization of an accumulated wealth of data, and convert your avatar presence into the ultimate embodiment of influence peddling"

17. Here the reader will immediately see how there can no longer be any question whatsoever that *I* am now writing the book and not Roussel. Obviously there are no "pin numbers" or "passcodes" (why passcodes? why not "passwords"?) in Roussel's world. But something in the auto-translation is triggering this reading, this writing, this remix. It is by no means a gratuitous translation, and I am being faithful to the original auto-translation in that I too, like all all translators before me (human and/or machine), am committing an act of betrayal. Translator = Traitor. Too obvious, you say? Let's face it, given the context this work is appearing in, if it wasn't for me, none of this would even begin to make sense.

"Remember, by locating yourself in this private retreat, you will have always already found yourself building network presence in the reputation economy"

"But before we can even go there, first we must perform a magic ritual using nothing but our roaming stylus and precise signature-effects"[18]

"How can I put this? Carmella—take this sharpened dagger and sign your name on Hello's buttocks. I want you to brand her, now"[19]

And without hesitation Carmella approached Hello's large and fleshy globe, as if she were ready to eat it, with a knife

Hello, always in undress, had conveniently positioned herself on top of the breakfast table, face down, and exposed her extraplanetary gifts to the rest of the world

But before Carmella dug in, she began to speak in something like twirling tongues, but with a rhetorical clarity that she was hoping would make sense to both herself and to those who were listening to her:

"This is the origin, I am the signatory, I am signing the documents, this is my name, my name is my origin, this is where I entrust everything identified as my Ego, this is where I reinforce the prestige of being asked to agree to the conditions that will determine how well I reign, this is my expurgation of both source and self all in the name of branding, branding what I will now own and what will always be owned by me, and this is also where the culmination of all my writing designates the lost sovereignty I will now rule over"

"Just fuck me with it," said Hello, and then hurled out a laugh that was sure to stick in Carmella's heart for longer than her memory would forbid

18. See note 2.

19. OK, maybe not faithful-faithful, but faithful to the writing process itself. This is me through and through, but me filtered through all kinds of auto-translation affects that I have come to embody over the years. It could be said that all acts of communication are acts of translation and that the translator is not just a conveyor of meaning between languages but a remix artist whose embodied praxis filters the process of translation as a durational work of performance art. My version of *Locus Solus* is actually a very conceptual work of art driven by my commitment to the idea of *definitively unfinishing* it, experientially documenting my performance of the work no matter its outcome, whether it be limited edition print book, freely downloadable e-book, or no-book-at-all (and instead, a mobile application that is meant to be looked at and interacted *with* more than *read* in the traditional sense of that term). Basically, this entire project is running parallel to my practice-based research into what it means to process a simultaneous and continuous fusion of durational achievements.

"Cut me with it"

"Then suture the memory"

Hello kept prodding her

"Don't hesitate. Predominate. Lightly claw me with your dagger. Then trace your index finger over the line and speak your cabalistic phrase. Really—I want you to engrave this so-called Ego of yours into my ass. This isn't real anyway. It's a digital inscription, no? So what if I don't feel it. I want it anyway. It's like you're gonna rip me open some new data stream and who knows what will leak out? Do it without precaution. Just imagine you're some new researcher who is given this great opportunity to enter an emerging field of undiscovered indexicality. Or that you know there's this dark, cavernous world behind the crack of my ass and you just don't know what to do with it. So you decide you'll just *own* it. For now. You'll sign for it"

Carmella was salivating and hated the way she felt but loved it too

She wanted nothing to do with any of this but these were the cards she had been dealt and when she spoke she had no idea why she was saying what she was saying:

"I'm reopening the exit wound, but will promptly close the grille behind me"

"You must mean grid—and while you're there, don't ignore my oblique axes"

While Carmella probed toward inscription, Hello, lying on her taut stomach, leaned forward on her elbows and began accessing information on Joel's mobile, first by typing in pin numbers and access codes and then looking into what kind of retirement accounts he had and eventually opening his digital notebook that included a recent entry detailing a trial he had been a jury member on

Apparently the trial was full of intriguing but ultimately mundane pornographic facts concerning a love triangle between a grandmother, a step-daughter, and either a mother or father or possibly both (which would quadruple it all), but exactly who was who was utterly confusing and Joel's mobile notes played no role in clearing things up

Innumerable nuggets of information from this trial were listed in digital shorthand and as Carmella continued to slowly probe Hello's abundant rump, the others in the group closed their eyes and meditated on the moment, hoping that breakfast would soon be served

Lying on her stomach, Hello kept reading from the last section of jottings in Joel's digital notebook but could not get a fair take on what the trial was ultimately about

transformational typeface

what did it mean when she said "open sesame"?

was that code for "everything is permitted"?

the smell of chlorine and a long black dildo that must have been imagined (or was it real, but camouflaged as a carpenter's tool?)

a fetishization of the video game as a sexual stimulant?

or was it more like first-person teenage ejaculation shooting whatever naked image entered her mind?

and who initiated things?

were they feeling self-pity?

avatar envy?

no specimen nor contra-semen staining the sheets?

no trace of blood

"Here, let me take that," Camera said as he took the stylus from Carmella and began scribbling monosyllabic lyrics right at the entry to Hello's murky cave[20]

20. Everything that has been going on here in the text, especially its sexual dysnarrative, can be traced to my early years working as an undergraduate creative writing and film student at the University of Florida with the French *nouveau roman* writer and cinema artist Alain Robbe-Grillet. As is often the case with students who learn and grow with their mentors but then, if they are capable, pullulate their own networks and fields of vision, I realize I cannot nor would I want to repeat the styles or narrative content of those who came before me. Rather, we may, if we so choose, mirror the literary-aesthetic neurons of the artists that most appeal to us and integrate the auto-affective modes of production we sense in these artists into our own *practice-based rhythm science*. This is no easy trick to pull off and is near impossible to perform at will. Even so, it's important that I be clear in what I am proposing here and that I discuss in a different context in Chapter Four of *remixthebook*, "The Renewable Tradition (Extended Play Remix)".

I could never mimic Robbe-Grillet even if I tried (well, I could try, but would it really be worth the effort?). Instead, I am more comfortable just letting his influence take me over whenever it wants to, perhaps in the form of a muscle memory as alien visitation. These visitations have happened to me in other long-form projects, so I was not the least bit surprised when they manifested in this work as well.

"What are you doing?" asked Hello

"I'm doing what I always do, I'm seeking clarity, clarity by way of your cavity, suggesting multiple samples of how one might consider *seeing as smelling* without necessarily crimping their style"

But Hello was receiving Camera as an anonymous pedestrian, someone who was so banal that any possibility of authoritarian reign over her or her story were now completely removed, and this too was part of her own attempt to brand herself an automated engine of compelling desire—The Bride in Full Formation

Finishing his imprecise fishing expedition and coming away with no useful catches, Camera declared to the group of morning onlookers that he was obsessed with every detail that would enable them to dissolve—or *melt*—inside *The Massive*—and he pronounced the word *massive* as if he were proctologically snaking into Hello's dirty canal waters

"*Massive*," he would again say while calmly resting the palm of his hand on Hello's right orb

It was as if his hand and slow moving, lubricating finger were a magic password, one that Hello would translate into "open sesame," at which point Camera would then bury himself deep in her rotating egg vault, muttering "keep faith in the future, know that you will not despair the inevitable losses that come with my oversupply of demand, and that every time I enter you is a signal that I give sanction to other potential rulers, that this is what I feel is most responsible for the continuation of my legacy in whatever shape I may leave it"[21]

For example, when I was embodying the spiritual unconscious of Lautréamont in my second novel, *Sexual Blood*, or when I was metamediumystically conjuring the hauntological presence of Derrida, Cixous, Godard, and many others in *GRAMMATRON*. Or the way Robbe-Grillet appears with alarming regularity in my unreleased feature-length "foreign film," *My Autoerotic Muse*.

21. This reads like a mangled mashup of *Fifty Shades of Grey* and *Story of O*, as well it should. That undergraduate "Special Topics: Pornography" course I took in the English department at UCLA in 1981 after having first studied with Robbe-Grillet at Florida (I studied with him twice, once before and once after the porn course) gave me the overview I needed to begin investigating the relationship between writing, sex, the body, and (even) theory. This one sentence from Camera (but does anyone at the beginning of the 20th century speak like this?) feels very gratuitous to me as a reader, but as writer, that is to say a reader-writer / auto-translator who is also an editor but not a censor per se, I keep it in the text because this is what

Even though this was all happening in his mind, and Hello was now half-asleep on the communal table, everyone had already accepted the fact that he was a pig

A down and dirty porker (but with the sheen and glow of an ultra-experienced guru of the *always-to-be-invented*)[22]

Already feeling the embrace of what could very easily turn into her own death, Carmella was mirroring Hello's neurons as the princess squealed with serious pain, or was she faking it?

Camera had the dagger up inside the cave

"I would like us to finalize Joel's estate," Monette interrupt the proceedings, "to expedite the execution of his orders, as well as take into consideration the many related recommendations he put forth, to do this without fear of retribution, especially given the uncertainty of who we determine is really meant to inherit what he has left us, or at least bequeathed to me since I was his last confidant"

---

the process has dictated to me even as I dictate the parameters I expect the process to operate under. Does this mean I am not accepting responsibility for my own text? Yes, but then I must ask: is it really mine? Sometimes it feels like it's definitely mine, but at other times it feels more like I am just the remixological filter that these stories and associated source material pass through. Again, for me, it's more like a performance art work that I must live through and that I am challenging myself to process as a durational achievement. You may think this is a kind of cop-out, a side-stepping of what could easily appear to be an ethical dilemma, but I am not writing this for you. I am writing this for Lautréamont, Roussel, Duchamp, Robbe-Grillet and whoever else gets hold of it one hundred years from now.

22. See? Even the auto-translation allows for self-critique. But still, why can I not take responsibility for it? I remember when, during one of the classes I took with Robbe-Grillet, a female grad student attacked him for his misogynist prose. His response was translated to the class as something like, "But my mind cannot control what my hands are doing." It goes without saying that Robbe-Grillet, whose narrative material is so different than Roussel's, was, like Duchamp before him, totally influenced by Roussel. In his essay on Roussel in the collection *For A New Novel*, he wrote about the author's "demented acuity" while admiring the fact that he, Roussel, really had nothing to say, "[n]o transcendency," and that "no humanist 'going beyond' can be imputed to the series of objects, exploits, and events which, at first sight, make up his universe." The same cannot be said of my inappropriate auto-remix of *Locus Solus*. However, we all live in different times, and maybe, looking back, we can pretend this is somehow what Roussel meant to say or would have wanted to say if he too were living in the early 21st century and had gone through the American higher education system in the 1980s and 90s. Robbe-Grillet might disagree.

While Joel looked on, she took the mobile out of Hello's hand and began reading:

Blind and hideous, shit smeared on the outer edge of the mutilated

Dressed always in pink, with yellow fingernail polish

A thin lip ring that betrayed her former youth

A charming and witty response to every offering as if it were enough to justify the next round of relentless pounding and coming a hard rain like never before

But still a child, needy—unconfident

"What's a rim job?"

"Don't worry, it's something aesthetic—you have to have a taste for it"

A soul who was generally thought of as straight and good, devoted to her step-grandmother, Godfather and brother-in-law

Mildly grotesque but not hard to imagine, though she would eventually choose to forget it, which is the issue, since memory plays a key function in determining who is and is not a reliable narrator here

If the court would please—our next witness[23]

Do you swear to approximate your fictionally remixed memory as if it were the truth, the whole truth, and nothing but?

A vile and wounded presence that holds a great secret

"Or so they would have you believe"

But where is the evidence to distill this into a crisp conviction?

Living through this entire process is cruel and unusual punishment

Good thing all of the characters are seriously disgusting because if she was a hot Lolita whose literary intelligence made it clear that she was seriously playing everybody involved . . .

You have been charged with using your avatar presence to set up a series of serious sex-death traps—how do you plead?

23. The trial I was a juror on is still fresh in my mind. It won't go away. And to think of Kafka's trial, or the unreliable narrators in Robbe-Grillet's seedy and seeding novels, is it any wonder the corruption-of-an-already-corrupt text is what I end up glomming on to at times throughout the discourse?

The familial cage

Further away from any insistence or threat to talk about—the value of (a) life?

Camera's probative signature-effect dallied around the inner sleeve of the crusty crack

"This is when what was happening was timed to act"

Hello now remembering being notified of the imminent arrival of the detective squad but first the arrival of the police to secure the property so nothing was compromised before the judge issued the summons and her stepfather was arrested

"Is Hello your daughter?"

"Yes"

"And the body belongs to her son?"

Camera now imagining Carmella taking out a sex toy and moving it over to the luxurious blue cushion near Monette who by this time has returned to meditating on the moment

Monette's opening the cushion's stitches, digging into the pillow's stuffing, and pulling out a small, mechanical puppet the size of a long finger with a thin pen on its tip

She holds it in her hand with a long, passive waiting

"What exactly did you find when you opened up the contents contained in the blue cushion?"

"At first I thought it was a heavenly signal to wait—or to write as a form of waiting"

"But then?"

"I imagined it was a sex toy of some kind. A vibrating puppet"

The object was without palpable consequence

Probing deeper we can hover over two salient features: the sex toy and the quick decay into decadence on a minor

Carmella wondering if maybe the trial Joel was referring to just before he died was really his own, but transgendered to protect the innocent

Another entry in the digital notebook on Joel's mobile had nothing but song lyrics that Hello thought nothing of but read nonetheless

Cockpit of reason

Paternal revelation

This is my secret

Uncle Fellation

Anarchy kingdom

Massive elation

Tricked out of rose

And into relation

Hello?

Mom?

Is that you?

Come again?

Hello?

Hello kept thinking of her own teenage years where she would never consider agreeing to a truce with the celestial symptoms predicted by her disappeared father

She remembers herself walking alone, her arms full of flowers, toward an ancestral castle where she lived each summer, sumptuous red sky and reflections born of a sun not quite gone, smothered by the long clouds lying on the horizon

Then, stopping to admire the magic of twilight, some falling leaves strangely bending under the angle of light and circling in a breeze as if generating random 3–D poetry formed out of vague letters that revealed a series of lines all beginning with the word ALREADY

ALREADY[24] *frayed into tatters and only just begun*

ALREADY an advertisement for submission and not even awake

24. In an interview regarding his book on Roussel, *Death and the Labyrinth*, Michel Foucault discusses "the fact that we live in a world in which things have been said. These spoken words in reality are not, as people tend to think, a wind that passes without leaving a trace. [. . .] In certain of Roussel's works nothing is given at the beginning except the possibility of encountering the 'already said,' and with this 'found language' to construct, according to his rules, a certain number of things, but on the condition that they always refer back to the 'already said'—that at first delighted me, and seemed to be the interplay of literary creation starting from a

ALREADY conducting penetrating research into the use of sex toys

ALREADY a tonal habit forming a halo around the empty orbit

ALREADY the mysterious doll evoking the putrescence of coming out loud

ALREADY an admissions officer at the Institute of Receiving Jesters

ALREADY transmitting cloud-core sentience in a very propitious time

But now she remembers being installed in a large cage with litter and newspaper and a strong deodorizer set on an industrial dolly ready for transport but where was she going next?

What was the real travel purpose?

Did she honestly expect to get reimbursed for embracing the inner workings of The Massive?

She was becoming impatient and wanted to see the more memorable events that would put an end to the mad ruins congesting the fatal landscapes marking her brain

She was such a young princess, always saying hello to whoever would listen, her outward gesture an offering to all passersby

And anyone with a mobile capable of opening the grid with an effective sentence uttered secretly in a low voice while mildly scarring more skin tissue

---

cultural and historical fact. It also seemed to me that it was worth questioning."

But in what way is it worth questioning? From the vantage point of the author in search of a function? This was not what crossed my mind as I started the process of auto-translating and remixing Roussel, but one that came to the fore soon after I got caught up in his novel as both historical and aesthetic fact.

In the same interview, Foucault tells us that that he wrote "this study of Raymond Roussel when I was quite young. It happened completely by chance [. . .] I was completely taken by the beauty of the style, so strange and so strangely close to that of Robbe-Grillet." So he reads Roussel *after* Robbe-Grillet, and sees a relationship between Roussel's *La Vue* and Robbe-Grillet's *Le Voyeur*, but only later finds out that Robbe-Grillet initially titled his book *La Vue* and not *Le Voyeur*, as an homage to Roussel. He goes on to state that "if I hadn't been preconditioned by the reading of Robbe-Grillet, Butor, and Barthes I would not have been capable on my own of experiencing this shock of recognition while reading *La Vue*." This is what I'm saying too, especially in relation to the Borgesian take on the writer inventing their own precursors, but my reading of Roussel is much more complicated in that I literally *cannot read him* and so must, out of necessity, remix him, sometimes through experiential filters provided by other figures including Robbe-Grillet but also Duchamp, Lautréamont, Acker, Cixous, Derrida, and various versions of "myself" writing across the media spectrum.

"Open sesame"

Come again?

The Multitude

The Massive

The Demultiplied

Many arms, feet, hips, elbows, hair, tongues, cocks, tits, teeth, deep anus projections from the milky way flesh of constellations coming from a distance, and still more coming, and Camera taking pictures of her coming, the gaping grid, the categorical imperative

Authenticating the signature before approving the next round of procedures that would change things forever?

"All of these unsuccessful suitors," Monette was now coming out of her trance, realizing that she was at the beginning of a fast

She started talking as if something had surreptitiously entered her body and now she was transmitting her fear of the inevitable

"Soldiers competing under the banner of feverish passion, a procession of raw insignia leaving nothing but their own trace, and even then, just scattershot disseminations of expedited release forms for the summarily acquitted"

Carmella abruptly stood up to signal to the group that she was now leaving without asking for permission, besides who would she ask, Hello?

If she asked Camera, then she would be his for good

"Long live the Princess," she said, softly stroking Hello's hair while walking past her pleasantly pert body

"Long live the Queen!" Hello roared back while tracing Carmella's movements out of the room

I'm still not sure if that was an entry or exit wound

Check beneficiaries on retirement accounts

At the bottom of some spacious niche, attempt a fitting despair

A sublime admixture of resilience and dismay[25]

25. While writing these italicized riffs, something exciting always opened up for me. I imagined myself running away with the text, with getting away with it—whatever it was. Clearly, the feeling is one I associate with how I wrote certain of my previ-

* * *

Momentarily veering off the path, Camera walked up to and peered deep into the crack of a cave and viewed its contents

Stored therein were the recent excavations carried out by the company that he himself was principal shareholder of

A quick survey of the interior revealed that there was a statue broken into thousands of pieces and someone, but who?, was projecting onto the dark interior wall a cataclysm of injected grass

He wanted this space and these objects, whoever triggered them, to be the beginning of something antithetical to the *long durée*, something more personally akin to auto-affective reincarnation

He thought of himself as the chosen vehicle trained to channel unconscious entities toward this venerable entryway whose mere existence confirmed the legendary status he had achieved even as he also thought it was entirely curious that this was indeed his reality

After a last glance at his redoubled conflict of interest, his believing and not believing that this was his reality, Camera continued leading everyone up the ascending gangway and he immediately forgot the cave even existed

---

ous novels, especially those sections where I am just letting the language speak itself, a kind of abstract expressionist stream of consciousness, but one that is still bound by certain parameters. In this case, the parameters of the story are being auto-translated for me. In composing these solo writing bends, I thought I would explode the volume further, max out its amplification so that the work ceased being an object and, in the process, revealed its own inner universe as a complex, remixologically inhabited, jumble of algorithmically generated words. These words were then filtered through a mangled reading-writing-remixing of Roussel, or what I imagined to be his linguistic machine, not to mention the coded behaviors of the various online translation programs I had at the ready. In some ways, I hoped it would just go on like this forever, that I would find three to four solid hours a day to devote to readwriting Roussel according to my own narrative predilections. But that was not to be the case. Everything was about to change. This first chapter was an aberration. I would now have to come out from under my own spell and align my writing with more precise data. I would now come under Roussel's spell and remain as diligent as I possibly could, relaying his story as a kind of vast playground of intermedia performance and installation art unlike any exhibition seen on the face of the earth. But I would do this as an outsider, which Cocteau thought was the best way to take Roussel on ("In 1918 I rejected Roussel as likely to place me under a spell from which I could see no escape. Since then, I have constructed defenses. I can look at him from the outside.").

2

As everyone climbed, the vegetation became more rare

Soon the grounds were stripped bare from all sides, and toward the end of this first part of the journey, the group became aware of the large esplanade as if collectively visualizing its architectural presence as part of some intersubjective hallucination that only multiple sets of eyes could conjure into being

They all took a few steps toward a point in the landscape where there stood a kind of paving instrument used to level roads

Within its all-metal sheen, one could, if they wished, make out the shape of a woman suspended by an object resembling a light yellow balloon that seemed to emit a small flame around its outer edge—a miniature hot air balloon tethered to the human condition ready to take flight

Below this part of the scene, the ground itself was covered in a totally defamiliarized work of collage art[26]

26. The use of the term "collage art" is by no means a literal translation of what the online program delivered to me when I first plugged in Roussel's original sentence written in French. Hardly. But I had already determined, from having translated the first chapter, what geographical location I would use as my model for the premises and that all of the ensuing scenes would be viewed through an *artistic exhibition context*. Though I had no idea what elaborate fiction awaited me, for some reason, I immediately associated the property Locus Solus with the vast natural and artistic grounds in the center of Brazil known as Inhotim. This property, a few hours south of the city of Belo Horizonte, is owned by an iron magnate and known for its many pavilions of contemporary art nestled within an expansive botanical gardens. As part of my December 2010 sponsored artist tour through parts of Brazil

Taking in the image of the entire sculpture, one could see a wide variety of human teeth in all shapes and sizes spread on all sides

Some were glowing white and contrasted with the incisors of smokers, and there was also a full range of browns and maroons

All of the yellow ones appeared as a bizarre stock of fake ornaments comprised of straw tones or, in the worst instance, tawny shades of proverbial decay

Blue teeth, some soft, some dark, fulfilled their quota and contributed eye-catching hues to this rich polychromatic display

The blues were complemented by a host of black teeth screaming their bloody roots ebony red

The contours and proportions differed in the vast infinity of molars and monstrous canines bordering almost imperceptible baby teeth the color of organic soy milk

Numerous metallic filings bloomed here and there

Next to the paver and its decorative dental sculpture of multi-colored teeth was an unfinished table

Taken together in the abstract, this group of objects evoked a sleepy retiree who was sunk inside a dark crypt and sprawled on the edge of an underground pond

---

where I was exhibiting and screening some of my video art works, my hosts arranged for me to visit Inhotim where the seed of a potential narrative was immediately planted inside my head, but when I eventually got back to my home in Boulder, I was unsure exactly where I wanted that story to go, so as is often the case with "great ideas" that never pan out into full-fledged projects, I put it on the back burner. But Inhotim's aesthetico-botanico landscape in the middle of the Brazilian state of Minas Gervais sprang back to life as soon as I began translating this novel. Since I had challenged myself to not go back and do any heavy revisions to my sequential translation of *Locus Solus*, which felt as though I were making it up as I went along, I had to commit myself to this idea of Camera as a kind of artist-inventor more than, say, a scientific entrepreneur (though there was no reason that he could not perform that function as well and, indeed, ends up performing *many* functions in my version). Fortunately, Roussel's narrative did not disappoint me and I was able to carry the more artistic angle all the way through to the end, introducing readers to Camera's eccentric sculptures, combines, abstract expressionist assemblages, performance art happenings, new media / interactive installations, literary and philosophical leanings, and much more. The image of Inhotim never left my mind, and I believe that the grounds there would no doubt be the perfect location for a film version of *Locus Solus*, especially one that remains faithful to my own translation.

An automated mechanism spraying cigarette smoke into the retiree's brain triggered a dreamlike ritual where a group of six or seven people were bending down as if hiding under the influence of a fear inspired by a chemical air ball that must have been responsible for the spot marking a slight shadow given off by a dead bird lying on the ground

An old, closed book lay next to the barely outlined figure of the retiree, both of which were lit by a weakly illuminated torch planted right in the floor of the crypt

From another angle, the yellow and brown ornaments prevailed in this unique dental mosaic

The other tones, rare, threw hints of other colors bright and attractive

The Dove, made of beautiful white teeth, was frozen in a quick pose suggesting graceful momentum and the retiree now seemed more like the paver, a piece of equipment melded into the collage, which also included a red feather adorning a dark hat slumped close to the closed book, not to mention a large purple cloak stapled with a copper loop that emitted a complex amalgam of aural sensations in collaboration with the blur of blue-hued teeth and a fashionable pair of jeans sinking in wide boots which was also made of black teeth

The soles of the boots were very visible where one could make out teeth made of assorted fragments of nuts and filings composed of bent nails

It was near the left boot that one of the property's staff members, a young woman, was currently stationed[27]

27. These property staff members appear throughout the narrative and are presented as cinematic extras who can be easily disregarded, but for some reason I always wished that we would go in deeper and reveal things about them that no one would expect and that would provide more information to the reader about Camera and, consequently, Roussel. The mystery behind the author and his protagonist are compelling aspects of the larger story that I am investigating as I auto-translate, mostly because I am trying to *put myself in his position* and in so doing unlock some of my own motivations for doing what I do. As Louis Aragon once remarked in a discussion of Roussel, "[f]or me, Roussel remains the man of the great secret. But this secret is one that no one will ever pierce." For me, that's a given, but this secret is also now my secret in that I have discovered the connection between Roussel, Duchamp, the Surrealists, Robbe-Grillet and the *nouveaux romanciers*, Oulipo, the New York School of Poets, and now the entire conceptual art and writing apparatus that comes before and after the Internet and that I am filtering through my Avant-Pop glitch aesthetics.

To the side of the unfinished table, random teeth were scattered in an inconsistent pattern with no pictorial quality whatsoever

Suddenly the paver took off by itself into the air, apparently thrust by a modest breath exhaled by the retiree releasing cigarette smoke, and immediately landed not far from the group

Camera, making a signal to everyone to take precaution, stepped over the rope line that separated the group from the sculptural contraption, and approached the complex air instrument

Everyone followed him, very careful to not kick or knock off any of the scattered teeth, since it was clear that the apparent disorder was in fact the laborious outcome of a more comprehensive aesthetic study

Upon close listening, one could hear clicking, performed by the young staff person who, standing just to the side, nervously snapped her fingers in her pockets while her face shone in the sun

Without being completely disruptive, Camera drew everyone's attention to the various organs of the device[28]

Below the yellow hot air balloon tethering the miniature woman ready to take flight, was a finely threaded net shaped like a webbed neck, and on top of it all there was an automatic aluminum valve that had a circular shutter near a small, barely visible chronometer dial

Under the vertical balloon strings now dangling on the net-neck, there was a thin cloth made of fine red silk with holes drilled in and around its lower edge as well as a round aluminum tray which contained an ochre substance resembling an inverted pickle bottle lid laying on its bottom

The underside of the shelf or tray was fastened to the top of a narrow aluminum cylinder post securing the body of the entire object

28. I can imagine that these technical descriptions of the mechanical devices that run many of the machines Camera depends on for his "wow" factor are much more intricately conceived and explained than what I offer throughout the novel. I decided early on in the translation-performance—in fact, right about this point in the text—to not get too hung up on trying to make perfect sense of the precise details of each object's mundane technicalities. There's a reason I never got into the technical writing business and decided to not focus on these kinds of descriptions in my own novels, so why would I obsess over them in this one? True, Robbe-Grillet, for one, probably found himself immensely attracted to the repetitive minutiae that Roussel laboriously pinpoints throughout his version, but for me it's just about getting through these sections—like slogging through the jungle in a rain forest during the storm season hoping that I come out on the other end in one piece.

A long rod—also aluminum—was planted in the upper region of the post and pointing obliquely toward the sky

It was higher than the circular plate and each of its extending three branches were supported by a large stopwatch propped against a round mirror of the same circumference

Three dials, each operating on its own, were externally oriented in three different directions

Three discs of tinned glass faced a common median space looking West and South

The first mirror was currently receiving the direct image of the sun which also drenched the second even as the third appeared to play no role at all

Each mirror was configured with four horizontal stems gently toothed and was routinely recorded individually at the top, bottom, right, and left in the back of their perimeter

All of these rods, in all three cases, crossed the stopwatch from side to side and pointed on the other side to the peripheral margins of the dial, a little lower in diameter than where the watch was moving

Is watching also moving? (Camera mumbled under his breath)

Operating via invisible gears in connection with the mechanism of chronometers and stems, as well as a variety of progressions and intentional setbacks, gave the mirrors a multitude of inclinations

The front of each consisted of a small metal ball trapped two-thirds by a hollow sphere itself incomplete and adhered to the back of the mirror suggesting some kind of heretofore still yet to be invented game

This method of attaching one thing to another easily lent itself to the autonomous movements of the discs reflecting the sense-logic of the sun

Every day the triple disc system followed the sun in its course, from sunrise to sunset

One could say the piece, as the antithesis to what one would call *art per se*, was discovering its own *mirrorical return*

One could also say the piece, as the antithesis to what one would call *painterly*, was discovering how one might have *an apprentice in the sun*

One could also say that the piece was a *delay-in-decay*

According to Camera, it was during the morning hours that the first mirror turned east collecting all of the sparkling lights

After the passage of the sun past the meridian it became inactive and the other mirrors took over

Activist mechanisms performing their own rituals from morning to night, a mirror gazing south, pointing in a fixed direction, catching a bright scent of light or mirrored reflection and moving without interruption, sometimes one, sometimes one of the others, or none at all, but then the eventual passing of the torch to a brilliant neighbor taking their turn at co-responsibility

In the middle of the oblique stem with its triple-branched end, stood a right bracket itself divided into two curving branches forming a half moon with zenith-pointing horns

This semi-circle, perpendicular to the vertical plan where the stem was ideally held in oblique relief, could serve as a partial framework for a powerful round lens which, assimilating its horizontal diameter, was set internally by two pins to the topmost portion of the curved branches

Placed accurately on the path of the light beam past the second mirror and toward the most distant mirror, the lens was lying parallel to the rays that flooded it

A minimal chronometer with a dial adorning the upper part of one of the curved branches, was set to turn the lens at such strictly determined times, that creating a subtle connection between time and the image-movement of the work as a whole indicated that the machine-as-event was in a state of *always becoming something else*

Further securing the stability of the entire contraption was a horizontal metal rod screwed into the aluminum post just opposite the lenses and mirrors

A huge magnetic needle that must have come from some giant compass was crossing the post at right angles and used its magnetism to maintain, during flights, the immutable orientation of the air pan

Its northern tip was placed right below the mirror facing south while its southern point coincided in a similar way but with a remote spherical counterweight

Was this a kind of metaphorical trapdoor?

At its base, three aluminum claws, curved and united, recalled in miniature the legs of furniture

Each claw supported its end on the ground giving a sufficient base to the paver and everything else including the cloistered stopwatch dial which was barely larger than the mirror tracing its every move

A little higher than the location where the claws were attached, at the extreme lower end of the post coming in from on high, there was a last chronometer dial

By this time the staff person had left and few seconds later the visiting participants were all stationed on the other side of the rope line

The sound of a low shock soon attracted everyone's attention and they all simultaneously moved their eyes toward the bottom of the art object

Things were happening that are difficult to translate

Everything joining everything else in a masterfully conducted synchronic choreography

A general feeling that the various parts of the mechanical sculpture were semi-working together but also feeling them to be stuck a little too close to each other

A single brown tooth left the ground as if obeying the commands of some mysterious power of magnetization and attached itself to a blue washer

For everyone's ears, two loud clashes seemingly layered into one sound exactly

Soon thereafter, a flash coming from the lens which then does a quarter turn by pivoting on the horizontal diameter's axis and then, cutting at right angles, an emitted light beam which then follows a downward skew toward the mirror pointing south

As a result of this maneuver, the rays, through what must have been special glass, focus with power on the entire area surrounding the sprawl of yellow under the balloon in the circular tray

Do you follow me? (Camera wonders—thinks aloud—questions himself)

Don't forget the webbed net i.e. the neck that performs the function of casting an imperceptible shadow as a sudden shimmer *resplendent in color*

Under the effect of an intense heat produced by the material conditions of the environment, a light gas is released and immediately transforms into a flaring ball shot toward the sky taking on the appearance of an upside-down aviator mistakenly igniting the initial bombardment

The upward force of the shot has the added effect of lifting the entire art object gently into the air while the lens, making another quarter turn in the same direction, obscures the amalgamated yellow mix whose rays were once identified solely as the sun

By this time the direction of the wind had changed where the rope line was demarcating the parameters of the art object and the woman staff person was brought back into the dental array

She led the group to a different perspective where everyone could now see the darkest corner of the crypt, that place where the retiree's posture suggested a new direction for the entire apparatus to orient itself

According to Joel's mobile notebook, found after his death, *Bottom, during the flight, one of the claws lay itself through an internal needle that went down to one-half*

To further confuse things, the balloon had substantially deflated and the unit, now lowered back down, was led by two additional claws landing on a set of black teeth belonging to one of the banks of the underground pond while a newly revealed needle settled in the middle of a space (intentionally?) left blank

At the time of the landing, the participants saw, on the top of the balloon, a still gaping valve which, having measured the amount of gas required, quietly closed its shutter

The visitors were now being asked to deduce how the rising of the contraption was perpetrated through the lens and the valve

Novice eyes[29]

Between the three claws . . . grey washers . . . blue? driven by its stem?

Proving once again that the magnetization was destroyed

As nicotine destroys teeth

And the woman holding the balloon?

Was she just part of an unfinished mosaic?

But then the adjacent teeth—and the unfinished table too—slightly advanced in the direction of (__?) upon landing

29. I have had enough. I am going back to what I do best: sample and remix. Remain suggestive . . . and lead the witness on.

The minimal contribution discounted prominently

Whose role now?

The lens performed another quarter turn as per usual and the fumes of the substance, luminously heated, revealed an insolent bladder

The ball was removed

The lens turned again

The needle extended and returned the claws to their rightful place

The breeze took his cap

The woman tethered to the yellow balloon ran in a straight line to a solitary and remote route

Taking root, pink, thin and sharp

The valve operating as if it would actually fit

And nobody asking anything, at all

* * *

Camera began explaining the reason for showing this odd work of abstract expressionist assemblage art

The apparatus, he told the group, was meant to test the limits of predicting the parallel possibilities of time and that these precise instruments indicated to him days in advance the specific location, direction, and power of the incoming wind gusts being produced in the environment

Sometimes he would be able to forecast the arrival of less condensation

"I myself am a kind of cloud in trousers[30]," he said, directing his attention to Camille who, like the others, was focused on how Camera would articulate the why and what of everything they had just experienced

He said his goal was to create an aesthetic environment designed to utilize the sun and wind as principal media

He started by building the woman holding the balloon and attached the five chronometers to adjust the work's evolution over and within alternate streams of time

30. Mayakovsky? Sure, but coming from Camera's mouth it sounds less poetic and more creepy. Nice!

The valves, yes, and the mirrors and lens, beautifully rendered with the solar light enveloping the balloon creating a brilliant yellow substance which, due to special preparation, exhales hydrogen

"The effluence of its mechanistic presence only came into being," he said, "when the lens would focus on the bright sun rays"

In this way, Camera had created an instrument that, without any other help except from the sun, could take advantage of planned air flows well in advance and forecast a specified route that the apparatus would follow

"I was looking for the material we're all born with," he said, a glimmer in his eye, "and only a fine mosaic seemed to enable me to structure the give and take of the device"

"These multicolored fragments, some with intermittent magnetization, can seemingly be attracted to each other or, alternately, left alone near the bottom of the piece, off to the side"

"It was an unexpected discovery I happened upon a few years ago that really enabled me to keep this all humming"

He explained that it was a curious system for extracting teeth without suffering and that avoided the use of hazardous and harmful anesthetics

As a result of lengthy research, Camera put two highly complex metals together, metals that irresistibly found themselves magnetized to each other and whose combined power could be exercised on the calcareous element of human teeth[31]

One of these metals was gray, the other had steel blue highlights

Carving a one millimeter slice of each metal enabled him to fix the gray substance to a thin, rigid handle that he would obliquely slide into the rim of the blue substance, symmetrically at equal distances, and then insert the ends of three short and divergent horizontal stems

He would hold on to the thin handle and, in time, using both hands, introduce the cylinder into the patient's mouth and, buttressing the device on the edge of two other teeth, employ the magic-like magnetization to extract the tooth under question

31. This is where the artist and scientist begin to blur for me. Roussel is really a 21st-century novelist, one that anticipates Modernism but that surpasses it in the same breath(lessness).

It would happen so fast and with such clean magnetic power that the decayed tooth would obediently dislodge itself and the patient would leave without even realizing the tortuous counter-option they had so successfully avoided

The participants' eyes were glazing over so Camera decided to speak in what he called "inadequate translation" or "conceptual language" as a way to spice up his presentation[32]

"When it came to the lower jaw[33], a dominatrix of dentistry would have to have her way, or at least she would have to be in control of the situation if she could move at will, but often she could not, and any maneuver on her part would require the complete overthrow of the cylinder and gray washer—which is exactly what you *did not* want to happen, since this could create a condition I call 'bald mouth,' where one side lacks the necessary support structure due to missing teeth—whether they were already missing or not—since I could extract very quickly and without notice in a matter of seconds—so you see, it was always better for my patients to make it simple and allow me to do my work, to choose from a batch of possibilities ranging from—for instance, right parallelepipeds whose full ivory tusk could offer the desired opposition, right?—and this is one of those instances where an elephant may never forget, but that's only because we have succeeded in simulating the experience of masticating as if the patient really had *an entire set of teeth in their mouth*, which was simply not the case, how could it be? Their teeth were actually, in my artwork, performing an entirely different function"

"Again, the pain was nonexistent because of the alacrity with which the procedure was executed, and the simulated row of ivory cubes I had left in their mouths gave the sensation of *actually having real teeth*"

"Of course, once the teeth were extracted we had to rid the patient of any proximity to the experimental magnetic substance less one false movement create an accidental . . . well, it's all there in the name, isn't it?, acci*dental* . . . "

32. This new literary device I employ here and in other locations throughout the novel, what I sometimes refer to as "[inadequate translation]," is my attempt to keep the performance going even though the auto-translation is making it nearly impossible to maintain narrative momentum/consistency. What I like about these periodic riffs that come after the phrase [inadequate translation] is that it gives both the reader and the writer a chance to take a breather, to let the senselessness have its say as part of the experience. Sometimes this senselessness can be beautiful too, in its own right. Like a cut-up or mangled email spam message (see my novel, *29 Inches: A Long Narrative Poem*, for endless examples of this aesthetic proposition),

33. It should be noted that translating this particular segment was personally difficult as I have some serious lower jaw issues myself. TMI?

According to Camera, word of mouth quickly started circulating about his patient-friendly procedures, especially the prompt and comfortable way the teeth were extracted, and Locus Solus had attracted a flock of unexpected visitors with sore mouths

Pell-mell—Camera would pile discarded teeth into different regions of his growing abstract expressionist assemblage art project and after awhile he had accumulated an embarrassing amount of rotting material whose extraction he would have to personally attend to

Soon the artwork started taking over the tooth extraction business and then there were successive delays that he began thinking of in terms of *a durational achievement*, something that was inherent in the making of the work itself, a delay in decay[34], and this became a central element in his practice

The entire group was quite enthralled with this last bit of personal trivia—or theoretical pretense—and since most of them had, up to this point, not made a strong connection with what they were seeing and why it was so important that they encounter it right from the start of their journey, it was somehow easy for Camera to take the party toward one particular tile made entirely of teeth

The shades and edges of each tooth differed enough to lend themselves to the overall fantasy that now included a complex and rich entanglement of roots attached to shiny fillings and other substances still not identifiable

Then he took out the instrument and, exercising great care, indicated where the gray and blue substances came together to form this magic magnetization effect that would—as everyone present was now witnessing—lift ran-

34. Given that this entire project is being conceived as a further investigation into Duchamp's *Large Glass* and that I intentionally remix some of Duchamp's notes from his *Green Box* with what the auto-translation provides me as I translate Roussel, these forays into *delay* or *durational achievement* are par for the course. In fact, these endnotes are a stylistic remix of Duchamp's *Green Box* in the way they serve as a key to the experience of the translation process. In regards to his *Green Box*, Duchamp has said, "All along, while painting [the *Large Glass*], I wrote a number of notes which were to compliment the visual experience like a guide book." Among these notes, Duchamp refers to his elaborate painting and accompanying conceptual apparatus as a "delay in glass" (these notes are often underlined in Duchamp's original handwritten texts as are many of the echo-references throughout this translation). This present work of auto-translation / remix, which I am processing as a kind of durational achievement, one that grows out of certain strains of performance art, could be conceived as another kind of delay effect. For more on these potentially revealing interconnections, see notes 9, 10, 12, 13.

dom teeth off the ground and vertically up toward the dental device he held in his hand

"Of course," he said, "these are teeth—but I could have just as easily adopted this technique to create an iron mosaic"

But teeth is what he ended up with

Effortlessly, teeth

Discontinuously, a delay in decay

Not to mention the flying aspects of the piece, especially with the cumbersome paver, all of it powered by a system of batteries that created their own serious drawbacks

"Basically, I went with the teeth because that's what was made available to me via my practice, and once I had them, they were readymade—cut and tinted—and this enabled me to build the object out of material that was devoid of any artistic intention or premeditation"

And as the work grew—one might say *organically grew*—it became more attuned to innumerable potential readings or interpretations, particularly in relation to the artist and emerging forms of contemporary practice in general—*but what was contemporary?*

Was contemporary 1914?

Or 2014 translating 1914 for an even smaller audience than one could have imagined a hundred years ago?[35]

These were a few of the thoughts that Duke was considering

Monette on the other hand felt as if she had been left behind somewhere and this limited field of presence she was occupying had more to do with time-travel or the metempsychotic distribution of innumerable selves she had unconsciously embodied while dozing through more than half of the tour

Camera continued getting into the details of what he termed *vital importance*, particularly the lower portion of the three claws, the small stopwatch, and what he referred to as *the inner workings of time itself as a mobile medium where interior micro-projections coincided with a temporality subsidized by—*[36]

35. Going meta, one hundred years hence.

36. Instead of asking—"What would Roussel write in the age of networked and mobile media?"—I just go ahead and do it. Not that he would write it, but that I decided I would experientially write it *through* him and, yes, he would refresh the

"The creative work process?"

Was that The Ghost of Joel speaking?

No, it was Carmella, but it sounded like Joel—as if she were already speaking for him

But Camera did not catch her question, in fact he was not intentionally leaving his prior sentence hanging on the elliptical edge of an exhausted brain fart nor was he deigning his "current status" as uncertain

He was not dangling his linguistic come-on to someone who, paying close attention to his every word and gesture, would finish his sentence for him, rather, he himself was not really paying attention to anything but a close-up detail of the esoteric artwork he was bent over, muttering something about "a claw can find itself on a tooth which already forms part of the mosaic" and "sometimes two claws will rise and engage with these teeth by way of this needle"

Joel's mobile notes[37] don't help:

Molars, pallets, a child's incisor

Two mobile appendages

The pictorial effect of the mosaic

The absence of any direct contact with the Earth

These too were part of the "inadequate translation" that the work had still yet to finally unfinish

---

page and continually *ghost-write* me through his own delay-in-presence, a kind of intersubjective, metamediumystic channeling process that is not as spooky as it might at first appear. In fact, the idea of muscle memory, embodied praxis, and mobile mediums is something I investigate in my spontaneous theories in both *META/DATA: A Digital Poetics* and *remixthebook*. This partially explains why I can read a mangled online English translation of a French sentence written by Roussel and immediately postproduce it into "*the inner workings of time itself as a mobile medium where interior micro-projections coincided with a temporality subsidized by*—" It should also be noted that Roussel's day-to-day lifestyle was (literally) driven by way of luxurious caravanning where he would immerse himself in innovative forms of mobility or what today we would think of as cruising around in a personally customized, high-end Winnebago.

37. The reappearance of Joel's mobile phone as a micro-computer that enables him to take notes and maintain his various accounts (financial, narratological, etc.) is meant to highlight the atemporal qualities of the live auto-translation as remix. It also opens up the text to more poetic renderings of the source material I keep receiving from the online Gods.

But given the intricacy of the these features one could say that Camera had most certainly put in a lot of exceptionally hard work

"She's still a slave to the air current," he said and was looking directly at the woman holding the yellow balloon

"And this valve has to always work, precisely on time, with the sun, for the experiment to become fully operational"

"I just wish I didn't have to use needles, or even these claws, and that the field would just denude itself, little by little"

"Maybe a little added soot would highlight the brown decay and further contrast the yellow staining"

Camera without even acknowledging the new visitors he had led into this alter time, continued talking to himself

According to Camera, around 1650, a rich Norwegian Lord, Duke Jerkz, was madly infatuated with the beautiful Crystal, wife of one of his vassals, Baron Skedual

Jerkz was without scruples and thought he was too good for common work

This rich prick of an Overlord exhibited irresistible love whenever he felt his heart pull away from him in the presence of beauty as embodied by Crystal

Her image continually haunted his dreams and knowing that the King would have no sympathy for his predicament and could, in fact, expose him to the most violent form of retaliation, Jerkz held back his secret desire from everyone, including Crystal herself

But he could not stop himself from wanting access to her and went to stay near the residence of Baron Skedual waiting for the perfect opportunity to have an encounter with her

One night, in the park of the castle near where he was holing up, he tried to visualize Crystal strolling silently by his side as if she were there with and for him

Then the moment actually presented itself to him, and he darted toward the ill-fated young woman whose hands could not cover her mouth in time to stop her initial shriek

Skedual heard her loud exclamation in distress and called several servants to his aid, all of whom arrived in time to rescue his wife as well as grab the aggressor

By order of the castle's commander, who himself was now in a drunken fury, Duke Jerkz was sent to the bottom of a huge crypt that extended under the park

The secret entrance to the crypt was in the middle of a high hill near the scene of the crime

This underground retreat had been unused for an ethernity[38] although it had served as a refuge for the castle staff and was considered the go-to shelter in case there was a major disruption occurring inside The Massive

At the center of the underground crypt there were other prisoners standing in the soil that was composed of an easily penetrable clay

A resinous branch was flicked like a light switch just as the descent was made

Inside the crypt which was more like an eerie, dank cave, a pond languished, full of unhealthy gases and chemicals

The space was designed as a tomb and the Baron, following his servants who walked before him, left the crypt and ordered them to seal the entrance with huge red stones that needed at least two men to lift up off the ground

These heavy rocks came from a nearby alley just off the edge of the park

It had been more than a half-century since any underground communication would make its way to the castle so once you were in there, you were essentially shit out of luck

After unsuccessfully trying to stir the red stones piled in front of the entrance opening, Jerkz toured his new, vast prison, and began scrutinizing the details of his surroundings as he began imagining his escape

During his exploration inside the crypt, Jerkz had picked up, in a dark corner, some old book that had started rotting in its place, and realized that there were actually volumes of works there although they were mostly destroyed by mold or rats

Back near the light, he examined the book he held and saw at its cover: *A Collection of Head Trips*—published for Queen Sophie and authored by Laurence Weed—1591

Having found a moment to read the dismal thoughts that might be lurking within its covers, Jerkz lay down on the floor, opened the book to a random page, and read about *The Legend of the Water Ball*

38. Alfred Jarry, who coined the portmanteau word *ethernity*, was clearly a contemporary of Roussel's, as was Proust. In fact, Cocteau refers to Roussel as "the Proust of dreams."

Prince Rolfing, known for his generosity of spirit and loyalty, used to live near Elderwood

Having amassed an immense wealth, Rolfing cherished his daughter Ultra, a 100% spoiled hippy teenager who nonetheless was virtuous and forced him to view his eleven sons, all treacherous young punks, as filled with vile and cruel instincts

At Rolfing's death, Ultra, although she was his youngest, inherited all of his possessions

The eleven brothers, mad with rage, went to find the evil fairy Genevieve and begged her to lay a hex on Ultra

The fairy explained to them all that she had limited powers and would not be able to directly cause the girl to just up and die

She could, however, try to morph her into a dove and exile her to the Kingdom of Birds

They were cool with that and, after singing her magic chant, announced that Ultra was now a dove and could be safely sequestered away in the Kingdom of Birds

All of their father's treasure was ready for plunder

Along with some practical advice, the fairy gave them a cage whose interior was sheathed in linoleum and inside was their sister

Before taking her to the Kingdom of Birds or what Genevieve now referred to as the Fugal Congeries, she shared with them a cabalistic word that she said they could use to protect themselves from sudden peril that might reveal itself as an immediate encounter with their mortality

Indeed, she explained to them, this Kingdom of Birds—this Fugal Congeries—was guarded by a terrible idiot who, in the form of a sphere of aerated water, prohibited access to the adventurous souls who desired entry into its environs

The guard would tell all who desired entry into the Fugal Congeries that every living being touched by the shadow of the water ball he encompassed would immediately die

But this guard was worse than illiterate and would say things that made no sense even though he might, for example, be issuing a stern warning

For example, she said he would go off in a crazed rage declaring that "the moon in drunken fury persists in the starry night revealing a pure sky moment of nothing but a sufficiently bright and appreciable clarity"

The brothers sensed that the magic cabalistic word would soon come in handy as Genevieve had told the brothers it would

"By uttering this word," she had counseled them, "you will force the liquid globe to flee"

For example, it would come in handy if they were to "encounter its shadow"

But the brothers were in no rush to put their sister away and risk rubbing up against the legendary shadow of the water ball

What mattered to the eleven bros was that they could now take possession of their paternal resources—that and the fact that their sister with her vacant hippy eyes had been transformed into a dove stuck inside a cage with linoleum

Forgetting that Genevieve had directed them to hurry, they spent the better part of the next year partying really hard, throwing gold around like it was water, not worrying about the future

Finally, after endless rustling of feathers and mad chirping as if they were in total denial of their ultimate endgame, they made it to the Fugal Congereies

It was broad daylight and the sun was glistening in a radiant sky

Suddenly all eleven of the brothers were terrified to see the sphere of water the fairy told them about and they unsuccessfully sought the cabalistic word that would preserve their lives

After countless orgies, the word was now long forgotten

The ball approaching, they collectively freaked out and threw the cage to the ground whereupon its door opened and the dove flew out

Finding themselves full of mad terror, the bros tried to flee the aerated water scourge that pursued them relentlessly

The chase would last awhile and the party animals could finally not shake off the fluid presence of the agile water ball as its shadow kept getting closer to them

But then, as if out of nowhere, a dove, rising out of the Fugal Congeries, raced in full flight to the place this agonizing scene was being played out

Hovering over the aerated sphere to avoid its own deadly detection, the new arrival, by lowering a spout, spilled some water onto the ball causing it to evaporate

The eleven bros, realizing they were in the presence of Ultra, bent to their knees, moved and repentant

Their sister, now a dove, led them back to where they came from

They meekly followed her and once the family estate was in view, the evil experience behind them, sweet Ultra resumed a feminine form and spoke a few words of touching conciliation, joining hands with her brothers who thanked her for penetrating the shadowy water ball

All eleven of them would now live with their sister who, back in possession of whatever was left of the estate, treated them with tenderness and generosity

At the bottom of the crypt underneath the park near the castle where Skedual had buried him alive, Jerkz felt the thrill of having lived through a small conquest, reading a long forgotten book that had survived time

Seeing himself start to doze off, he lay himself down on the ground and soon fell asleep

A dream, inspired by the recently assimilated text he had just read, revealed to him the eleven brothers and their legendary story of having been terrorized by the sphere of aerated water but were then saved by the snowy dove who dissipated the ball and its deadly shadow and rescued the boys from their inevitable death

Little by little the dove became more accentuated within his dream and he felt totally touched by her presence

Opening his eyes, he saw bending over him Crystal, who pressed her hands into his chest to awaken him

With just a few words, she told him about the events that led to the affixing of the heavy red stones to the crypt's entrance

Obsessed by the thought that her assailant might die a terrible death, Crystal had snuck into the castle's library and grabbed some old manuscripts that contained the interior design of the crypt and a secret plan to smuggle illegal goods through its labyrinthine network

"I hope these documents reveal something illegal," she said, "at least enough to show that there has been some indiscretion in how this all relates to a foreign aid scheme I know will implicate them all"

His slow, patient research had brought him the complete realization of his desires

After burning in his memory every word of a significant passage that indicated just how implicated these others were in the foreign aid scheme, he watched her press her hand against an invisible spring hidden behind a rough edge in a corner of a dark wall

Soon the slab started moving higher and then stopped, supported above by four thick vertical rods that revealed a small area filled with water

Crystal pushed another spring just to her right in the same area of the wall and the water started lowering, whereupon they discovered a few steps leading to an even further underground passage

Crystal stepped in first and entered the dark tunnel and began sloshing through a thin layer of icy water that filled the entire length of the path

Now walking carefully on an angular surface that bordered the slick and icy surface of the sheet of water, she pulled the prisoner who only moments ago was lost in heavy sleep

It was as if the moment in his still fuzzy dream where the dove and Crystal became one attested to a vibrant and liberating force that enabled the simultaneous rescue of both the eleven brothers in his dream and his own persecuted presence as well

While he was engaged in these reflections, Crystal, gesturing him to follow, projected an air of confidence as she led him through the underpass that had opened up to them and presented the incredibly shallow and icy pond

After a quiet passage, they both felt relieved to find themselves hidden in the cellar of the castle

Crystal pushed another spring to fill the pond in the underground crypt back up with water

The water came in via a hose connected to Lake Cuomo and when the levels had returned to their former height, the secret slab entry, now at the other end of the passage, descended and closed with a hermetically sealed tight shut

A delicate system of rods and sinks obstructed the length of the hose that was drilled deep into one of the walls of the pond

Over the years all of the young women affiliated with the castle admired the foresight with which the architect devised this secret passage that was quite useful to many of them as they would undoubtedly need their own escape routes to and from the castle

Once they walked up some stairs, Crystal, who had two keys that she was able to use to open a door to the porch and then the park, granted her assailant complete freedom and forgiveness

Instead of giving in to an earlier temptation to abduct this beautiful creature before him, Jerkz, influenced by the story of the dove and the eleven brothers, threw himself at Crystal's feet and begged repentance

Then he fled into the night while Crystal quietly returned to her quarters

Camera seemed to take delight in this subject of the underground crypt, its secret passages and hose mechanism, and the instability of the direction everything was going in

It might be an "inadequate translation" of what was really said—or written—he confessed, but at least it was a story

A story (inside of another story ((inside of another story)) (((and so on))))

The unpredictable nature of the contraption both before him and that he had immersed himself in as part of the larger story informing his creative process, had somehow stimulated the transformation of his life-work into an organic form of ongoing composition, and this had, in time, completely overwhelmed him

He was patient with his art work just as he was in telling his stories, he told his hostage audience, all the time knowing that one's experience of the entire apparatus before them could be altered at any given moment by an excessive wind or an undue amount of rainfall

Any combination of effects could increase the chances of disturbing the flight of the balloon and tarnish the functioning surfaces of the mirrors and lens

Over time, he would collect and store in a large box all of the teeth he had extracted since discovering the magic process of magnetization enabled by combining the gray and blue metals

But he was never really able to predict the future accurately which meant he had absolutely no control over the direction—*the literal direction*—this art work would take

Everyone could see that this inability to forecast was weighing heavily under his eyes, even as he admitted to spending entire nights full of nonstop work perfecting the admixture of multi-colored hues of light made out of these dental materials and that through a strange and prodigious glowing effect would produce an improvised lighthouse that would revolutionize the world of artmaking by allowing any artist to work under the stars with the same security as if they were in daylight

From dawn to subsequent dawn, long black hours and complex preparations were turning into prophetic light

Serene evenings heading toward zero necessity

La Demoiselle

Careful not to waste a moment, an applied aesthetic concurrent with the philosophy of creative evolution[39]

Recombinatory potential[40]

A model run

A gaseous eros

A ferocious tease looking from high above

The future mosaic (of teeth, of all shades, ready to be extracted, to be caught in the various pilgrimages of the paver paving its way toward the sky, toward new heights)

In advance (of the broken arm)[41], *the teeth, wisely directed according to the exact meaning that they collectively expressed via their different contours, their constant chattering, not to mention their roots, always separated from the crown, instantly, via a high-tech saw*

By this time Camera was imagining the future clutches of a supplemental motor mechanism loaded with new chronometers which, once installed, would work nonstop for exactly 233 hours, a superior device whose accuracy

39. There can be no doubt that the philosophical investigations of Henri Bergson were of significant interest around the time Roussel composed *Locus Solus*. It's not my job to elaborate on what connection, if any, was ever made between the two (Jarry, though, was at one time Bergson's student). For my own open-ended, speed-edit remix of Bergson, see *Creative Evolution: Natural Selection and the Urge to Remix* at http://www.livingbooksaboutlife.org/books/Creative_Evolution

40. Go there if you dare: http://www.grammatron.com

41. An obvious reference to Duchamp's *In Advance of the Broken Arm*, the first and one of his best known *readymades*, a gestural form of conceptual practice that intuitively subverts the traditional notion that beauty is a defining characteristic of art. The strange use of conceptual titles in Duchamp's readymades indicated his adherence toward art as an intellectual operation that would experiment with language independent of the object. The object's status as art thus came under question and the linguistic encounter one faces when coming upon a readymade title could be related to Camera's description of his elaborate art objects and performances that are then intellectually contextualized after one witnesses their functioning presence. This series of notes performs a similar function and is written in the spirit of titling a readymade object, one that seems to have chosen me as much as I have chosen it. In fact, as Duchamp once remarked, "[t[he object chooses its author as much as the author chooses it," and this idea is something that entangled itself in my thoughts throughout my speed-translation of Roussel's fabricated, textual objects.

could be maintained to the thousandth of a second, phasing perfectly with the solar year—from the lively expectorations of the first sunrise to the final adventures of the last sunset

The time-setting of the valve could be applied to violent blasts that would cause partial deflation of the balloon which would complicate the air travel creating a backlash that would corrupt the lens and oblige the viewer to accept being dazzled by the yellow glow that materialized as a result of the loss of hydrogen

Down below, the two washers made of the two magical metals who had found each other unabashedly attracted to each other, would always be tasked with easily extracting and dropping the various teeth scattered in, on, and around the sculpture

On the other hand, the strange arrangement of the three chronometers and their prefabricated internal extensions produced scary calculations

Was this due to some faulty moralistic mathematics? (Camera—questioning, again)

As for the mirrors, their perfectly regular tips would follow the sun in its course, a mechanical operation that would take place day in and day out

Ideally, the appliance would invariably remain stationary from sunset to sunrise, and would never be touched, since the chronometers would be set to advance until the project was once again finally unfinished[42]

The dials, left visible, would constantly move about but, also, free of disturbance, continue to reliably deliver sameness in realtime

Camera the alchemist filled the balloon with a fundamental balance of hydrogen and, taking advantage of the vagaries of the wind, slowly pieced together the toothy mosaic so that it grew as necessary, and when appropriate, the retiree would take a positive breath and lift the woman up along with the rest of the artwork

By the time it ended, the experience with the work would last between seven to ten days and, thanks to the wonderful adaptation of his chronometers, perform a beautiful choreography where the teeth or roots were always moved to their appropriate place

42. A point of convergence for Camera, Roussel, Duchamp and myself. See note 19.

Depending on the whimsical face of the wind, ones journey with the work would alter course, a breeze finally staying resolute in its one direction creating an opportunity for the unit to resume its flight as if being directed by the unnatural conjugal forces of chance and destiny

From time to time, Camera would entertain small groups of strangers like the group he was with now, and several people would be quietly approached and asked to spy on the next ascent of the balloon reporting all they had seen

As Camera was finishing up his improvised presentation, a familiar popping noise caught everyone's attention

It was the three claws supporting the yellow balloon woman who was undergoing a boost at the stem of her body, powered by the added timer set in the bottom of the post

The lens turned as usual to create supplemental hydrogen—and then turned a second time while the apparatus began to fly, stealing the root

* * *

A slow breath drove the woman to the feathered pen that was deployed in the hat of the retiree who was still smoking[43]

The valve functioned as it was supposed to and Camera, posing as cameras do, dropped spreads of washers thin and light on to the preying apparatus thus completing a pink square that subtly degraded while forming on the edge of the feathered pen that was lodged within a ridge of scarlet roots growing from another view of the hat from a different angle

The claws found their three suitors and the internal extensions were simultaneously released upon contact

43. Is it any wonder that it was the Surrealists who were the first vocal proponents of Roussel's work? Once Roussel moved his creative arsenal into the field of theater, his work could no longer be ignored by the public, but it was still heavily shat upon by the cultural cognoscenti. The Surrealists, however, accepted Roussel's quirky monsters as simpatico souls worth nurturing. As John Ashbery notes in his postscript to the translation of Foucault's *Death and the Labyrinth*, Paul Éluard wrote a review of one of Roussel's plays where "[t]he characters are all marked with the same sign: each is prey of the same imagination, which carries earth and heaven on its head. All the stories in the world are woven out of words; all the stars in the world are at their foreheads, mysterious mirrors of the magic of dreams and of the strangest and most miraculous events [. . .] May Raymond Roussel continue to show us everything which has not been. We are a small group for whom this reality alone matters."

Almost immediately the lens performed a new maneuver as if parasailing—and this was followed by a second turn even as it seemingly wished to take on a different meaning by moving counterclockwise

The paver, continuing its flight in a straight line, dropped from its position above the small crowd a canine pearl that, according to Camera, came from the mouth of an enthusiastic American inventor who had completely misread most of Camera's intentions but wanted to collaborate with him nonetheless

Then a fast cloud covered the entire disk of the sun bringing an array of different disturbances in the airstream and mildly disrupted the mechanical environment so that it began exuding a field of New Currents

The passage of a veil of mist came in just as the presentation was ending and left the impression that Camera had planned for it to happen all along

Joel or his ghost kept taking quick mobile notes:

Militant hub glass station

Sun free of all vapors

A hearty diet of hydrogen

The dove of a dream

Lowering herself now to the tip of the ground

A balancing act

The other one claws

A soft grinding of teeth

Subtle masticatory sensation and the sound of animal pleasure

The protruding needle extension

Decay signaling and tethering a connection to yet still more decay

Bluetooth

The cloud, moving quickly enough, ceased to veil the sun, which then regained its full power

This resurgence of the prehistoric yellow monster marked the end of the contrary currents felt during the momentary eclipse and the breeze resumed its former orientation while the mist disappeared

The lens had no need to try to cause the flight of the errant machine that still appeared to ready itself and, defying both its operational collaborators and gravity, leapt gracefully up toward the illusory underwear of the retiree where a choir of steamy acts further stimulated the valve

Once again the claws and their penetrating extensions found three new points of entry—the ground and two foreign teeth of different thickness

Under the influence of the chronometers and what had already been programmed to happen, two needles plunged unevenly toward the ground but one landed on one of the foreign teeth

Now an indigo deposit fell just where it was needed

The other yellow ball(oon) embedded in the artwork and gratuitously pretending to emulate its extraplanetary master, was immediately bequeathed more strength than it knew what to do with and continued its journey toward an inevitable black and hideous void

Advertising, chances to purchase memorabilia, an endless waiting in line—none of this would be necessary as the insider group was encouraged to attend the next automated spectacle

Camera led them to another region of his vast property

3[44]

At the direction of Camera, the group approached a giant diamond which, at the end of the esplanade, had already drawn everyone's eyes on repeated occasions

It's tremendous brilliance revealed a monstrous jewel, two meters high and three meters wide with a rounded, ellipse-shaped figure that, when thrown under the rays of the sun, would create an almost unsustainable profusion of lights that adorned it with aesthetically manipulated streaks of lightning heading in all directions

As the party stared at it all, they could see that the diamond was supported by an artificial rock that was set low and served as a relatively small base from which to secure the gem

44. Chapter Three was by far my favorite chapter to translate. It was the moment in the performance when I really began seeing how one could learn to co-create by way of translation. The readwrite remix process took off right from the first sentence, and I was reminded of something the American-in-Paris Harry Mathews once said in an interview: "If the reader is the only creator, the writer gets to share and in fact participates in that act of creation in the stage of rewriting." For me, translating *Locus Solus* is all about rewriting *[readwrite remixing]*. Of course, it was Mathews who funded and assisted Ashbery in editing an experimental literary journal titled *Locus Solus*. Mathews even translated the first chapter of the novel for the premiere issue. Just as Duchamp has said "Roussel showed me the way," Mathews has said "my reading Roussel enabled me to write prose as if it were poetry." My version is also self-consciously examining a more poetic, line-by-line, rendering of the text, although the term "poetic" is loosely applied here and is more in tune with my larger Conceptual practice as a remix artist.

It was cut like a real precious stone and appeared to contain within its materiality various moving objects

Little by little, in approaching it, it took on the aura of a musical wave emitting its wonderful effects that consisted of a strange series of strokes, arpeggios, and other ranges that would rise and fall

In reality, as everyone could see as they rendered it into clearer vision, the diamond was actually a huge container filled with water

What was not as clear was the array of exceptional elements that were undoubtedly being cleverly remixed into the liquid composition contained in its thick, irradiated, walls of glass

Applying one's eyesight into various aspects of the glass would accentuate how the piece itself embraced every circular glance while simultaneously sharing everything that was going on inside

In the middle of the piece, a young woman, graceful and thin, coated with a flesh-colored jersey, stood upright on the bottom and was completely submerged in the internal environment, gently swinging her head as if algorithmically coded to emit a certain aesthetic charm

Wearing a cheerful smile, she seemed to breathe freely in the liquid element wrapping her from all sides

Her hair was the star of the permanent exhibition, blond and beautiful, rising above her as if a mossy sea vegetable delicacy but not quite reaching the surface above her

Her slightest movement would cause every hair on her head to vibrate in its own aqueous viscosity and her entire body would vibrate under the friction of the fluid sheets of circulating *aqua-micans* whose subtle waves played her like a voluptuous reed instrument

Her rising mass of hair would occasionally transform into a kind of thick and mesmerizing rope dance

This musical and vibratory hair phenomenon explained the seductive sounds one heard as they all approached the diamond

The clever young woman was deliberately producing these soundscapes, carefully adjusting the crescendos or diminuendos by varying degrees of force and speed signaled by the oscillating movements of her neck, itself enthralled with the head it was attached to

Ranges, traits, behavioral characteristics—the arpeggios, in their ascots and melodious tumbles, could shatter an aural field of at least three octaves

Oftentimes the performance would turn simply with the soft, light gait of the skull as it maintained its very limited register

It was as if some late 19th century machinery had printed a large, attractive 3–D body that, in realtime, rapidly prototyped itself as the central figure in a composition designed as one simultaneous and continuous movement, and the woman's body, slowly simmering in its self-motivating experiential broth, would conduct a complex water instrument that freely gave itself over to maximum extent and tone

This mysterious companion of an instrument was ideally suited to the plasticized poses of the young woman who would play the instrument with her unique dance style that further accentuated the liquid medium where the surround sound would spread in multiple dimensions

Sometimes in passing, a surprised animal must have explored the huge tub and its ideal swimmer, for there were serious claw marks on its outer structure

Pink and free from any clothing, her impressive skin was a call from the wild—and a call *to* the wild, easily diverting the attention of any observer whose eyes would attach themselves on to the scene before them like a cat identifying its next bird kill

On the right, there was a tiny object submerged at a depth of five decimeters hanging at the end of a wire

It could have been the internal residue of a human face with no vestige of bone, flesh or even skin elements

Under the brain everything remained intact, the nerves and muscles still developing their complex networks

Thanks to a thin almost invisible carcass gently supporting its lower corners, it retained its original form even as nothing of this plexus-configuration could be clearly recognized as cheeks, mouth, or eyes

Each and every fiber appeared to be wrapped in its own watery envelope

The wire above would occasionally connect with the blond mermaid causing an odd lightening effect which would then cause the formally flaccid bachelors hatching in the head below to take on the *apparition of an appearance*, a peripheral row of miniaturized, ghostly skeletons that would light up just below that part of the head belonging to the brain

Once again the wire extending from this loose kelp brain would touch the towering Bride of the Underworld and spark a connection

Continuing the review to the right, everyone could see a tiny column of drums, or barrels, which stood perfectly erect and motionless in the animated *aqua-micans*

On the bottom of the vast tank lay a long metal cone that had apparently been drilled with several very sharp holes

Camea was checking out the left side of this sculptural object that now consumed everyone's attention, and each participant began closely examining a series of small individuals, some of them couples or even a few groups bundled together, who would rise vertically through the water tank and then, unable to reach the surface, fell to the bottom where they would briefly rest before starting their next ascension

Dr. Cam, fully comfortable playing the just-mad-enough scientist or artist-inventor, was watching a synchronized couple rise and fall and then rise again, before giving this explanation:

"A superstar athlete, let's call him Michael Jordan, impedes the momentum of a robust bird whom, affecting a kind of criminal chic, attempts to strangle Alexander the Great"

Not exactly, and Camera was certain that the "inadequate translation" he was always depending on to make his stories up was now going to try and relate the tale of a hero in a tragic scene that begins with a man softly sleeping on a sumptuous oriental bed

Still, every air bubble floating inside the chemically altered Waterworld circulating within the precision cut diamond held out the potential for any story to be told and, if one so wished, translated

For example, in one air bubble, one could see attached to the wall next to a bed, an extended gold wire that, on its other end, was wrapped in a noose around the sleeping hero's neck

The noose was held tightly by the talon of a gigantic green bird that spread its wings whenever it wanted to tighten the potentially deadly embrace of the tense suicidal thread

But this was not a slam dunk by any means and, yes, after a flap or two of the wings resulted in a further tightening of the wire around the hero's neck, the bubble burst and the bird fell into the powerful hands of the superstar athlete who was once again using the incident to further promote himself and further supplement his endless endorsements

After the air bubble disappeared, the descent began, and the hands of the superstar athlete deviated from the norm releasing the bird to its original place

Once placed on the bottom of the container, the bird-turned-inanimate-object remained stationary before making its next ascension that, at the same height, ended with a recurrence of the already observed movements, coinciding with a sharp expulsion of air

"Here we have Pilate feeling the burn of the terrible seal marked with strokes of flame singed on his forehead," said Camera indicating a Cartesian diver vertically moving straight up toward the surface

Standing, hands raised to his face tense by suffering, Pilate, with half closed eyes and an expression of anguish mixed with terror, reaches the highest point possible, a globule of air escaping through some occipital opening while a luminous sign, due no doubt to an electric light placed on his head, was dazzling on the front of his avatar-presence

During the slow fall of the diver trinket, the neon sign blinking on his forehead went blank, ready to return to its former brightness at the next escalation

Camera's index pointed to a new figure and articulated in this brief announcement:

"The emerging literary artist, Gil, stirred on the ruins of Balbek with the famous sistrum of the great poet Missir"

And then, to indicate the multi-directional trajectory the narrative could take at any given moment, he auto-remixed himself:

"Gil spun his poetry on the ruins of Bilbao, most especially the famous sister museum designed by the great architect Gehry"

This time, at the height of its ascending route, the air bubble played out a short scene where the figure, undoubtedly Gil, made a gesture by raising his arm and, with that gesture, cheerfully waved the sistrum he was firmly gripping in his right hand as if vibrating his entire arm the way a jackhammer might penetrate a hole into a pliant sidewalk

Camera nonchalantly dropped another line: "Using a knife concealed in his bed, the dwarf Pizzarrhea slyly performs a series of light taps on his body so that his annual blood sweat, watched by three village observers, appears more abundant"

This comment by Camera applied to the current group lying motionless in a bubble on the bottom of the large tank

Prominent among the immobile group was the scruffy runt-being lying in bed, sheets up to his chin, as if cocooned in a sort of cradle made for a child

The dwarf maintained an expression of animated cunning expressing his desire to show off before the three fixed monitors watching for his body to signal the appearance of bloody sweat that would immediately be decoded for its symbolic value

A very small pearl of blood-sweat formed on the hideous face of the runt whose linen skin, dyed an artificial red, appeared to be on the verge of hemorrhaging

Intense scarlet coloration came across that part of the tank where the drama was playing itself out—eventuated by way of a light powder suddenly released by a mass of microscopic holes that together formed a foaming eczema over the surface of the dwarf's face

Another group of four inconsequential characters whose bubble had gone up to the top of the tank, now returned to their deep starting point, nestled into the incarnate dust, dissolving into the vestige of red-dyed water

"Here," confided Camera, "Atlas has just temporarily unloaded the weight of the world by taking the globe off of his shoulders and, with a furious kick, sending it to the constellation of Capricorn"

Highlighting Camera's words, a new diver, shooting upward, was under review

This figure, bending his knee and showing the sole of his right foot ready to kick, was obviously Atlas who, seen from behind, turned his head to give a furious look at the glistening globe which had fallen behind him, and that was connected by an imperceptible and rigid wire to a multitude of small stars, each one illuminated in a network of genuine cosmological togetherness

Atlas kept hoping for a higher phase of experience when, suddenly, out of the top of his skull, came the designated output: several centimeters of cubic air (which was much better than, say, several centimeters of pubic hair)

Atlas abruptly placed his heel right into Capricorn correcting the displacement of stars that must have been inventoried without the attention of an authorized uranography

His leg came down, returning to its initial position where all of the issues of the world reappeared without a moment's notice

Camera, watching Atlas fail yet again, succinctly changed the subject yet again:

"Voltaire's moment of doubt came when he came upon a girl lost in ecstatic prayer"

Voltaire, his hand gripping a companion, was lost in profile, contemplating the anxious teenage girl who was fervently praying and who, from the side, was now facing the sky

After resting on solid supports at the end of the dive, this minor scene taking place inside yet another air bubble, once again flew up gently and upon approaching the top of the tank's surface, was halted by the latin word *Dubito*, which escaped Voltaire's lips in the form of numerous tiny air bubbles which, as a group, created six perfect letters in the most elegant calligraphy ever seen

"Five months old," Camera kept pointing at other air bubbles and digressing, "Richard Wagner, sleeping in the arms of his mother, was already placed before an inspired charlatan who would curse out his predictions of what the baby's future life would be"

And there, inside another air bubble, a man, whose left arm was extended toward the child, pointed his index finger at the baby

He was an old man with long grey hair who looked like a crooked nosed magician hovering over a small table where an inkwell containing a grayish powder and iron filings was opened

This time, a defective wave from an undivided air mass spun the figures in the bubble around, creating a disturbance that twisted the mother's wrist and the old man's index now giving three tweaks to the inkwell on the edge of the table

Out of this random turbulence, three words appeared as if rolling some ashen dice: *Will be plundered*

Exactly what forces or figures had produced this prophetic outcome and whether or not it would have the desired effect of predicting the future no longer mattered as the entire scene became enmeshed in what was clearly a mechanical ballet

Or at least a choreographed water sport with irreproachable aesthetic intentions

This last review with the old man, mother, and baby completed, everyone's attention was now drawn toward seven delicate sea creatures who would soon reveal their athletic capabilities by making their continual comings and goings, moving up and down and twisting around without any set agenda—each occupying with varying degrees of height and depth their own sense of self-actualized space and self-generated momentum

Camera pointed to the top of the diamond container

The edges were disproportionate and framed a central circular opening

Next to the opening was a bottle of white wine whose label bore the word *Sauternes* and a big jar where the seven seahorses were now idly floating

The chest of each sea creature was finely crossed in the middle of their protrusions with a long wire, the end of which was stuffed inside a tiny metal case resting nearby

Each of the seven fragile circus performers had their own color, evoking the rainbow spectrum

A fishing net lay with the jar

Camera cautiously opened a small bottle containing several large red pills

He took one and after shuffling around, skillfully engaged the large hole at the top of the huge diamond

A scarlet nutmeg light permeated the air

There was a soft singing coming from a choir of watery ventriloquism—

—a randy domestic creature was tracking through the water—

—and then—

—the animal slowly descended—

—his skin pink and naked, touching bottom . . .

It was at this moment that Camera introduced the onlookers to a life-size cat named Wong Kar Lens[45]

45. Doubling down on the name Camera in conjunction with all of the descriptions of lenses that have already appeared in the text, why not refer to another artist-director, Wong Kar Wai? At this point, the project has become both a durational challenge and a daily dose of ritualistic fun. Is that allowed?

Due to a special oxygenation formula composed of a variety of exceptional properties he was not at liberty to discuss, Camera explained that this made it possible for purely terrestrial beings to breathe unconstrained within the waves of the tank

This is why the woman with the musical hair who, Camera suggested, was a postmodern dancer, could support with impunity—along with the cat—a prolonged immersion

Leading all eyes toward the right of the tank, Camera pointed out a human head composed solely of brain matter, muscles, and nerves—and he brought the group closer to look at it

It was the head of Danton that, everyone would soon find out, Camera had become the owner of through odd circumstances

While Camera spoke, the hair of the dancer created a musical accompaniment of melodious vibrations further electrifying the entire tank as if sheathing the device in a microfiberous sleeve of residual sound

Now came a silence as he motioned to Wong Kar Lens who, having risen again, immediately dropped to the bottom of the tank and secured around his face, ear to ear, a metal cone whose tip leaned against the wall of the container

Then the cat swam to Danton's head

Camera said that due to the effect of a specific chemical composition, our eyes would now see how the cat could expose Danton's head to a strong electrical power concentrated in the cornea of Danton's eye by slightly touching it on the surface tip with a conductive substance emitted from the cone

Thanks to a subtle prodding, Wong Kar Lens knew to touch Danton's features gently with the tapered part of his strange conical mask causing the brain's muscles and nerves to undergo a vigorous discharge making them act as if under the mnemonic influence of old habits

Having achieved this with a delicate touch, the cat would once again put the tip of the metal cone on a part of the brain exposed before him

The feedback relay that the cat, cone, and cornea created would trigger certain movements that must have been exciting for Wong Kar Lens, because he would suddenly execute an impressive water gymnastics the more he got into it all

Some of the twitching muscles seemed to trigger Danton's absent eyes into a flash of illumination while others would periodically upset the face causing lifting, lowering, convulsing or relaxing of the eyebrow and forehead

The lips on Danton's head churned with a crazy agility undoubtedly signaling the prodigious oratorical faculties he formerly possessed

Seen in profile, Wong Kar Lens, with a few aquatic moves, stood staring beside the head without keeping it hidden from the observers and would occasionally prod the cornea of Danton's eye and then quickly pull away

Someone must have been thinking that by playfully tweaking Danton's head, the cat would inadvertently reveal how life inside the tank could be construed as the theatrical residue of an historical facility stuck in motionless time

During a lull after the cat's ongoing agitations had ceased, the tank resumed its normal fluctuation of currents

Throughout the repetitive exercises he kept performing, the animal seemed to keep its cautious optimism while also enjoying its freedom, maintaining its balance at the end of a wire that connected to the top of a simple suction cup adhering to the transparent ceiling of the immense gem

Camera, who had previously, in similar experiments, used his lip reading skills to interpret the movement of oral muscles coming from the great orator's lips, cherry-picked some of the incoherent fragments of speech that kept coming out of Danton's mouth and that bespoke a vibrant patriotism

Pell mell, catchy pronouncements previously postured in public now launched memory waves that would automatically infect all of the activity at the bottom of the tank with its eclectic debris

There on the bottom of the massive water sculpture, air bubbles carried within their ranks multiple flashbacks from a variety of times gone by and, in Danton's case, one particular bubble was filled with a drama where significant hours of full parliamentary activity had clearly taken place

Meanwhile, the remainder of facial muscles masking Danton's potential tirades were clearly indicating how much his hideous muzzle was dead set on expressing its volumetric opinions

On Camera's command, the cat disconnected from the metal cone and lazily fell to the deep bottom of the tank

While asking his guests to remain immobile, Camera proceeded toward the monstrous diamond and ascended its luxurious nickel-plated exterior ladder until, standing above his patrons, he took command of the post near the top of the circular opening

With the help of the fishing net, he lifted one of the seahorses out of the jar to immerse it in the *aqua-micans* where an unexpected event occurred

To the right and left side of each breast there existed the edges of two artificial openings from which the sea creature would breath

This unusual breathing method seemed to be put to use when necessary—for example, when an athletic event was about to take place

Slowly, over time, these racing events, which had occurred only periodically, would happen with extreme frequency

Camera, taking hold of the bottle of Sauternes, began to pour a trickle of its contents into the strange reservoir

Gold wine, with no indication of any additives, solidified once it made contact with the manipulated tank water and suddenly coagulated into a cluster of magical chunks as if borrowing its essence from the material world of realtime objects, and soon these golden chunks fell in sunny blocks to the bottom of the pool

Finally, having released an adequate dose, the strict sommelier corked the bottle back up and placed it near the jar

The remaining seahorses held their own, forming topological shapes via their constant self-kneading out of which occasionally emerged a solid yellow ball measuring three centimeters

Turning on the spot in all directions, it was as if the ball of seahorses were a professionally managed operational system that, when coated with wax, would form a perfect roundness without defects

But before long, they were collectively embodying a sphere of absolute homogeneity stripped of all interior difference

Unfurling in abrupt agreement, the swarm now stood individually, side by side, in a single row that delineated the ordered color of a perfect rainbow

Below the spherical opening up top, there ensued a liberal descending of the horses

Arriving to the level marked by a double wire attached to two columnar barrels, a strange attraction magnetized all of the creatures toward the enormous dancer and they responded as if performing with algorithmic certainty the prefigured acts anticipated by a matchmaking service that has already accounted for the laws of seduction as they relate to the collective mettle of a herd or bachelor apparatus that would unconsciously give way to the blond desire-engine transmitting its gaseous eros in waves of hair music

Resistance was futile and resulted in the brusque acceptance of an experiential élan (without knowing—or with an inexplicable animal knowing)

A cry of surprise sprung forth from Danton's dead lips

The sound evoked Apollo's chariot putting on the brakes

Having ardently participated in the brilliant program produced in this liquid underworld, the ball, yellow and diaphanous, continued emitting blinding rays transforming its seer presence into a temporal day star

On the surface of the water a continuous hatching of tiny air bubbles were being expelled from the breast-piece of all of the sea-bachelors as they circumvented the small columnar barrel with fixed intensity

The tension of the stringwire across their breasts tugged at the nearby metal cases

The bright yellow solar sphere whose mass formed a perfect curve was now sonically droning low frequencies which remixed well with the avant-garde hair composition of the postmodern dancer

Slipping by both Danton and the postmodern dancer successively, the seahorses passed in front of Camera's guests in a kind of show parade of almost-synchronized swimming performance

Camera then announced the race, requesting each of his guest participants to pick a seahorse, and then declared that though all of the small creatures were athletically handicapped, they would be slowly pulled by a thin wire toward the finish line and so, after giving each horse a simple, temporary name, everyone chose one merely as way to bet on the possibility of having the distinct honor of having won the race

Once the wandering row of seahorses had perfectly aligned, Camera indicated three complete solo circuits that would comprise the length of the race and then made a gesture with his arm that the intelligent animals understood as the start of the race

Delicately initiating their three pectoral fins and dorsal, the competitors hastened to accelerate their march

After a stylish turn, the competitors ran impetuously to the left

Tertiary was leading the pack followed closely by Sextus, Primus, and Quinella

Despite the disarray in the squad's original attempt to line up in coherence, the stringwires, endowed with a certain elasticity, remained absolutely rigid and all of the competitors were free of delays even as they may have had to undergo the occasional light bump

Faustina, the postmodern dancer, continued to melodiously bob her hair that served as the band providing musical accompaniment to the mythological ride

A brilliant air bubble revolved around the scene and revealed the figure Pilate whose face was illuminated by the shining yellow sphere

The Oculist Witnesses[46], who had until this point kept a lower profile, viewed this all as what could be termed a "flexible translation" of what was really happening all around them[47]

The position of one of the Cartesian divers was too close for comfort and the solar ball was close to brushing up against the celestial sphere at the foot of Atlas who was always on the verge of unleashing his automated kick-blow

The seven horses formed a unified bachelor apparatus that could have easily been eight or possibly nine, and together they created a mass of soft, fully-oxyengated pearls which in numbers alone proved how much excitement the race had activated just in terms of respiratory exchange

At the first turn of the horses, a new air bubble once again was filled with the word *Dubito* as it escaped from the lips of Voltaire

Camera left his high command post and descended the luxurious ladder before taking a new position in front of a special place filled with a very small circle marked in black

46. The underlined phrase refers to the extreme right lower section of Duchamp's *Large Glass*. The splicing of the Oculist Witnesses into this narrative suggests that the reader (and writer/translator) have become voyeuristic accomplices with the group touring Camera's property. It also resonates with being a juror at a trial (see notes 9, 11, 12, and 23 above) as well as becoming the artist's voyeuristic accomplice just by performing a parallel durational achievement *with* him (for example, as when one reads the work of Robbe-Grillet).

47. Flexibility is key. As is balance. As is emotional ballast, even as one's head continually finds itself drifting toward the clouds.

Moving three steps back, everyone could clearly see in the tiny, dark circumference a drumlike column, now converted into a winning post

On the homestretch, the horses, seemingly aware of the next stage of the fight, put in amazing effort and, to the applause of the one who had their money on him, Second-To-None came out of nowhere and suddenly took on the final advantage

Camera declared the winner and then decreed the end of the race by chastising the rest of the docile bunch who then nonchalantly turned away and began their idle flâneur trick by floating back to wherever they imagined they came from in a way that suggested everything was just fine and dandy

Keeping a distance from the spirited drift of the curvaceous saunterers, Wong Kar Lens, seeing the restored calm, began to pursue the solar sphere with bullet speed, mischievously kicking the soft yellow ball with his leg

This created erratic lighting in the tank and heretofore unexpected scenes were now becoming nouveau cinema

While the special visitors to Locus Solus felt their eyes held captive as they watched everything from Faustina the postmodern dancer to the Cartesian divers and the cat gymnastics to seahorse races, Camera began a more detailed narrative discourse on the diamond and its contents[48]

* * *

Camera said that after endless experimentation, he had actually found a way to invent his *aqua-micans*[49], a type of fortified chem-water that, thanks to a special and very powerful oxygenation technique he had discovered but that needed to be renewed from time to time, would allow any terrestrial organism, man or animal, to live completely immersed in the pool without interrupting their standard respiratory functions

48. Roussel's narrative style, whereby exposition is invariably followed by explanation, takes hold at this point in the story. This Rousselian approach to narrative has been covered in all of the important close readings of his work. Lucky for me, it's not my job to read through them all and tell you which ones I think are best. My translation, being something different than a close reading per se, can only invite the reader to Google "Roussel+method+writing" if they so wish.

49. The introduction of *aqua-micans*, along with the previously (un)translated *semen-contra*, not to mention the soon to arrive *résurrectine*, form the perfect admixture of chemically-altered substances I need to fully render the genetic relationship between the various linguistic components that, together, auto-compose this narrative machine.

Once the water had been invented, he then wanted to build a huge glass container to make visible some experiments that he planned to conduct on several specimen contained in the foreign liquid

From the outset, he confided, the most striking feature of the imaginative waves that undulated in this magic liquid was its prodigious brilliance

The slightest drop would shine in a blinding way and, even in the dark, would glisten as if from the cleanest fire imaginable

Anxious to emphasize his findings, Camera adopted a multifaceted structure that, once completed and filled with its extraterrestrial water, would resemble a gigantic diamond

For the indispensable role of water sprite, the guru-inventor chose a seductive yet graceful woman who, according to his precise instructions, then manifested as the postmodern dancer Faustina, known for her harmonious and beautiful attitude toward life

Wearing a flesh colored one-piece that fit naturally and accentuated her flowing blond hair, Faustina ascended a luxurious and delicate double nickel-plated metal ladder that was installed near the large diamond and entered the wave

Despite Camera's encouragement, who in immersing himself in the tank had often experienced easy underwater breathing that took advantage of the manipulated oxygenation of the water, Faustina sank with caution, grasping with both hands the edges at the top of the tank and shook her head a few times before taking the final plunge

Finally, after several tests, each one longer than the last, and feeling reassured about the conditions of the experiment, she let herself go completely and gained a permanent foothold at the bottom of the container

Her thick mass of hair gently went up above her, facilitated by the extreme lightness of her being and the recalibrated liquid pressure in the contraption

Little by little she would be taken over by an intoxicated laughter after having absorbed too much of the oxygen

But over the long run, a continuous resonance in the forms of waves shook her hair that then bulged and retreated or simply went wild as her head moved, more or less

The strange music she began emitting soon took over her body and was intense

Each hair vibrated like its own string instrument and, at the slightest movement, would create a symphonic sound resembling a wind harp that played an infinite variety of long threads of sound

Depending on their length, the silky blond strands would emit different notes that spanned more than three octaves

After half an hour, Cam, perched at the nearby ladder, helped Faustina by grabbing her with one hand by the nape of the neck so as to move her near him at the top of the container so that she could then get herself back on to the ground

Camera, who had followed the developments with great focus and care, examined her splendid mane and discovered a kind of excessively thin aqueous sheath formed by a subtle deposit of chemical salts that had, by now, dissolved inside the liquid underworld and coated her every hair

Violently electrified by the presence of these imperceptible envelopes of magical sonic emission, the full mop of hair was now set to vibrate under the frictions of the brilliant water and—as the innovator had stated previously—united a fantastic acoustic power with its incomparable luminosity

Since then, Camera wondered what effect would produce a similar phenomenon on a cat fleece, already so easily electrifiable in its own right

He had a white Siamese cat named Wong Kar Lens, notable for its intelligence and who, in no time, was immersed in the container

Although frightened at first, Wong Kar Lens sank gently continuing to breath normally and quickly adapted to the new atmosphere

He touched bottom and began to wander around curiously

Soon, feeling lighter than usual, the cat started executing large jumps to entertain himself and, little by little, he succeeded and, a short time later, had actually taught himself underwater swimming which soon became quite familiar

The shock of the fleece was accomplished according to expectations and the cat's hair, a little ruffled, began to vibrate—but due to their uniform shortness in length, they gave off only a humming drone sound that came across weak and confused

This was contrary to Faustina who, with her raw, at times platinum blond and phosphorescent hair-glow, was totally intense, especially in the daylight, where each strand would slice violently on the bright bursts of water she immersed herself in

Still, dazzling micro-flames of aqua brilliance seemed to surround Wong Kar Lens who, when left to his own devices, would swim with ease and continue to develop his underwater motor skills

Noting the cat's inevitable sensitivity to the intense oxygenation of the water, Camera wanted to interrupt his play for now and, retaking command of the ladder atop the giant sculpture, he called Wong Kar Lens who immediately swam to the surface

He grabbed the cat by pinching the skin behind the neck and went back down the ladder to place him on the ground

But during the short trip down the ladder, constant electric shocks shook his nervous system due to the contact his hand had with the cat's white fur, each hair of which was surrounded by the thin, transparent aqueous sheath

Still sore from the shocks, Camera suddenly thought he would share a tale with his visitors, one that was directly related to the violence perpetrated by his constant curiosity and subsequent commotion

Philbert, Camera's great-great-grandfather, had grown friendly with Danton since they were both born at the same time in the small town of Arcis

Later, during his political career, Danton never forgot his childhood friend, who had become a financier and led an active life in Paris, albeit obscure and consciously avoiding publicity so as to not come across as just another yes man of the famous and powerful orator his childhood friend had become

When Danton was sentenced to death, Philbert penetrated the state bureaucracy to receive his friend's final wishes

Having got wind of some of the rumors circulating among his enemies, namely that they were determined to throw his remains into an anonymous grave without any tombstone or indication that these were, in fact, his remains, Danton pleaded with his loyal friend to attempt the impossible—to appropriate his head with the complicity of others loyal to his legacy

At once Philbert went to find the executioner Sanson to expose the supreme wish of the prisoner to him

A fanatical admirer of the illustrious orator, Sanson decided to commit himself to the cause and gave the following instructions to Philbert that he should communicate to his condemned friend:

Just at the fatal moment when he was to be executed, Danton, with an emphatic and eloquent bravado that would surprise everyone present, would request that Sanson show the head to the people as a way to showcase the ironic pretext of the proverbial ugliness that accompanied such executions

After the fall of the guillotine, Sanson, obeying the orders of the tormented soul, would put the bloody head in a basket and for a small fraction of time, reveal it to the greedy eyes of the crowd

At the same time he was doing this, Sanson would skillfully transfer the head to a second basket that contained the cloths to wipe the knife as well as other tools used to sharpen the blade or make repairs to the head-chopping apparatus

This risky subterfuge would happen so fast that no one would realize what he had done

Pleased with the outcome of his mission, Philbert went back to Danton to notify him of the plan

His good friend had one wish: if the plot succeeded, he wanted his head embalmed and then transferred to Philbert's son in memoriam to the heroic dedication that was at this point in time not immediately forthcoming

Philbert promised Danton to punctually fulfill his desires and began weeping a string of long goodbyes because execution was imminent

The next day, before bowing under the cleaver, Danton, complying with the orders he had received, told Sanson: "You will show my head to the people—it's worth the pain!"

Moments later the blade did its work and Sanson had quickly taken the head and shown it to the shivering crowd

Then releasing it high at an oblique angle, the head fell into the second, adjacent basket with the tools in it

Only Philbert, in the first row of the curious onlookers, knew the fraud that was taking place

The evening came and Philbert went to see Sanson who handed him a shapely mass in the form of an unsuspicious package that was easy to carry out without arousing any attention

The financier went home and sought a way to embalm the head without revealing his secret

Knowing that Danton's features were too popular to just hand over to any professional embalmer, Philbert decided to do everything himself and bought several embalming treatments specifically for this purpose

Once he understood the more commonly used method, he gave the head multiple chemical baths and preparations that would ensure optimum conservation

Since that time, and in accordance with the great patriot, the strange remains have been ensured by five generations in Camera's family

But Philbert, a novice at embalming, had undoubtedly accomplished his task in an imperfect way, because the putrefaction had taken over all of the skin's fabric little by little, however respecting the actual brain and some of the facial fibers which after more than a hundred years were still intact without one being able to recognize anywhere the least vestige of flesh or skin

Seeing the flawless complexion of this material brain and these facial fibers, Camera, led by his research spirit, had long experimented with many electrical processes to get across some kind of reflex movement

Achieving some success in these experiments would have attracted great interest in the fact that the death had been so long ago and that the person whose head was being kept was of major historical importance

But all of these attempts remained unsuccessful

However, undergoing a series of strong jolts at the mere touch of a wet cat's nose made him wonder if a sustainable immersion of the famous head into the diamond water would not trigger a shock powerful enough to make available, under the temporary influence of the water's current, the production of the desired reflex

He carefully detached the legendary brain with its mass of muscles and nerves, leaving aside the osseous parts as useless clutter, and then cut into the light matter as a sculptor might so as to preserve the primitive form

As the experiments continued, eventually everything was immersed in the splendid water at the end of a fine cable with pneumatic suspension whose low end was split and caught just below the brain

After a whole day voluntarily devoted to waiting for the immersion to take effect, even smaller filaments were covered with the aqueous sheath, although these were thicker than those already put to use on Faustina and Wong Kar Lens

Camera then brought out this weird conical object unearthed from the depths of his laboratory and strongly electrified the brain

To his deep joy he obtained some imperceptible bursts in the nerves forming the lower lip

To prove to himself that he was committed to this project and that his efforts were not being made in vain, he continued the experiments in hopes of achieving greater results

The reflex would occur in different regions of the face depending on what part was intentionally being agitated

By nature not being able to settle for anything less, Camera reasoned that to send a current to the entire head during its immersion in the blinding wave would require him to wrap all sides of the conical hat with a high voltage electricity so as to increase the magnetic power of both the facial fibers and brain

He again drowned Danton's head into the large diamond installing it so that it would be easy to make contact with the cerebral lobes

The consequences of this experiment were far superior to anything he had conducted thus far

The trigeminal nerves seemed to outline some words while the muscles of the eyes and the eyebrows moved timidly

The guru-inventor, excited, began to repeat the experiment

It was always in the mouth region that things were set into motion

Obviously, the brain, by a kind of routine, made its preferences for an amazing glibness known on the lips of this glorious speaker whose entire life made speaking the most dominant feature of his legacy

Seeing the latent energy that preserved time in a strange cluster of cells, Camera tried hard to extract the maximum level of intensity and effect

And it was always nice to be able to test the various kinds of currents and to constantly increase the strength of the batteries he was using as a way to move beyond his initial discoveries as noted during his early tests

He then began looking among his precious human relics to see if anything else could be put to the test

His old research into animal magnetism returned to the front burner

He remembered a red substance that he invented, dubbed by him *tetranitrate*, which absorbed the volume of a pinhead and would enliven the spreading tissues of a subject in need of living cells

When he was at first investigating its potential, he thought it was enough to place the face of a patient into the flared portion of a large, special metal cone

He would have drilled a few holes into the cone for ventilation in hopes of obtaining a concentration of all the electricity stored in the body

As soon as the tip of the cone could, by simple contact, create such a current or strike the motor-functions of the subject in question, then undoubtedly . . .

. . . but the discovery would probably have to have a practical application as well—or so he thought—and so he had put the research aside but still held on to the formula used to create the *tetranitrate*—which he was now thinking of using for his new research!

Indeed, that part of the research he termed *animal magnetism* was designed for a targeted biological structure that would experience a kind of *artificial resurrection*[50]

But the mediocrity of the physiognomic reflexes provided by the strongest battery had proven that only a huge dose of *tetranitrate* would act effectively

Also, an exaggerated consumption of the red drug would unquestionably result in serious hazards and the test would have to be made on only one expendable animal

Camera, referring to the easy way that Wong Kar Lens had learned to move in the respiratory wave, wanted to exploit the intelligence of the cat and his obvious skills prompted a new initiative

But before trying anything he had to remove the thick white fleece that, by its too intense propensity toward electrification would inevitably produce multiple detriments

50. This particular sentence is confounding. My own take on it is that it must relate to the 18th century physician Franz Mesmer who is credited with coining the term *animal magnetism*. Mesmer's parapsychological research into interpersonal energy transference could be attributed to his interest in discovering a "life medium" or "fluid" that would spontaneously cause one human to become *mesmerized* with another.

Therefore a very active coating of a substance that would enable an automatic transformation would have to cover the whole animal so as to create a radical and painless shedding of his hair

He then shaped the conductive metal into a cone sized to fit the snout of the cat

Drilled here and there with several holes so that the feline was free to see, the cat was able to maneuver the liquid concoction inside the cone while circulating through the always renewed oxygenated pool

Wong Kar Lens, now pink and freaky, was again engulfed in the great diamond, his nose surrounded by the metal cone though still without a drop of the *tetranitrate* ready to resuscitate the human subject

Camera prodded the cat to graze Danton's brain with the tip of the cone

Understanding quickly what was being demanded of him, the Siamese cat, with a few movements of its legs, was, before long, making such delicate contact with Danton's brain that it almost seemed to barely touch it

He also taught the cat to use the cone as a muzzle and how to put it on once he was situated at the bottom of the container

After having gone through these various tests and seeing the ensuing results, Camera composed a batch of *tetranitrate*

But, instead of dividing the substance into infinitesimal fractions, he made strong pills out of it

Increasing the dose, though, could have catastrophic effects on Wong Kar Lens

Being prudent, Camera parceled out micro-pearls of the substance, subjecting the animal to a progressive training, giving him tiny pieces initially but then increasing the ration every day

When for the first time the cat had actually swallowed a pill, Camera plunged the cat into the radiating aquarium and then waited to watch the effect

Immediately, Wong Kar Lens went perfectly upright and sank to the bottom to grab the cone whereupon he swam to Danton's brain which he touched gently with the tip of the metal end

Camera, ecstatic, saw his greatest hopes realize their potential

Under the influence of the powerful animal magnetism embedded in the cone, the facial muscles fluttered, and the lips began stirring eventually pronouncing energetically delivered words devoid of any intelligible resonance

Using the lip reading tricks employed by the deaf, Camera came to understand different syllables being parted with

Slowly, over time, he discovered chaotic bits of speech that sometimes coalesced into a singular focus

Dazzled by his own success, Camera, at various intervals, would start the experiment again, this time beginning by immersing the cat in the tank and then randomly dropping a pearl of *tetranitrate* into the underwater as a kind of daily feeding ritual

* * *

Dreaming about potential new uses of the aqua-stimulators, Camera thought about producing inside the large diamond a collection of Cartesian divers who would be able to automatically rise to the surface via a streamlined gaseous effect where little by little a portion of the abundantly widespread oxygen would accumulate inside vertical pockets channeling through the environment

Upon reaching the surface, the divers fall back down until hitting bottom thanks to the sudden departure of rising gases

Adapted to each aquatic figurine, a subtle mechanism would be driven by the sudden leaking of oxygen in order to generate a variety of movements and performance art phenomena

For example, a typically short sentence that would be written in fine, graphically arranged air bubbles would transform into a kind of fluent *calligramme*

Searching his memory, Camera had chosen many different things likely to provide him creative research subjects worth investigating

1) *The curious adventure of Alexander the Great reported by Flavor Flave the Fifth*

In 331, while victorious in Babylonia, Alexander had greatly admired a huge bird with a gorgeous green plumage that belonged to Governor Eduardo Said who always kept it in his room, the bird's leg held captive by a long golden wire attached to the wall

The King appropriated the wondrous bird and named it As-If-It-Were

Gazoleen, a teenage slave girl, was assigned to service the bird, feeding and caring for it as if she herself had given birth to it

Shortly thereafter, during the occupation of a conquering army, the bird was installed in Alexander's apartment where he continued to marvel at the bliss-effect produced by the splendid plumage

The end of the golden wire was again attached to the wall not far from where the Great One slept, and As-If-It-Were, wandering all day across the room to the extent that it could do so amidst the various obstructions, slept the night away perched a few meters away from his master

However, the bird, apathetic and cold, showed no affection for his new master, who really only kept it for its radiant beauty

At this time, amongst the Persians that Alexander had admitted into his entourage, there were certain brutes who deeply hated their new master and thought he was too hypocritical in his various remarks

Driven by something they imagined to be patriotism, the brutes thought of bribing one of Alexander's servants to stop his momentum by assassinating him

They set their sights on Gazoleen, especially given her close proximity to As-If-It-Were, freely coming and going into and out of the royal chamber, and they offered her, a young slave, tremendous riches if she were to destroy the oppressor of Asia

Having accepted the offer, Gazoleen sought a way to make it work without compromising herself

The teen slave had noticed over time that As-If-It-Were seemed very docile and was easily persuaded to do things

She imagined a kind of terrorist training program that would bring *the bird* to kill Alexander whose death could not then be attributed to anyone in particular

Whenever she was alone in the sovereign house, Gazoleen would lie on the King's bed and patiently teach the bird to make a slipknot out of the gold wire which bound him to the wall

When the obedient beast was able to accomplish this feat, the slave kept extending the precise training so that after multiple sessions, the bird was making huge loops by placing one hand on his neck and the other against the top of his head, eventually expanding the size of the noose he was able to create so that it would successfully fit around the neck of the Great One

Pretending to sleep, he would seize the opportunity to slowly, little by little, wrap the gold wire around the nape of Alexander's neck and when the right time came, facilitate the task at hand

Alexander, a notorious restless sleeper, would essentially hang himself by shifting around in the dark with the noose around his neck

To be sure, having managed to get everything to this point, Gazoleen would still incite the bird to flee in the right direction at the right time, drawing on the entire force of its wings propelling its body forward so as to tighten the noose at the appropriate time

Gazoleen had full confidence in the resistance of the wire which was extremely firm in its braiding preventing any loosening of the animal powering its feathers to finish the job

When everything was ready to go, the young slave hastened to carry out the deed

From the start, all of the training was set up so that the bird would view the recumbent man as a strong signal for action

Up until that point, Alexander had no reason to fear even an accidental execution like the type entrusted to the bird and so was quite content to sleep through the night, even if it were accompanied by a predictable restlessness

At the desired date, the adolescent administered a simple drug to stay awake while in the presence of Alexander who was now asleep on his bed with no clue of this secret operation that had been meticulously planned

As it became obvious later, everything was done according to Gazoleen's forecasts

Once the King started dozing off, As-If-It-Were deftly made the noose and managed to pass it on to the neck of the sleeping giant by beating his wings

But in a burst of nightmarish agony, Alexander, unconsciously hit his hand on a nearby metal cup that was still full of the drink that was prepared for him each night, and it made a vibrant sound

The noise was loud enough that a nearby housemate, the athlete Virus, rushed into the room, now barely illuminated by a low night light, and saw the King's purple face going through convulsions

He ran to the bird, released the gold wire that was now gripping Alexander on its other end, and then returned to that mere mortal to provide immediate care and resuscitate him

An investigation led to the arrest of Gazoleen who clearly taught the bird these none-too-subtle amusements

The slave, when pressed, confessed and was named the instigator of the murder

But the brutes, having learned of the failed attempt at homicide, hastened to flee without a trace

By order of Alexander, they put Gazoleen to death as well as the dangerous As-If-It-Were who would never perform similar acts on any sleeper

2) *An issue regarding a Saint named Pilate who, after the crucifixion of Jesus, would throughout his life endure a terrible torment without being able to taste the benefits of a soporific snooze*

According to the evangelical lore, when evening fell, Pilate, feeling awful from his own bad cooking, would lay awake until the morning light or if not light than some kind of phosphorescent signage blinking atop his forehead

The mortal torture of experiencing physical pain made Pilate obsess over his own remorsefulness

The neon mark of fire in the middle of his forehead extended to the eyelids where with unmitigated symmetry he held out one hand to the dress of Madeleine and one to the Virgin

The only resource that was therefore left to the poor Saint was exposure to this bright light blinking on his forehead

But this perpetual clarity that pierced his thinking was itself the ultimate in excruciating martyrdom and Pilate could barely find time to drop off into radical slumber

When, during these restless nights, he was unconsciously trying to avoid the tiring irradiation covering his forehead by moving his hands over his face and eyes, a pounding headache would return with even greater force as if cooking his brain

During the course of the waking day, he would still be cursed by the great light on his forehead and he would seek a dark corner but the striking pain would rise into him with even more intensity, imposing the seal of infamy on his scarred vision

The situation eventually became intolerable

Almost forgetting that sleep was even a part of the human equation, Pilate, his eyes severely damaged by the uninterrupted electronic billboard playing on his forehead, had tried everything in his power to lose consciousness in an immense and immersive darkness

But even when yielding to his irresistible desires and finally entering the mark of total blackness he had begged to situate himself in, eventually a sumptuous corrugation of light would suddenly shine and this only reminded him how much he hated anything that could make him see things as they really were

Up until his last hour there was nothing but this repetitive and incurable evil for him to endure

3) *An episode noted by the poet Gil referring to his living in the Orient*

In 1778, Gil, being curious and hungry for the nomadic artist lifestyle, went on an important trip for several months where he was engaged in deep studies into Arabic in Asia Minor

After visiting both major and secondary sites, he came upon the ruins of Balbek, which was the reason for his journey in the first place

The main attraction was the dead city that was satirized by the great poet Missir

Satirical himself, Gil was a Missir fanatic, whom he considered his spiritual ancestor

On the first day, the traveler was riding to the public square where, according to tradition, Missir had come on certain fixed dates to recite his newly created diabolical texts before attentive crowds swarming in the droning murmurs of their religious incantations

Gil had read many of Missir's self-contradictory pages full of vehement passion that had inspired a lot of commentary and notoriety

According to Gil's historical readings, the testimonials Missir had unleashed on his listeners was meant to distinguish himself from everyone else in attendance by the way he manipulatively layered the poetry on his papyrus with the accompanying sounds he was emitting by shaking his beautiful sistrum—all of it signaling his own embodiment of personal emancipation, power, and continuous good luck

Sending his guides away, Gil remained alone and meditated on the sanctified spot where his distant master had once left his shadow

In the ruins that surrounded him he sought to find the ancient populous and splendid city while feeling emotional at the thought that he was now walking in Missir's footsteps

The night was falling, and Gil, losing the time while lost in his extended reveries, was now sitting motionless in the middle of the street amidst the scattered stones that once held up great buildings

When night finally came down upon him, he finally thought it was time to leave this inspiring space

As he rose, a little light in the distance flashed before his eyes, thin spokes moving inside it, grabbing its source from the depths of the earth and revealing a kind of vertical gap

He went toward the light and soon took several steps up on to the raised pavement near a destroyed old building

It was through the gap of two disjointed brick plates that he saw pass a strange yet clear figure of shadowy mobility

The poet, plunging his eyes into the vertical slit saw a large room with two strangers, one who was lit by a lamp and wandered among a curious cluster of objects, fabrics, and what appeared to be tree or bush trimmings

Listening to the two companions, he could tell that they were both men of the region, and he detected some kind of plot in their conversation

The youngest of the participants had unexpectedly found in underground apartments all kinds of antiques that were now safely ensconced in his room

The older one, a star figure of the State, had come every year to take some of these old riches and load them on to his ship where he would set out to sea in hopes of selling them off for gold

The two friends shared in the profit and kept the plot to themselves since, according to rationalizations that they kept repeating, everyone had some rights to these communal treasures

While browsing the gallery, the two men chose different pieces that they wanted to move in the middle of the night so they could get them out to sea

Gil tried in vain to get closer and see exactly how this whole drama would play itself out among the ruins but had to contain himself

Instead, not hearing anything now that the two had begun carrying pieces off to the ship, he realized he had become taken over by a mad curiosity and immediately had the idea of touching and admiring one of the pieces within his reach

The moon appeared and flooded rays of its light into the room seen through the vertical gap

Looking closely, he saw that a piece of the wall below his face seemed to be stripped of any remnant cement and used his hands to take hold of a large, embedded heavy stone and slowly pushed it aside

Now his fingers were clinging to the edge of a new opening that he pulled himself through via an act of acrobatic contortion made especially for this occasion and, once slipping his body through the hole, fell down into the ruined space

With lunar light streaming into the room, he became an enthusiastic browser checking out with delight various pieces of jewelry, fabrics, musical instruments and statuettes in what felt like a ghost museum teleporting through an n-dimensional space of time

Suddenly he stopped, trembling with surprise and emotion

Before him, in pale light, standing among various trinkets, was a sistrum with five stems!

He hastily took hold of it and began examining it closely, discerning on the sleeve the engraved name MISSIR and knew it was authentic

Dazzled by his find, Gil, erecting a temporary scaffolding by stacking up pieces of furniture, made his way back up to the opening he had created so that he could make his exit

Again treading the ground of the town ruins, he returned to the place where his reverie had extended his presence into the night and there, drunk with joy, intoned in its original language, an especially beautiful and provocative stanza of verse written by Missir, gently waving the sistrum once wielded by the great poet

Under the intense moonlight, Gil, exalted, thought he felt the breath of Missir revive inside his own chest

He was occupying the exact location where his God had previously and melodiously recited his new stanzas before the crowd, punctuating his delivery with swings of the same instrument that was now ringing in the nocturnal air!

After reviving the poetry and memories of his guru-mentor, Gil went back to join his guides and told them about the existence of the treasures in the underground room and the arrangement the two men he had seen conspiring with each other

A trap would be set for the accomplices, one that would surprise even the night their clandestine work took place in

In gratitude for revealing this scheme, Gil was given Missir's sistrum whereupon he piously retained this priceless relic

4) *The Lombardi legend offers a gripping remix of the story about the hen that laid the golden eggs*

In Bergen, there once was a dwarf named Pizzarrhea

Each year, on the first day of spring, Pizzarrhea saw his pores dilate under the influence of climatic renewal, and his whole body began to sweat blood

According to popular belief, this sweaty blood, when it happened with force, signaled a plentiful harvest season, but if it was weak and limited, would instead predict a drought followed by famine and ruin

This system of forecasting was considered the gold standard

At the time of his strange illness, Pizzi (as some would call him) would get an intensely bad fever that inevitably made him bed-ridden

During this time, he was always being spied upon by a few local farmers who, seeing the amount of blood he was sweating, would exude either joy or dismay

When the prognosis was satisfactory and word had spread throughout the region, the country people would thank the dwarf by sending him many gifts of appreciation

This superstitious giving ritual was performed as if giving offerings to God

They figured that by giving the dwarf these gifts of appreciation, he would treat them kindly the next year and sweat enough to predict another fantastic harvest

But what if they gave him these gifts and the following year only a little blood and sweat was released from his pores?

Pizzi was getting lazy and debauched from attaining much profit for little effort

Once the blood in his laundry was washed away and he began taking advantage of all the gifts he had received, he would immediately begin living a copious and extravagant life of serene idleness

But he was being too improvident to save anything and would soon fall back into misery and poverty whenever his annual sweat was but a mere trickling

One year he came up with a scheme that would guarantee him unabated profits

Before getting on the bed for his feverish sweating, he hid a knife under his sheets to assist the phenomenon in case of need

As luck would have it, upon his opening sweat he noticed that only a few rare droplets of blood were shining on his face, so, frightened by the prospect of the long months of indigence that would soon await him, he took out the knife and, under pretext of nervous movements due to his high fever, managed to cut a series of deep wounds into his upper body without arousing the suspicions of the observers who surrounded him

The blood flooded the sheets to the total delight of everyone watching

But the injured dwarf could not stop the bleeding and this left him feeling self-abused and half-dead

Many new offerings made their way to Pizzi who, weak and anemic, was frightened by his own terribly white complexion

Meanwhile, a terrible drought did not cease its horrific reign throughout the season and the cruel famine persisted

For the first time ever, the sweaty blood prediction had contradicted actual events

Some of those who were watching Pizzi during his sweating had suspected some deception during his fevered gestures and they forced him to show his body whereupon they discovered the scars left by the voluntary cuts he made on himself

The disclosure of this subterfuge unleashed a huge outcry against the impostor who, by accepting beautiful gifts from his fellow citizens that had led to their own increased poverty, felt they had been cruelly betrayed

But given that his actual condition did in fact predict the future, Pizzi was exonerated from serious reprisals and they all vowed to more closely inspect his vermillion seepages

The dwarf, laughing under his cape, continued with his copious ways in pursuit of the next big payday while across the country the crops were failing despite his dishonest ways

Meanwhile, his pale exhaustion still remained extreme even as he continued to habitually engross himself in endless orgies

The following year, at the spring deadline, Pizzarrhea was being closely watched as he spread himself on the bed

But the waiting was in vain

His hemorrhaging was not to be

He no longer received gifts or even donations

About four months later, a superabundant harvest proved the incapacity of the dwarf to prophesize the future

Doomed to loneliness and contempt, Pizzi, now contrite about his inability to continually *lay the golden egg*, was therefore deprived and incapable of seeking a cure

Never again did the blood appear as it had once profusely presented itself in times of lucky yields

5) *And now a passage from mythology concerning Atlas who, exhausted by constant fatigue, would one day let fall from his shoulders the terrible celestial sphere he had been saddled with and in one swift kick rid himself of the burden he had been forced to eternally carry*

6) *An anecdote on Voltaire, drawn from the correspondence of Frederick the Great*

In the fall of 1775, Voltaire, then in his eighties and full of glory, was the guest on his era's version of a reality TV show focused on Frederick and titled "Fred at San Souci Castle"

On the show, one day the two friends were walking around the royal residence and Fred was charmed by the lively speech of his illustrious companion that was full of verve and expertly articulated an intransigent, anti-religious doctrine

Forgetting the time, the two continued their stroll until they found themselves out in the countryside

At the moment, Voltaire was immersed in one particularly virulent rant against the old religious dogmas that he had been fighting for a very long time

Suddenly, in the middle of a sentence, he went silent and remained still, taken over by a deep disorder

Not far from him, a barely adolescent girl began to kneel at the ringing of a remote bell that, from the top of a small Catholic chapel, rang the angels awake

Fervently reciting her prayers at a high volume, hands clasped, and face turned sideways toward the heavens, she was unaware of the presence of the two strangers

Her out-of-body ecstasy was being transported in a luminescent dream of nothing but blind faith

Voltaire looked on with an inexpressible anguish that spread throughout his whole face as it turned into a parched yellow field full of earthy hues pock-marked with tiny craters

A terrible emotion further contracted his features as his whole body responded to the utterance of a word within the flow of words coming out her mouth

The word she kept returning to was, in a sense, blowing his mind

The word was in Latin

The word was *Dubito*

Doubt

His own doubt was being aptly applied to the scene before him

Doubt nothing but doubt all of it clearly connected to his theories on atheism

Looking at the girl was a kind of impromptu revelation that took him to a beyond-place

A beyond-place that was triggered by the simple subjectivity of an expression assumed by the girl lost in prayer and that forced him to deal with his own quandary of aging to the point of near-decay and what was undoubtedly an indication of how close he was to his own imminent death

The terror of eternal punishment seized his entire being

The crisis lasted only a few moments

Irony again made its way to the lips of the great skeptic and his next despondent sentence started and ended in a biting tone

But the tremor had occurred and Fred never forgot the short and precious vision of Voltaire experiencing a mystical emotion

7) *A fact directly related to the genius of Richard Wagner*

On October 17, 1813, in Leipzig, a truce between the French and Allied troops interrupted the terrible fight that had commenced the day before and certainly would have continued over the next few days

On a boulevard outside could be seen a crowd of jugglers and nomadic merchants that moved in parallel with the armies, and the animated scene had the feel of a pop-up fair

In the crowd a merry swarm of young women told their extravagant tall tales to each other and that amused them all to no end

One of them carried her son who was almost five months old, a certain Richard Wagner, born in Leipzig on May 22 of that year

Suddenly, an old man with long grey hair, standing behind a small table, was called by the young mother who asked him to predict the future of her child

In what appeared to be a pure French accent, the man spoke in a comically painful German that made everyone laugh and, consequently, having gained their attention, insisted that the group make their way in front of him

Taking on a mysterious air, the old man, after examining the child, picked up from his table a flat-bottomed cup and inside the cup spread out a thin layer of bright iron filings

Holding the object near the mother's foot, he asked her to strike it three times with the edge of her finger while thinking of the destiny of her son

The charlatan carefully rested the cup on the table and with huge spectacles examined any disturbances that the triple blow had produced in the filings

Suddenly he made a grand gesture signaling amazement at what he discovered—and advised that a desk be placed in front of him as he took a white sheet to copy in ink the feint figure drawn in the metal dust

Then he handed the paper to the young woman who was able to see these two French words: "*Sere pille.*"

"Will be looted"!

It was quite readable despite the inconsistent contents of the letters unevenly splayed in every direction (as if a secret password that only a human could read and comprehend)

At the same time, the charlatan, pointing at the paper copy, made note of the similarity between the model and the reproduction

Indeed a spindly and circumvented ravine had grown hollow in the cup of metal dust and this had formed the two transcribed words

Giving his client the Germanic translation of the short phrase, the old man attempted, in his poor German, to give them the entire scope of what this phrase was prophesying

According to him, the highest artistic destinies resided in this germ of a phase, a kind of to-be-expected formula applicable to any powerful innovator who, as leader of an historical movement, would inevitably generate a plethora of imitators

The proud mother, stroking her little baby like a valuable fetish, generously paid the soothsayer and carried the paper that would become a valuable document

Later she gave it to her son telling him of the adventurous event that had produced it and intimating that he had become a kind of unconscious hero of the story

At the end of his life, Wagner whose work had finally become known and appropriated by a network of unscrupulous plagiarists, liked to tell this story, admitting he had counted on this odd translation to lift up his spirits throughout his career

He said he viewed the story as a beneficial influence providing him with just the right amount of superstitious encouragement during the endless years of disappointments and sterile struggles he had gone through, especially when a wave of despair had often taken him over

* * *

After having chosen to share all of these material fragments with his visitors, Camera had the Cartesian divers perform specific moves

From their judiciously weighted base that provided them constant balance, each of them had a small cavity carved inside their body that was then topped with a special metal to chemically capture and isolate all of the extra oxygen in their immediate vicinity

Little by little each figure would use their personal gaseous desire to excavate themselves from their position from the bottom of the tank up to the surface

But during the rise toward the surface, exactly ten seconds after their calculated upward start, the diver would be forced to create a stir in their self-generating mechanism by essentially popping out of the top of their isolated bubble and, once devoid of the special air chamber, sink back down by the effect of their own weight all the time oxygenating themselves so that they could soon rise again

Some of these automatic mechanizations were programmed to delicately arrange particular events inside the tank

So, for example, the appearance of the luminous sign on Pilate's forehead could be produced by the momentary flaring of a small flashlight necessarily produced by a passing studio assistant

The word "Dubito" that appeared in the important story told about Voltaire, would be projected out of the half-opened lips of the great thinker via a skillfully crafted globule of subdivided air bubbles

To mimic a bloody sweat, like the procedure the dwarf Pizzi had experienced each spring, required a minimal amount of red powder that, when released in the abundant waters of the tank, would immediately disappear through the phenomenon known as dissolution

As for the cup of the charlatan in Leipzig, false iron filings would be represented according to the assigned figure performing their three finger strikes

* * *

With all of these many digressions within digressions clarified for his viewers, Camera reminded himself that he had not recently tasted the water and made a small liquid reserve for his careful swallowing

Once it was poured out, the magical elixir from the fluid diamond seemed readymade for his thirsty throat

Taking the first mouthful, Camera discovered a remarkable lightness and exquisite flavor, and greedily consumed three consecutive glasses of the sparkling beverage whose excessive oxygenation got him totally high

Camera then wondered what it would be like to add some wine into the intoxicating mix

Pouring the very heady Sauternes into his glass, he filled it to the top

But there had already been a little bit of the water at the bottom of the glass and the first bit of white wine to touch it immediately transformed into a compact block

Apparently the composition of the diamond's liquid prevented any admixture of the two ingredients since the sudden oxygenation of the alcohol would instantly harden the sturdy Bordeaux

Camera, wielding the block with his fingers, found it very malleable

Forgetting the experience of dual impairment that he had just designed for himself (wine + water), he imagined forming a new project based on the docile flexibility and solar irradiation of solid wine

He had recently engaged in multiple tests of acclimation including trying to introduce some oceanic life forms into the fresh water

A very slow, gradual desalination of natal liquid temporally suspended any organic disorder that could be observed in the actions of the sea creatures and required a great deal of patience and tact

Camera's patience paid off and his first triumph was with a group of seahorses whose adaptation was already complete

Three of the ten had died during their initial, perilous inhabitation, but now the seven survivors were permanently without discomfort nor felt the need to revolt inside their jar of natural water

Their master, Camera, offered to immerse them all in the large diamond so that they could trace a sphere around the newly solidified Sauternes globe which would then, thanks to the fire-light hue of the water, create the appearance of a miniature sun

First he carefully dipped a seahorse into the magic liquid diamond to see if the new wine element was detrimental to their health

After a while, the graceful animals manifested great suffering as they tried to flee from all sides of the contraption

Camera suddenly understood the cause of their anguish (something he had not expected)

Being appropriate for purely terrestrial breathers, the spectacular liquid concoction was too oxygenated for aquatic creatures, and the seahorses immediately sensed the hazard and looked for a way out

Using a net, Camera hastened to pick them up and put them back in their jar

And then, seeking any remedy against the huge and potentially destructive downside to all of his projects, he wanted to cross each seahorse breast with a stringwire which would create two air passages that would allow the excess oxygen to escape right out of the seahorse's bodies

He first attempted this trick on a single seahorse with a provisional stringwire and the experiment was a success

Small bubbles would force open a passage in one of the two new ports as soon the animal had plunged into the pool relinquishing any discomfort in the sea creature

In ordinary water, the edges of the two outlets would cease to expel the excess due to an overflow of indoor air that would completely adhere to the wire and, from each side, hermetically close everything in

By tying two stringwires together, Camera was able to secure a mode of attachment that helped him begin mythologizing the project even more than he had originally imagined himself capable of producing

The stable of seahorses, he thought, would graciously circumnavigate the interior space of the diamond and he decided to spice up the show by establishing that initial race of the creatures around the sphere

The relative elasticity of the wires allowed the nimblest competitors to take their victorious leads, leads that were minuscule given the generally poor means of transport available to the seahorse species

So that the gamblers could easily recognize their race pick, Camera had ingeniously given each of the seven creatures a name indicating one of the seven colors of the rainbow prism, thereby replacing the imaginary seahorse jockeys with an imaginary visual cue[51]

51. The seahorse races are almost as exciting as the Faustina character for me, although my reading of both is deeply intertwined with two as-of-yet unreleased art projects I have been working on forever. These two projects are, in fact, the two longest ongoing projects I have yet to *definitively unfinish*. One is a long novel whose working title is *My Oblivion, The Life and Times of David Star, Conceptual Artist* and relates a great many stories sampled from my teenage years as a full time employee at the Greyhound racetracks in Miami, Florida, in the mid-1970s. The novel switches between various historical time frames: the turn of the 20th century when David Star is about to have his major retrospective at the Guggenheim, the mid-70s, which feed off my own adolescent adventures into the underworld of gambling, prostitution, disco, and the drug trade at the Greyhound races, and the emergence of AIDS in the early-mid 80s. By no means is the work truly autobiographical (but then how can any work be truly autobiographical?). I prefer the term *pseudo-autobiographical* and, in the case of *My Oblivion*, the personal narrative data that I sample from the experiences associated with the teenager Mark Amerika [sic] reveals my relationship to racing, pari-mutuel wagering, and the drug-addled free sex environment that permeated the South Florida culture I was immersing myself in at the time. Roussel's seahorses were a pleasant surprise and rather easy to relate to.

The other ongoing project that informs this project is a feature-length "foreign film" whose working title is *My Autoerotic Muse* and features a character that I imagine looks exactly like Faustina. In fact, the film version of my unique translation of *Locus Solus* could expand upon the Faustina character so that it becomes a kind of non sequitur sequel to *My Autoerotic Muse*. The Faustina-like character in the *Muse* film goes by the name Kat Wolf, a live, Web camera performance artist who uses her Upper West Side apartment in New York as the ultimate location for her ongoing artwork. The narrative is driven by the subtitles which do not translate dialogue from a foreign tongue but, rather, slowly reveal the interior monologue of a voyeur who is watching the live Internet performance. The title of the film refers to the two longest scenes in the film where Kat Wolf gives herself autoerotic pleasure. The connection

He was particularly pleased how his earlier tests had predicted the varying speeds of the seven horses so that when the race was finally on, the horses would stagger in from best to worst in the exact order of the rainbow colors

Reflecting on the best way to weld bizarre traits to the yellow sphere in the tank, Camera wondered if the electricity transmitted by the oxygenated water to everything it wrapped in and around would not be enough to create a certain magnetization between the solid wine and some other conducting substance that could be fixed to their ends

After groping around, he brought together both ends of each stringwire creating a brilliant envelope made of a metal chosen for its superior results, and this enabled him to create a spontaneous illumuniscence inside the tank

In order to create a clearly defined path, Camera had to make, not far from Danton's head, a small and simple column of barrels whose density he had carefully calculated so that once it was fixed at a low depth would not willy-nilly ascend and descend at random

To carry out a lap of the track without crashing into the perpetually rising and falling Cartesian divers was a huge stumbling block he had to find a solution for

Just for kicks, he would pour in more Sauternes which quickly solidified after making contact with the magical tank water and this would then change the environment for the free-range seahorses who would themselves appear to turn to wax or at least take on the color of wax as soon as the wine had coagulated and blocked their potential passage

---

between this film and some of the nouveau roman and nouveau cinema of Robbe-Grillet as well as Duchamp's *Large Glass* and *Étant donnes* will become apparent to the viewer who is familiar with the context the work is made in and that some of these notes point toward. For me, when the figure of Faustina enters the narrative, she further amplifies the way artists unknowingly generate their precursors when making their own works of art.

Both projects, *My Oblivion* and *My Autoerotic Muse*, are sexually charged investigations into the performance of identity as the central component in an aesthetically manipulated conceptual practice and have been in a state of near-completion for many years. In some ways they are as *definitively unfinished* as they will ever be, but there's still a chance that either one of them, or both, will go through further transformation. Still, to take them further would be to essentially *finish them off*, and I have chosen not to kill them just quite yet, though I really have no problem with the thought that I may have stopped working on them forever. For now, they are being kept in my archives so that only I can savor them.

The demonstration having been successfully administered—coupled with the welding of blocks that outlined a strange steeplechase of a course, the seahorse-pupils would suddenly unravel from their swarming sphere of amalgamated collectivity and immediately line up in a single row so that together, bound by common stringwire, they could stick side by side against the tide of waste that surrounded them

Finally, he taught the seven sea creatures to perform at the start of the signal whereupon they would attempt to surpass each other over the desired course

Their goal—or finishing line—would be the column of barrels which they could see out of the corner of their eye as they swirled and declined at an almost level angle toward the designated marker

Seven shades of the prism were now programmed by Camera to aesthetically align themselves as one collaborative movement toward the endgame

Racehorses not being able to do without names, the guru-inventor, hoping to avoid exhaustion of memory, gave each of the potential champions their virtual name in Latin, a kind of digital baptism

Wearing the purple string was Primus, the slowest, who took his place at the extreme left of the row and was thus given a positive handicap

The ultrarapid Second-to-None, on the other hand, was wearing the red string, and had the disadvantage of being positioned all the way to the right

The perfect amount of handicap privilege and positioning was equally dispensed between the five intermediary horses

It was a fair and somewhat subtle handicapping that would keep the race close but always with the same outcome

* * *

While Camera spoke, Wong Kar Lens had been slowly dragging the solar ball toward the seahorses

Having completed his show, Camera closely approached the gem and, rolling up his right sleeve, made a sign toward Faustina who then placed Wong Kar Lens on her shoulder and went back up to stand on the ladder

Grabbing with his fingers the solar ball, the connection broke its adherence to the metal sleeves that had guided part of the action and soon this dwarf sun rested next to the bottle of Sauternes

Next, the seahorses were taken out of the net and returned to the jar where any inhalation of air bubbles was summarily dismissed

Camera put his hand near Faustina's genitals as she now faced him[52]

Soon she threw her head back while Wong Kar Lens lightly brushed against her cheek

She kept raising her neck as if experiencing some uncategorizeable sensation beyond pleasure and/or pain

Then she came, quickly, as if on sexual impulse, and the water changed again just as she knelt down on one knee

Camera dried his pungently-moistened hand with a handkerchief which then quickly disappeared into his pocket

52. I have no idea if Camera put his hand near Faustina's genitals in the original, nor do I care. The point is that I wanted him to put his loving hand near Faustina's genitals and the auto-translation made it easy for me to do that.

4

After having followed Camera across the esplanade, the visitors descended into the middle of a rich yellow lawn that sloped gently and then widened out horizontally where there sat a giant, rectangular glass cage approximately ten by forty meters

Supported by a strong carcass made of iron scaffolding, the transparent construction was the utmost in geometric simplicity consisting of four walls and the ceiling, a monstrous box without a lid and turned upside down on the ground so that its mass coincided with the main axis of the valley it was nestled in

Walking around the edges of this grand species of sculpture, Camera gave everyone a serious glance as the group circumnavigated the fragile building

A group of people standing upright against the glass captured the group's attention

Upon closer inspection, about a meter away, there appeared to be a square room that took on the appearance of a chapel in ruins, a kind of indefinite detention area

Directly in their line of vision they could make out a window halfway down the wall, an eroded pavement, two pallets, a coffee table and a stool

On the ground, an altar that had fallen leaned against the wall, broken, a large virgin whose baby Jesus had been torn away from her

A bear of a man wearing a cardigan sweater and bonnet was wandering inside the enormous cage and Camera uttered a couple of words to an assistant who went inside toward the unfolding action

Lying on the largest pallet, a stranger with grey hair seemed to be lost in thought

Soon, as if making a decision, the man stood up to walk toward the broken altar, his left leg obviously in pain

Near the group, sobs erupted, coming from a woman wearing a crepe veil who was carrying a young child in her arms, crying: "Gerard, Gerard . . . " her hand desperately stretched toward the chapel

As she came near the altar she approached the separated baby Jesus and sat down on the stool

Out of her pocket she held in her fingertips a round metal box that, when its lid was taken off, revealed a kind of pink ointment which she began to spread a thin layer on the childish face of the statue of Jesus

Immediately, after applying the strange makeup on the statue, she said something to the boy in her arms who tearfully, affirmatively, nodded:

"This was for you—to save you"

Gerard seemed to fear the unexpected and before long the statue was smeared in the pink ointment

Setting the statue on the smaller pallet on the wall to the left, she closed the container of ointment and put it in her pocket before moving toward the window

Corpulent forms filled the space near the bars of the window as she leaned into it to look outside into the nothingness

Taking a few steps to the right, the group's curiosity led them to look at the opposite of the wall where the woman was looking through the window

There, slightly indented, the window was located between two corners and they could see a cluster of refuse including pear peelings where Gerard, reaching through the window and neglecting the peels, kept picking up all of the inner filaments with their seeds and stems

His harvesting completed, the group moved back to their original observation post

Nimble fingers parted the stems and collected filaments of the fruit revealing the stringy, whitish guts which were then patiently divided into a large number of edible wires

Using these strands of white pear wire to tie together one lengthy piece, Gerard, lacking a certain degree of professionalism, instead passionately pursued a simultaneous and continuous work of abstractly weaved fabric art

Finally, by dint of narrow tangles and general tampering with these odd substances, he had in his hands a decent cap made for an infant and that could have been mistaken as being made of linen

He then capped the pink ointment-smeared statue with his improvised bonnet over the backside of the stone-haired figure until it was hidden and took on the appearance of a real baby

The woman, meanwhile, took great care to pick up off the ground the waste he had left behind while working, and threw the lot of it out the window to her left

Afterward, Gerard's attitude—for a brief instant—seemed to adhere to a certain vagueness and emitted an overall sense of absence

But he quickly gained lucidity and suddenly lowered his left hand, the high elbow and fingers stretched out tightly together so that he could slip his wrist into the hollow of a gold bracelet attached to a chain where an old coin hung

Stroking the coin with his other hand for a rather long time, eventually he was able to collect a steady dose of gold powder in his other hand

On the table near his gold stroking, there was a big old book whose spine, in large letters, read: *Errant Glossolalia* by Ludwig Calvino[53]

It was next to a jug of water and a nondescript flower stem

53. Here, as throughout the performance, I take great liberty in inventing new names for most of the characters. The names are in some instances very loaded with what the sophisticated reader may sense is intentional art/literary historical referencing. Any well-attuned, early 21st century reader will immediately recognize the allusions. In this particular case, the character is a cross between Ludwig Wittgenstein and Italo Calvino, but in name only. The character is really, as are all of the figures who appear in *Locus Solus*, more of a loose caricature or conceptual persona, a pure linguistic construct that materializes in the narrative by way of unforeseen circumstances triggered by both Roussel's <u>texticles</u> and my own hyperimprovisational jam session with the auto-translation I am constantly being fed by the Network. This is all fine by me since it resonates with the kind of critifictional presence my work generally explores. What's a real character, anyway? Especially in the context of a story that is anything *but* real? For a sense of what I mean by conceptual personae or concept-characters, see my 1995 net art work *Hypeterxtual Consciousness 1.0* (now the "companion theory-guide" to *GRAMMATRON* at grammatron.com). The concept *hyperimprovisation* is explored in the opening "Spontaneous Theories" section of *META/DATA: A Digital Poetics*.

My experimentation with character in metafictional form reminds me of something my former mentor, friend, and artistic co-conspirator Ronald Sukenick once wrote in a short story he published titled "Random Access Memory": "They all avoid the one identity he can't invent. His own. That's why the more [he] loses his

Burying the bracelet in his pocket, Gerard crawled up a kind of ladder on to the table quite close to all of the onlookers and, balancing himself against the wall near the window, stood in front of the odd dictionary that he then repositioned so that he could open up it up at the beginning and start quickly rotating himself around its axis without once buckling

The whirl of boy and book revealed the distorted white sheet of the first blank page

After slowing down, Gerard grabbed the flower stem from the penholder and held it between three fingers and then soaked one end in the jug of water while almost tipping it over

Then, with the tip of the spine, he began to write on the white sheet of the faux dictionary with a kind of anxiety and haste

After writing a few lines in water, he sprinkled a few pinches of the gold powder that he had still held on to in his other hand over the page and soon the invisible handwriting started to take on its golden color

Under the word ODE, drawn in bold, he had written a stanza of six Alexandrines

After having completed this first short work, Gerard put the sharp end of the stem back into the jug and then after pulling it back out continued to invisibly write on the page

The second verse was soon lying on the sheet and also sprinkled with gold

This same procedural scribble-work proceeded until he reached the bottom of the page

Giving the work time to dry, Gerard momentarily lifted the sheet by rolling half at an angle so that the grains of gold that had not been absorbed by the water-writing could collect in his passive hand

Delicately yet sturdily lifting the dictionary up a bit enabled him to accumulate a decent heap of gold powder

Released of its fuzzy excess along the edges of all of the letters, the golden text now appeared in all of its purity

---

character the more he finds himself. The more he finds himself the less of a character he is the less a caricature. But it's not so easy to find yourself the self beneath the hard crust the hot magma beneath sudden eruptions of feelings the source the base on which everything rests. Not easy to find and impossible to escape."

Gerard then rearranged the objects on the table so that the dictionary was more stable

Without changing his process, Gerard was able to create perfectly delineated stanzas written in gold

The gold dust he had returned to his hand was now put back in the reserve

Au, gold (Chemistry)

prep. on, to, toward

art. the, definite article used to specify one person or item in particular (Grammar)[54]

Gerard, like a penguin, dipping and writing, gilded and guiding, filling and filing, invisible then visible, packed with layers, little by little, an erratic (*erroratic*) dictionary opened to a virginal page that came to life with the gift of gold

After what appeared to be a final, routine recovery of the remaining gold dust that had not been caught by the essential text, Gerard began distorting his movements and took on the posture of a strange scribe whose designed artifice was signed in a typography still in development

Now only a few grains of the precious powder remained in his hand, and he just let them fall to the ground

When his gold signature had finally dried at the bottom of the page, Gerard let the time pass by randomly cleaning the page of everything foreign to the essential text

After a long time had seemed to pass, he appeared to engage in intense discussions, advising the inanimate objects around him until he reached up and grabbed another nearby volume titled EOCENE

He placed the book before him but behind the dictionary and flipped it open until he came across a two-column index

Here he encountered a nomenclature followed by a series of numbers, and he started quickly using his finger to touch each word while counting out loud

54. Occasionally, I would accidentally cut and paste only part of a word into the auto-translation program which would then misread it and just give me a kind of simplified definition of what it thought I was looking for. Whenever this happened, it would usually be the first letter that was cut off and in this instance I liked what I saw because it (a) resonated with Gerard's clever use of the gold powder and (b) played into the idea of Camera as an alchemist always moving toward the next discovery that awaited him.

Then, on the following pages, where the index continued, Gerard, without skipping a beat, kept reciting the numbers while touching each word

Walking away from his audience toward the window, he momentarily unveiled from his pocket the gold bracelet and, again, stroking the hanging coin, collected in his left hand another dose of the gold, this time a minimal amount of the bright powder, and immediately relocated to the EOCENE book

On the index page where his prior count had ended, he wrote in his usual way, but this time in capitals, up top and centered: DAYS IN CELL and then below that, to the left, ACTIVE, and to the right, PASSIVE

The last word was plotted with a geometric simplicity of easily designed characters

Then Gerard crossed out the first printed word with which the column began

The minute provision of gold powder was barely enough to start browning the water markings

Even when it was so light it was barely perceptible, Gerard would crawl down the table, find some loose grains on the floor, whisk them up, and bring them back to the book for potential sprinkling

After his finger rested under the figure that immediately followed the first crossed out word, he flipped the book to its beginning, pretending to search for a specific page

* * *

Camera had the group walk along the edges of the immense, transparent cage, and stopped them all in front of a well-decorated Catholic altar where a figure behind the glass wall suggested the presence of a priest standing before his tabernacle

It was here that the not-too-subtle use of a piping hot apparatus was about to be applied to Gerard who had in an instant appeared in the room

Meanwhile, on a sacred table to the priest's right, there was an ornate metal box that looked very old and on its front, below the lock, was written these words formed out of garnets: "Vise of the Golden Anniversary"

The priest walked past Gerard and, raising the lid on the metal box, withdrew from it a rather large vise which, though a simple model, functioned by means of an elaborate wing nut

Descending the steps of the altar, the priest stopped before a very old couple who stood up to him as he approached, leaving empty the two ceremonial chairs they had sat in side-by-side

Presenting their files to the priest, the old man was not wearing a hat and wore a simple tailcoat

To his right was a woman wearing a black shawl wrapped around her head and who, in deep mourning, wore a heavy coat despite having, like him, bare hands

Putting the two old people face to face, the priest united their right hands and placed them between the splayed open jaws of the vise, at which point he began slowly turning the wing nut, ostensibly gearing this demonstration for the audience watching on the other side of the glass

But the old man, smiling, intervened with his left hand and forced the priest to let him take control of the metal ears which he then merrily turned a few times with a mischievous strength while the old woman began sobbing emotionally

The jaws must have been made of some imitation iron because they performed without inflicting any serious torture on the two intertwined hand-holding lovers

Once again free to do as they please, the priest meticulously took hold of the vise who then carried it up the altar and moved toward the metal box while the couple sat back in their ceremonial chairs signaling the end of their extended masochistic handshake

* * *

Alongside the giant cage, Camera led the visitors a few meters further along and stopped before a sumptuous room where they all saw the old couple attempting to escape the scene with alarming alacrity, taking an indirect route behind the altar

Near the glass separating the scene from the viewers, they ran into what appeared to be a luxurious bathroom from a castle in the Middle Ages

The absence of any slope or any encumbrance whatsoever made it easy to enter and exit before using

Toward the bottom of what could have been mistaken for a well composed cinematographic shot that everyone saw exactly the same way without thinking about it, a little to the left, and sitting at a table placed diagonally, a lordly gentleman's naked neck could be caught in momentary profile annotating a book opposite a wide window

On the man's neck appeared a dark grey tattoo whose Gothic Monogram type spelled these three letters: B, T, G

Now in the middle of the shot and toward the bottom, there appeared a courier delivering some documents—and it looked like a man who was standing earlier before the closed door but was now to the right of the seated gentleman separated by just a few steps

The costumes of these two players fit them well and meshed with the decor of an older, more formal time

Without interrupting his annotations or, for that matter, changing his attitude in any way whatsoever, the gentleman said, in a distinctly ironic tone:

"Really? A contract? Some kind of offer to sign my life away?"

The voice could be heard by the participants as it was carried through a round opening as big as a dinner plate and that was topped with a disc made of a durable tissue with bent edges

It was sticking outside of the glass wall about two meters above the ground

Posted below this disc where what had just been spoken had entered the exterior environment was a professionally printed image of a young black girl whose stare devoured all who encountered it

The courier now replied to the well-to-do gentleman:

"A cob"

Just at that moment when the courier muttered his words, the gentleman, opening his fingers to let go of his stylus, confidently turned his head to the right and immediately used both of his hands to take hold of his own neck in some kind of mock gesture as if to emulate a kind of auto-strangulation, an unusual looking act full of self-inflicted pain

But that too was quickly forgotten as he then stood up, walked to the courier, and looked at the document where the word "Contract" appeared followed by a few lines of text and, then at the bottom of the paper, a crudely drawn picture of a horse with a short, thick neck

In a tone of supreme anguish, the gentleman repeatedly pointed his finger at the equestrian sketch:

"The cob! The cob!"

* * *

But Camera had already moved on and had now stopped before a seven year old child whose head and legs were bare, sitting in a simple blue suit on the lap of a young woman covered in mourning, installed on a chair positioned as an extension of the floor

The courier, who had taken a detour behind the scenes, was now approaching the child with great strides while the actor who had just played the gentleman with the loose neck in the prior scene was also now present in this new scene

Another exterior disc topped with the durable tissue extended from the glass where this new scene took place and allowed the group to hear the young boy say, "Viral conceptualism of the radical kind," at which point he then proceeded to recite with 100% accuracy the entire verse of a famous poet while sharing glances with the young woman on whose lap he sat, his gestures totally appropriate for the occasion as he stressed each word's underlying intent while his inflection of the text as a whole demanded every ounce of pure conviction so that the end result could be fully experienced as a work of high performance, spoken word art

When the childish voice had suddenly stopped without warning, the group continued to traverse the property in their usual direction and in a short time came before another station that Camera indicated by stopping before it and standing alongside a young observer who was looking at a man in a beige shirt sitting at a table embedded into the wall of glass, facing it

The noble head of this artist in the beige shirt, with its long grey hair, was resting on a completely black sheet of paper composed of dry ink, but on closer inspection one could see he was meticulously scraping at the paper to reveal specific fragments of a white surface as if unconsciously losing himself in a compositional process that would oust all remaining remnants of anything even remotely resembling time

The more of the white that was revealed, the more the man seemed to be experiencing some kind of rapture

Little by little, under the blade which he wielded with supreme skill, the emergent white figure was coming to life on its slowly disappearing black background, and in the process began indicating an image that could have easily been modeled on one of de Kooning's "Woman" portraits

Among the group of observers, watching the young man who they had come upon nearly press his forehead against the glass, some appeared awestruck by the subtle actions of the artist who, on occasion, seemed to utter something that at first was unintelligible, especially as he began laughing at himself

But the sentence he kept uttering in a kind of on/off sequence eventually became clear: "The big ditto!"[55]

This phrase also came out into the environment via a third exterior disc covered in the sturdy tissue

The artist's work went quickly as he thoroughly executed each flick of his wrist and subtle twist of his fingers that, in spite of its strange eliminatory process, soon revealed the image of the "woman" whose gradual appearance suggested a full, exuberant—even erotically charged—life, almost as if the scraping gestures and manic laughter of the artist were somehow shaping this aesthetic organism into its very becomingness

The delicate steel strokes scratching the dried black ink slowly constituted another kind of imaging method, one that would create a masterpiece of metaphysical violence and biomorphic dismemberment, something all of the visitors could appreciate the value of, although from everyone's angle, the piece seemed to be upside down

55. Again, it's impossible for me to know how close my auto-translation is able to capture the literary meaning being conveyed in the original, but this is not necessarily a bad thing and relates to other translators' experiences even if my own process stretches what is an appropriate translation beyond the point of no return. For example, Walter Benjamin, after translating Baudelaire, writes, "[n]o translation would be possible if it strove with its total being for similarity with the original." I agree, and for me, what comes across in this one sentence ("The big ditto!") as well as the lines that immediately surround it, is that developing a commercial art practice has, for the most part, not changed much over the last hundred years. The mediums have changed, the content has changed, the formal strategies have changed—but too many artists get stuck in the grind of repeating themselves over and over again, of doing what they have always done as a way to monetize their studio-based routine. I, on the other hand, go out of my way to create work that has very little to no relevance to the studio-art world and the commercial gallery scene that pretends to support it. Instead, what I make relates to a pseudo-autobiographical version of my life as a conceptual artist who uses the act of writing (as performance art / as remix / as auto-translation) to tease out different aesthetic tendencies in my day-to-day research practice. ("You could have pursued a more literary-oriented trajectory as a dissident novelist instead of becoming this digitally-processed performance artist that others seem to think you are," my wife told me after I read this note to her. "You chose not to. Isn't that dissident enough? At least you're not repeating yourself.")

When everything was finished, the scraping knife, in the hand of the artist who controlled the gestural action in a way that only he could, had also, without anyone noticing, created a backside view of the woman on the other side of the previously covered black sheet, and the absolute symmetry between the front and backside of this "woman" created this sense of a performance art painting that had simultaneously become a kind of live-installation designed by the artist for the viewer's pleasure

Here again, what was omitted during the scraping process could somehow be read as a kind of intentional suppression timed to the imaginative foreplay of the artist who knew his performance would allure his audience just by the pure elegance of the experimental sounds he was creating and that were coming out of the disc

With the two-sided modeling process of his meticulous practice revealed, the artist, letting go of his scraper, stood up and took hold of the sheet, extending it a bit farther away from his audience, and placed it on the pivot of a sculptor's saddle, where a small, reinforced wire frame, shaped like a torn apart human subject, stood near a pile of paring chisels and a box of white paperboard without a lid and that, on its side, had these words written in ink: "Night wax"

Manipulating the frame, held in place in the back by a solid metal rod whose base, connected via a blossoming washer, was subject to a core group of screws embedded in a wooden shelf resting on a rotating platform, the artist moved with ease thanks to the flexibility of the wire frame, and this seemingly natural yet intense bodily movement synced with the vibe of the two-sided image his wild scraping had just created

Then his hand, diving in the box, pulled out a thick stick of some tiny, white grain-speckled black wax which, reminiscent of a starry night, justified the name written on the outside of the cardboard box

With this night wax he successively molded the head, trunk and other parts of the frame and then put the rest of the stick back inside the box

Thus prepared, he then began to create a fairly accurate shape using only his fingers and then continued working the material with a paring knife until he formed a piece that properly took advantage of the material's special grain which could be dried and hardened with a serious smattering of stale bread crumbs kneaded and eventually aged within

As the work progressed, the visitors kept getting a better picture of what was being made before them, in this case an actual figure of an abstract expressionist “woman” modeled after the scraped-image the artist had previously rendered on paper

All of the paring chisels were now being put to use, minutely reshaping the hardened wax-bread

As he worked, the artist slowly accumulated some of the excised wax in the fingers of his left hand which he began rolling into an exiguous ball that he occasionally accessed for simple touch ups

One got the feeling that in addition to performing a necessary artist function in the creation of his significant oeuvre, there was an even purer occupation he was embracing now, something that had become a compelling routine—an indispensable daily ritual transfigured in time

On the surface of his piece he began picking at the details so that they aligned with the ink model he was using as his guide

Even when he got to what would be the interior of the woman’s face he seemed to be more immersed than ever, delicately paying attention to every detail of this singular persona’s outward being

Sometimes he would rotate the saddle platform where the piece was resting so that he could tackle another side of the work while turning the sheet of paper from one side to the other so that he could always have both sides of the figure in his mind at once—and meanwhile, when necessary, pushing the box of night wax out of his way whenever it obstructed his fluid dance with the material before him

The sculpture progressed quickly, acquiring an incomparably smooth aesthetic quality

At times it was as if the artist were losing himself in the wax, here molding in with the whiter grains of sculptured flesh, there slightly digging in to the surface to get beyond that which abutted him to material reality

By the time the artist had finished, all eyes were looking at an exquisite blackish figurine that was the perfect negative of the white on black figure revealed in the paper scraping

* * *

After getting the signal from Camera, the group was now positioned before a square iron cage almost two meters high contained within the transparent wall that separated them all from it, and bathed in blue light

A bit away the group could see an invalid laying in a robe and sandals on a stretcher

He was wearing a kind of weird helmet that almost looked like a wig or toupee, and the tour assistant, always ahead of the group, reached into his pocket and pulled out a key that he put into the lock on one of the four sides to the iron square and turned it

After turning the key, he opened what became a tall iron door that, when everyone looked at it, revealed these words engraved on a wood panel: "Fecal Jail"

The patient got up and stood before the stretcher and removed his bathrobe so that he was now only wearing boxer briefs

His helmet of hair was holding steady

It was a small sheet of metal poised on the top of his head and secured by a strap of leather passing under his chin and that was attached to a mobile and round horizontal needle that, according to Camera, had a powerful magnetic force

Above the right shoulder of the patient an old square frame with four smaller squares inside of it was suspended by two small remote hooks screwed vertically into the extreme upper edge of the ceiling

In the frame, devoid of a protective glass, the uppermost left square contained a silk engraving, clearly an antique, that had these words on it: "Plan de Paris"

The uppermost right square had a detailed map of the Paris metro circa 1929

The square on the bottom left had an abstract geometric shape with a thick black horizontal line running through it

The square on the bottom right offered something like a print containing a multilinear curve but one that was quite straight for something so bent out of shape

Also without protective glass, another frame with nine squares was suspended above the left shoulder of the patient

These squares included a gross engraving on paper with these words underlined as a kind of caption: "Feeds into the role of Anus"

More squares included a used Trojan condom, a profile lost in the bliss of seemingly boundless space, a terrestrial globe, an image of a solitary singer mesmerized by their own violent vocals, the boot of Italy leaning up as if kicking, an immense open mouth with various dots coming out of it like elliptical vomit, a deviant version of something resembling planet Earth, a group of stars that had the word "Nadir" situated in the middle of their cluster, and a treble clef with an acute *C* note and three *F*-iliations

Taking a few steps into the cage, the patient was now, without fear, entering the prison-house of language indicating he was ready to read

The door was closed and double locked by the assistant who left the patient alone and, taking the key, went back to the prior artist who was still occupied with his black figurine

Passing the newly imprisoned patient, the group walked three meters to the right to a space that ran parallel to the glass wall where they came upon a huge round lens that went as high as the circular iron cage

The entire edge of the lens was circled with welded copper that, at its center, was firmly connected to the floor by strong screws

Intrigued by a light source that existed behind it, everyone moved back a few steps and could now examine, without obstacle, a black, heavy cylinder that was standing upright off the floor and was topped with a large spherical glass bulb from which emanated a blue clarity that was visible despite the bright daylight

The bulb, accidentally turning off for a second, displayed that the glass itself had no color and that *the clear light itself* was blue

The three respective centers of the bulb, lens and jail were horizontally connected by a perceived straight line

Wearing a heavy fur coat and a down hat, the famous doctor, Petiot, whose popular features identified him immediately, moved on the platform of the black cylinder which caused it to rattle, and proceeded to tweak some buttons behind the bulb in view of the lens he was facing

He kept looking at himself in a round mirror that was positioned in front of him and to the right of a vertical metal rod attached to the floor

Brought back in twos to the prior scene, the group came up to the glass wall and saw the patient giving signs of extreme excitement no doubt caused by the action of the blue light which was now more intensely filling the space he was in because it was now the focal point (which in the mess that was his mind he sometimes thought of as the fecal point—or even the fecal joint)

Behind the jail a man wearing wool gloves and a loosely buttoned hood whose cap enveloped his head held horizontally in his raised right hand a short iron bar that, Camera indicated with few words, was a magnet

Targeting the helmet of the patient, the man arranged for the earlier mentioned engravings to become magnetized to each other

Once again, as with all of the other demonstrations Camera had exposed his willing victims to, he tried to encapsulate what was going on, but as he spoke, the specter of an "inadequate translation" haunted the conversation, and he seemed to take a certain amount of glee in seeing this dysfunctional linguistic mechanism return at such a crucial moment in his showing and telling of the story:

"If we observe the engraving which feeds the protagonist . . . Already very pale since having been incarcerated, and by protagonist what I really mean is *the patient* . . . for example, his fading eyes . . . Now, as I keep repeating, it's partly due to the greater, or in some instances, lesser rapidity of his gradual deterioration, that Dr. Petiot, seeing himself perfectly situated in front of his mirror . . . which separated him from the lens . . . but based only on an indulgence . . . right? Meanwhile, he was tweaking the buttons of the cylinder, maneuvers that seemed to be connected to the serious fluctuations of blue light whose intensity should be considered invaluable for the look and feel of the event as it transpires . . . The slow discomfort literally transforms into a kind of magical revelation where more of the white imagery appears as if working his way back to the blank page that started his frustrations in the first place and that only an artist can conjure up after having been in the dark for so long . . . but then somehow got turned on to this very specific method of creation and proving, once again, that by ceasing to let the dark take over within, he can eventually shape it into the darkness without . . . and over time, that the development of a blue clarity was finally made. As for the Plan de Paris, how else to keep it in circulation, to accentuate the mobility of his nomadic practice in full force?"

As Camera spoke, the garbled translation became semi-clearer, and everyone watched the patient little by little reach the height of his intense agitation as he became more and more possessed

To quickly relieve himself of his suffering, he sought to break the bars of his prison with the full strength of his feet and hands only to turn all of his energy back on himself whereupon he would crumble into a ball of unbearable anguish

Despite all of his gyrations and pirouettes of cumulative force, the magnetic needle hanging around his neck never pointed his destiny in the right direction and the engravings seemed only to serve as an aesthetic ornamentation full of gratuitous symbolism as if that would somehow make his story more complex and meaningful . . .

. . . but he knew that this was not to be, and like so many others, his outpouring of emotion was now animating the supposed tableau vivant that could no longer be controlled because he desperately needed to gesticulate and even give voice to the role of a madman struggling to deal with his demons

Meanwhile, Petiot, a kind of Wizard of Oz, was back tweaking buttons, looking in the mirror, manipulating the magnetic force, monitoring the engravings, and generally fading into the background noise as Camera noted the exorbitant force of the works as a whole while reclaiming his own authority by abruptly intervening in the viewing of the greater work-in-progress

* * *

Continuing along, everyone saw that behind Dr. Petiot was the back of a decorative object that forced them all to stop and look closely at what appeared to be a rich facade of plaster painted and moulded into the wall of glass at a perpendicular angle

Very close to everyone viewing this facade two great wings opened, a genuine gateway which was topped with these words: "Hotel Europe"

The lobby was paved and its walls consisted of simply painted fabrics hung on uniform frames

At the top of the entry, just above the middle of the horizontal part of the frame, pointing outward and perpendicular to the facade, was a short stem made of wrought iron

A lantern was fixed to the stem and painted on one of its four glasses to whoever came up close to look at it was a red European map

High above the entrance was a large glass canopy that let in bright rays of light one of which was reflected off an iron crosspiece and that created an oblique effect on the map

It appeared as if the ray maintained its presence despite the fact that a cloud was now covering the sun

A large black man, dressed as if waiting for a freeze, was stationed in front of the entrance near the threshold while a young bellhop, by contrast, looked like he was living in the middle of summer

The tour assistant who had appeared in the scene with the earlier patient had advanced quickly into this scene as well, running down the paved hall and moving far off toward the left where everyone who followed his movements could see him running toward the Fecal Jail in the distance

Wearing an elegant and light beach outfit, a beautiful young woman whose nails were sparkling with various colors and glitter as if turning her fingers into mirror reflections of each other, was being pursued by a hotel employee wearing his usual livery and who was trying to give her something before she left the scene

Despite holding on to a rose stem in her right hand, the woman, wearing gloves and sunglasses, took hold of the letter which, due to its close proximity, one could read the words "Lady Albert Exeter" written in red ink

Obviously disturbed by some detail in the superscription, the seductress, feeling something take root, quivered as if stabbed by a sharp thorn in the stem she was still holding while trying to open the letter

The sight of blood was suddenly absorbing into the paper, soaking into the secret words held within, and she let the paper fly while she attended to the horrific site of her thumb lightly dampening everything around her red

The visitors heard the woman say something off-hand like "in the lacunae . . . there is still Red Europe . . . the whole of it," the words coming out through yet another extended disc topped with sculpted tissue poking out of the glass wall

Watching, one could see the map on the lantern as it glinted behind her back, the sun still spraying its pseudo-rays across the makeshift architecture creating the illusion of a tremendous reflection that hinted at an alter-world beyond the speed of light

Immediately after they had fallen to the ground, the hotel employee had tried to grab both the letter and bloody rose

However, given the fact that he was at least octogenarian, he could not bend sufficiently enough to reach them

He looked promiscuously at the bellhop and said "Tiger," pointing to the pavement with his finger

The obedient teenager went over to pick up the two small things that belonged to the woman

But after having shuddered at the name "Tiger," a kind of sick old man reference that he was uncomfortable with, the boy, overtaken by a sort of violent hallucination, began a looping series of hot-tempered pronouncements under his breath, saying "I'm not your fucking Tiger, and this bloody shit you always ask me to do, why must I pick it up, you're not my father, you old fuck . . . "

The insanity only got more intense pouring itself into a well of absolute dementia, at which point the black man who had been there since the beginning, dressed as if ready for a freeze, took the stage in an emotional reappearance, making small steps toward the interior of the hotel

* * *

Once again stunned by Camera's continuous performance-art exhibition, the group, after journeying a few seconds forward, suddenly stopped near a common man and woman who were in a rectangular room that had no ceiling and where one of the two longer walls was actually the wall of glass through which everyone could see clearly

Inside you could see the assistant who had, at the previous stop, run out toward the scene we were now in front of

His slanting skip across this room led him to a door that he exited through as he quickly poured his fluid image through the lobby of the Hotel Europe

The new scene playing before everyone's eyes gave the appearance of some kind of office

Strangely, near the back wall was a magnificent library that on first view contained a spacious set of black shelves but that on closer inspection revealed what were rows of black skulls collected on each shelf

On the mantelpiece above the fireplace without a fire, and between two pieces of nondescript tchotchkes, a globe of glass was housing something that looked like the Head of Death Itself, and this head was wearing a toque carved out some old newspaper

On the wall to the left there was a wide window that faced the door

A large rectangular table was installed *into* the wall on one of its short sides and there was a man sitting at the table with his back to everyone shuffling some paperwork

Soon, getting bored with this kind of work, he stood up and put a cigarette in to his mouth that he had taken out of a leather case pulled out of his shirt pocket

In a few steps, he walked to the fireplace where out of an open box he pulled out a flammable starter which he lit and then used to light his cigarette with, immersing himself in the voluptuous volumes of smoke surrounding him, and after a while extinguished all of the flames and threw them in the hearth

But it was during his last action that he noticed that the skull with the odd headpiece resting on the black shelf above the fireplace was giving him a restrained look that shook him to his core

Under the spell of intellectual undecidability, he lifted the glass globe to readjust the skull's position, seizing the macabre object without upsetting the toque, and returned it on to his table while revealing to all of the onlookers his young face, that of a man of about 25 years old

A common man and woman who were somehow nestled closely to the visiting group were, in fact, a guy with his mother whose role-playing position in this particular scene was crucial—and they too avidly watched the action across the glass wall

The smoker, reinstalled at his table, turned back to stare at the skull he had taken off the shelf and placed before him

On the visible portion of the skeletal forehead, a kind of fine weaving was sunk into the bone where a metal tip was clumsily installed amidst meshes of fragmented fishnet

Camera called everyone's attention to some Runic manuscript letters, a list of similes written on the vertical edge of a page which was actually part of the material made to create the odd looking toque adorning the skull

"These pieces are made with old newspaper from the *New York Times*," he said

Then he showed the crew that, upon closer inspection, there was a resemblance between the Runic manuscript letters and a piece of *Times* newspaper, except for the obvious way they deviated in their titling and spacing of letters and the odd form of the actual letters in the rune

"Except for that," he said, "and maybe . . . " but then he trailed off

He was distracted as was the group by the presence of the young man who, still smoking, was hovering around as if spying on them all

His look was hard to describe except to say he was living on the edge of a mysterious hairstyle

Now he indicated his desire to interact with the audience and advised everyone to watch him take hold of a small tablet that came with a foam-tipped stylus that he used to transcribe letters on to the sensitive glass screen that by way of subtle touching would transcribe his movements into letters of the alphabet and foreground a kind of live textual performance, constantly touching the screen with both the stylus in his right hand as well as his left index finger as if prodding language into a typographical dance of visual complexity beyond meaning per se

When he had temporarily finished, no one could really situate themselves in any ideal way that would enable them to see the entire screen, but on closer inspection from a particular angle, one could make out two large words in all upper case letters: RECTO and VERSO

Compelled to align himself with his writerly performance, he extended his choreographed remarks by walking in toward the library and then returning back to the table where he presented a large volume that, following an extremely long title, had the subtitle “A Commoner’s Condition”

“Come sit at the table,” he teased the group

“Excuse the skull,” he said as if intentionally creating a kind of mock alienation effect

He sat down and, placing the book on the table, opened it to the first page which consisted of several distinct paragraphs printed on rich, brown colored paper

Then he began to count the letters in one paragraph by mimicking the same touch-screen movement he had just performed on the other side of the glass only this time he used a white pen to touch the book instead of his finger

Sometimes, when he reached a specific number, he would look at the letter he was pointing to and immediately reproduce that letter with his foam-tipped stylus on to the digital tablet

One could see that he was now pointing to a place in the book where a very heavy type spelled two fragments, the first “technique first appearing in the year” and the second “alchemy or similar diversion into the subliminal”

When the young writer had finished his arbitrary procedure, a series of white letters appeared in a moldy type at the bottom of his now black slate, all very crisp in their milk-tone flesh punctuated by pulsating ruby buttons spaced between each letter for aesthetic effect

On the table, the lush book—opened to what appeared to be a random page—seemed to be a self-contained art object

It was a little bit longer than it was wide and appeared to have bound up within its pages certain facsimiles of theater posters

The surface cover of the book had a gold enclosure with countless tiny gems embedded in its surface

Clear emeralds formed the bottom and readable text was made out of darker emeralds

Other words were created out of gems of various sizes, characters made out of sapphire set on diamond backgrounds, dimensions variable

“The thought crossed my mind: how can I make a diamond tape, and what would I tape it to?”

The young performer who had been shuffling his way through the scene said this aloud to no one in particular as he carefully looked through a magnifying glass on the table at what must have been more tiny gems

After quite a long time, he appeared to make another remark, not by speaking per se, but by raising a loose ruby into his fingers and immediately letting go of it

He proceeded to do this with quite a few rubies

He must have been trying to find the perfect ruby to restore back into the book or else why would he be going through these repetitive motions?

Finally he began reading from the book remembering he had just extinguished his last cigarette in the improvised smoky haze he had started near the fireplace

(The thought crossed someone’s mind that this scene being played out before them was an imprecise version of a larger story, one that they anticipated would eventually penetrate into the depths of some hideous, unsuspected secret)[56]

It was with difficulty, trembling, and uncertainty that the young man continued turning pages, each successive page becoming more quickly devoured by him as he swept through the text

By the time he reached the end of his unusual reading of the material, he stopped cold dead, enmeshed in an unconscious stupor

Then he had a delayed reaction and, wringing his hands, seemed to be invaded by a flood of demonic thoughts

Finally, recovering his composure, he put his elbows on the edge of the table and thought long and hard while pressing his forehead into the palms of his hands

He emerged from this meditation with a cool assurance that made one think he had come upon a steadfast plan

The last handwritten sheet he had looked at was drawn with very broad letters and the final line of the text contained a signature: *Frank Court*

56. Who this someone could be is still open to question. Could it be one of the colleagues being toured through Camera’s alternative art compound? The person reading the book? The person readwriting the book? What book? Which persona?

. . . and there was no postscript

Now dipping a pen into the inkstand, the young man began to write excessively on a white page until it was almost all black

Then he signed this name into the black: "Frank Court"

Around the capital *C*, he spent a while drawing a curved serpent which served a diacritical purpose by doubling as a kind of hook

All eyes were keyed on what had just been written

When the ink was dry, the young man began collecting all of his paperwork and assorted gems and placed them with a stash of gold into their proper carry case which was then closed with a snap, although the sound of the snap was not present due to the absence of any extending disk made of tissue

Soon the cumbersome portfolio, the huge book, the art object—whatever it was—was placed back in its exact former location and shone the way an embalmed face shines while laying in an open casket

After having made his way back to the library where he got lost inside the book and finally returned to his table, the young man was rubbing the tip of his right index finger with his thumb, getting ready to trace his riff-reading practice across the digital tablet's glass screen

He thought about donning the toque resting on the small death skull—or becoming the glass globe that encased it

Could he not also function as the main ornament near the fireplace?

A moment later, his right hand, searching one of his pockets, came out holding a revolver, while he used his other hand to unbutton his jacket

Moments later, he pointed the gun at his heart and pulled the trigger, everyone seized by the noise of the gun going off—the sound of which, when coupled with the image of the man falling stiff on his back, caused varying degrees of near-incontinence

Camera left the group, opened the door and entered the room

The common woman and her son, who had paid close attention to the entire scene as it went down, stood erect, embracing their emotions

* * *

The group went on the way they had been, moving along the transparent wall behind which appeared more open space awaiting their next set of new characters

Having reached the end of yet another huge cage, Camera turned left, then began walking the entire length of this side of the glass, about ten meters in all, before turning right and leading the pack toward the esplanade where, slowly, everyone walked alongside one of the two last walls that was still new to everyone

Soon Camera stopped, his finger tightly taking hold of the inside of the cage

He pointed out a significant piece of dark, cylindrical, metal mass that measured two feet in diameter and five feet high

He informed everyone that it was some kind of electrical appliance that radiated intense cold and indicated to the group that there were, in fact, seven of these devices in total

But by this time the entire crew was on overload and Camera, who had led them through the performance-art installations every step of the way, was clearly quite happy with the way he envisioned himself lighting up everyone's minds by providing an accompanying narrative context to what their eyes and ears were hungrily devouring

* * *

Seeing what wonderful reflexes he had obtained by experimenting with the facial nerves of Danton who had been locked in death for over a century, Camera had imagined giving the complete illusion of an active, emotional life coming out of the bodies of recent corpses that would be preserved by an intense cold that fought against deterioration

But the need to keep the scene at very low temperature made things difficult for the diamond tank and its *aqua-micans* which tended to freeze up and made most of the action inside that exhibit totally impotent

After lengthy tests on corpses subjected to the intense cold, Camera, after many attempts, ended up composing a kind of vital form of biomorphic stimulation he termed *résurrectine*[57], a reddish substance containing *érythrite* that he would inject into the skull of a deceased subject by laterally boring a hole

57. The thought immediately crosses my mind as I write this that my auto-translation is a kind of literary *résurrectine* that's being applied to metamediumystic acts of writing as an embodied form of *hauntology*. Octavio Paz, in *Appearance Stripped Bare*, writes, "Jarry is and is not Ubu, Duchamp is and is not Rrose Sélavy." I would have to disagree with Paz, though, who thought the same did not apply to Roussel who, to him, "is no less unreal than the character [Camera]." Come to think of it, can I not also be and not be all six of them (Jarry, Ubu, Duchamp, Rrose Sélavy, Roussel,

into their skull until enough of the fluid would have formed a mass surrounding the outer layer of the brain

After the *résurrectine* was injected it was then easy to insert in the porthole a short stem coated in an alloy-like substance that would infuse and surround the hole he had drilled and that, when powered with electricity and triggering an alchemical transformation inside the cranium now loaded with the *résurrectine*, would stimulate the brain to such an intense degree that the body would bypass its signal to decompose and, instead, endow the subject with quite an impressive artificial life[58]

Camera)? My sense of an embodied praxis that readwrites experiential forms of post-identity into the field of distribution suggests that I can be *all of them at once*, and that, in fact, it's my job to be oscillating versions of them all—and others—at once. Rimbaud writes that "I is another," but for me it's way beyond the I per se and another always leads to another and many another, a simultaneous and continuous fusion of conceptual personae flickering filtered signifiers without even blinking. These conceptual personae are discharged from a fictional state of unconsciousness that has yet to be located inside the brain-body as it performs its ongoing creative act(s), its parallel processed durational achievements. In *remixthebook*, I relate this fictional state of unconsciousness to a neural mechanism that Amiri Baraka, writing as LeRoi Jones, refers to as the *trigger inference*. Specifically, I quote Jones as he responds to Jack Kerouac's "Essentials of Spontaneous Prose" via a letter he writes to the *Evergreen Review*:

> This is the consciousness that supersedes or usurps the normal consciousness of the creator (though even the usual or uninspired consciousness of the creator can hardly be called normal). For it is during this so-called normal state that the artist's peculiar and/or latent impressions are gathered; but it is only during this 'unconscious' state that the writer's voice becomes his only voice . . . and the creative act itself is accomplished.

His use of the term "the creative act" syncs with the title of the lecture Duchamp delivered in Houston in 1957, but is most likely coincidental in that regard. What's strange to me, though, is how tapping into this trigger inference or supraconsciousness, has become my (pre)occupation over the last few years as I investigate spontaneous forms of performance-making. Even more bizarre to me is that I actually get paid for it as an elemental American. But at what cost?

58. There's an underlying sci-fi vibe running throughout *Locus Solus*, something that Robbe-Grillet seems incapable of tapping into or at least uninterested in pursuing. Duchamp, on the other hand, seems to have had his pump primed by these fantastical musings. In his 1954 book, *The Bachelor Machines*, Michel Carrouges employs a remixological reading of Duchamp's definitively unfinished *Large Glass* by circulating it through a kind of cybernetic filter and mashing it up with readings of the work of writers such as Roussel, Jarry, and Kafka. These writerly bachelor machines are a-teleological auto-translation programs that strip language of its formal desire, leaving them "incapable of operating in reality." Instead, they become conceptual apparatuses or "*mental machines*, the imaginary working of which suffices to produce a

As a result of the curious awakening of very short term memory, the subject would immediately reproduce with strict accuracy the slightest movements they had made during the crucial last minutes of their existence and then, without any rest, indefinitely, repeat this same unchanging series of actions like a live loop[59]

The illusion of life was absolute: mobility of the gaze, continuous breathing of air in and out of the lungs, unconscious proprioception, the various actions, a sense of presence in a general economy of meaning—nothing was missing[60]

When word of his latest invention got out, Camera received many letters from alerted families who wished to see their loved one, whose death sentence had already been spoken, revive their eyes again after what had clearly been their fatal moment

He had decided then to build a viewing area in a good location in his park, itself a kind of privatized outdoor museum that had an interconnected series of pavilions displaying his techno-scientific aesthetic installations

---

real movement of the mind." But my experience is different in that, rather than being completely disconnected from reality the way, say, an *a-cognitive creep* like the concept artist Henry Flynt might imagine himself to be, the perversion is more indicative of an innate urge to experiment with the inner workings of one's unconscious creative potential, a potential that is always already erotically charged by an urge to remix. Duchamp, in "The Creative Act," referred to this unconscious potential as being related to a *pure intuition*, and the curator Harald Szeeman suggested that this aspect of Duchamp's aesthetic vision, and the way he applied it to the functionality of his bachelor machines, grew out of "a belief in eternal energy flow as a way to avoid death, as an erotics of life: the bachelor as rebel-model, as antiprocreation." And yet when one reads through Roussel, Jarry, Robbe-Grillet, the writings of Duchamp and even my own novels, digital narratives and films, one cannot help but sense the sex happening everywhere, even when its noticeably absent.

59. The extent to which Camera by way of Roussel creates these installation environments so that they continually loop with very little variation is ingenious. He's essentially resurrecting the past by creating live-action scenes that are part theatrical but also a kind of expanded form of cinema that anticipates audio-visual performance art (and here I am also thinking of the extended discs made of tissue paper that leak sound out from the enclosed installation spaces—a very museological / zoological approach to preserving the narrative elements).

60. As the reader might have guessed, here as elsewhere throughout the text, there is no way in hell this sentence has much of anything to do with the original. But the truth is that I did write the line after having read whatever mangled script the auto-translation gave me and am quite happy with these kinds of spontaneous riffs. In fact, I prefer them to much of the more idiosyncratic historical narratives that populate the story. Whenever the performance process would produce a sentence like this, I would often think of those "affirmative ironies" that Duchamp once referred to.

This glass pavilion, like many of the others, consisted of a huge rectangular room made out of a metal frame that supported a ceiling and walls of glass

Inside the room, the electrical coolants would keep the subjects at the appropriate temperature and Camera and his live assistants would dress in super warm clothes so that they could effortlessly stay inside the installation as long as they needed to

Transported into this large cooler doubling as a glass house, each deceased subject approved by the artist would suffer through the cranial injection process

The introduction of the *résurrectine* took place via a thin hole just above the right ear and would then receive the follow-up plug of the vital alloy which would harden in and around the opening

Once the alchemical process of remixing the *résurrectine*, alloy and electricity forced these elements to make contact with each other in the guise of a subject coming back to life, various gestures and words began appearing and repeating themselves, and this enabled the artist to conduct a cluster of very specific episodes

During the initial phase of researching the possibilities these episodes might have for a series of performance-art installations, Camera and his assistants would closely surround an animated corpse and help with any of the movements they were once again becoming reacquainted with

Indeed the exact execution of their muscular effort to, say, pick something heavy up off the ground, resulted in them inevitably losing their balance which, without immediate intervention, would cause them to fall over

In addition, whenever their legs would take them from a flat surface to an imaginary staircase that would require them to lift their legs to climb, some help would have been needed to stop them from falling forward or backward

A prompt hand was always at the ready to catch any subject who had become too reliant on a wall to lean their shoulder on and who would unknowingly lean back into the space with nothing there to hold them

After identifying how each of these scenes was repetitively playing out in the various pavilions, Camera carefully documented each work and once he had achieved what he imagined was a desired framework to the let work go live, he attempted to recreate as close as possible the original circumstances and objects in each location where the subject was last seen living out their lives

He kept practicing and building the sets and where he found an appropriate opening, he would fabricate the externalized discs made of tissues that would leak sounds out of the glass interiors and into the viewing stations

After awhile, the corpse, dressed in accordance with the spirit of the role it was playing, would find its way around the furniture, locate points of support and resistance, conduct its normal business, employ its usual motor skills and avoid false gestures or accidental falls

After a loop had ended and it was back to where it had started, it would just begin again without variance (a perfectly looping digital file but embodied as a performance-art spectacle)

If one of the corpses ceased to conduct its bio-loop or started "losing information," and this happened frequently, the artist would have to go in, refurbish the alloy-coated stem so that it connected and covered the hole properly, patch it with the simulated hair, and send another jolt of electricity to the strange attractor that would then trigger an immediate resurrection of the same loop that would now play from the beginning

Whenever a scene would require it, the artist would pay extras to play the necessary parts

The bodies of each performer were wearing the latest in high-tech alpine performance underclothing and donned thick, heat-inducing wigs so that they could play their character in the ultra-cool compartments

The finished work now consisted of eight scenes developed after eight deaths, the subjects of which had endured the new treatment so as to revive their last moments and summarize a random set of patterns that kept repeating themselves

1) *The poet Gerard Lowry, led by his widow, whose only obsession, conveyed in a voice full of pain, was that Camera apply the résurrectine to her man*

For over fifteen years, Gerard had successfully published his remarkable poetry in Paris where he excelled at capturing the local color of the land he came from

The nature of his talent included traveling incessantly, a nomadic bard who would take the world by storm, and to avoid the continuous heartbreak of separating himself from his family, he instead convinced his young wife Chloe, who spoke many different languages, to allow him to occasionally take their young son Florent, who never seemed to tire of the wandering, on his trips

One day, while he was driving his van through the mountains of Calabria in southern Italy, Gerard was robbed and attacked by a group of thugs led by a character who went by the name El Grocco, an undesirable known for the audacity of his attack method and the ransoms he would extract

Suddenly stabbed in his left leg and unable to escape, Gerard was captured as was his two-year-old son Florent

El Grocco immediately notified Chloe that he would not set them free unless, before a date he indicated would be the day of execution, she arranged to deliver to him a sum of one hundred thousand Eurofrancs

Then he took out a device reminiscent of what, in the early 21st century, would be referred to as an iPhone, and forced the poet to write a message facilitating the transfer of funds[61]

Abducted with their luggage at the top of the steep mountain, Gerard and Florent were imprisoned inside a former chapel that was part of an old fortress and had become the hideout where El Grocco and his gang camped out

The poet, reflecting on his situation, saw no way out

Grocco, being a greedy pig who thought highly of himself and naturally assumed that he was entitled to a rich life, had actually demanded too much money, about 4/5ths more than Chloe would be able to obtain

And if and when the money did not arrive, the idiot creep decided he would not delay the hour of execution for one minute

After a long meditation on the reality of the situation, Gerard thought of a risky proposition that he hoped would at least save Florent's life

By promising 10,000 Eurofrancs[62] that he knew Chloe could easily put together, the poet tried to win over one of the gangbangers who initially cap-

61. My original remix of the auto-translation for this sentence read, "Then he took out his iPhone and forced the poet to write an email facilitating the transfer of funds." My thinking at the time of production was, "a hundred years from now, when this text is read by visitors from another planet, the mention of an iPhone will not seem cute or coy or even problematic for the author who seemed to thumb his nose at the potential longevity of his literary enterprise. Rather, these polite visitors, seeing the scorched remains of a formerly green and blue celestial body whose best days were now in the past, will figure that the author or whatever sentient form of life transcribed the words contained herein, must be referring to a device that transmits messages, much like the device you are using to read this work in its present form."

62. When it comes to technology, I have no problem, say, calling an iPhone an iPhone, but with financial currency, who knows? Best to hedge ones bets.

tured him and now was his guard, a guy named Leo Castelli[63] who, along with his girlfriend, Marta, seemed more astute than the rest of the band of thieves

Gerard gave it his best shot and detailed a plan whereby Marta would secretly remove Florent from the scene and meet Chloe where she would exchange the baby for the smaller sum, which Leo Castelli and Marta would keep for themselves and then take off on their own to start an entirely new life together

The poet had thus come up with a plan to relinquish his own potential escape as a way to ensure his son's survival

Grocco, meanwhile, frequently passed in front of the chapel which was located at ground level and, through the window, could see Gerard who intentionally stayed within his sight so that when the time came to sneak out the baby and send him on what would undoubtedly be a long and arduous journey through the countryside, everything would be normal

Afraid of his prisoners having any communication with the outside world, Grocco banned all writing utensils and anything else that resembled what in the early 21st century would be referred to as networked mobile devices

Leo Castelli, defying his boss, arranged for the poet to write out his instructions to his wife, Chloe, which would include the plan of returning Florent to her for the set amount of money

The next day, before dawn, Marta, equipped with the letter, left with the child hidden under her coat

But that day, Grocco, suddenly learning about the imminent arrival of a group of rich travelers ripe for the picking, called on Leo Castelli to help him coordinate the planning strategy for their next attack

A new guard, Laz, was assigned to Gerard, who trembled at the thought of Florent's escape being discovered so soon, especially since there was still time to catch up with Marta

63. Leo Castelli is positioned here as a both guard and accomplice. One of Manhattan's most successful art gallery directors who was able to monetize various forms of Conceptual and Pop Art, Castelli was once quoted as saying, "There is nothing that has been done since Duchamp that doesn't bear a little of his influence." Perhaps that's a bit of an exaggeration, but even if it's partly true, then it would also be partly true that there is nothing that has been done since Roussel that doesn't bear a little of his influence as well (remember Duchamp: "Roussel showed me the way.").

When Laz brought the first meal, he seemed to not care about Florent, who was supposedly still asleep in a small pallet over in a dark corner of the room

But Gerard knew that this new guard would eventually realize something was up, and probably sooner rather than later, and that Marta was still vulnerable to being caught—with or without the baby!

Gerard sought a way to create a subterfuge that would ward off the danger

Against one of the walls of the chapel where it semi-stood in place inside the remains of an altar next to a life-size statue of the Virgin that was broken into several pieces including the broken arms, was a baby Jesus that remained intact

The poet decided to use this stone child as a kind of ersatz infant that would give the impression of a baby being in the room with him

In order to soften the wound that his left leg experienced during the attack, he had received a flesh-colored ointment from Grocco

Naturally, he took the divine child and began covering it with the pink ointment all over its face, ears, and neck before settling it into the pallet previously occupied by Florent

Not fully satisfied with the resulting illusion, he thought about ways to better conceal the stone hair

Only a little white cap would do the trick

But how to make such a thing?

Gerard, following a habit he picked up while nomadically wandering the landscape, had access to some linen that he carried with him everywhere, and out of this he imagined could be created something approaching a kind of bonnet

A window was all that lit up the chapel

It had a strong grid that was installed there to protect its prior inhabitants from invaders

At its bottom a narrow alcove had formed over the years and was littered with bits of rejected scraps, clippings, crusts, cores, and peelings

Just in case, the prisoner decided to find some useful material he could use to form a little baby outfit should the guard try and closely examine the faux child

Seeing at the top of the heap some pear peels, he remembered that the day before one of the thugs had stolen a cart full of delicious fruit, which the entire gang was thrilled to have access to

In fact, Leo Castelli had included one of the pears in his dinner the night before

An idea suddenly crossed Gerard's mind: he could take the white filament, cores, and stems of the fruit that nobody wanted and separate them into a material that he could combine into primitive cords or thin wires that his novice fingers would then weave and knot into something like a baby's cap

Covered with this linen and fruit cap to the neck, the statue gave the illusion of a real child

The ointment imitated the flesh well enough and the cap seemed to be as good as any 21st century thing you could buy online and that was made in China

After securing his folksy arts and craftwork, he restored the scrap heap to look similar to the way it did before he accessed it

When Laz later came with lunch, Gerard, suppressing his worst fears, begged for silence so that the baby could sleep, since it had been suffering earlier

The guard threw a glance toward the dark corner and was fooled by the ploy

The same scene was renewed at night when dinner was served

In the early part of the night, Gerard heard something of a ruckus and saw that El Grocco had succeeded in his latest attack and that there were new prisoners put in neighboring rooms

The next day, Leo Castelli, resuming his duties as the guard, admired the resourcefulness of the poet who, despite the unexpected developments of the narrative, somehow found a way to keep his cool

Taking precautions, the statue was kept intact on its place in the dark corner so that it would easily satisfy the quick lure of any unexpected visitor

Marta returned after being away for five days and said that Chloe had handed over the sum of cash plus a letter for Gerard in exchange for Florent

One morning, charged with the task of going back into the mountains and locating another opulent traveler as their next mark, Leo Castelli, who was told to take as long as two days to complete his mission, saw this as an opportunity to run away with Marta and the money they had already kept for the transfer of the baby

Gerard thought this was a great idea and gave them both his most grateful adieux

Thanks to the skill of the poet whose fake child ensured the successful desertion of Leo and Marta without any hindrance, Laz, now on guard duty again, assumed that the bulk on the pallet was Florent

But his suspicions came alive as he awoke the next day and after approaching the berth immediately realized what had gone down

El Grocco was notified and came in to survey the scene whereupon he deduced the role played by both Leo Castelli and Marta who, by now, were well on their way and had escaped his recriminations

Pretending to not care about what was quickly emerging as his inevitable death, Gerard sought solace in the act of writing as a way to defend himself against Grocco's all-encompassing presence

The same day that his van had been attacked, before leaving the village he was in, Gerard had come across a group of poor children whose arms were filled with freshly picked flowers

He had bought a bouquet for Chloe and this included a rose that he still had in his possession and that he turned to as a way to preserve the sweet memory of what he, now a prisoner, had hoped to reconnect with again, in one form or another

Gerard now thought about how he could use one of the rose's thorns as a pen, and tore them all off but the longest one and, with his fingernail, lopped off the stem, and soon found himself holding something like a stylus or impromptu writing instrument

He had been granted, upon request, a few books he had kept in his luggage for enjoyment, and among them was a large dictionary that ended with two double-sided white sheets so that he now had four large blank pages ready to receive his important disseminations

Gerard knew that his blood, caused by a prick of the thorn, could serve him as ink, but he also feared being discovered were he to stain his clothing

It is generally thought, or so Gerard convinced himself, that by reducing to powder a durable matter like metal, one could color the letters they had traced with water and that they would soon appear on a surface after natural drying as a readable and sustainable text

But which metal to pulverize?

As far as steel goes, the bars of the window were unassailable and the chapel only had external locks that were too obvious to steal

Fortunately, when all of Gerard's possessions were taken from him by the gang of bandits, they had mistakenly left an ancient gold coin in one of his hidden pockets

During a summer in the south of France, Chloe, a child then, played in some old feudal ruins under the thick shadows of what had, at one time, constituted a classic gold promenade

One day, while digging in the soil with her spade to playfully surround some ditches with a simple fortress made of dirt, she unearthed a gold coin that was later determined to be part of a shield used by a commanding warrior from the 14th century

Proud of her find, Chloe wanted to wear a bracelet with the coin hanging from a chain of gold

Being a girl, she kept the frail gem attached to the gold chain around her wrist

After receiving an engagement ring from Gerard, she then decided to give him this special jewel that had been on her wrist since childhood

Night and day the avant-garde poet hid the sentimental relic from his captors by slipping the bracelet inside a secret pocket circling the inner lining of his cuff

Maintained by two curved abuttments sealed in the wall, the bars of the window ended with steel quills that could, when the coin was rubbed against them, provide a gold powder

This coin, which was so precious and created a deep emotional connection between the loving couple, would be totally destroyed

But later, in the eyes of Chloe, the special value of her bracelet would only increase since the written words she would eventually come across could only have been scripted due to successfully pulverizing the gold coin into a powder that would translate into her poet's Swan Song

Given the fragility of the situation, as well as his desire to scramble any potential signal that would reveal his actions, Gerard decided to take advantage of the solid framework of the bookbinding, promising himself that he would fill the white pages at the end of the huge dictionary without detaching them from the entire volume

His work would live on since Chloe, coming upon or receiving his last possessions, would surely look for his words at the back of the old book

To avoid degrading the volume, which, worth a lot of money, deserved to be properly maintained and not devalued just to provide a few blank pages with his final ramblings, the poet decided to really focus on what he was writing as if it would become a kind of *necessary supplement to the dictionary itself*

If he were to write something so personal that it felt estranged from whoever read it, he would risk someone feeling the volume had lost some of its value, which could then jeopardize his intent to keep it in circulation until it somehow found its way back to Chloe

The book, after all, was in part valuable because it had been composed by the mythological researcher Ludwig Calvino

After a lifetime devoted to the study of a deep and personal mythology, Ludwig Calvino, famous philosophical investigator and experimental prose writer, had mashed up two remarkable dictionaries: one, referred to simply as *Glas*, the other *A Dictionary of Errant Forms of Transmission*[64]

Over time, he had accumulated countless new material that he fed into the remix, which he continued composing—or *compostproducing*—over thirty years of patient research and writing

There, sorted by alphabetical order, one could find concept characters, animal vocabularies, corrupt lines of pre-Internet object-oriented programming languages, and sampled bits of misspoken rhetoric from long gone diaries or what in the early 21st century were referred to as blog sites

Through this hodgepodge of unrelated words and phrases, he used the formal characteristics of experimental metafiction to hypertextually link readers to an array of subjects, ranging from supernatural visitations to neologistic puns to the process of transmission executed by troubadours sharing anecdotes on the rich variety of stories that had been transmitted over time

Any foreign word that attempted to force its way into the dictionary as a representation of the real was excluded from the nomenclature

Written as a kind of deconstructive artist-theory composed in a praxis-based creative tongue, it was a rare print book published by the author and could only be found in illustrious libraries and private collections

But thanks to circumstances related to the father of a writer he knew, Gerard had come into possession of this book whose title most believe refers to the

64. Calvino, Derrida, an old dictionary on the pre-history of glitch aesthetics, what's not to like?

elusive and vagrant use of language as just more data to be structured into a mangled sequence of digressions within digressions that may or may not make sense

Taken in its broadest sense, "Errant Glossolalia" signaled an adherence to an anarchic imagination ready to risk its stability in lieu of generating a poetic context for the flow of meaningless utterance

However, to throw more fuel into the fire, why not just use this strange dictionary as source material to indicate that his, Gerard's, death was but one more randomly composed element in the psychogeographical drift of history toward its inevitable event horizon?

Gerard drew out a plan to write an ode that would poetically trace a form of pagan survival connected to both his conceptual use of language and what he thought of as his "soul," a work that would indicate the power of transforming his always errant ways into an undisciplined, stylistic tendency, most especially related to the multitude of visions he would always blend into his *desire to write*, a desire triggered by reading different sections of the dictionary while under the influence of mind-altering substances

Is this not what it meant to be a textual alchemist?

(*translator's note*: I was feeling this myself, just by *writing it out*—by *becoming* it while blending)[65]

To produce new work, the poet had to be a kind of rebel of the time-clock, someone who would methodically work according to their own schedule, even if that meant sacrificing normalcy in the everyday robotic world of getting somewhere on time so they could perform a cog-like function in the wheels of industry

Of course, the poet would actually end up working more hours than most, including entire nights of not sleeping and most especially endless weekends and supposed holidays (in name only), a kind of self-administered sleep deprivation that would literally lead the artist to "lose themselves" in the heat of composition—and this was further complicated by the fact that in addition to not sleeping, they would undoubtedly begin to also *starve* themselves because there was simply no time to eat—until the work was done or at least finally unfinished—*this* is what it meant to exhaust ones creative self (as if there could

65. I decided to keep this translator's note in the text itself instead of turning it into a footnote, to let the translation wear its metafictional presence on its sleeve, as it were, and *let the various layers of reading-writing-translating-remixing blur.*

ever be a self) to the point of no longer being able to think—at which time it made perfect sense to just crash and do nothing for days on end[66]

Endowed with an excellent memory, Gerard mentally imprinted the ode deep inside his mind before taking hold of the pen

In sixty consecutive hours, every second would be used, and Gerard, following his own rules, would compose and continue composing, until his ode was finished at the beginning of a new, albeit delayed, dawn

He carefully collected, near the window, a dose of the gold powder by scraping the bracelet against the sharp pricks of the steel bar

Then, with the long thorn dipped inside the water in his pitcher, he began to write his ode on the white page, followed by his sprinkling of gold after each verse was traced with fresh liquid

Gradually he made his way to the bottom of the first page, which soon dried and revealed a clear, golden text, and Gerard quickly manipulated the book to recover whatever gold dust had not been absorbed by the water

Filling in the same way the back of the initial sheet he had composed on, then both sides of the last sheet, the poet completed his ode and signed it

Jealous again of the life he was about to leave, he was overtaken by a marauding pack of cruel thoughts focused on his own rapidly approaching oblivion, and even as these thoughts took temporary leave, they would also signal their willingness to totally assault him again without a moment's notice

Gerard, practically brain-dead from having composed from memory his crucial ode, decided to occupy his mind with dull, mnemonic exercises

The dictionary offered many odd stories that would be easy to remember, even for Gerard who, after a writerly performance similar to the one he had just conducted, would rarely find himself trying to memorize passages from a book, let alone a huge fictional dictionary devoted to glitches in the transmission of meaning

So he looked in his baggage for another book and found a scholarly tome on the Eocene

He tore into the book and got dizzy with its heady and colorful imagery

66. Who is relating to whom here? I must have been getting tired but also looking for an opportunity to express myself, even if this is what was happening in Roussel's text as well. One thing is for sure, I was clearly under Roussel's spell and had lost complete touch with anything remotely resembling a routine existence.

He thought about creating a mixed media collage by secretly composing tiny, obsessive texts inside the color images[67]

But Gerard felt that in order to perform such a difficult task, especially given his circumstances, he would need to force himself to stick with it every day until the last day, an endless, irremissible daily labor

At the end of the book, dragged across two columns, was a fine alphabetical index of all the important topics relating to sounds made by animals, substances, machines, and weather phenomena—each providing, as a result of its name, an indication of what pages focused on these issuances

Fifty days including the current day having passed, and still distancing himself from the immutable date of his inevitable death, Gerard sought an entry in the index that did not offer just some obvious word that linked to a section inside the book

On the one hundred and fifteenth line he encountered a phrase that synced with his feelings as well as linked to his own predicament: "Sound of an animal locked in a cage"

Then he viewed two new words, "Active" and "Passive," that were subentries below the entry just mentioned above

He wanted to keep them all, every line of the index, but then he decided to redact on a daily basis, one line a day, as a way to mark his imprisonment

Was it really necessary for him to now, each and every day, count the redacted lines of the index as a way of recounting the number of sunrises and sunsets he had been incarcerated?

And what about the fact that he was only just now starting this process of redacting?

And what exactly is meant by the word "now"?

There was no mention of errant accounting in the index nor in the errant glossary of terms found in the dictionary for that matter

Perhaps it didn't matter, but the key thing as always was for him to follow through on his commitment to do what he was programmed to do, that is, to simultaneously embrace and defy the so-called discipline he had staged for himself

67. Clearly, Gerard was a kind of avant-garde artist whose work was ahead of its time. Or, sampling from Cocteau, maybe the time was just behind the work? It happens.

(*translator's note*: I was feeling this myself, just by *writing it out*—by *embracing* it while defying a kind of rigid discipline)[68]

The prisoner that he had become approached every hour on the hour as an avid exercise in personal transformation and enduring wish oblivion

Three weeks before his fatal date, he had a very believable, lucid dream where he was holding Chloe in his arms

She was mad with joy since she had brought with her to the chapel the necessary sum of cash to liberate him

She had once been connected closely with a particular convent of modest means that, thanks to its utter beauty, had come into an unexpected inheritance of great fortune

Chloe had lost touch with the convent and had no idea of its change of fortune

Meanwhile, the rector, browsing through various magazine and newspaper reports of her and Gerard's dilemma, was moved to help the woman who once devoted herself to his place of worship and had generously sent her the amount required for Gerard's ransom

Released immediately, the idiot creep who went by the name El Grocco and who, in the dream at least, also happened to be a poet, proved to be a fair guy after all and gave Gerard permission to take with him the remnants of his memorable captivity, specifically the child in the strange hat, the two gold-trimmed writing books, and the single thorn he used to write out his ode

As for the gold coin, still unnoticed by all, it secretly hung inside the cuff near his wrist, as always

However, it was the main episodes narrated in this makeshift prison that the actors performed in this art installation

The desired decor was built into the cool room and supplemented by simulated accessories and tchotchkes that the real poet had kept until the end, which, it should be noted, came by way of kidney disease

68. You may want to refer to note 65 above and then, if you are so inclined, rewrite the line "(*translator's note*: I was feeling this myself, just by *writing it out*—by *becoming* it while blending)" in a style that suits your own remixological tendencies. After having rewritten this line, take the writing utensil of your choice and cross out my line and replace it with your own. You are now becoming part of the imaginary solution to a problem that does not exist.

The scene included a certain amount of *cinema verité* in that it contained the ruined altar, the broken statue of the Virgin, and other artifacts that made it all seem so real

To give free reign to the actor playing the deceased, one first had to remove from the child the flesh-colored ointment and the strange hat that adorned it for so long as well as delete the two books of their fragile gold characters

But sometimes things would go wrong and, for example, the corpse would appear to be alive while Chloe was pretending to be crying over his dead body

At the end of each loop, the stone baby with its strange bonnet made of pear guts and linen threads, and the two books with their golden text detailing his ode to life, would be readied for their next repeat performance

* * *

2) *Chairman Mao (not that one), who died at the age of 80*

Quickly recognized as the widow of the Chairman, the actress playing his wife, Roz, achieved a touching performance

Mao and Roz had spent all of their lives in Brittany in their hometown which was still faithful to old traditions especially the celebration of the so-called golden anniversary

In this small town any couple who had been together for fifty years straight would be required to participate in a ceremony that would take place at a mass at the oldest church in their town

In the middle of the church ceremony, the priest, after a brief speech, extracted a large and old vise, a simple iron-red model contained in a precious metal box and that he placed before both the man and woman before having them shake hands inside the fake jaws of the wrenching tool

The letters made of garnets that fill the words on the cover of the metal box that contained the vise were "Vise of the Golden Anniversary"

All three components were made of real iron, the nut—the screw—and the spring, and this insured the proper functioning of the equipment as a whole

The priest activated the device and clenched the jaws which, due to the angle and the way the two hands sunk toward the crevice in the bottom, did not cause any significant pain and yet still could be enacted as a way to symbolize the strength of their fifty-year relationship

After a short time, the married partners were released from the firm grip and stood before the congregation, whereupon the mass ended

For every golden wedding anniversary celebration from time immemorial, the object that was used was playfully referred to as "Undue Advice" and highlighted the perseverance of the old couple through thick and thin

Of course, Mao and his wife, as a young couple, had already figured out how to play-act the scene in the chapel and for years rehearsed a way to seemingly put the screws on each other even while they both knew nothing of the sort was actually happening

Shortly thereafter, Mao was to die in the arms of Roz

And the moments replayed in the Locus Solus exhibition were those where the vise had fulfilled its role as a potent symbol of their bond

A reasonable request to the old church to lend the vise out was often approved

Roz, intent on making sure the scene that would be performed was the best one to encapsulate their love before Mao's death, agreed to brave the cold, icy room and play herself just so she could feel his hand pressing against hers inside the jaws

A figure wearing a tonsured wig played the priest

* * *

3) *The actor, Lee, who died after fifty years of pulmonary congestion, is led by his daughter, Antoinette, still a child*

Pushed by an enthusiastic worshipping of her father and following through on his desire to be resurrected if there was any possible way to make that happen, Antoinette fulfills his wishes and inserts her father into the role of an historical character named Roland Systems whose life is edited down into five acts

Roland Systems was born in 1148 to a noble family of the Bourbon province where, at that time, following a singular regional aesthetic, every child would mark their appearance into the world by giving themselves over to an astrologically-minded tattoo artist who would, identifying what star had guided the child's arrival, employ a special process that would literally burn the name of the star into the child's neck in the form of a monogram

Taking great caution, the astrologist, using ad hoc instruments, introduced a clamp into the very front of the skin at the back of the neck, holding it perpendicular while applying amazingly tiny needles, creating a bulky mass visible beneath the epidermis until the desired figure of composed letters would be fixed there forevermore

The purpose of the operation was to put the subject in constant contact with the designated star during their entire life

Meanwhile, the star would reciprocate and also maintain a relationship with the tattooed figure, using its magnetic effluvia to protect and guide the creature through the rest of their lives

The neck was chosen as the ideal location for the mark because in most cases, the odiferous emanations, falling from the sky, would first have to cross the brain before reaching the thin needles, and this would pour invaluable clarity into the thoughts of the receiving agent

Roland Systems, from the time he was first squeaking, was nurtured by the astrologer Oberlin, who upon Roland's birth, engraved the letters *B*, *T*, *G* into his neck

This early event not only set the tone for his own astrological trajectory with the star he had been appointed with, but also was responsible for what soon became an obvious taste for science

Twenty-five years later, the master of his own domain, Roland married the one he loved and was a father of two boys living a quiet and happy life in the castle of his ancestors when, out of nowhere, a serious event brought about his ruin

Not being a micro-manager, he gave control of his estate to his family's old steward who had always behaved honestly in all property-related affairs

It was standard operating procedure for Roland to regularly hand the steward some blank checks with his signature already on them

Every night, when everyone was asleep, the steward walked around the castle to inspect the property and made sure everything was properly secured

One evening, after performing this duty, he discovered the traces of a contained fire and immediately knew what caused it to happen

Since the residence sat on top of a hill, it would sometimes experience very gusty winds and, in this case, it must have knocked over a lit candle on the oak table in front of the window, whereupon the curtains were ignited, the flames being fanned by yet more gusts that enabled the fire to spread to the table, which quickly burned too

It was only when it moved toward the stone walls and pavement that it finally died out

That day, Roland had given the steward a blank check, which he had quickly put in a drawer in the oak desk

Convinced that the valuable check had been consumed by the fire, and that he shouldn't worry about the consequences of the event, which was now under control, the next day Roland handed him a new blank check

In fact, the fire was the work of a lazy and somewhat vile valet named Quentin who had been specially assigned to service the steward

Quentin had once seen the steward fill a blank check from Roland and thought that if he could stealthily get hold of one of these checks, he could make a fortune

Always lurking around waiting for an opportune moment, the valet noticed that the steward was quickly putting a blank check into the drawer of the oak table and later, forced his way into the drawer, extracted the check and, looking for an easy distraction, thought that a small fire near the window would be rationally attributed to a strong gust knocking the candle over

As part of every signature on any paper that Roland signed, he drew a corn cob

In the 9th century, it was quite normal for many Lords, not knowing how to read or write, to sketch out a rough design of some image that would indicate their having signed an important document

It was much easier for them to, for example, use their pen to form some familiar symbol than the long assemblage of letters that filled their name

This was even better than, say, trying to turn the different component parts of their fragmented writing into a seamless signature

These illiterates would choose from a variety of vignettes or symbols, including animals or objects related to war, or perhaps the arts or science of nature

Once a subject was adopted and officially recorded as the official signature of the illiterate Lord, then this image would become identified with the family and, over time, would accompany even a signature by a descendent who was now capable of signing their name

Some families gradually deleted the special seal, so it was becoming more rare for these symbols to appear with a signature, but in this case, even in the 12th century, the image of the cob still remained

However illiterate his ancestors may have been, Roland maintained the cob in all of his signatures the way a stud farm maintains the precise genetic trajectory of a horse, disseminating his lineal value

The valet Quentin knew about this detail of the cob and wanted to turn it to his advantage by profiting from the one check he had stolen—by writing into it the total sum of Roland's worth—sure that any suit against him would hold up in court specifically because of the inclusion of the cob with the signature

By agreeing to share half the future proceeds he would soon come into, the valet would buy out an accomplice named Ruckus who was a leader of a group of marauders who had recently stormed through the country

He was to capture Roland, who would no doubt be spending most of his days reading his science books, and at some point in the afternoon take a solitary walk in the forest

The plan was to abduct him and force him to fill in the coveted text that would release his net worth

Quentin knew that Roland would rather endure torture or even his own demise than give away his worldly possessions, which he planned to pass on to his children, so the valet decided to trick the Lord

The cob on the blank check was supposed to go just under the middle of the leaf of paper, so Quentin folded it in two and, with a transparent glue, fixed one side against the other, sealing the high and low ends of the backside to the front

Now it looked like a thick, short, single sheet that he would present to Roland for his signature, which he already had but that he also assumed Roland would give since no one would believe it anyway

This way, the ruse being deployed would convince Roland that by filling in the coveted text with his written signature, he would never really have to pay the amount, since they would not ask for the accompanying image of the cob

Apprehended during his solitary forest walk, Roland was taken to the camp where the marauders hung out and Quentin was nowhere to be seen lest Roland recognize him and become suspicious of the entire scene and smell a trap

Speaking to Roland, Ruckus gave him the choice between death or his immediate signature, indicating the paper leaf next to an inkstand on a bundle of wood being used as a makeshift table

As expected, the prisoner, wanting to save his own life, figured that he could get away with little suffering if he would just put his John Hancock on the paper, and seeing no real significance in what he was being asked to do, willingly signed his name

This did not make the story's plot twists any easier to comprehend or translate: unexpected things were bound to take shape with *mechanistically generated language as the trigger device*

Still, Quentin was on the verge of pulling an amazing act of fraud on Roland, who, having children, could not really legally disown them, even if he wanted to, and was about to inadvertently squander his riches and his heirs' future inheritance

Little did Roland know, but he was essentially signing away his entire fortune: about 800,000 Eurofrancs

The money would be split between Quentin and Ruckus

Roland signed his name at the bottom of the note and then Ruckus forced him to trace the words "Pay to the order of" above it and to include his total net worth

After vowing he would not seek any form of retaliation against his perpetrators, he was set free

The next day, sitting at his desk, he was studying one of his favorite scientific authors when, to his surprise, it was announced that he had a guest, a certain Mr. Ruckus

Presenting his agenda, Ruckus demanded what he was due as outlined in the agreement that he held in his hand

Roland wanted to mock his oppressor from the day before, making him aware of the fact that he hated to disappoint him, but the paper required a certain traditional symbol of the cob at the bottom of the signature

Continuing his marginal note-taking while going through the scientific book, and without even turning his head toward Ruckus who was standing in front of the closed door just to his right, Roland said, sarcastically:

"Really? A promise to pay to the order of . . . ? But what kind of signature do you have?"

"A cob," responded Ruckus

On this last word, Roland immediately knew that if were true, that he had a signature with a cob on it, he would be ruined

He turned his head toward the beast in his room and was consumed with a formidable sense of violence mixed with violation

At the same instant, he experienced a sharp pain in his neck at the exact spot where his three letters representing his guiding star were burned into his flesh

Without thinking, he got up and, feeling livid, walked toward Ruckus to see how he could have obtained an authentic drawing of the cob as part of his signature

The paper, now with no trace of the glue and folding that hid the text he was signing yesterday, was actually a blank check similar to ones he wrote for his steward

Whatever it was, under a text written by his hand and with his signature—even if it was a piece of paper that essentially gave his entire fortune, accumulated over 300 years of family business without ever indicating he would disown his heirs—constituted a formal commitment that, as Quentin predicted, would be followed through on since he was a man of his word

Besides, they were clearly prepared to take what they wanted by violent means if necessary

After dismissing Ruckus with the promise of prompt payment, he called for his steward

His steward proceeded to explain what he figured must have happened, first by detailing the fire and then realizing that it was started by Quentin who had a specific plan in mind

Quentin, when questioned about this, frankly and cynically admitted his guilt, revealing his arrogance by insisting that a signature was an oath that required Roland to follow through on while remaining neutral to his perpetrators

The valet was expelled from the property immediately

Roland, wiped out, realized that all of his assets would need to be transferred to Ruckus, and so the transaction took place and Quentin got his half share

Moving from his castle into a poor neighborhood where he lived a life of penury, he immersed himself in his scientific studies, learning the lessons of physics and chemistry

Often, when looking back at the transformative events that had essentially ruined him, he thought about that strange, sharp pain he had felt in his neck as soon as Ruckus had uttered the word “Cob”

From that point on, there were times when he turned his head as he did back then that the same pain would return

But there were also times when a turn of the head was painless

Roland discovered for himself how the arrival of evil—or its failure to arrive—could be attributed to what he was feeling in his neck whenever he turned his head

After a multitude of experiences where he could quite confidently measure the data associated with his head turning and the pain or painlessness that could prophesize near term events, he was forced to admit to himself, despite the stubborn revolt of his reason, this incredible conclusion: when facing north, whenever he turned his head east or west, if the pain appeared, then he would need to reorient himself toward whatever inevitable future difficulty he would soon face, and not try to swivel himself in different directions just to pretend the pain was really not there

In fact, Roland recalled how when, on that fateful day with Ruckus in his room, he was facing north, looking toward a window

Upon closer inspection, he realized that the tingling pain he felt consisted of many distinct and localized feelings in the neck and that, in fact, the site of his discomfort was the tattooed letters on the nape of his neck

Roland, vaguely recalling the tiny needles burning into his neck at the hand of his great master, Oberlin, knew that the letters marking his skin had been placed perpendicular to a vertical plane that touched his two shoulders

After having many deep, meditative thoughts about his predicament, he deduced that the magnetic tip of the needle had undergone a strange attraction to the north and that since he was optimally aligned with his special star's movement, any time he abruptly turned his head and neck to the side this caused a violent reaction from the magnetism of the star he was moving, which then created this acute reaction in his neck, one that would otherwise just not be of any significance were he not so aligned

Roland was convinced that he had unraveled the real cause of his capricious pain

Being a man of the 12th century, this strange predicament he found himself in actually led him to believe that he was on the verge of some great scientific discovery, and the more he thought about its implications, the more drunk he became with the thought of penetrating some secret fact of life

To test the accuracy of his theory, he would fill a water container and lay it transversely on two small wisps of straw that ran parallel where floating in the surface of the water would be a magnetic needle—a situation that was open to discovery

And Roland, dazzled by his own developing discovery, where he was able to foresee a sublime marine navigation system, one where the needle would move in any direction but that always made its way back to its fixed position tipping to the north, brought the experiment to King Louis VII and revealed his huge discovery, something that would transform navigation forever, saving many lives at sea and assisting in the exploration of many new, still unknown lands

Thrilled by this discovery, the king gave him a reward that made him a fortune

Of course, his so-called *marinette* was a more primitive version of the modern day compass that only came into the world three centuries later

Repurchasing his castle, Roland, rich again, began to bless the strange circumstance of his last disaster

Without that financial catastrophe, none of this would have ever happened

On its own, a quick turn of the head accompanied by pain would reveal nothing of significance

However, to determine how the brutal revelation of the word "Cob" could trigger such intense pain in his neck just as he was about to go into financial ruin was the perfect process-based research subject for him to consider

By a bizarre sequence of events, the perception associated with hearing a monosyllabic word spoken curtly—the word "Cob"—was enough to trigger this sharp pain in his neck

Had the word being spoken by Ruckus been longer or less immediately connected to his psychic comfort zone, his legendary head turn might not have felt any pain at all, and his future scientific discovery never revealed

After the two accomplices, Ruckus and Quentin, had blown all of the money on gambling and drinking, they were eventually imprisoned for new crimes

Modeling this entire historical narrative, the playwright Mamet designed a living room set and helped create the installation at Locus Solus

This particular performance-art installation would consist of a prologue—where Oberlin conducts his ritual astrological tattooing of the boy Roland—and the five acts that would take place later

The five acts, when taken together, would evoke details that helped depict Roland's tragic adventure, including the fire, the blank check, the valet's trick, the ensuing financial ruin, and the eventual discovery of a magnetic process that could produce tremendous results for maritime navigators and that made Roland a wealthy inventor who was his era's version of The Comeback Kid

Wearing a low collar suit that revealed the stellar tattoo-monogram, the actor, Lee, had repeatedly played with great success the complex character of Roland, alternately portraying the calm and happy family man living with his wife and sons, the ruined Lord who was struck with misfortune, the scientist obsessed with trying to understand how this could all happen and why did he have the pain in the neck at the crucial moment, and the noble inventor destined for legitimate glory

One could see the artificial reenactment of the most memorable scene, where the word "Cob" was thrown by Ruckus as he revealed the signed note that simultaneously created the acute neck pain in Roland's neck, as one that resonated with eternal global consequences

Careful attention was paid to various details played out in the looping scene: the illustrious head turn, the pronouncing of the word "Cob," the role of Ruckus, and an accurate rendering of the costumes, decor, accessories—not to mention the make-up on the neck of the corpse so that the actor playing Roland would embrace the role with full fanaticism and keep the illusion alive, as if Roland himself were alive and kicking

* * *

4) *A seven-year-old child swept away by typhoid, Hubert Shelby, whose mother, a young widow now alone in the world and overcome with thoughts of suicide, experiences a personal tragedy concerning the body of her son*

A poignant emotion captured her unhappiness as soon as she realized that her son, sitting on his knees, was about to recite the conceptual poetry in as tender a way as the material would allow

In the work of poetry, which had achieved an absolutely perfect mistranslation of a series of scenes written by a well-revered, famous writer of some one hundred years ago, the child-poet hit precise chords that suggested an intense attempt to express his thoughts by scoring a kind of "screaming arrangement" of the words he was rewriting from memory while speaking

How to create threads of sense and sensibility while simultaneously loosening the ties that artificially bound language to predetermined forms of figurative "meaning" per se?

Would his stylistic attempt to tap into an alternative form of poetic spontaneity be rewarded by the audience he was building in his social network?

The tree of knowledge was loaded with inquisitive worms ready to eat away at all preconceived notions of plot and character and anything else that anchored the story in a traditional trajectory destined for meeting easily negotiated expectations

Better to violently dismember the words themselves, or at least their relationship to one another, no?

The recitation that the boy immersed himself in while embodying the great conceptual poet's text could be sustained by graceful integration of intonation and gesture along with some simple staging, like having a chair available where the boy's mother, warmly covered so that she would not freeze inside the art installation, sat down while her son seemed to be totally enjoying the trance-like illusion he was creating for himself, as if lost in a kind of utopian form of supra-happiness

No one would care what, if anything, got lost in translation[69]

69. Only now, after the auto-translation performance, do I recognize these last words of this short section as a subtle reference to the movie *Lost in Translation* which, when I first saw it, I thought was a remix of one particular aspect of my life from the first two years of the 21st century. During that time, I was—in addition to maintaining my new role as a professor of digital art and writing—touring various parts of the world as a VJ (visual or video jockey) where I would use my laptop to access handmade snippets of video art loops and filter them through a software program that enabled me to create on-the-fly moving image collages and, while I was at it, expand the concept of *live cinema*. These live audio-visual performances I was conducting became the experiential source material I investigated for various "spontaneous theories" I eventually remixed into the opening chapters of my book *META/DATA: A Digital Poetics*. The VJ figure then reappeared as a hitchhiker in my 2007 novel-cum-long-narrative-poem, *29 Inches*. I say that I experienced the viewing of Sophia Coppola's *Lost in Translation* as a remix of my own life because some of the lines that the male lead, Bill Murray, uttered, particularly while laying in bed talking to his wife on the phone in the luxury hotel he was staying in, were close to verbatim the same words I had used in a similar call I made to my wife while I was lying in bed in a similar luxury hotel in Tokyo. These trippy, jet-lag moments that Murray's character must have been experiencing in that film and that I could intimately relate to, take place in what I refer to as *unrealtime* or *asynchronous realtime* in *META/DATA*. Specifically, I write that

"By *asynchronous realtime* I am referring to what *at times* feels like a perpetual jet-lag consciousness or timeless time, a blur motion of experiential metadata that indicates a formal investigation of complex *event processing* where the VJ artist, always gyrating at a pivotal location in the narrative, becomes a multitude of flux identities

* * *

5) *The Midwestern sculptor, Jerzy, who died suddenly without any family, was brought to Locus Solus by a young man, Jack Pole, who also happened to be his former and excellent Grad student, one of the few who greatly admired his mentor*

Thinking about the ten hours a day that Jerzy had, from time immemorial, devoted to his unique brand of *hauntological sculpture*, one question about this particular installation was whether or not the performance loop, junked up on vials of *résurrectine*, would somehow reveal how the great artist was able to subtly manipulate the details of his work that, when taken together, signaled a series of aesthetic breakthroughs over the course of an entire lifetime

Camera had developed an interesting way of showing just how overwhelming the master's methodology was and attempted to exude the absolute rigor that was required to reconstruct these slices of life in his performance model

---

nomadically circulating within the networked space of flows (both geophysical networks and cyberspace networks). Living in asynchronous realtime often produces a feeling of being both avantgarde (ahead of one's time) and time-delayed or even preempted.

[. . .]

"Perhaps this is what it means *to become an artist-medium nurturing the field conditions for my creative potential to unconsciously play in*. These trance narratives that float through my body as I sleep or write or navigate my various digital art personas through the cyberpsychogeographical regions of The Network are an essential part of this everyday life I am constantly launching my asymmetrical phrasings and rephrasings in. This is the experiential space, full of rapidly reconfigured sense data, that I feel most at home in and will do anything in my power to have access to at all costs. I know I'm in the process of activating its full readiness potential when my internal superclock makes me feel pregnant with the synchronicity of everything happening right now, in realtime, although my intuition tells me this is not realtime at all but something that resembles realtime even though I know it's totally fake. It's what I would call *unrealtime*."

It should also be noted that this entire mini-section, 4, succinctly captures much of what was going through my head at this point in the performance. Amazingly, most of the text in this section was what the auto-translation program spat out to me and all I had to do was sample and lightly manipulate it to suit my immediate needs. What, one might ask, were my immediate needs? *To write*—my only need, not very unlike what Cocteau declared "a sickness." As Bataille once wrote, "I write not to be mad," and the best way to write these days, especially for the conceptual artist focused on displacing intentions, is to remixologically inhabit the source material one happens to be embodying as an act of pure intuition. For me, this auto-translation performance is what it means *to come to writing*, the *ready-to-be-readymade*.

He felt it would be a good idea to focus on the intense labor required to make a work of art and over time, slowly reviving the corpse in the scene, would spy on the idiosyncratic methods of the artist as he came back to life

According to Camera's story, six months before the scene in the glass box was (re)enacted, Jerzy was living in Paris, where he was visited by a collector from Toulouse named Ball who was a kind of fifty-something boy-inside-a-man's-body and who was expecting to marry a girl from his home town who was clearly seduced by his big fortune

Terribly in love at fifty-something with a girl who could have been a teenager, the collector wanted, on the occasion of his marriage, to give to each of his friends some precious souvenir—a jewel or work of art—which would help them remember the date of his illustrious wedding

In the eyes of Ball, a work of art signed by a celebrity artist would be something that would pass through several generations of whatever family owned the artist's work

Specializing in the production of waxlike sculptural artworks, Jerzy, whose international reputation was growing, was commissioned to create these art objects

It was agreed that the artist would sculpt three samples as possible iterations of the work and, if Ball thought they fit the bill, he would be commissioned to create a bunch of them for Ball's network

To appease the Toulouse collector, Jerzy began cranking out the artworks using his bizarre compositional methods, most of which he picked up when he was just a kid and that had since turned into a productive habit

Growing up a poor orphan in his uncle's Midwestern home before breaking out on his own and eventually landing in Paris, Jerzy really had no deep connection to his family anymore

The finest joys of his childhood, though, were long visits to museums in nearby cities that he would visit with his uncle

The aftermath of these blessed, often rainy Sundays, left in his memory certain objects that he would try to reproduce by drawing in his notebooks and then kneading a block of bread into a sculptural rendition of the drawing of the object he was copying

Alternatively, he would look at books that contained abstract painterly works from such prestigious venues as the Museum of Modern Art, where he would find work by the likes of de Kooning that he would then subsequently copy from memory

But he often was not content with the sketches he reproduced after viewing the pictures of paintings in art catalogues

Instead of feverishly consummating his passion with the canvas by liberally applying his brushstrokes in wildly abstract gestures, he created a kind of subterfuge to at least give off the illusion that he was performing a heartier task

He would blacken an entire page with ink, then, with the help of a scraper, when everything was dry, start redacting the black so that soon something like a de Kooning would appear

Right from the start this particular creative process was a success that could be traced to the gradual appearance of the biomorphic figure coming to life out of the darkness of the ink-stained canvas

He would occasionally deviate from the model and, for instance, use his scraping to mimic the erasure technique of Rauschenberg, whose "Erased de Kooning" was another can of worms he chastised himself for unthinkingly opening[70]

Informed by his gut instincts, he knew he was on to something special with this technical method and was quite content to diligently use the scraper on the black paper to create a variety of portraits modeled specifically after de Kooning's *Woman* series[71]

By employing this strange method that left a milky residue all over his blade, he was able to obtain astonishing, sometimes grotesque, facial expressions in the model

70. The atemporal aspects of the translation were not just my insertion of early 21st century technology like the iPhone, but intentional splices of other tidbits like post–World War II art history into the story. Rauschenberg, whose experiments in collage, combines, and collaborative art-technology-performance are reimagined in this novel, seemed like a natural fit here, as did the ghost of de Kooning who also haunts this section of the text, though a de Kooning filtered through an overdetermined *Jackson Pollack filter*. Having said that, I was also hoping to keep the European-American abstract expressionist connection alive (Jerzy instead of Jerry) as a way to further complicate the composite-composition-combine-character.

71. A future area of practice-based research might trace a direct lineage from Duchamp's work, specifically his *Nude Descending a Staircase* and *Large Glass*, to de Kooning's *Woman* series.

Given his childhood attempts to create replicas of statues by kneading and shaping coagulated breadcrumbs, he had a clear vision of where he wanted to go next

He had always preferred sculpting objects more than drawing anyway, so he figured the next step in his trajectory would be to use the scraped image that had unveiled the portrait as a study for a more elaborate work of sculpture and that this might actually make him even more rich and famous

But how would he really create a lasting work of art using only bread and his fingers?

He had once taken a class in botany with a Professor Brotherland who, stuck in nowheresville and a lover of her scientific studies, devoted all of her time to investigating the processing of greenhouse crops

It wasn't out of the question that Brotherland would, on occasion, be so lost in her work that she would bring to class some rare specimen of plant life

One day in class, standing before Jerzy and his classmates, she spoke a long time about a flower, which she took out of her special case: it was a large, Vietnamese flower that, like the tulip it resembled, evoked its sad state of mourning by way of its white and black petals

The flower she was sharing that day was primarily known for the bottom of its corolla, which secreted a black wax containing numerous white granules and was often referred to as "nocturnal" or "night" wax on account of its resemblance to a starry night

Having from her lectern shown the class this unique wax substance by simply tilting the flower in front of them, Professor Brotherland announced that the wax would slowly reform after having subtracted some from its total mass, and to prove it, picked up a low dose of it with the tip of her knife and had the students pass it around so they could study it closely and investigate its soft-to-the-touch malleability

When it came his turn to hold on to the knife, Jerzy was suddenly struck by something he could not explain

Glad to see that all of the students were amazed at the odd capacities of the exotic flower, Brotherland promised to give this flower, which would grow over a long period of time, to the winner of the next competition

Thinking about the huge advancements the night wax could help him make in his art practice, Jerzy had one goal: to win the flower

Risking punishment for avoiding all of his other duties and lessons, he devoted himself to study nothing but botany, and when the time came he attained the highest score on the designated test and received from the hands of his professor the strategically important flower

Providing detailed care and adequate doses of water until the flower eventually gave way and died, Jerzy ritualistically collected the night wax from the bottom of the corolla where more of the sooty wax would always reappear

He envisioned a compositional process that he would finesse with extreme precision over the years, using his odd collection of instruments on the breadcrumbs, which he would shape with small doses of the night wax, first using his hands and then following up by applying his precise use of the paring knives to produce an art work that would be fixed in time

Putting this unique methodology into practice, his detailed precision led him to triumph

Equipped with tools that he himself had designed as well as the stale bread, he could—with the addition of the night wax and bizarre drawing/scraping process—dip into his spiritual unconscious and shape into being unique art objects that were modeled on de Kooning's *Woman* series

Feeling himself lost in the heat of a continuous creative groove, he would create thousands of variations of this work

As soon as the work was finished, the extra wax in the palm of his hand was rolled into a ball and ready to be used in the making of the next art object

Jerzy became attached to what he viewed as the growing importance of the drawings that led to his sculptural creations

He would scrape these portraits from both the front and back so that he would produce two extensive studies that could serve as a step-by-step guide for modeling—which he himself put to great use by transforming the images revealed by his rapid scraping into soft black figurines that would align with the starry night of wax and do great justice for the evocative lines he had left after redacting so much of the black ink on the paper study

There were times when, feeling the need to experiment with the sense of texture that evolved from the various transformations the object was going through, he would draw into the night wax itself, forcing it to do things that further supplemented his unusual aesthetic

This *plasticization* process was a fertile component of Jerzy's work and eventually led him to create what are now considered by many to be masterpieces, which he always knew would never have been made had it not been for the luck of his odd beginnings as an artist who would invent his own use of materials

This means that Jerzy, who really had no major mentors to speak of, was able to piece together a resourceful approach to making aesthetic objects that led to his quick success

Yet interestingly enough, he could not, no matter how hard he tried, change the way he worked

He would only make a double back and front drawing using the scraper so as to begin to model his latest version of the biomorphic "woman" transformed into a figurine made of breadcrumbs and night wax

Basically, he kept copying himself

Once a woman portrait was completed it was then used as a model to create another, similar piece that, when looked at in relation to the thousands of other pieces he had made and distributed to his network, made him a powerful figure in the commercial art market

(It should also be noted that not only did he not have any mentors to speak of, he did not have an MFA either[72])

This too made him—as an artist—a unique presence in the upmarket commodity scenes

You could say that he was a marginally situated outsider artist—a kind of remote brute, yes?

He thanked his lucky stars that he was able to come upon the night wax so early in his development, especially given its rare snowy spray of stars shining on the black tarmac and that in many ways was an irresistible substance to hold on to and own and that had great appeal and could be used to create a wonderful negative replica of the scraped-away drawing that had guided the process so early on

His name indelibly connected with the substance he was known for using and the pleasant myth of the botany class helped secure his reputation

Jerzy quickly sent Ball the three slightly different sculptural figures that had been requested, all made using his typical methods

72. Cheeky, but true.

Ball found the style of the works quite amusing as they reminded him of the rough edges and refined surfaces of his own life trajectory as a former trader of luxury goods before he was focusing exclusively on collecting art

He texted Jerzy a somewhat naive note: "I am content with your three women and order you to create **A Big Ditto** of each one for my immediate social network"[73]

Jerzy loved that phrase: "A Big Ditto!"

He was accustomed to dittoing both himself and his works, processing the possessed, possessing the processed

Cheerfully expectorated by Jerzy's corpse, this short phrase helped Jack Pole prepare for this looped scene that he too was performing in the background, and that was initially triggered by Ball's text message

Equipped with all of the instruments and material that he needed, Jerzy, now reembodied as the frozen corpse resurrected by the vital fluid injected by Camera, created identical women within minutes of each other

The procedure, repeated over and over again, revealed the smooth operation for what it was

Thank God he had found a market for his work[74]

* * *

6) *The sensitive writer, Claude Calvados, who before expiring had reached a point of such stomach pain that he was nervously anticipating and yet still terrified by the*

73. As always, I am remaining faithful to what the auto-translation program is dishing me as source material, and manipulating it to keep this part of the narrative groove intact. And since I am already simultaneously betraying the "original," I have no issue bringing in texting and the social network. In fact, one thing that became an issue early on was how to write in a style that was simultaneously modern, anticipated postmodernism, and moved beyond it into whatever it is we are experiencing in the early 21st century. Instead of worrying about proper chronology or consistency of affect as it might have been played out in fictional rhythms over the course of the last hundred years—especially in relation to what is considered to be avant-garde, i.e. both *of* and *ahead* of its time—I decided to just let the rhythms flow together, but separately, that is to say in parallel, occasionally out of sync, unintentionally in sync, with and/or without purpose while highlighting play, performance, and the kind of energy transmission one might now identify as a kind of *glitch aesthetics* circulating in the field of digital distribution. By letting the work take on whatever shape the process demanded, I was able to sustain my own engagement with Roussel's source material during the ongoing postproduction process.

74. Amen.

approach of death, had requested to be put inside the cooler of Locus Solus as soon as he breathed his last breath, and knowing that he would be there was just enough comfort to keep him from completely losing his mind

When the time came, he realized that knowing he would be able to sustain himself in the artificial environment was also a form of psychological treatment

The previous year, a famous practitioner, Dr. Petiot, had found a way to issue a blue light that, although it had a low brightness to it, contained a wonderful therapeutic power that when transferred by a huge lens, would cut to the chase and perform a kind of laser-like, nanotechnological procedure on the patient

Placed at the focus of the lens, the subject was always embroiled in a mad overexcitement while simultaneously suffering from a general ill-health that they were trying to escape

The apparatus was locked on to a kind of cylindrical cage with strong bars which helped establish its name as the focal jail but that, due to its occasional incontinent effects, some referred to as the "fecal jail"

Even when one was fragile in handling the equipment, it was still incredibly dangerous, and the strange light, if used in an irresponsible or insidious way, could actually kill the anxious patient-cum-prisoner by sheer force of its strength

The blue light could quickly delete whatever subject it touched right at the point of contact, so Petiot came up with a procedure using an old engraving that could withstand the ray and serve as a kind of warning signal if things got too hot

Thanks to some active research, he found in an antique shop a Plan de Paris etched on a piece of silk-embossed wood

But the Plan was actually superimposed on another map, the city of the London underground map

In order to attract attention to itself as a work of manipulated art, the Plan had a long thick line extending across its width, a broad stroke from a pen that gave the appearance of a secant

This line marked the length and location of an avenue made for idle drifting, a swarming death march that would undoubtedly attract all kinds of diseased inhabitants plaguing the already foul air

Imaginary psychogeographical wanderers would tread these anonymous social lines that would slowly, over time, create an environmental ambience in the middle of an urban landscape disguised as a palimpsest where multiple cities were randomly superimposed on each other

More cities could also be superimposed on the map and a long avenue stretching across all of them at once would suddenly reveal poor areas that instantaneously transformed into breezy, light, and insanely valuable neighborhoods

This would inevitably change people's lives, for example, a poor writer named Hadassah who was actually the artist who made the piece now in Petiot's possession

Hadassah's world was overwhelmed with the serious condition of her only daughter Bland, a fragile hippy child who, since she had been about one year old, was pale and shaken by coughing and whose health continued to decline day by day, nailed to the bed by her own weakness

Running out of odd jobs that helped pay the bills, Hadassah had resolved to kill herself after her child died since the kid was really all she had—that is, until the gentrification began and transformed her house into what locals referred to as a "hot property"

The spring began and Bland rose from bed and dragged herself to the open window to inhale both the oxygen and rays

She was so happy, she cried, and her mother knew that something had changed

Eventually the mother found a rather easy home equity line of credit that enabled her to smartly renovate their place so that it had more windows and a general Feng Shui openness that created an overall sense of more light and clean air coming into their lives and potentially curing both of their ills

In this imaginary landscape, it was the thick pen stroke signaling the Avenue of Everywhere that really made the difference

To properly record the transformation that had taken place, Hadassah recognized the healing nature of the avenue by drawing on silk a few layers of urban maps she was recalling strictly from memory, and when she was done she drew a thick line that ran right through the entire multilayered map

The engraved silk artwork was matted onto parchment and then meshed into soft wood and finished with a varnish before it was then framed and eventually placed at the altar of their sacred home's entrance

She was so impressed with the quality of work she was now producing, that she began creating variations of this work just to suit her fancy

For many of the works, she started incorporating text into them

Since she was also a contemporary writer who experimented with image and text collage across various media, Haddasah was excellent at creating these very specific kinds of framed artworks[75]

However, how exactly would the work serve its function as a gesture of appreciation for the healing that had taken place?

With her best ink, Hadassah had lavishly taken her time to meticulously engrave the image on silk, an image that tapped into what she thought of as "the dreamworld of international culture," something that related to an old idea she had as a young woman about a utopian city created for artists where all of the world's most vibrant cultural capitols would be sampled from and remixed into a magical space for wandering and losing oneself in an abundance of aesthetically-enhanced life experiences as a simultaneous and continuous fusion of art, love, sensuality, and peace

If they were working as planned, these engravings and their framework could be used as enchanted healing objects

Due to the precious, detailed work she had put into her silk engravings, the one with its special inks and rare silk that Petiot came upon in the antique store was the perfect material object to use as an unaltered effigy, a symbol of unconscious spiritual release

Petiot read the long letter of ownership that went with the engraving and studied it as part of his research

In his notes, he wrote

blue light

focus

lightning eyes

75. Is it just me, or are there are a lot of artists populating this text? And Jewish artists? Hadassah is probably a name that Roussel would have never come across, but I felt it necessary to at least acknowledge that somewhere way beneath the surface of this text there lurked a Jewish-inflected, utopian dreamworld of international culture, one that Benjamin would have been aware of and in the process of investigating while translating Baudelaire.

solar plexus

heralding the danger

Out of these notes he had concocted the blue light fantasy apparatus that would magically heal his patients of their stress (often caused by the poor conditions they were living in), but why did the artist reference a blue light emanating from the gentrification of her neighborhood, somehow suggesting that it was something other than what it was? (this was an illogical shortcoming that he refused to try and make sense of because it would immediately undermine his credibility as a character or, were he to assume the role, a narrator)

Petiot loved the story of how the engraving he found was made and its fictional history—its narrative provenance, including the language used in the long letter that only he read—became very useful to him as he imagined applications that might sync nicely with the engraving

That was all fine and well, but to enact the engraving process as part of another performance art loop inside of a living installation powered by *résurrectine* at Locus Solus was another story

For each session, Petiot needed to conduct a less impressionable marking into the fabric

He also needed to successfully phase out some of the less practical ways of producing these silk works over and over again

For example, drawing copies on a single stock of paper would require . . .

—but what kind of paper?

He had an idea: what about a well produced book of maps that had already been remaindered?

Could he use a bunch of those as the stock for his looping productions?

Of course, it would change the nature of the "engraving" but writing was writing, and drawing was writing too, was it not?

Collage was mixology for the eyes and could subsequently intoxicate the brain

He felt uncomfortable drawing such simple conclusions

But at least the works inside the installation weren't going to be made on silk, and they weren't too expensive either

"A picture," said Petiot, "is worth a thousand reproductions"

* * *

7) *A young beauty from across the channel, accompanied by her rich husband Albert Exeter, who was still tender from the realization that their dream life had since become a tragic moment relived over and over again*

She was a poor bride who had become a heady socialite, light in spirit but weighed down by money and titles, something she had not thought possible, since marrying a rich man was supposed to be the road to perfection

She had recently procured a fashionable trace of the swinging London culture, namely a sequence of artificial nails made of tin that a machine would securely place on the tips of all her fingers

They would sparkle in the mirror reflection and the adroit operator of the polish machine that she had access to was quite professional in the way he could use his mechanical invention to separate the original nail from its flesh connections, coat it in a fine and abrasion-resistant tin, before sticking it firmly back on to the finger using another innovative product that he also invented

The tin nails were skillfully endowed with a semi-transparency and even retained some of the whiteness associated with the inner cuticle, which could be cut into with scissors for precision styling that was at once discreet and nuanced for each client

As the nail grew, it was necessary from time to time for the inventor to remove the nail and re-coat it with a new strip of tin

To the casual observer, the beautiful young woman's mind was vain and fragile and could be viewed as having a weak faculty when it came to reason, primarily because of something she experienced as a child

The intensity of her psychic discombobulation could be traced to a scene that took place on the southern coast of India where her father, a young colonel, had died before her eyes during a tour of duty

His throat was crushed by the jaws of a tiger whose sudden attack came out of nowhere

Inexhaustible waves of scarlet were gushing from his carotid artery, which freaked his beautiful young daughter out forever

She froze at the sight of blood and was struck with horror at most things that were colored red

Not being able to keep red things in her house or even wear a red dress, she had always tilted her personality toward the strange

Her rich husband, Albert, was an affectionate son as well as a considerate husband, and was inseparable from his mother, whose precarious health concerned him

It was in August that he traveled with his mother and wife to the huge Hotel Europe overlooking one of the best beaches on the Normandy coast

An accomplished sportsman who was an avid equestrian rider, Albert was able to access the hotel property's stables

One afternoon, preceding his wife who was still preparing herself for the day, he had grabbed some local travel guides and met with Ambrose, a young bellboy, who was positioned at the head of the horses, ready to lead them on the climb

He was away awhile and soon, his wife, confused by his delay, appeared in frantic disarray and seething with a vitriolic psychosis

Her gloves were still folded and she was holding a rose that was most assuredly not red and that had been given to her earlier that morning as an homage

Interrupting her momentum as she was rushing out of the hotel was an octogenarian man wearing the hotel livery and who was trying to catch up with her so he could give her a folder

Having worked in the hotel for over sixty years, the old man was clearly more than a courier of letters, but this was important

The folder, a large envelope, provided by the old man, showed, in black superscription, the socialite's name traced in red ink: *Lady Albert Exeter*

A year earlier, Albert's unmarried older brother had died without any heirs

However, the enclosed letter came from a young woman who was the older brother's childhood friend and who was reluctantly begging for some relief money that she said she desperately needed and was hoping to keep the request a secret

To complicate things, the odd relationship between Albert's mother and wife made the request even more problematic since who had the money?—and the fact that the name written on the letter was composed in red ink did not help matters either

Her umbrella and gloves in her left hand, she took the letter in her right hand that was holding the rose whose stem, pressed by her thumb, was now being applied to the envelope

Seeing her name in red ink, she tried to forget about it but, in the process, unable to suppress her nervous reaction, pricked her thumb with a thorn that the florist had forgotten to take off the stem

Detesting the sight of blood from the puncture, the sudden appearance of red everywhere had increased her chaos and confusion and, repulsed by the entire incident, she instinctively let go of both the rose and the letter

While this was all going down, she had somehow managed to twist the nail on her index finger so that the tin coating was now reflecting the red off of a replica of a famous old lantern found throughout the countryside

At the end of the 18th century, Bill Cassidy founded the Hotel Europe, and it was still being operated by his family

Above the entry to the hotel, he had positioned a broad and high lantern that had on one of its side panels, painted right on the glass, a map of Europe where each country was highlighted in a nuanced shade of red

During wartime movements and shifting of government control, the map would need to be repainted various shades of red to indicate the redesigned borders

As news of the war's entry into Moscow spread, that part of the map designated as Russia started turning purple, signifying France's offensive

Proudly, Cassidy, inspired by the monochromatic movement across this part of the world's shifting borders, renamed his hotel by adding one additional word: *French Europe Hotel*

When Napoleon finally lost and was in retreat, he renamed the hotel yet again, this time back to its former name, but kept the sea of red on his map painted on the large lantern

During a reconstruction of the hotel, the lantern was given a modest facelift and was placed prominently back at the entrance, where it served as an effective advertisement for the entire enterprise

The beautiful socialite, meanwhile, upon her arrival to the hotel, had noticed this very provocative red object and whenever she passed by it was sure to avert her glances toward it

However, the red map was illuminated by a burning ray of sunshine piercing through the wide canopy sheltering the entrance and now all of red Europe was reflected in her tin nail

Already upset at the multiple layers of cruelty that had fallen upon her, the young beauty just became mesmerized by this brilliant red spot shining its continental shape in her eyes

Immobile, and feeling anguished, she said, without any affect but instead choosing to just go with her instincts as if immersed in the French atmosphere where only a mother tongue could speak:

"In the lacunae . . . there is Red Europe . . . the whole of it—"

Hard of hearing, the old hotel employee did not hear what she had said

He seemed oblivious to everything around him and just bent down to pick up the rose and letter

But the stiffness of his fingers as well as a small pain in his kidney stopped him midway, and he mustered a strong yet brief voice asking for someone to quickly help him

Having been a young man himself once, one who would play the role of an assistant and assist a romantic dandy of his immediate needs, he figured the young man he was calling now would respond favorably and act accordingly

He called the young helper "Tiger" and pointed to the objects on the ground before him

Obeying the gesture and glance but ignoring the nickname, the bellboy left his station at the head of horses and came over to grab the rose and letter

On his way over, he suddenly felt paralyzed by the term the old man used, and it caused him to momentarily hallucinate so that he was lost in an earlier part of his life where his father was struggling with a fawn who was about to be slaughtered, and he started spouting a looping series of hot-tempered pronouncements under his breath, saying "I'm not your fucking Tiger, and this bloody shit you always ask me to do, why must I pick it up, you're not my father, you old fuck . . . "

Adding this to the three destabilizing shocks earlier experienced in the scene—all of it bloody morbid and continually recurring—no wonder there seemed to permeate within the player's minds a kind of mental weakness that would leave them vulnerable to high level stress attacks

The beautiful young socialite had by this time shown signs of falling into total madness and could not even acknowledge Albert, who had returned with the bellboy and the horses

Albert had the bellboy return the horses on his own while he took hold of his wife and gently led her back to their suite

From this day forward, her condition only got worse, with everything around her taking on a blood red color

Transported to Paris, she was seen by a specialist who, after hearing the whole story from Albert, diagnosed the cause of her special disorder

Everything was coming down on her at once, first the red ink, then the blood from the prick of the thorn, then the reflection of all of Europe in her nail until the entire universe was awash in nothing but red

She had accelerated down a slippery slope into crimson madness until finally the disease turned her own eyes completely red

Combined with her own tendency to always blush, it was no wonder that her life had become a perpetual hell

All treatments failed, and undermined by the martyrdom that she endured, the poor mad woman wasted away and died

Overwhelmed with grief and thinking of the huge role that the sequence of events at the hotel played in her demise, Albert thought about the tinsmith whose machine created the fashionable faux nails that ultimately caused a lot of this grief

However, it was his wife, the gorgeous socialite, who had ultimately attained such a disastrous ending to her life and who abruptly lost all sense of purpose and direction

Apprised of all of these details, Camera was keen on faithfully reenacting the scene

He made sure the nails of the young woman would appear to grow, even in death, and imported them special from London at a heavy price

Then he employed the services of a clever manicurist who, at Camera's request, applied the required tin coating first to the thumb and then, so as to not bring attention to what he was doing, to the other nine fingers, but slowly, so as to maintain designer continuity without drawing Albert's attention to it all, since to Albert it was the nails that had caused most of the problems in the first place

Lovingly owned by the widower as a memento, the rose, if used in the recreation, would need to be washed repeatedly so that the blood on the stem was constantly being removed

But the actual rose was a faded memory of an object that really held very little value anyway, so Camera produced an unlimited run of artificial copies that always looked fresh and stiffened with a hard spine

Then he procured the use of envelopes, one by one, all of them identical to the one whose front had been labeled in red ink

He also paid special attention to other details such as the thickness of the paper stock the letter was written on

Albert was quite content playing himself in this particular performance-art installation at Locus Solus and performed in the company of two extras—a very old man and the other a teenager

A fake radius was projected into the faux lantern and the sun would shine into the red European map

He also added some fake flesh to the young woman's thumb so that when it was lightly pricked, it would spill an imitation red liquid masquerading as blood

But the stem of the fake rose could not be washed and each flower was only used once—as was each envelope, easy to ditch after being stained by the red substance[76]

* * *

8) *A young man, Frank-Jules Court, committed suicide and this was presented at Locus Solus on very special conditions*[77]

76. This particular section creeps me out. Seahorse races I can relate to, but this crowd is beyond me. How they have managed to survive as long as they have, throughout the ages, is something I'll never figure out. Part of me wants to command, "Off with their heads!" but I am basically a mellow West Coast kind of guy and believe that we can all peacefully co-exist if we try. Still, if you try to stab me in the back, there's something in my radical Eastern European blood that might respond to your attack in ways I have no control over, and then that's it, you're gone. Obliterated.

77. This section is *much* less creepier than the last section. For me, it's the funniest bit in the whole novel. Preserving the humorous aspects while totally rewriting the novel was not easy, especially some of the very dark undercurrents that lay beneath its complicated renderings of the *tableaux vivants* that resurrect scenes produced in the past. How can I put this? It's as if I am auto-translating Roussel while

Working hard to get the actual corpse, Camera came upon a quite valuable handwritten confession that allowed him to rebuild from scratch the penetrating drama which had, up until that point, been hidden

Already quite a while ago, this man of letters, Frank-Jules Court, who went by the quicker Frank Court, was a widower and father of two young children, Frank Jr. and Lydia

He had acquired a property in the French countryside that enabled him to absorb himself in the quietude of his villa rising in the middle of a large garden

Featuring a remarkably salient entryway that he was very proud of, Frank became an expert and advocate for phrenology as a serious science and this benefited his reputation greatly

In his office, a broad black shelf was full of skulls neatly arranged so that he could refer to them as needed while developing his expert discourse

One January afternoon, as the writer continued working, Lydia, then nine years old, came to ask her loving father if he would like to play and pointed out the window at the snowflakes that had begun to fall

---

reading him, and that as I readwrite him and his narrative, *Locus Solus*, I am also producing it as a kind of movie, or movement, in my own mind, and that what emerges is a mixed media performance that becomes my own 21st century novelization of that movie, or movement. This novelization is created in auto-affect mode, that is, I attempt to mirror Rousell's literary neurons as I compose it, but given that he himself may have been at least slightly autistic, this then means that what I am mirroring is a body that may not itself be mirroring what goes on around it. This means that I am attempting to mirror the way I would engage in a conversation with an interlocutor who simply *just can't relate to me*. This further complicates the versioning aspect of the performance because this translation is, in fact, being produced by an individual, *me*. In fact, it's only upon rewriting the draft version of these footnotes that I think I am beginning to fully see the relationship between what I have called an auto-translation and something that approaches autobiography or, what in *META/DATA* I refer to as *pseudo-autobiography*. Somehow, even this translation of *Locus Solus* and its accompanying footnotes has too become another (potential) version of me.

It should be noted that one of Roussel's other translators, Mark Polizzotti, has spoken about trying to "capture the pleasure of reading Roussel, the humor embedded in the narrative" and how his version of Roussel, "for better or worse, differs from Heppenstall's and from Ashbery's precisely because it was produced by an individual, me, with a specific background, sense of humor, set of linguistic associations, and so on." To repeat: translators are traitors, some sloppier than others. We leave our imprints, our traces of idiosyncratic blood, our marks, our *fingerprints*, everywhere.

She was holding on to an oddity, a kind of lawyer-doll that was a mass-produced model of a woman lawyer who had broken through the glass ceiling and was directing the bar

Frank loved his daughter and went out of his way to show her tenderness since she had to spend a lot of time alone now that her older brother, Frank Jr., was placed in a harder class and spent almost all of his time intensely studying at a private school in Paris

He said "yes" by kissing the child while not promising the world

Anxious not to distract her father from his work, she went around his large table and sat behind it so that he could not see her

Playing quietly with her lawyer-doll, she was pitying herself while thinking of the fresh snow falling outside that, if only she could run her fingers through it, would turn her hand into a wet porcelain glove . . .

. . . and now, quickly, as if becoming stiff, the lawyer-doll was sleeping on its back in front of the flaming fireplace inside her father's study

Soon the heat from the fire started melting the doll, turning it back into a kind of glue or soft glass, and quickly the heat was reaching the bottom of the head

The child, chagrined, pulled the doll away from the fire and closely examined what had occurred

She then detached and placed the melted lawyer head on the black shelf next to the row of skulls and was struck by what she perceived as the similarity between the vacuous expressions of the skulls and the artificial pink face of the doll whose eye sockets were now empty orbits masking the void

She took hold of one of the skulls and was very happy to invent a new game where she would recognize these similarities and ponder their connection

As was required by the austerity of the persona taken on by the lawyer, the doll's hair was pulled back into a serious bun and placed under a business woman's hat

Being a cheaply manufactured object, the toy lawyer was simply accompanied by a net-like fabric that went under her hat but that also stuck to her face, and this made the entire model seem stiffer than it already was

Lydia decided that her first duty was to copy these lines she examined in the interlaced netting and to apply them to one of the skulls right near the empty eye sockets so that she could then further investigate the connection between the death heads and the play-lawyer

The little girl, who, under the direction of her housekeeper, had learned some basic embroidery skills, took out of her pocket a small kit of instruments that she put to use

She pulled out the punch and began guiding her hand over the frontal bone of the skull, slowly tracing the various short and oblique lines she had copied from memory and that represented the netting on the head of the doll

Mesh by mesh a kind of net was eventually scratched on to the region of bone she was focused on and the end result did not betray the amusing clumsiness of being a kid who had no sense of imperfection and even relished the strange zigzags she was composing as part of her creative process

The skull now needed a hat similar to the one worn by the counsel

Under the writer's desk, a wastepaper basket was full of old newspapers from a variety of foreign countries, some of which her father did not speak the language

Eager to deepen his appreciation for the way stories have been written in all languages, he was particularly interested in accessing the original texts in their native tongue and to just push his relationship with narrative and rhetoric as far as it could go

During the course of the entire previous month, every day he would buy a foreign newspaper and read—or pretended to read or even inappropriately translate—the abundance of events that the papers contained, as well as the commentary that ran parallel to all of the stories

In an age of social media networking, which this was not—although it could have been—depending, again, on the translation—these comments might have been more useful than the stories they supposedly were responding to and riffing on

One story, for example, was about a British traveler, one Damien Hertz, who had just returned to London after a long polar exploration that was noteworthy for, first, its not having failed, but also for discovering new ecological developments in the ice lands that were occurring as a result of climate change

In particular, after hitting an unexpected ice barrier that had broken off from a main piece of ice-land, Hertz, realizing the hazardous track he was on, surmised that he had come upon some new territory absent from all of his maps

Near the shore of this icy island, on top of a mound, was an iron crate laying at the bottom of a red mast that was planted in the ground as a way of signaling the presence of someone else

There among these living objects was a rune written in Old Norse that came with a signature and date

The antique nature of the entire sculptural construction there on the shore could be traced back to the Norwegian navigator, Gunderson, who departed for the pole back in 860 and had disappeared forevermore

This new discovery, that centuries earlier an explorer would have planted his mast in the icy island only just now being rediscovered, captured world attention, for suddenly, this document became a kind of contagious media meme that, even though its lines were fuzzy and nearly erased, gave rise to a multitude of conflicting interpretations

All of the newspapers of the world turned the idea of interpreting the document into a kind of game by posing an "Absurd Question of the Day" just to see what kind of comments it would generate

The *Times*, for example, in addition to publishing multiple versions of the obvious hermeneutic readings of the ancient text, even managed to share a daily facsimile of the original document's old parchment and fill it with a large type that would take up a half page

This large type was designed in three columns that inevitably included language that also referred to the discovery of the text and the seemingly endless interpretations it triggered

Frank, who was well versed in the knowledge of old Norse culture as well as its runes, was spurred on by these controversies and was a bit turned off by the sound-bite nature of these faithful reproductions of the original parchment set alongside all of the interpretive hype

As a protest, he would write his own thoughts on the subject on the back of the page highlighting the parchment and in doing so overloaded the paper with ink, which seeped through unevenly on to the commercial version, thinking to himself that at least he was capable of disseminating some interventionist hack of the pseudo-real

The runes ended up being entirely elucidated and many intimate details were revealed in the process of analyzing its text

Yet the tragic outcome and the disappearance of the explorer was never cleared up nor was there any real indication of how such a miraculous exploration could have taken place at that moment in history

The story, having been left behind for the next media meme, led Frank at one point in the morning to just throw the papers and some of the cut-ups he had made into the basket along with a couple of copies of the various newspapers he was "reading" / auto-translating

Lydia randomly took a few of these celebrated newspapers from the trash and sticking out of them, without her knowing or wanting to know, were three runic cut-ups made by her father, somehow lodged in the interior of the thick last fold of one of the papers

She took one of these intact cut-ups and placed it perpendicular to herself before folding it in and scissoring the paper into a shape that resembled a toque

For the narrow vertical edge essential to finish her design, Lydia used the mock bands framing the borders of the original parchment facsimiles—and they fit perfectly without having to cut them

She then took a needle from her kit and started sewing the bands into the lower part of the hat, exposing the other side of the paper annotated by her father

When the work was finished, she laid the fragile paper hat on the skull and, satisfied with the resulting similarity, cleaned the mess she had made on the carpet

Once she had accumulated all of the newspaper cuttings, she put them back in the wastepaper basket

As for the extra light clippings she made after making the intricate net, she threw them into the fireplace

She then proceeded to exit the room with a kind of raunchy sound of accomplishment

But at that instant, as a result of having thrown the clippings into the fire, the ensuing combustion caused a corner of a piece of paper already in the hearth to catch fire and jump out of its pile, lightly brushing her skirt just enough to set it too on fire

She screamed and Frank threw himself at her

He was totally livid but acted spontaneously and leapt on to her trying to put out the fire, without worrying about the fact that he was burning himself in the process

He thought of wrapping her in curtains and tried this even though it was foolish and could only make things worse

The wind and the curtains only fueled the fire more and the flames thundered for what seemed like an eternity

The empty orbs peering from all of the skull heads were watching attentively as the father finally succeeded at extinguishing the blaze and was able to lay Lydia in his bed, whereupon two doctors were called to the scene and pronounced her near-dead

Taken over by delirium, the girl endlessly recounted the scene from the beginning, first her father saying "yes" with a kiss, then the remixing of the lawyer-doll and the skull head, and finally the fatal conflagration

She died the same evening

Frank was ridden with the madness caused by great pain and on the top of his cabinet, above the black shelves, sheltered inside a glass globe, he kept the skull with the zigzag markings wearing its fragile toque

Symbolizing the beautiful last hour of his beloved child, these two objects had become priceless relics

Shortly after this horrible tragedy, Frank's pain was compounded by the death of one of his best friends from high school

His friend had died on the same day of the year that his asthmatic wife did a year earlier

Arp, his friend, left behind a daughter, Andrea, who was the exact same age as Lydia and whose only close relative was a poor uncle who had a family of his own

Suffering from his own loss and experiencing continual grief, Frank found a way to simulate the return of his beloved Lydia by taking in the orphaned indigent, Andrea, who was herself a soft child who had a delightfully playful streak in her personality that was contagious and created a tenderness in the household that spread to Frank Jr. who was filled with joy at the arrival of his new sister

The years spent developing the elegant presence and beauty of Andrea resulted in a wonderful teenager whose athletic body, gorgeous long blond hair, and huge green eyes matched her candid interactions with the world in the most perfect of ways

And this was about the time that Frank realized his paternal affection for this orphan girl had become somewhat obsessive as his thoughts became devoured by unrealistic senselessness and imaginary futures

Although their relationship was sincere, he felt his conscience pull at him every time she called him father, for a new feeling had taken him over now that she was becoming a real woman

Controlling his desires, he tried to savor the taste of her mere presence in his home, to feel content with having her grow up under the same roof as him, and to hear her voice every day—meanwhile uncontrollably imagining what it would be like to fuck her, everywhere, especially her tempting face, all day and all night

At eighteen, blossoming even more than at sixteen, Andrea was about the same height as Frank who, unable to contain himself any longer, decided to pursue a double strategy: faux father and potential sugar daddy

Nothing, he thought, would violate their evolving relationship since theirs was potentially an ideal union

The absence of all love was beside the point

The magnetic attraction on his part plus the outpouring of gratitude she had come to show him over the years had no doubt pleased him and, indeed, he was glad he could help

Meanwhile, choosing for himself the same career as his father, who had passed on his gifts as a writer, Frank Jr. was devoting all of his time to getting his BA in Creative Writing

After dinner, he would leave his father and Andrea to go back to his room to focus on his writing before catching the last train back to Paris so he could lock himself in the library the next day, take his classes, and eventually take the train back home

One evening, while his son was working alone in his bedroom, Frank nervously stammered out a line that synced with his rising heartbeat:

"Andrea . . . dear child . . . you are old enough now to get married . . . and I want to propose to you . . . with all of the happiness I have had in my life, to give to you . . . but, alas . . . I know . . . if you accept . . . "

Blushing, the young woman shuddered with joy mistaking what he had said . . .

For she and Frank Jr. had become lovers

Since they were children, taking vacations together, they had found time to sneak away and steal kisses, share readings, and play all kinds of games that led to a variety of sexual intimacies

They entrusted their dreams to each other and lately, feeling very dependent on each other, they swore to unite, expecting that a propitious time to let Frank Sr. know of their plan and to gain his enthusiastic support was fast approaching

Andrea, thinking that Frank Sr. was referencing some kind of eventual marriage to Frank Jr., replied immediately:

"Dad, you can be happy now, because I have anticipated your wishes and they have been carried out. I love Frank Jr. very much, and have promised myself to him, and he to me"

Frank the Elder, of course, had thought that up to this point, the mutual love that his son and Andrea had for each other was purely Platonic, like all brothers and sisters

Blown away by these developments, he had no choice but to accept the reality of the situation and not jeopardize their appreciation of him in their future life together

Soon after she revealed this to him, young Frank Jr. went to the train station and now, standing at the threshold to his room to say goodnight was the stunning Andrea, who Frank Sr. realized had sunk him into a deep emotional crisis

Highlighting the scene was the fact that his son was a younger version of himself, that the resemblance and imagined allure were quite profound, and that his own declining health and aging could only be filled with a tortured jealousy

"She loves *him*!" he gasped to himself once he was alone, the image of Frank Jr. with his Andrea taking over his mind

For hours on end he kept looking around his room, tensing his hands into two balled fists, and moaning softly at the pain he felt droning inside his whole body

Suddenly, he came up with a bold plan that gave him some hope

He would make it clear to Andrea that despite her love for his son, it would be in her best interest to actually marry *him* instead, since he was the ultimate caretaker of the family fortune and could determine who his ultimate heirs would be

But he had to express this tenderly and in a way that made it obvious to her that he was only doing this for her and, she, then, out of pity, especially due to all that he had already given her, would agree . . .

Feeling resolved, an indomitable urge took him over to just go and do this immediately

He felt he had to end his torment ASAP and if he succeeded, then her one word could change his hell into an inexpressible happiness

Still feeling livid, his trembling, haggard presence climbed a floor to join Andrea

It was now daybreak

She was sleeping, a beautiful angel, her gold hair scattered around her bare neck

Awakened by Frank's approaching footsteps, she smiled at him first

But suddenly realizing the odd hour and anomaly of the visit, she became scared, and this fear only increased as she focused on the disheveled insomniac in her room

"What's up, Dad? You look really—*bad*—like an unkempt ghost."

"What's up?" he mumbled back at her

Chanting words as if in a deep, multilayered dreamtime, he began to describe his uncontrollable love for her

"You will be *my* wife, Andrea" he told her, taking her hand inside his, "otherwise, I will die, me, your benefactor"

Annihilated, the poor girl had become the lead character in a horror film

"But I love Frank Jr.," she whispered, "and want to share my life with him"

These words, piercing Frank's overly sensitive heart, were like setting a burning iron on an already festering wound

"Oh, no, not him," he began pleading, "me . . . *me*"

She repeated herself in a firmer voice:

"I love Frank Jr. and want to be with *him*"

This sentence was like a curse ringing in his ears and an all-consuming vision of his son with his fantasy wife was so appalling that he almost—

But he took a deep breath and said, between trembling lips: "No, not with *him*, with me. *Me.* Your benefactor," and went to hug her, but she was totally distraught now and felt naked in her own room

She tried to just cry hoping it would end but then he took her throat in both of his hands and said, in a threatening tone:

"Not to *him*, to me . . . *me*"

His fingers were dug deep into her flesh even after she was long gone

Then he fucked the corpse[78]

An hour later, situating himself back in his bedroom, Frank, trying to erase from his mind what had just happened, was horrified by his crime

The agony and sorrow of having just killed his fantasy mingled with the dread of the punishment he would certainly face not to mention all of the shame that would now be associated with his name and reflect poorly on his son as well

Then the unfortunate murderer began to calm down a bit, thinking that everything happened in absolute silence and there was no testimony that could emerge against him

No one had a clue of the deep love he had for the girl and he could easily defy any suspicious activity, especially given his reputation as an honorable citizen beyond reproach

At eight o'clock every day, the housekeeper used to wake everyone up, including Andrea and Frank, and so she would do so the morning of the murder as well

A careful examination of the site would reveal with absolute certainty that only two men had been on the property the night of the murder: Frank and Terry Foucault, a young helper who had recently been hired

Frank would be considered innocent given his reputation and lack of probable cause and Terry, in spite of his fervent denials, would be arrested on both rape and murder charges

78. This is the one point in the performance where I wanted to consult another English translation, but I resisted. "Eros, C'est la vie."

Rushed from Paris to the countryside after receiving an urgent call from his father, Frank Jr. stood before the corpse of the woman that was supposed to brighten his life forever, and began a deep, painful screaming like a possessed lunatic

The case followed its course and at the trial, where absence of premeditation was admitted, Terry, who vehemently denied any connection to the crimes whatsoever, was nonetheless found guilty and condemned to life imprisonment

Convinced of his innocence, his mother, Penelope Foucault, an honest farmer near Frank's property, swore to her son that her sole purpose in life would be to get the charges reversed and rehabilitate his reputation

Plagued by remorse, Frank became obsessed, day and night, with the image of the poor convict undergoing thousands of torments in his place, and so he started losing sleep and his health deteriorated quickly

His liver went bad and within a few years he approached the ultimate threshold before the tomb

Realizing his life was a lost cause, he wanted to write a confession that could, after his death, reveal Terry's innocence

The young man's undeserved pain and atrocious predicament continued to haunt him more than his own dying ways

Forced to remain silent lest his life be filled with the horror of the criminal justice system, he had refrained from admitting anything, mostly because he did not want what would inevitably turn into a heinous scandal to negatively affect Frank Jr., though now he had accepted the idea of a frank, posthumous, mea culpa

But he was resolved to confine his writing to a special hiding place that could only be discovered at the end of a series of operations suitable to an honorable confession

He once achieved an amazing success with a comedy that he wrote and that was performed for an entire season in Paris

It was his hundredth show, and he decided to take out of the folds of his portfolio the poster from this hugely successful work that, when fully presented, measured about two-thirds of his height

His plan was to have a local jeweler, who everyone loved, recreate the poster as a unique work of art that featured various gems whose color tones would spell out the text of the poster

Thanks to a dense multitude of emeralds offering two distinct color tones, the text stood out clearly as a dark green on the pale green background

Inside thirteen white rectangles of various sizes, all made out of diamond dust, were the names of the actors, including twelve in more or less large blue letters made of sapphires, and one, the first and biggest of them all, in light red characters made of many small rubies

On top of the piece it was written: "100th Presentation of . . . "

Frank thought that by choosing this object as his ultimate cache and that commemorated the most triumphant day of his creative life, it could, better than anything else, be used to wrap or frame his muddied confession

After detailing his long and precise orders to a clever Parisian goldsmith named Goldsmith, the art object was altered so that it was top loaded with a secret gold-lined pocket that could only be opened by pushing on a barely visible nail camouflaged on a single star ruby that now had a spring set beneath it

It was in this secret pocket that his confession would be placed

As for the operations that would, little by little, lead the motivated sleuth to the hidden pocket, Frank decided that, in part, they would first have to make connections between gradually revealed historical facts

In 1347, shortly after the famous siege of Calais, Philippe VI of Valois wanted to reward the heroism of the six burghers who, barefoot with rope around their necks, had voluntarily gone to Edward III to participate in what was clearly a death march as a way to satisfy the demands of the enemy monarch

Their efforts thus saved the city from ruin and, to their surprise, were also saved by the intercession of Philippe of Haunaut

Initially, Philippe VI planned on conferring an official nobility on all six, since they had shown such courage and were willing to give their lives up for the cause

But then there was the fact that everything turned out OK and no one was really hurt

However, a feat such as theirs, accomplished without forethought of how they might survive their march, would not be properly addressed with something as simple as an honorary award

He thought there should be some kind of monetary reward as well

Choosing to meet him half way, the king vowed to award the six heroes their nobility by maintaining them in their commoner's quarters but giving them distinct privileges previously denied to them

In this kingdom, there were several large families and almost all of the family elders in the most paramount branch of these would invariably share the same first name, which would be registered on official documents that would evoke aesthetic details designed for a specific letter: for example, depending on the circumstances, the name might include a letter **t** that would affect the shape of a sword standing on its tip, or an **o** designed to resemble a shield, or even the letter **z**, ornamented with the appropriate flourishes, could render into view a subtle dislocation transformed by a lightning strike

Sometimes an **i** would refer to a lit candle and a **c** would morph into a sickle while an **s** would become a watercourse

All concerned parties, when signing their documents, could then routinely carry out their branded flourishes promptly

Then, this individual could add additional attributes to the coat of arms, creating unique marks of distinction that would be appreciated for their rare design and, for example, could be transferred by a bishop's hand in a marriage ceremony

The bishop would wear a red undergarment, which was ostensibly longer than the normal Pontifical tunic covering it and was embroidered with these special designs

These tunics and subtunics were used for only the highest ecclesiastical ceremonies

And so, the king, following his fancy, declared that the principal first name of each of the six Calais heroes would be transmissible via the undergarment during matrimonial ceremonies

However, in the famous Group of Six, there was a certain Frank Court who was a direct ancestor of Frank Court

Frank was there to witness how Philippe VI changed the **C** in Court into a kind of inflected aspic

Since then, as passed down through generations of progeny, all of the elders in the Court lineage were named Frank, with another name added on for distinction—for example, Frank-Joseph or Frank-Jean or Frank-William or, as in this case, Frank-Jules and his son Frank-Charles (referred to here as Frank Jr.)

Philippe VI had set an example and was followed by his successors so that it became an historical tendency for burghers, after having participated in significant achievements, to receive—without changing the class they were born into—a few aristocratic benefits

Also, when under Louis XV Mark Lemon wrote his colossal work on arms, he made sure that his tome, 25 volumes in all with the first 23 devoted to the nobility, included, at the end, a penultimate volume on the most prominent segment of the common man's population and a last volume on everybody else

The author then decided to publish his work by accessing the best paper available for the first 23 volumes and a cheaper stock for the last two volumes

But on further reflection, he ended up using the luxurious paper for the penultimate volume and only used the cheap stuff for the final volume on the public rodents and other assorted riffraff

The beautiful reproductions of the first 23 volumes that he published were collected in only the best houses and were better looked at as book objects than as something someone would seriously read

The noble volumes were paginated on one side and had a limited edition serial number on each page along with the words recto and verso imprinted on either side of the paper

This made it clear to all who paid attention to such things that one side was delivering a brand of superior preponderance and the other side was quite inferior

After a short hesitation, the publisher agreed to apply this same unusual watermarking on the last two chapters as well, thinking that it would at the very least provide some aesthetic consistency for the work as a whole

Things got weird, though, and the 24th volume included the names of the Calais heroes, and their unsurpassable seniority was explicitly referenced in the first paragraph of page 1, recto, volume XXIV

Lemon, along with Philippe VI and others of their ilk, had figured the heroic Group of Six would benefit from milking their noble privileges as much as possible

In fact, the original Frank Court of the Group of Six managed to procure a copy of the bulky book which he then passed on to his descendants and which had, over the centuries, been transmitted from one Frank to another, all the way down to Frank-Jules, the necrophiliac murderer

Frank-Jules was very proud of his origin, its historical and illustrious narrative, and used it when necessary as a kind of corrective measure of opprobrium while dipping his head into the pot of skunkweed he always turned to when tapping into his hallucinatory visions of excess

So was the case at this moment as he took out his pen and, eyeing a loose sheet of paper, wrote down, in a clear formula, clues to the hidden pocket:

"You are to read Marc Lemon's volume XXIV on the more distinctive commoners and refer to the recto of page 1, specifically the subparagraph devoted to Court, the letters 17–30–43–51–74–102–120–173"

Sampled wisely from the salient words cited, these letters when sequenced would constitute this short phrase: "Star ruby"—which, if they were clever, would undoubtedly lead them to find the location of the spring that would then release the pocket hiding the confession

On purpose, Frank had ordered the Goldsmith named Goldsmith to indicate, within his precise composition, the unambiguous location in the overall design that would most reflect the crimson color he would be pointing to in his game of clues

But as part of his mixture of clues, he also wanted to point the investigator toward an even luckier find, that is to say, the one object that most resonated with the story of how this all got started in the first place: the skull under the globe in his study that included the weird scratch marks on the forehead bone and the light newspaper toque balanced on top of the skull's head

This object was, after all, the last work of art created by his child prodigy, Lydia

Didn't the fact that he had, almost childishly and piously, preserved this relic mean that he would never betray the memory of his beloved daughter and, in fact, indicate that he was full of the touching, fatherly love one needed to transmit in order to show sympathy?

Conjuring a precise image of an emotional memory he now equated with the series of events that brought him to this point in his life, he sought a way to have the investigator interact with both the strange toque as well as the lattice network of pell mell lines created by Lydia on the skull's front-end, something that would infuse the adventurous spirit of the search with an attention to detail that might otherwise be written off and overlooked

Soon, he became almost obsessed with the idea of remixing the zigzag network of lines engraved on the forehead bone with the faux runes visible on the vertical edges of the impromptu and rather flimsy toque made of old newspapers

Inspired by this thought, Frank decided to approach the globe that contained the collaged skullwork with a knife whose tip he put to use as an engraver or meticulous scraper devoted to transforming the work, adding and deleting things so that it no longer maintained its former traits

He thus managed to settle on to the face of the skull the entire runic formula that was printed on the newspaper, in French no less

There were readable characters and mashed-up words leaning in all directions, aesthetically deformed and metaphorically welded

Each of the two words underlined in this replica were skillfully put between two quotation marks and, considering that he had successfully deconstructed the runic figures, now what could be read were numbers appearing in letters

The job basically completed, there were still a few stitches left to put into the work and he painstakingly put them in as well

Then he relocated the skull to its new post on the mantelpiece above the fireplace but inside the globe where it was still somehow balancing its paper hat

With its net-like neckline generally preserved, the newly constructed lines on its face offered to the future investigator the cut-up paper runes that if read correctly, would awaken the reader to a point that needed immediate attention, namely that the culprit would soon be revealed and the monstrous secrecy that the search would have already generated would soon be revealed

Clarity would prevail over eternal *irrevelation*[79]

A fine, tightly executed handwriting that covered several sheets detailing his confession was the next part of the intricate work

He chose to write the confession on a fancy, ultra-thin paper stock that was at one time used for messages transmitted by carrier pigeons

Veracity, elegantly composed language art, palpable culpability, it was all there, and when he was done, he folded it up perfectly to the edge along its

79. Whenever the auto-translation program would bring up words like *irrevelation*, my heart would skip a beat or two, since I immediately felt like I was on the right track again and had made a good decision to persevere through the duration of the performance.

permanent crease and buried it into the narrow, velvet-lined, hidden pocket studded with its precious gems

Having not eaten for what must have been an eternity, Frank managed to achieve a degree of weakness that compelled him to lie in bed

He kept with him the key to his office, which he locked so as to preserve the relic skull's clue and defer any premature interaction with the modified notes he had carved and cut into the object

He had hoped to maintain the feasibility of his cryptic plan before he died and within two weeks his body was discovered

When the time came for dealing with his father's estate after he died, Frank Jr. entered his father's office one evening after dinner and sat at the writer's desk full of cluttered paperwork

After two hours of uninterrupted sorting, he allowed himself some time to take a break and, getting up, he put a cigarette in his lips and went in search of a light that he correctly thought would be in a nearby box close to the board that opened to the chimney

Having had his first puff, as he shook the match to put out the flame and throw it into the ashes, his eyes fell absentmindedly on the skull with the toque, which was now well-lit by a chandelier hanging in the middle of the ceiling

Ready to be seized by the least unusual aspect of the familiar object he had seen all throughout his childhood, Frank Jr. suddenly felt himself aroused by the marks on the front bone that had once seemed random and insignificant but that now appeared to reveal a series of strange signs that resembled some of the odd textual material imprinted on the toque

Intrigued, he lifted up the globe and put it aside, taking the skull with its light toque into his hands and immediately sat down with it at the desk

There, at his leisure, he was in a convenient position to closely examine the front bone, whereupon he realized that indeed, the lattice network of lines had undergone some subtle changes and, in fact, had brought into view several lines of runic text

Sensing that there was some kind of revelation hidden within this network of lines, a feeling that was initially triggered by the fact that he was now crying, Frank Jr. experienced an impatient curiosity pure of any apprehension because in his eyes his father had always embodied the ultimate in righteousness and honor

Being too much of a high achiever as well as a well-read young man to ignore the runes, he quickly transcribed the French letters on a small black slate with white chalk decorating the desk, and upon seeing the not too mysterious statement that eventually came into view via a series of underlined letters and symbols, realized he needed to go retrieve the volume written by Marc Lemon and to find the paragraph that spoke of the first Frank Court to join the honorable nobility, wherein he would immediately decode the assigned letters to reveal the next part of the clue

Back at the desk with the huge volume, he applied the numbers to the letters in the paragraph in the book and, writing on the slate, jotted down two simple words in quotation marks: "Star ruby"

Then, he realized that there before him on the desk was the large display of jewels modeled after the old theater poster—which had been there all along even though, large as it was, he had never really paid any attention to it

Seizing this opportunity, he grabbed a nearby magnifying glass that was lying among an assortment of pens and pencils and looked closely at the poster, particularly the name in red

After a lengthy perusal, he discovered in the golden plate one imperceptible circular notch closely surrounding one of the rubies that, once some mild exertion was applied to the nail that held it in place, slightly raised the hidden pocket

Consequently, jimmying the magnifying glass into the thinly opened groove, he was able to uncover the rest of the secret compartment and, gently releasing it so that it snapped open, was able to access the enclosed contents

Throwing his finished cigarette into the fireplace, Frank Jr., very interested in knowing what his father had written, leaned back in the writer's chair and began reading the excruciating confession

Little by little his face started cracking, various parts trembling with rage

Andrea, his cherished partner, his fiancée, was loved by his father—and then murdered and raped by him!

A sort of catatonic daze took him over as he finished reading the confession

Then he was mauled by an infernal anguish—he was the son of an assassin!—these words, he believed, were stigmatized right on his forehead

Incapable of surviving this shame, he decided to end his life that night

But who, if anyone, would he inform about the confession?

Once revealed, he would have essentially become the narc who properly denounced his father, but if he destroyed the document, then an eternal life of torture would be visited upon the innocent young man already in prison

Frank Jr. was, it seemed, being sentenced to his own odious role in the whole affair

All that remained in him at this moment was the fuzzy desire of becoming-something-other, anything-other, in its most primitive state

He could just be passive, like that, a human numbskull inconspicuously continuing his bio-trajectory, and do nothing, leave it all to chance, evolution, mutation, inheritance, whatever total sum was destined to stay in formation, with or without him, nothing more, nothing less, honor, dishonor, alive and/or dead and/or alive-but-dead-inside, potentially reincarnated, summarily executed, imaginatively resurrected, the looping horror spinning in his head over and over again like a bad performance art spectacle played in a mad man's theater

These thoughts, whosever's they were, tenderized the meat in his brain

Feeling resolved, the document was placed back in the velvet interior of the hidden pocket and the enclosure was sunken back into the jewel display

Then, having replaced back on the library shelf the volume written by Mark Lemon, as well as erasing everything on the slate, Frank Jr. restored the globe to the mantelpiece above the fireplace where it now sat enworlding the marked-up skull and its barely balanced paper hat resting atop it

It was then that he took out of his pocket a loaded revolver that, given the isolation of the countryside property, he always took with him

He opened his jacket and soon fell dead, shot in the heart, while blood ran rampant at the site of the detonation

The next day, the news went viral all throughout the region

Penelope Foucault, convinced of her son's innocence, suspected that there existed some mysterious, unexplainable relationship between Andrea's murder and this suicide

Knowing via press articles that Camera was running experiments that would resurrect the dead, she thought that artificially reviving Frank Jr. so that he would then relive the last moments of his life would inevitably reveal some precious details that could benefit her son Terry's case

What, she thought, would have pushed this young man who seemingly had everything so far beyond the brink that he would kill himself?

Thanks to her feverish, persistent ways, voicing her concerns to the media and anyone else who would listen, she obtained a ruling from the justice that approved the transfer of the body from its transitory state in the city morgue over to Locus Solus

She had managed to make this all happen in spite of heavy resistance from the extended Court family who were becoming more and more concerned about a possible scandal staining their reputation

The troubling case of her son, now referred to as The Foucault Affair, was stirring up troubling possibilities and uncertain outcomes

Frank Jr. was thus reincarnated as someone "like himself" by Camera

But the version of Frank Jr. that chose to reappear in the performance-art installation triggered by the *résurrectine*, though clearly under duress and experiencing something along the lines of a real, unexplainable tragedy during the last moments of his life, did not indicate anything specific that would help with the case

It was generally assumed that Frank Jr. must have always been lonely and given that he had not uttered any words in these final moments, there was no detailed account of what it was that was quickly leading him to his suicidal moment

The scene that was being played out, though accurate in its own way, did not necessarily reconstitute anything remotely close to a motivation

Objectively taking into account the information available to him, Camera went back to the scene of the suicide where Frank Jr.'s corpse had been found

He meticulously retraced all of the steps and movements of the resurrected corpse in his own simulated installation and it was then that he noticed Lemon's book on arms

Once moving inside the office with his fragmented bits of notes and a basic deductive reasoning, he also realized that Frank Jr. must have made his way over to the fireplace mantelpiece, where he saw the constructed skull head of the faux lawyer-doll

Camera's attention was drawn to this odd looking object and his own immense knowledge did not exclude his embrace of runes too, and he immediately recognized the signs covering the edge of the toque that eerily resembled the latticework on the frontal bone of the skull

Removing the globe, he peered in closer at the runic characters to make sure he read them exactly right and, looking at the scratched bone surface as well, soon had a clear idea of what the clues were and copied the numeric formula down in his pocket notebook

Following the same subtle chain of clues that had been previously tracked the movements by Frank Jr. during his cadaverous loop in the performance-art installation, Camera eventually found the confession, which he handed over to the justice officials who then read the text in full to Penelope Foucault, thus explicating the effusive confession of the father and explaining the dark postscript of the son

Extracted from the prison, Terry, whose conviction was quickly overturned, regained his freedom along with an honorable reputation

Penelope could not find the right words to express her gratitude to Camera and his artistic reenactment of the final moments in the life of Frank Jr.

It if it wasn't for Frank Jr.'s encounter with the cranial runes, whose deciphering revealed the true murderer, the only chance her martyred son's innocence could have been proven would have disappeared forever

Feeling the total horror that came with being related to the purveyor of these revolting crimes by blood, the cousin-heirs took great care in not reclaiming the corpse of the assassin's son from Camera, and sold at auction the contents of the entire estate, which were otherwise old and not worth getting sentimental over

In fact, given the ignoble nature of the crimes and its aftermath of wrongful imprisonment and suicide, they would have been quite content to see the whole lot of it completely demolished

Eager to replicate the scene that led to the suicide, Camera acquired almost all of the contents of the library and other assorted artifacts available at auction

He was thus able to restore a great deal of the original material in his temperature-controlled performance-art installation

Working from the newspaper publication of a perfect facsimile of the entire, handwritten confession written on the fine sheets of paper used by carrier pigeons to deliver messages, Camera made a large stack of copies that he reproduced in a specific way, one that would leave a blank postscript space at the bottom of every page so that with each performance the actor would be forced to fill something in for the absent dead

Forcing Frank Jr. to write a postscript into the blank part of the page during each and every performance loop was something that Penelope and Terry never got tired of watching

Eventually the resurrected corpse would write in a prayer for the mother and her innocent son

But it was the fatal act of using his revolver that served to punctuate the end of every loop

It was always loaded with blanks

* * *

Wrapped in furs, an aid to Camera would go around to all eight performance-art installations and revitalize the corpses with a fresh shot of the vital fluid, one scene after another without interruption, and as each installation came to life, the aid would move on to the next one and animate the subject waiting for its cue to reenact the very last moments of its past life as a form of post-studio art remixed into the present[80]

80. A transcribed note: "Now that I have reached this point in the performance, I feel like the performance has itself become a kind of heavy drug whose sole purpose is to keep me laser-focused on the task at hand as I continually write my way through the text. Finishing this final line of Chapter Four, I realize this entire project is becoming one long high, the ultimate immersion into the dream syndicate." Re-reading it now, the line strikes me as a cross between William Burroughs and Duchamp, and that my imagination was properly lubricated by what emerged as a mechanized routine fueled by a new *pharmakon* invented by a mad scientist who just happens to be an artist-entrepreneur: a book, a narrative, a procedural composition with no predetermined outcome. It reminds me of recent tweet of mine @markamerika where I intentionally remix something Duchamp once said in an interview: "People always speak of 'great' art with a meta-reverential intensity, but why? Art is a drug, That's all it is." But in the case of Roussel, what a heavy fucking drug it is.

5

Dusk arrived while the group of visitors to Locus Solus continued to listen to their presiding artist-guru, who was now leading them up a steep path

A ten-minute climb brought the crew up to a small building whose facade, with its top facing a huge expanse of trees that appeared to be a manmade forest, included just two closed shutters, whose wide grid was secured by very rusty hinges made of solid gold

Between the walls, without any signs of an exit, there stretched an enormous single room that was adequately furnished

On an easel, an unfinished canvas could be seen, and it appeared to have painted on it an allegory focused on a new dawn where there was a young girl, whose body was transmitting rays of light that metaphorically connected with a wing-tipped horizon that signaled another life beyond

With brief comments, Camera pointed to the middle of the room where a certain Lucius Jackson stood

Jackson, the story went, had recently gone mad after having witnessed his one-year old daughter being trampled to death by a group of gang members dancing the jig, and had taken up a self-admitted treatment plan at Locus Solus for several weeks

At the end of the room, a guard stood motionless

Very bald, Lucius, revealing his left side, was sitting in profile before the end of a marble table on which a kind of mini-hearth rested

Imagine an andiron with a pair of metal supports for firewood and made of a horizontal bar mounted on short legs with a vertical shaft surmounting the front end—topped with hot coals

Thrown as a bridge above the andiron was a meter-wide piece of long grey window screen, and the madman, trying to avoid any contact that would cause him to burn himself, slipped his face under the screen and adjusted himself accordingly until he reached the perfect tension of his upper head locked into the object as if framing his portrait into the hot apparatus

Compared to where his audience was located, his face appeared to gently slope down toward the coals

Marvelously painted and modeled, twelve figures a few centimeters tall and dressed in thin balloon skins and who, at the corner of the table, evoked a band of merry pranksters, were taken by Lucius one at a time and carefully placed on top of the screen resting above his head

Hot air was passing through the screen via an infinite number of fine, tight holes

Having been transferred from their resting place on the corner of the table, the miniature hucksters were held upright in space thanks to some ballast that had been melded into their feet and, soon, they were circulating across the screen according to the whims of their insane maestro, whose fingers wandered around the top of his fabricated device

Deprived of the vertical air currents, whenever they passed very close to the back or mid section of his head would disorient them off their axis and each figurine would take on a life its own, moving back and advancing forward or even to the side while occasionally plunging down but, then, temporarily avoiding obstructions, popping back up to their initial stand-up state as if citing the repetition and randomness built into this jittery design

Some would swivel under the sway of certain air currents tangentially skimming the surface underneath the screen while others would be suppressed of any such movement and, projecting their presence in a more stoic way, would jab an elbow into their neurotic bandmate

Once they were rearranged so that they stood opposite each other in two rows of six, the nearest of which had their backs turned to the onlookers, the figures would start to perform a more classical dance that reminded some of the visiting onlookers of an old Scottish jig

Only Lucius operated the mechanism, walking his fingers on the screen as if it were a subtle keyboard that he had been born to wear atop his head so that, over time, with great patience, he would become a kind of virtuoso

From opposing diagonals, two figures danced toward each other and then, before touching, regained their superior individuality and skipped backward to their starting positions

Several times an alternative square-dance style would emerge as the figures became differentiated by a set of spinning movements carried out in the center of the screen, two pairs of two randomly determined by who happened to meet who while bouncing around

Lucius was very agile at controlling the screen and made sure to heavily curve his wrists so that he would not break the current of some of the hot air streaming from below and that ultimately supported the stability of the inactive players

Then the idiot savant gradually brought in to the mix the two most distant figures by having them dance with the figure opposite and slowly switch partners until they had moved across the expanse of screen that was their stage

This kept the dance machine operating as a continuous performance generating new combinations of dance partners in constant turnover

With great facility, free of any awkwardness, Lucius was able to animate an intense liveliness in the jittering figures dancing without a parquet floor and whose initial quiet pace would gradually build into something incredibly fast and, eventually, impetuously aggressive

Developments suddenly ceased

Removing his hands from the screen on top of his head, above which the dancers hung aimlessly, Lucius, exhausted and with terror filling his eyes, turned his face away from his audience and, as Camera told the group, was now undergoing a kind of strange capillary crisis fueled by hallucinatory reflexes that accompanied his recent performance

These cruel obsessions that overruled his every rational move were always there, despite himself

Under the empire of fear, he now imagined six hairs on each side of his near-bald head jumping from one pore to another, sometimes from one side of his head to another

Uprooted by some deep relaxation technique that he must have invented himself while acting out his performance art madness, he imagined every one of his twelve remaining hairs would rotate their position in the dance program

Each hair would loosen, then eject itself into the air before tracing a tiny path vertically upward until it would fall back down into an open pore, which would immediately receive the acrobatic hair

The deep relaxation of unconsciously performing with the balloon-dressed figures as if immersed in a trance ritual was more than enough for his body to hunt down a new hair, launch it into the air, and consequently receive it in the gaping asylum of his porous head

Totally uptight and suffering from some nervous, uncontrollable tic, Lucius, trying to stop the infuriating hair dance from continuing, would try to drape his hands over his head, but a wicked terror would overtake him and prevent him from touching it

And, despite himself, he would conduct this jittery choreography in both reality and in his imagination, a simultaneous and continuous fusion of aesthetic intensity, bouncing things into the air at will, nonstop, relentlessly, twelve hairs moving according to an auto-affective illogic of sense that if he were to stop would disempower each element from conquering its spatially motivated moment

In a low voice, Camera reported to the group that the enormous anatomical interest in this project was currently focused on how the madman's reflexes were triggering a kind of "simultaneity-effect" in the formal choreography of the piece—something that might be attributed to an ongoing obsession resulting from electrical shock therapy

Painfully aware that his hair dance was somehow cursed, that he was destined to perform the piece with an impeccable, some would say maniacal precision as the work built up over time toward its passionate crescendo, Lucius would inevitably start experiencing volcanic tremors and begin groaning in agony

After a moment of acute paroxysm, the crisis would appear to finally dissipate, and while the madness would be soothed in a balm of semi-normalcy, his individual hairs would find refuge in their porous homes on the edge of his baldness

Then Lucius would break out in long sobs, his face in his hands, pouring a stream of tears brought on by his nervous relaxation

Soon, rising with a beaming smile, he took a few steps to the left and sat in front of the side wall, in front of a large table where several crystal bottles without caps, each with a brush dipped in a colorless liquid, sat side by side with many pieces of cloth cut in advance and clearly intended by their dimensions to be used to compose a baby outfit

He pulled something out of his pocket and threaded it through an imperceptible hole on the table

It was a long white stem as thin as thread but as rigid as steel

With quick tongue brushes, he licked the top end and then, without delay, placed vertically above it, one hand held high, the edges of two pieces of cloth applied one against the other

Suddenly taking on the attributes of a rigid Pharaoh snake, the hard wire lengthened itself with fast, tight undulations, and did not stop moving in each direction as he successively pierced the two layers of cloth, running up and down a fine sewing line, perfectly completing each minute gesture in less than a second

The phenomenon came to an end and Lucius broke the thread whose captive portion spontaneously formed a small ball resembling a stopper knot

He had clearly acquired an on-field flexibility that fed into his seamless performance

Camera showed the visitors a white rod wrapped in something like thread that, when combined with certain chemical properties contained inside the colorless liquid stored in the crystal bottles, would transform the object into a rocket

Lucius, wetting the top of a new white stem with a thick brush of his tongue, stood upright in his desired place like a perfectly positioned bookmark

Amounting to a small, closely packed spire, this fast, white rocket-in-the-making required a hem stitch, achieved by piercing twice round the apparatus and alternating through the linen first a singular then a double

Made the break . . . two rocket-balls . . . obstacles disappearing . . . the sewing softens . . .

The artist-cum-tour-guide stressed to everyone what he perceived to be the readiness potential of the madman who, working with haste creating an abstract artwork modeled on the imaginary presence of his baby daughter, whom he might have believed he was giving birth to yet again, was not being deviant but was still deviating from what must have been a nagging thought, or series of nagging thoughts, all different, all colorless liquids stirring in his own bottled-up rocket of a brain

In haste, generating his own temporary stitches that would never mend whatever word there is for futility beyond fatality . . .

Singly, doubly . . .

Almost like a fourth spindle, by the effect of the colorless liquid generating an energy still not quantified, crossing the first hole at each of his gestural descents, followed by the rise of a double length and always with rocket-speed

One bottle rocket, two, three, four

A fifth, due to a new vial, got a whip stitching by enclosing one side without any space, the outer line marked by two edges of cloth bonded exactly together

The formation of the two balls of judgment and the phenomenon of triggering unconscious readiness potential as a deep relaxation technique never failed to usher in a new sense of accomplishment

But—two balls of judgement?

Where did that idea come from?

Make or break . . . rocket-boosters . . . obscene appearances . . . threaded associations of nervous thought . . .

Lucius' infallible glances, each time exhibiting subtle differences, were accompanied by his wetting a tiny fraction on the top of the white stem and proceeding to follow through on his instinctive, calculated moves, without error

The perforated path he had assigned himself was leading to the creation of a set of multiples, this time in the form of bottle-rockets that also doubled as projected versions of a baby modeled after his daughter

A rocket from a sixth bottle made of stitched linen, recalled his prodigious zigzags of thought masquerading in his mind as a rhetoric of ranting pyrotechnics whose chaotic meanderings oscillated widely and carried with them an air of explosiveness

All of the rockets, moreover, resembled—when reduced to such simplicities—some complex fireworks whose curvaceous formations were capable of generating multiple twists, coils, and staggered lines of flight

The perfect realization of each seam showed the overwhelming excellence of his method, something that easily would have matched the work of a laborer mass producing a hundred times the amount of stitched cloth on the very best sewing machine on the market

After having executed his focused work on all six bottles, Lucius, feeling exhausted, stopped for a moment and looked at the very shortened white rod of thread

Turning as if by chance, he seemed to be seeing for the first time the visitors through the grating:

"Sing" he commanded, as if conducting the players

The artist, Camera, now becoming a kind of Happening director, asked Monette, who he knew had a background as a singer, to perform a lyrical phrase to satisfy the whims of the madman[81]

81. It's as if this work cannot help but become a kind of dys-eased Happening (the phrase *dys-eased* is a remix of Robbe-Grillet's concept of dys-narrative which, in my undergraduate Nouevau Roman / Nouveau Cinema course that I took with him, he attributed to *Last Year at Marienbad*). Conceptual art as installation-performance. But oh so cruel, and where exactly is the artist's responsibility to be located in all of this madness? That's what makes the work so beautiful, and what I like about its effect on both Duchamp and Robbe-Grillet, that is, there is no moral to the story, no political agenda per se, certainly no attempt to be politically correct. Having already experienced the intensity of higher arts and humanities education right at the height of gender / ethnic / identity / cultural studies, I would sometimes feel the latent effects of that mostly useful propaganda stir inside of me many times throughout this performance, but I welcomed the chance to rid myself of the responsibility of having to seriously acknowledge it. What a fucking relief, to just let the story tell itself with me as its filter, but not as a vessel being filled with otherworldly or Godly inspiration—hardly! I'm a remixologist, not a religious poet, and so I go into the performance knowing that I could tweak the source material any way I wanted to. Is how I tweak the knobs of the remix machine I become when embodying another text also my responsibility? Is this where my political agenda can finally make itself known, by what I do and do not let pass through with the least amount of politically-motivated adulteration? But then what about this strange feeling, this overwhelming sensation that runs through my body as I watch the madman, Lucius Jackson, perform his esoteric rituals in front of me and all of my other colleagues taking Camera's Dadaist tour? Remixologists, or what I also refer to as *artist-mediums*, are *co*-respondents, that is, they share in the responsibility by way of a *transgressive shareability*. This latter term I sample from Bracha Ettinger who, in a lecture in Switzerland at the European Graduate School, said:

> Some artists are imprinted by, operating on and produce traces of the trauma of the world and of others, at the same instant that they are realizing a work as beauty and wound, tableau and cicatrice, in a sphere which with-in the artist is from the outset transgressive. I propose that archaic psychic matrixial borderspace and metramorphic borderlinks between partial and shared subjectivity and trans-subjective-objects open aesthetic channels for transmissions, exchange and inscriptions via artworks, but it is artworking that offers this sphere the means for seizing itself.

A creative collaborator of some of the best performance artists of her time, Monette, who was always more understated in her personal presence than when she was playing the role of performance artist, began to sing:

"I'm . . . waitin' for my man . . . " stretching her measured vocal chords very slowly so that it sounded as if she were embodying the spirit of Billie Holiday[82]

"Ahhhmmm . . . waitin' for my man . . . "[83]

Brusquely interrupting her, Lucius made her repeat that line over and over again, paying particular attention to the pure vibration of the pause after "I'm . . . "

Then he sat down right in front of the onlookers, before a table supporting these objects[84]:

1) A lamp currently without light

In other contexts, I have referred to this as *transubjective neural shareware*.

But for now Ettinger gets the last word in what would be a pre-Freudian, post-Lacanian remix of the emotional disturbances being exhibited by Lucius Jackson (and others who appear in Chapter Four):

> A matrixial trail, skirting on sensation's edges, is vibrating at the edges of visibility when a passion based on marks of shareability becomes affectively transgressive again and labors anew in com-passion, to perforate the screen of Vision. When a world, internal and external, from which the artist has to transfer and to which she has to transmit, is shared with-in-difference via the tableau, this world is being presenced at the same instant that the work awakes its strange beauty, pain and languishing, languishing as both yearning and ebbing while swerving.

82. Billie Holiday mashed up with Lou Reed—as it must be.

83. The drugs are still prevalent in my system, not as liquid narcotics, but as words being auto-translated into art.

84. In his essay, "Engimas and Transparency," Robbe-Grillet discusses the world Roussel creates for us and that we cannot escape: "We are in a *flat* and *discontinuous* universe where each thing refers only to itself." What excites Robbe-Grillet most about Roussel is that he conducts an "*investigation* which destroys, in the writing itself, its own object." But then there are the objects within the-world-as-object, the statues, the lamps, the postcards, the pile driver, the extracted teeth, the skulls, the fabrics, the paintings, the tablets, *the people brought back to life*. These objects too are no longer anything but mechanisms reproduced for the reader so that the composition may proceed according to its predetermined function as indicated by the procedures he develops within the parameters of the specific rules he has created for himself. In this regard, his world-as-object comes to me readymade and the rules I have set up for rendering my own version of his transubjective neural transmissions enable me to create much more ambiguity in the text than one might otherwise find in its original form. The use of ambiguity becomes central to my auto-translation when the object of the text per se, *the text as object*, becomes subjectively filtered in ways no one could have anticipated one hundred years ago.

2) A prodigiously thin golden punch needle

3) A small ruler of a few inches with some lard showing on one of its sides along one of its main divisions marked by numbered bold lines

Each division contained twelve subdivisions that were indicated in lighter, shorter marks

The red lines and numbers on the ruler were chopped off by an encroaching piece of whitish grey bacon

The tool, when carefully executed, reproduced in miniature an old apparatus divided into six feet and seventy-two inches

4) A thin, green and square tablet made of some hardened wax

5) An acoustic apparatus consisting of a simple short needle attached to a membrane shaped like a round cone

6) A small rectangular sheet of white cardboard with an opening at its center encircled by a garnet-layered flat line that, when redoubled, gave off the appearance of something like a makeshift ace of diamonds

Lucius then found a way to support—in the middle of the green tablet laid flat before him—the small white rod of thread held on both ends between the thumb and forefinger of his left hand—and that he compressed lengthwise by shortening the divisions and subdivisions he eyeballed

Choosing with great care, by examining the red lines, different places on the same line, he held the punch vertically in his right hand, making seven superficial marks in the wax by leaning the needle into the bacon

Having achieved these milestones, Lucius arched slightly, clenching his two fingers, letting the elastic rod give, and then stretched himself a bit more so he could take in the scope of his measures

Then he interposed new marks among the previous ones he had just made, repeating his exact procedural method

For what seemed to everyone a long time, clutching the rod and deforming it into various phantom shapes, the crazed artisan passionately pursued his task, questioning the red-lined subdivisions while lightly attacking the wax with the punch, stamping his straight marks on to the blank areas by subtly varying his unique style of touching the material[85]

85. The whole time I'm translating this, I'm thinking, Lucius the Genius, inventing his wax 'n' bacon iPad with its own metamediumystic remix-app and, not

Finally, the green tablet exhibited a short and thin line formed by tiny punctures resembling a phonograph roll with a single voice impressed upon it

After Lucius rearranged the ruler and punch to meet his specific desires, he had the guard light a match as he approached the lamp

While the flame licked the wick, Camera slipped his arm between two bars in the grating and turned himself toward the left against the wall so that he could bring something up to the artist

It was a faded silk sheath, long and flat, with one side covered in old embroidery with the Latin word "Mens" surrounded by religious symbols and flowers

He also pulled out a very old piece of wood that had some text carved into it and that he showed everyone

Covering both sides of the wood was the full text of a mass ceremony finely engraved in Coptic characters

The relief carving was returned to its sheath and then passed back through the grating where he leaned it against the wall

By triggering a simple release, the guard was able to shake a small mechanism in the lamp, which then threw off a series of fugitive flares regularly separated by three second intervals of near-extinction

The green tablet in his left hand, the ace of diamonds between the fingers of his right hand but held at a distance, Lucius moved closer to the lamp, raised his arms, and turned a little to the right

His profile now lost on his audience, he began to wave the two objects alongside each other as a way to use the ace of diamonds as a shield between the flame and the tablet

The performance's initial burst of energy was starting to subside

Microscopic points of red light, projected from the ace of diamonds with its tiny garnets encircling the opening, emphasized the surrounding shade of the paperboard

---

only is he capable of constructing the synth-device, but he's also got some kind of metempsychotic/poetic rhythm going, one where he's discovering a unique sense of measure while performing his live audio/visual remix. This brings to mind Robert Creeley, who once wrote: "I want, as Charles Olson says, to come into the world. Measure, then, is my testament." What Lucius wants, though, is to invent a mechanism that will enable his daughter to *come back* into the world.

As he moved the two objects in parallel before the flame, the experimental light show exhibited varying degrees of intensity, depending on what region of the garnets the flame was able to catch in the midst of his gestural dance

Moving the strange paperboard with its diamond cut right in the center, Lucius jabbed one of the gems at the highest mark of the tablet and kept it there for three loops of the fugitive flares

Various iterations and impromptu filter effects were conducted by the degree to which he waved the objects between and during the flare-ups

All of the marks from the punch on the wax tablet informed his sense of measure as he spontaneously decided which detailed spot would create which kind of effect as a result of how it was being shaped through this odd interaction between the various elements

Sometimes he would use two or more of the marks successively to create a specific lighting effect

Camera commented on the level of exertion being employed by the mad alchemist's live remix

Having taken responsibility for meticulously modeling the desired shape of the tablet by mixing an amalgam of red and green light synced with the fluid movements of his gestural dance with the two objects he still held in his hand, he was also imperceptibly heating the already softened wax tablet under the various marks, and in so doing completed the first work in a new series that would improve the future quality of his sound-art projects as well

Turning to his audience, Lucius placed the green tablet flat on the table and grabbed the acoustic device, which he then stroked gently over the tablet with the hanging needle dropping from the membraneous cone

The needle tip, stirring on the roughly grooved wax road, started transmitting vibrations to the membrane and escaping out of the open end of the cone was a woman's voice, similar to Monette's, clearly singing "I'm . . . waitin' for my man"

Through a process he was experimenting with before everyone's eyes, he kept moving the needle over the various impressions he had made on the wax and out of the cone came a variety of artificial human voices

He kept trying to find the right combination that would amalgamate into a replication of his daughter's voice

Earlier attempts at this oratory experiment led to multiple bouts of trial and error in hopes of discovering by sheer chance the stamp, the mark, the groove—the serial code closest to his ideal, one that would translate into a transmissible success

That is why, pronouncing the word "Sing," he quickly attempted to reproduce the sonorous model generously donated by Monette

Camera led the group away from Lucius, who was now out of sight and would, no doubt, obsessively pursue his research in solitude, using these latest vibratory tracks of experience to remix with all of the other moments that had come before

Wanting to stay within earshot of the guard just in case he needed to be alerted to any unexpected developments with the madman, the artist *cum* curatorial tour guide, Camera, wandered behind the group and began narrating some painful stories

* * *

A young visitor, Flora Jackson, had once begged Camera to use his illustrious scientific discoveries to save her husband who had gone mad as a result of a sudden misfortune

She said she was tired of visiting leading "specialists" and proceeded to share an emotionally gripping story

A fanatical member of the Leonardo da Vinci Society, the patient, Lucius Jackson, was simultaneously immersed in science and art, just like his idol who had made a unique mark on world history

Lucius, she said, was a painter and sculptor of considerable talent and as a scholar had made some valuable discoveries

He was a tender spouse and together they patiently waited over ten cruel years to finally conceive a baby

The birth of their daughter, Jeanne, filled their most ardent wishes

Neglecting his work, he became a devoted father watching his baby smile and absorbing the happiness that she exuded from the moment she was born

At last, there she was: the child they had so long desired

A year later, Lucius took Flora and Jeanne to London where he was commissioned to make a series of unique portraits and busts

Twice a week he went to a sumptuous residence in Kent County to paint a young lady, Lady Raleigh

One day, he requested and was approved to bring to the estate his wife and daughter who was still being breast-fed

The recipient of a warm reception, Flora, guided by Lord Raleigh, admired the details of the property grounds while Lucius was working on his model's eyes

Invited to stay for dinner, the visitors, who were about twenty miles from the nearest station, thought they should cut out at about ten that night

Midway through their passage in a thick, wooded area, they were forced off the road by three cars full of a lot of drunken voices screaming in unison

It was the rallying cry of the Red-Gang, whom had just a few minutes earlier been chased by a group of highway troopers

Impulsive and nervous, Lucius got out of his car and began shouting at the worked-up gang that surrounded him, but he was soon made aware of his own impotence

Flora, meanwhile, was fearfully clutching the sleepy Jeanne

At this point, seemingly out of nowhere, the gang leader was shot at twice by one of the other car's drivers and was critically wounded

Meanwhile, the nimble driver who shot him took off and disappeared into the night, trying in vain to swerve his vehicle away from the sound of bullets that were now tracing his exit

Reaching slightly in front of himself, but exasperated by the sight of his own blood, the drunken gang leader came over to Lucius and threw himself on top of him, accusing him, Lucius, of attacking him, and then, for no apparent reason, snatched the baby out of Flora's arms while he ordered his men to search their vehicle

Seeing the wounded gangbanger start punching his baby, who was now awakened by the contact and began to cry out, Lucius, freed of any need to embrace his nonviolent demeanor, jumped toward the attacker

It was at this time that he revealed a small dagger he had concealed in his hand as soon as they were surrounded by the gang, and which he at first aimed at the chest of Jeanne to distract the kidnapper, but then immediately brought the knife tip up to the face of the attacker and notched the blade into his cheek

He then moved the blade upwards so that it deeply penetrated his left eye

Discombobulated and mad with bloody rage, the gang leader single-handedly apprehended Lucius and moaned like a wild beast

Crazed beyond simple grief, the gang leader had dropped Jeanne, who was now screaming on the ground, and figured that, given all of the options at his disposal, the best way to weaken this couple would be to first execute the child

In a choked voice, he commanded to his band of thieves—while pointing to Jeanne:

"Let's do the jig"

At this point, the group of bandits, twelve in all, took their positions, two rows of six standing across from each other, and began a hellish, jittery dance around the child, who was sitting in the middle of the space they now controlled

Leaving two opposite corners, the gang leader and one of his sidekicks came diagonally into the middle, hopping and skipping toward the baby whom they fiercely struck with their boots and then their heels before hopping and skipping backward to their original posts

Then the next set of two diagonal partners skipped their way to the middle and performed an identical set of violent kicks

This routine was then followed by another set of partners until all of the gang members had participated in this murderous dance

The same couples then alternated a few times, performing various spins and/or mock greetings to themselves or even the baby before continuing their monstrous assault, destroying the tiny victim they angrily trampled and crushed under the weight of their entire bodies

The wounded gang leader was especially brutal, directing each one of his kicks at the baby's head or abdomen

After two went, another two would go, and then the rotation changed as they entered the stage from varying directions and positions and moved around from one end of the row to the other and sometimes across to the other line, exchanging partners completely

At some point, one of the more aggressive gang members provided a new element to their brutal game that would enable him to make more appearances while trampling the infant martyr

Everything began again as in the beginning, and the frightening jitter dance of the gang continued unabated before the disbelieving eyes of the parents

Thanks to the rotation established by the more frequent return of the aggressive dancer, all of the performers began successively hopping around the space like jacked-up pogo sticks, and as part of their drill-like choreography managed to torture Jeanne into an early and unforgettable oblivion

This cruel exercise was a sadistic version of the classic jig mixed with the jitterbug, various Scottish dances, and portmanteau punk moves that were probably still in cultural vitro

The atmosphere seemed to accelerate their nightmarish ballet as the madmen mutually cheered each other on, especially as new blood spurted out due to the nails embedded in their shoes ripping into the disfigured red blob on the ground

Suddenly there came into view a group of armed troopers waving revolvers, and the gang started to flee

Flora, rushing to her daughter, picked her up, alas!

What she was holding was a hideous, disfigured corpse covered with multiple bruises and wounds

Touching and looking at the child, Lucius was hit with total madness, and burst out laughing, imitating the dance steps of the heinous dancers

Bewildered, Flora threw Lucius and the dead baby into the car and drove off toward the castle where they had just come from while the troopers took off in all directions chasing after the cold-blooded murderers

Devoted and sympathizing, the Raleighs, staying up all night, sat with Flora and watched over Jeanne's body while trying to make sense of the demented minds that inflicted such a grave outcome

After the burial of the child, Flora, signing her testimony against the murderers, who had been deftly captured the night of the assault, made her way back to Paris, where she began trying to find a treatment that would cure her husband's intense mental illness

Now believing that he was the living embodiment of Leonardo da Vinci[86], the misfortune that had struck his family and killed his daughter obsessed

86. But is he not also projecting both Camera and, beyond all reason, Roussel as well?

Lucius' thoughts and this, he insisted, would lead him to more creative breakthroughs in both art and science

For two years, his treatment deemed unsuccessful in five asylums, Lucius tried to accelerate his research, but despite all of his attempts he was denied access to his art supplies

Extracting from this story the certainty that a cure could be found, Camera, instead of viewing the slightest annoyance as an enemy of progress, was, on the contrary, resolved to slavishly access even the most extravagant desires of the patient

To provide Lucius a deep, quiet and calm environment, he quickly built onto a high point in the park an adequate studio space with basic furniture and a large grid with two winged doors forming the facade up front from where he could view a vast expanse of green forest stretching out as far as the horizon

Once the patient was transferred, he was carefully guarded during the night hours, when he was able to absorb the invigorating smell of the outdoors

The next day, many disparate elements that he had laboriously compiled in a list were eagerly given to Cam

Not without traces of his past talent, he began painting a subject that could have been a future, more developed image of his daughter, spreading her wings toward the horizon as she reached out to take hold of a new dawn

As Camera learned during a series of healing therapy sessions that were soon started, the patient-as-painter evoked various iterations of Jeanne, who had been stolen in the wee hours of her life

With carving tools, he had fashioned a series of small, light figures dressed in various fragments of torn, thin balloon, and then used a metal tool to push the clothing into the figure while maintaining its delicate shape

Having patiently obtained the desired look and feel of one figurine, he continued working each successive piece that, thanks to its elasticity, allowed for a carefully detailed outcome

Blurring the edges in order to weld them, without forgetting to ballast each foot with just enough fine sand to assure its relative stability, he blew inside the body before quickly closing the hole completely—but knowing he could reopen it as necessary in case he needed to readjust the interior elements—then proceeded to engage in a detailed and colorful customization of each figure's costume design

Soon he had twelve almost imponderable subjects evoking all of the harmful beasts he had previously encountered

Then, laying the figurines down on the marble table, he created a series of vertical heat currents

He put to use one plate sheet that was adorned with red charcoal, two andirons, and a piece of grey window screen that was wisely pierced with many tiny holes so that he could run his dolls via a clever carousel derived from the movement of his fingers on the screen, thus mimicking the hodgepodge jig of the bandits by way of the figurines that, becoming more animated over time, made obvious this important fact to Camera: besieged by the double sense of grief and universal otherness, the pseudo-Leonardo, as a sculptor and painter, was creating characters that were able to reproduce the image of the fatal jig

In requesting on his list a piece of window screen for his collaged object d'art, and specifying a grey tint that would be indifferent to the flitting dirty ashes from below it, Lucius revealed an intuitive and practical sensibility that Camera considered to be a positive step in his healing process

He thought his patient had chosen a material that would resist the embers below but also maintain enough flexibility to accommodate the vagabond fingers traversing on top of it in order to find clever shortcuts for the figures to make their moves and skew in various directions

Suddenly, whenever he dropped the screen, Lucius went through a terrible crisis in which, due to reflexes that accompanied the powerful effects engendered by hallucinations of the deathly scene that kept agitating him, twelve hairs on his balding head stood up and began dancing an uncontrollable jitter on the top of his smooth head, similar in all aspects to the assailant's

Therefore, at the end of every day, under the influence of a reverie caused by the disturbing events that had taken place, the progressing virtuoso would burn the embers below his head and slowly perform with his fingers a reenactment of the fatal jig, inevitably followed by the same capillary crisis

* * *

An eccentric morning would consist of a piece of cloth, scissors, and a complex array of chemicals and laboratory instruments

Engaging in numerous manipulations, he would create with one hand more colorful mixtures, and in the other, a rigid, white Pharaoh snake made of loose wire that he could use to perform a series of fast cuts and stitchings that then enabled him to successfully make many works of magical fabric art that to some resembled something like explosive lingerie

A skillful question was being proposed by the antics of the madman and Cam, the artist-doctor, had come up with the answer to the patient's riddle: sometimes believing in the imminent rebirth of his daughter, the result of a peculiar obsession associated with his mental disorder, Lucius would sew together a pseudo-baby in haste, tapping into the scientific side of his bicameral personality, and in the process conduct a remarkable invention

In spite of taking ultra care with his meticulous performances and necessary upkeep of the facility, a phenomenon of oxidation occurred, due to the continued manufacturing of the strange chemical mixtures in the room, and soon even the iron grid was rusting, including its hinges, and the routine was eventually paralyzed

A bunch of other hinges were made out of various metals but they all too completely deteriorated except for, finally, ones made of solid gold, which Camera adopted due to their perfect functioning

Lucius then received, to cut his cloth, a pair of solid, well-sharpened, gold scissors

* * *

Flora had been receiving updates on the patient's therapeutic recovery without having to visit him

One day, at Camera's request, she brought over some strange vessels and other materials, the purpose of which, according to Lucius, who had requested them the day before and that he had been working with before the fateful trip to England, was to create an artificial language that would be transmitted via a vocal device that would literally speak this artificial language

Not satisfied with the package he had received, the madman, with an insistent tone, uttered this word over and over again, each time more nuanced than the last: "rod"

When informed of this detail, Flora remembered that when, back in saner days, he was diligently handling these materials, Lucius planned to manufacture an elastic material that one could manipulate at will as part of an alternative measuring scheme

When matched with a subtle phono-arithmetical logic, this elastic measuring instrument would have, even when reduced in scale, the same cutting effect as older measuring apparatuses still in use

The next day, with his sharp gold scissors, the nutcase of a man carved a piece of bacon fat brought to him at his request and that he then dried thoroughly

He embedded a small ruler into the lard that he then transformed into a customized measuring apparatus with red-lined divisions made on one of its sides

With this measuring rod and the last items he received, he then sequestered himself into his delicate practice which, based on some whacked-out calculations of distance and heat, tended to print on to the green tablet an artificial code generating newly fabricated verbs intoned from abstract musical marks

His wise preference for bacon was highlighted by the fact that, as a material, it had a more resistant elasticity which, for his purposes, was a desirable quality

Now the sole purpose of this unfortunate man, and this came out in his incoherent soliloquies, was to reproduce the voice of his daughter as it had been revealed to his ear the last time in her life she was talking to him

With an endless variety of tones and intonations created out of all kinds of fragmented markings, code, stamps, and measurements that would ideally translate into something like his infant daughter's musical voice or at least something resembling baby-speak, he was hoping to find, by sheer luck, among all of the elements he was experimenting with, a sound indication that he was on the right track

These procedures, when combined with all of his other obsessions, were still related to the second coming of the scientific and artistic genius he imagined himself to be

In the meantime, he worked on this mechanical baby vocoder by implementing the rusty metal dissimulation machine with its hanging needle, thin wooden handle, vibrating membrane, and unalterable golden dream

* * *

One evening, Lucius described and soon claimed some heavy old piece of memorabilia that in his mind he associated with the baptism of his child

Once, in Egypt, some Coptic priests, who were then officiating, had made for themselves an engraving of their mass text on both sides of a nicely cut piece of old sycamore wood

The engraving was in their specific language

Piously considered the spirit of the holy sacrifice in power because it contained a hauntological aura among its carved phrases, the piece of wood was carefully slipped into a sheath of silk adorned with the Latin word "Mens" and placed gracefully among other embroidered embellishments

Lucius had given Flora, remembering the baptism of Jeanne, a replica of this work that he had once found, its sheath intact, in the collection of an antique dealer

The wood and sheath were given to the patient who, often taken over by delusions and manic depression, would smile at these priceless artifacts that unconsciously provided a kind of serene escape mechanism devoted to the memory of his daughter

The glory of discovery associated with these very peculiar methods convinced Camera that this sick soul was well on the road to a complete recovery

* * *

At this moment, a loud cry from Lucius was heard and attracted the entire group back toward the big room he was stationed in, and soon everyone was standing before the large grid with its rusty gold hinges

On the green tablet the onlookers saw a new series of marks, evidently due to the slow melting away of other lines, as well as his use of the punch, the small rod, the lamp, and the ace of diamonds

Very agitated, Lucius slid on this newest series of markings the tip of the needle and touching on the extreme bottom portion of these marks produced a vocal projection, the vowel "a" being drawn out in one long syllable that, recalling the beginnings of a smile and sound made by eager young children who are still learning to speak, slightly resembled the vocalization of the word "I'm," but pronounced more like "Aaaaahm"

The demented artist uttered a second cry similar to the one caused by what he had heard earlier when first encountering the monosyllabic yet joyful accent

Distraught at the thought of having achieved his immediate goal, he murmured:

"Her voice . . . it is her voice . . . the voice of my daughter"

Then, panting, he felt her presence and uttered these tender words:

"You, my Jeanne . . . they have not killed you . . . You are here . . . near me . . . Speak, my dearest . . . "

And between these interspersed elliptical phrases, repeated endlessly, was a wordless draft that responded in kind

Camera, speaking low, suggested that everyone quietly begin to leave this beneficial scene in peace

He congratulated Monette for the way her singing and openminded participation in the creative process led to this happy event that would likely hasten the recovery of the patient[87]

Then the group made its way to a new path and began a long descent

87. Why is Camera so attached to the recovery of this one specific character? And why does Roussel give him his own chapter? In "Trans-Subjective Transferential Borderspace," Ettinger writes:

> The artist is a patient [. . .] The therapy that the artist offers consists in inventing, through 'a new vision', a people that is lacking, inventing 'a possibility of life' hollowed out by a kind of foreign language within a language, by 'a becoming-other of language' that opens 'an outside or flipside consisting of Visions and Hearings . . . These visions are not phantasies, but veritable Ideas constituted by the passage of life into language'. The Ideas are not phantasies, but they are analogous to them.

"This sick soul" referred to in the novel could be all three of them (Lucius, Camera, Raymond). Immediately following the quote above, Ettinger continues: "The artist is *a doctor and a patient*, re-distributing a multiple-several and shared *sinthôme* where the drive and desire meets a Thing on the screen of phantasy, or where the symptom and phantasy share a fate, offering this conjunction, diffracted and transformed, via artwork." Ettinger footnotes the term *sinthôme* and writes, "*Sinthôme* is Lacan's return to an ancient term which he uses to describe the symptom, as transformed by the writer into a piece of literature. It plays on *saint homme* (saintly man) and the English *sin* (sinful man), and refers to psychosis." Normally, I would avoid this type of Lacanian reading of anything remotely literary, similar to the way I have taken leave of other responsibilities as touched upon in note 81, but something I have turned to time and again in my auto-translations and remixes is spontaneous sampling of source material encountered via random searching and surfing of the Internet, and Ettinger, who has appeared in my prior works, keeps popping up, so in a way, her inclusion here is the result of another kind of determined indeterminacy.

6

The night came readymade with the moon, almost full, shining beautifully in a cloudless sky[88]

Once again treading the lower regions of the large park grounds, the group saw, at some distance away near a river lined with rocks, an old pauper with a mop of gray hair, working away while sitting at a cluttered table, some-

88. It gives me great pleasure to readwrite this opening line of Chapter Six, to remind myself how the auto-translation triggered an unexpected poetic use of the Duchampian term *readymade* and meta-reflected on one of the central discoveries I made during the writing of *Locus Solus*, namely, that all of Roussel's text was my own readymade, one I had at first intuitively selected for reasons that had more to do with escaping the headaches I was experiencing from my sudden call to jury duty, but that I then became more invested in as I began filtering (flirting with) the novel's source material through my remixological apparatus. The idea of "treating" Roussel as a readymade patient was one of the principal motivating factors that kept me engaged with the performance throughout the four months of its making. Having said that, with Duchamp, the readymade was usually selected through a filter whose emotional effects might best be expressed as *indifferent*, whereas for me, the translation process, the creative act of sampling and manipulating Roussel's linguistically triggered machine-fictions through a palette of signature-filters, felt absolutely subjective, and became a kind of ritualistic practice that channeled my energy in the direction of a series of chance occurrences brought about by the online programs I was using and that I came to embrace as my daily bread to feed of off as I sustained the / his / my / our narrative.

In this regard, the readymade is transformed into the remixological, and thus ceases being a modern gesture.

how positioned between a svelte black woman showing off her bare arms and a beautiful child who must have been about twelve years old and who was dressed in rags

Camera introduced the group to the three characters, who were quite far away

One Sunday evening, in Marseille, at the end of a recent trip, the artist had noticed in the middle of a rally there, a certain Meta Bliss, the popular new age sorceress who was trying to exercise what she deemed "the art of divination" out in the open air with the help of her little grandson, Luke[89]

Taking into consideration the charlatan qualities of her practice, Camera was struck by some of her methods, which he imagined using in his own artwork

When she was through, the crowd dispersed and he made a deal with the sorceress that would include his unreserved support for the child

Brought to Locus Solus, Meta Bliss and Luke, by their good offices, were able to help realize the hopes of the artist-guru, whose direction they were now under

The black woman was a young Sudanese named Samiya[90]

* * *

With everyone watching it happen in realtime, Bliss was arranging a page that she covered with mysterious numbers and figures

Then, taking four medium-sized eggs with thick hard shells, she put them in a basket as if aligning them with the tilt of the table and opened the door of a large cage where a bird came out in its multicolored plumage

89. Once I realized that I would be able to translate the sorceress as Meta Bliss, I knew it would open up my ongoing interest in the relationship between what the new age community refers to as creative visualization and what I, in *META/DATA*, refer to as *unconscious readiness potential* (see notes 57 and 58). I have already explored prophetic writing in relation to sorcery in "Nutrience," the opening section to my second novel, *Sexual Blood*, where the Medicine Woman opens her womb up to the play-giaristic performer, Maldoror, who I ripped from Lautréamont (in fact, the follow-up section to "Nutrience" is titled "The Songs of Maldoror" which was actually the original title of the novel). I was hoping Meta Bliss would easily become a kind of fictional reincarnation of my own Medicine Woman, but this was not to be. Still, in many ways, they are two sides of the same coin.

90. The character, Samiya, was perhaps the most difficult for me to write *through*. Roussel came from a different time and it shows here more than perhaps anywhere else in the text—and this note has very little to do with my higher education experiences referred to in note 81.

There was a vague similarity between this bird and a peacock, and the animal was presented to the group as a rare tropical bird whose name meant something like "the thousand tones of its integument" or, alternatively, "the varying tones of its integument"

Prodigiously developed, the caudal apparatus appeared composed of a kind of solid cartilage frame expanding vertically up and creating a shield-like canopy

In the inner part of the shield was bare skin-like material while the outer layer had long tufted feathers thrown back against a thick bush of fabulous hair

The extreme anterior portion of the frame was very sharp and ran parallel to the table, forming a kind of small arched knife

A horizontal gold plate was set under the canopy and secured by several screws piercing its edges and swung around as if being manipulated by some strange magnetic force

On the plate moved a heavy mass of water, perhaps half a liter, that also behaved oddly, as if despite its volume it were composed of a simple drop on a fingertip

Stopped in front of the first egg, the tropical bird (referred to as an iriselle or iriseaux), inclined to play it safe, gently attacked the egg with the edge of its knife-like tail, which it utilized from over and beyond the front of its head

Encountering resistance, she began again, approaching it with all of her energy and singleminded goal to penetrate the solid shell that she was prepared to cut into with the sharp edge of her tail

These inconsistent movements disrupted the water mass on the gold plate, which furiously tossed about in all directions, enveloping the egg and then spreading on the table but without ever separating itself from the gold plate even taking over parts of the nearby air, which the bird then followed, all of it happening without leaving a wet track and recomposing as soon as the bird's tail had stabilized and gained back its steady momentum

After a series of efforts, meticulously measured by the iriselle, the shell finally began to show a slight crack

Moving a few steps over, the iriselle attacked the second egg in the same exact way and cut into the shell immediately

She performed a similar triumph on the third egg, always proceeding ahead with caution, and incisively made a thin cut as if now performing the procedure on autopilot

During the entire culinary dance, despite the occasional fluttering and performative gyrations, the water remained faithfully glued to the gold plate

Placed back in the cage by Bliss with only one single egg remaining intact, the iriselle began to sit on the egg, so it would eventually hatch, while Luke took the other three now worthless eggs and threw them into the river

Camera spoke to the group about what he perceived to be a surprising amount of volatility from the bird, which, behind the bars of the cage, was still attracting everyone's intrigued looks

* * *

In Marseille, Luke, for a minimum wage, would sometimes help with the unloading of ships albeit under the watchful eye of Meta Bliss

Contributing his labor one day among the panting of steamers, on the boy's tenth trip he appeared at the end of a footbridge carrying a crate, whose interior contents had fascinated him, on his shoulder

As he ran to his grandmother to share with her the amazing crate he had on him, a crack in the structure gave way to two eggs that fell out of the crack and hit the ground without breaking

The eggs were immediately picked up by Bliss

Luke showed her the insides of the container that, topped with water and grain, had two birds with a spectacular plumage and that were adorned with an unusual tail that formed a canopy above them

A few eggs, finely cut, lay beneath their feet, while others remained intact and were collected by the sorceress

Meanwhile one of the captive birds went back to hatching and seemed satisfied that its task would no longer be interrupted

Thinking about how she could exhibit birds similar to the ones in the crate, Bliss thought about how the two eggs she was holding had such strong shells and had resisted breaking when falling to the ground

She decided to have these eggs hatched by a hen and eventually a male and female were born that would enable her to reproduce these unusual creatures

As soon as they were adults, the two birds, given room to roam a spacious cage just like their own parents, were successfully presented before curious onlookers

One morning, Bliss noticed the female, who was a great layer of eggs, strangely attack a group of seven eggs with the natural edge of the anterior part of her knife-tail, and she successfully cut into four of the seven shells

The three eggs that stood firm during her assault were then chosen to be hatched by the beautiful beast

The new-age prophet in her wanted to take advantage of what she was witnessing, to view it as an emerging form of freaky performance bird-art, one that she would just ride out for its weirdness and that she mentally recorded without fully understanding its true purpose

With all of the egg laying, the public exhibition would come across with some confusion, since there was only a partial breaking of the shells, which led to speculation about why the bird was so anxious and if she was perhaps revealing some kind of prophesy tied to the number of eggs that remained intact and ready for hatching

Camera wondered about the causal relationship between these instinctive maneuvers, which were being performed right under his eyes, and he brought this issue up with Bliss the night of his first interview with her

Being a patient observer, he discovered that small creatures, instead of using their beaks, which were always fragile, would break the shell with a bold assault of the front of their tails

Moreover, even in adults, the atrophic weakness of very short beaks were contrasted with the extreme force of the caudal gear

In the presence of their new artist-master, one of the iriselles[91], once having to fight against a dog, had employed the use of his over-the-head knife-tail as a weapon of defense and attack, not once using his mandibles

This was the way they would act against all of their enemies in the forests this eccentric species had come from

91. The emergence of the iriseaux / iriselles in the story gave this section a different hue, one I had not anticipated, but then again, who knew what to anticipate in this narrative of endless surprise? I was delighted with their presence the way I was delighted to visit Flamingo Park while growing up in Miami, hanging out with the beautiful peacocks and other assorted fauna. Little did I know as a child chasing the peacocks in Flamingo Park that only a few years later I would be working full time at the Greyhound race track (for more on this time of my life, see my novel *My Oblivion, the Life and Times of David Star, Conceptual Artist*, unpublished).

Camera realized that the female, to prevent premature births, eliminated the relatively frail shells, which were prone to breaking early, and would birth insufficiently developed babies who would be sentenced to a life of rickets and suffering

By artificially hatching all of the eggs of a clutch before the attractive mother, he saw that indeed those who tried to escape their oval prison too early were born quite small and sickly, while the others who burst forth notably late appeared full of exuberant strength

The shells of these stronger, latter babies were endowed with a thickness that would remain intact when clashing with the carefully calculated attacks by their mother who, however, would also cut into those early arrivals who were more delicate and fine

More than anything, the extravagant stirrings of the female that had caused her eggs to reveal the destiny of those inside had impressed Camera in his study of the iriseaux

Convinced that nowhere in nature were there similar mixtures of supreme swiveling and perfectly calculated movements, the artist wanted to take advantage of the opportunity to fully highlight the full value of a certain property owned by the troubling subject of a recent discovery that this passage of Herodotus had suggested for prosecution:

In the year 550, after conquering the Medes, Cyrus, visiting Ecbatane, saw in the palaces and temples—in a thousand different renderings—a striking profusion of gold

Wanting to know the provenance of so much precious metal, he learned about the existence of an opulent but now exhausted mine resting under Mount Arouastou

As one might have anticipated, he really distrusted the rumor suggesting that the deposit mine had been rendered sterile, so Cyrus figured that a potentially rich vein as that mine was probably still worth something and, ignoring the stories of it being totally depleted, went with a host of workers to the mine's location near the mountain

Having actually found the mine stripped down to its most secret impasses, he had his men dig further into new galleries and was soon able to admire a huge, weighty block of gold captured at a great depth by one of his teams

But subsequent explorations into the mine that led the teams in many different directions were ultimately unsuccessful in their search, and so he returned to Ecbatane with his one unique specimen

In keeping with an ancient tradition, Cyrus was forced to capitalize on his find and would soon receive with magnificence the top of a makeshift throne on the public square, a humble tribute to this great kingdom in the presence of the people assembled there, and then, in a single gulp, he would be asked to drink from a precious vessel filled with water from the most significant river artery in the region

The conqueror, by equating his own presence with that of the nation itself, would take symbolic possession of the conquered country

Eager to keep digging in the mine at Mount Arouastou, in the event that it may not have been exhausted—and could just as easily be extracted in haste by some future exploitation of Mother Nature's devastating floods—Cyrus would leave Ecbatane to its usual solemnity, where it would channel the water of Choaspes into a large tributary of the Tiger River

This time, instead of taking any bowl for his iconic swig, he forged a cut into the block of gold he had brought from the mine

He would drink the water from the Choaspes, in a container made of recently extracted precious metal from what was also the slave region, as a symbolic gesture of strengthening the significance of his act

On the said day of his coronation, before a huge crowd, a draped throne full of rich fabrics shone in the sun in the heart of Ecbatane

Cyrus took his place at a marble table where there stood the golden bowl filled with water from the Choaspes and a parade of Medes dignitaries presented themselves to the new ruler

After the parade ended, Cyrus, amid great silence, brought the cup to his lips

But it was all in vain as he threw his head back to drink the water only to find that it was retained in the bowl by a strange force that would not allow it to enter his throat

Confused and disturbed, he threw aside the gold object and immediately heard a collective cry of surprise from the crowd: the water in the bowl, without falling, actually hung below the bowl, which turned on its side and, at first, frightened Cyrus, who then passed it around for everyone to see

The water had slipped outside the parameter of the precious metal but was somehow balanced in parallel to it

The gold was an invincible and mysterious attraction on the body of water

Convinced that, by decree of the Gods, Cyrus was not being permitted to drink the water from the Choaspes and therefore had no firm ground to stand on, the Medes were now emboldened, and immediately outlined their revolutionary movement

It was with great difficulty that the Persian soldiers attempted to defend Cyrus's throne against the attacks of the multitude

Annoyingly impressed by the sequence of events, the conqueror left the next day to another country, but left a strong garrison in place to resist the nascent rebellion

Whatever the case, from that point on, Cyrus never managed to gain the respect and submission of the Medes dignitaries who, approaching each day with more confidence after having witnessed the episode with the golden bowl, would now work secretively and tirelessly to take shake the yoke off the Persians

Herodotus therefore presented his legend as pure fact

But according to Camera, even though nothing in the scientific literature suggested that any gold compound was composed of special chemical elements that would lead to the powerful attraction of any liquid mass, he still considered the wild idea to be plausible and, aware of the risky nature of pursuing this line of inquiry, he still thought it was defensible to examine the most secret recesses of the famous mine for a secondary ingot that would abduct the water in such a manner

He shared his plan with the archaeologist Derrida, and soon they were ready to undertake a series of excavations not far from Mount Tough, which was none other than the former Mount Arouastou

Excited by the entire program, Derrida, once on site, dug the ground at what he was sure was the exact place suggested by Herodotus where Cyrus and his team had extracted the solid block of gold

After long and active surveys, the archaeologist found a heavy nugget, which he showed to Camera, who hastened to dispatch it and draw water with force

The artist vigorously shook the precious specimen around in a full bowl and saw the mass of water collect and jump out in all directions and then faithfully return to the subdued state of gold

Continuous and stylized gestures being necessary to highlight the gravitational virtues of this curious metal substance, Camera tried to force the point by playing his most capricious hand as it frequently enacted new twists and turns

But his gestures, by being so self-conscious, appeared to lower the potential of maintaining the rendered effect, not leaving to chance a more unexpected state of turmoil that would unreservedly lack purpose and thus seem more random and natural

However, any person, even the dim or insane, would perform similarly if they were acting with the full knowledge of the facts playing out before their eyes, turning themselves into something like a machine that would invariably and inevitably repeat the same precise procedure and go against the grain of a randomized natural phenomenon

Only an animal, alive and uncomprehending at the same time, could give to the experimental operation what it required to successfully measure the discovery's potential impact

Having received the nugget shortly after his return from Marseille, and coincidentally right at the time of his increased studies of the iriseaux, Camera used his judgment to determine that the crazy caudal developments of the female with her eggs would give him unexpected results by bringing with her the anxious feelings necessary to launch these water antics

He transformed the nugget into a special plate that he then set underneath the bird's natural canopy and poured the entire contents of a bottle of water on to the plate

The strange tail, too powerful to suffer from its double overload, ardently attacked the egg shells and in the process created a kind of transitory 3–D print of the water as it hung in mid-air with each strike of the knife-tail

These were exactly the kind of visual effects and scientific renderings Camera was after

Seduced by this quick scene in the distance, Camera indicated—for no apparent reason—that today's events had contributed to "a faithful recovery "

Quiet in her cage, the iriselle was simmering her egg so calmly that the water barely moved under the gold plate

* * *

With both hands on the table, Bliss grabbed a bunch of nettles and seized them by the stems so that they looked like an intentional assemblage joined by a thin rod of wire coils extending from its midst

The old woman, committed to guessing the character of each member of the visiting group by reading some magic into whatever data presented itself to her, extended the flowers to Duke, the experimental poet in the group and who was clearly captivated by her presence

She presented the free end of the floral arrangement as if they were all of the same moving piece, constantly using her hands to shift each flower between or behind another with a rare dexterity

Having chosen one for himself, Duke, at the behest of Bliss, accidentally poked the spiky end of the nettle against the bare arm of Luke who had just appeared near the transaction

The sorceress then showed the group that the nettle sting prompted some red marks to form on Luke's skin, and these spelled out, in small, uneven caps, this phrase:

WAVERS

COWARDLY

Then, in a sententious, accusatory tirade, she proceeded to "treat" what she described as Duke's "indecisive mind"

That one aphorism followed by Bliss's slightly overdetermined freak-out caused a unanimous laughter to rise from the group and Duke pretended he was some kind of victor, even though he knew he had somehow failed

The poet was, in fact, a spirited conversationalist, whose main enemies were the stereotypes he held on the tip of his tongue, though he delivered his dialog with an unexpected charm, suffused with a thousand preposterous theories

A mystery still wrapped itself around the sudden appearance of the letters on the skin because the nettle, when seen in close-up, did not appear to be abnormal

Seeing everyone's slight discomfort, driven by their pity for poor Luke who was now scratching at the bruise, Camera stopped Bliss and indicated that he was ready to continue his investigation with his excited audience so as to reveal the secret behind the stinging skin inscription

The sorceress, meanwhile, having studied her audience members from the beginning of the shenanigans, had quickly discerned the behavioral traits and attitudes of each flâneur

Seeing Camera finish his remarks, she approached the spiky bouquet with skilled movements and presented another nettle as if *forcing a card* on the hand that was about to pick from the stack

Leaving open different spaces on the nettle head so that it formed a kind of printing block with all uppercase letters, Bliss had previously brushed each nettle with a mysterious, colorless potion that would both clean the leaves and cause the plant to secret some of its sharp hairs

The end result was what appeared to be a normal nettle but was in fact a customized typographical head that she had coated in such a way that only certain parts of the head would actually sting the skin

So when Luke's skin was momentarily branded by undergoing the irritating effect of being stung by only those places that were still active, the red inscription would magically appear as a harmless result of the inoffensive brushwork of the perpetrator, whom she was clearly fooling

Strongly-worded categories of personal defects were thus included in the whole bunch

However, one could better symbolize the paradox of cowardly behavior by tapping into the most intangible histories of military glory

Still, several disconcerting traits exhibited toward the iriselle by the imperturbable Duke must have guided the fateful nettle his way

* * *

Storing the nettles away, the sorceress brought out a high, narrow box made of old leather with its cover missing

This was a game of tarot and she put one of the cards flat on the table

Soon a kind of Argentinian music was being transmitted from the map on the card, although there was no abnormal thickness there to suggest the presence of an inner mechanism

Amidst the seeming incoherence triggered by the whims of the improviser and her living creatures, the air, tinged with a fault free harmonization, softly unfolded its ambience

A second tarot, placed near the first, played a warning sound

Other, successive cards were played and emitted their own discreet piece of pure and metallic sounds

The effect was similar to a kind of avant-garde noise band[92]

92. Roussel's use of audio throughout the novel further piqued my interest. Don't forget, I was reading him for the first time, and coming from an experimental sound art background (among other things), the inclusion of these devices such as

An indie noise band sound emerged as each card took its place in the set and, sooner or later, took over the symphony by dragging its sound out or brightly raising its volume with happy tones or even dark drones, including the unexpected, almost hesitant, extended note that would betray the personal intentions of its maker's animated style

Never quite overstepping the imaginary boundary that would crush the listener's ear and just confusing enough to alter one's aural state by layering the audioscape with multiple ensembles, those who had already been sapped of energy due to everything else that had been going on throughout the tour were too weak to really let something like this orchestration of simultaneous effects annoy them

The blatant localization of each sound emitting its spirited noise from within the confines of each tarot created, against all probability, a miraculously flat musical apparatus

As Bliss kept her groove and randomly displayed, side by side, the main face for the *hermit* and the *sun*, the *moon* and the *devil*, the *fool* and *judgment*, the *Pope* and the *wheel of fortune*, Camera opened, after taking it from the table not far from an ivory spatula, some round metal box full of white powder, which he indicated was a faithful reproduction of one of the famous inventions of Paracelse, that is, a magic preparation to assist in the secretion of a variety of organo-therapeutic remedies

The spatula served him well as he used it to withdraw from within the box and then extend into the light a heavy dose of the powder, which he then spread on the forearm of the negress Samiya covering a large area of her skin

Then the mad scientist patiently waited until the effect of this external application took hold while Luke picked up a large black cover standing on the ground against one of the table's legs and hid himself in it

The tarot cards, exhaling at will their defamiliarized noise composition, performed an amplified concert that was now being gradually decomposed by

---

the sound-art cards, Lucius' wax tablet and rudimentary phonograph, and the discs made of tissue projecting from the various glass walls enclosing the *tableaux vivants*, indicated a sensitivity to the aural capacities of the various installations and scenes in the literary composition. A question I had asked myself when writing *Sexual Blood*, was, "How can I literally get sound into the novel?" I had to settle for placing it in the text *literarily* by way of typographical composition tricks, and it was only when I eventually opened up *GRAMMATRON* to the World Wide Web that I was finally able to put real sound into my fictional narratives.

Bliss who, listening to each card closely, began comparing the talent of each and took to eliminating those whose pace went against the rest of the group, abruptly silencing them by simply picking them up off the table

Soon all that remained was an elaborate horn section which were themselves picked off one by one until all that was left was a tarot designed as the *House of God*, a kind of *allegro vivace* prevailing in its joyful gusto

Gifted with its strange powers of penetration, the powder quickly found its way into the skin of the Sudanese[93]

When the last grain was absorbed, Camera made a sign to Bliss who, leaning toward the table, sang very close to the transmitting *House of God*, vocalizing a tender, melancholic pattern that immediately disrupted the card's allegro, which didn't seem to matter much since the tarot, now abandoning any harmonic convergence, just kept flawlessly playing at full volume its acute and grave octaves, a slow blowing and plaintive melody that, when imprinted, would symbolize a great nostalgic charm, which could be noted as thus:

From the first notes, eight circles of bright emerald green, smaller than rings, had appeared horizontally above the tarot, deprived of any visible link with them

Thin halos about three millimeters wide then dominated the colored surface, marking the center of eight imaginary squares that, two by two, symmetrically divided the entire area of the card

Bliss indefinitely repeated sixteen measures, leaving in her wake the docile tarot performer

The halos, very intense, generated a powerful green light

It seemed like the same melody was constantly being emitted by this enigmatic green brilliance operating on autopilot

Luke, suddenly prompted by Camera, came out of the black cover he had hidden himself in like a kind of loose jacket, holding a lavishly framed painting that he offered directly to Samiya

93. WTF?

The moonlight on the canvas was splendidly rendered and the piece was signed by Vollon in stricken relief

In an African setting, a young black dancer, surrounded by some wild monarch installed right in the middle of the image, was perilously balancing on top of her head three simple baskets, each containing a heavy stock of native fruits arranged in a slender pyramid

A big red berry appeared to be accidentally falling off the top of the heap, which terrified the ballerina who, at gunpoint, must have been rushing to move the goods to their destination

The entire painting was loaded with a rare energy and the expression of fear in the dancer's eyes exhibited a supreme intensity, though the fruits above her also revealed the special gifts of the artist to create still-lives while, rising halfway from the back of the landscape, a dazzling purple suggested the fugitive bay

Suddenly, everyone's eyes were drawn by a deafening moan that came from Sayima, who was suffering from a terrible crisis

Her eyes assiduously affixed on the table where the horror was unfolding, barely able to breathe, she started convulsing

Camera, eavesdropping with visible joy at the sight of these sudden symptoms, showed the group that, under the grip of an unrelenting terror, the Sudaese's arm was full of goosebumps

With half closed hands, Bliss was now holding the *House of God* tarot at the extreme end of her ten fingers

Applying her voice to the same tune she had been singing as a counterpoint to the musical tarot, the old woman was able to keep alive the vital halo-effect

Lowering his head to look from above while horizontally holding out the arm of Sayima, Camera slowly angled a halo on the tarot over a portion of the skin hidden by the white powder until it touched it

Observing the manner in which things were evolving, the group saw the halo dig into the skin, without causing any apparent pain or bloodshed, while it formed a deep cavity in the shape of a cone whose bright green circle had constituted its base

Soon, from the very top of this crater, a red blood cell formed and fell on the *House of God*, which led to a triumphant exclamation by Camera, who then slightly raised the arm of the Sudanese only to lower it again after a slight horizontal displacement

Over the same halo, a new cavity was formed and another red blood cell appeared on top if it

The same swift maneuvers were executed as before

Without necessarily repeating the same experiments of Paracelsus before him, Cam faithfully stuck to his strategic action, forming and opening cavities in Samiya's skin and always holding her black arm in parallel to the tarot card by mounting it with a slow vertical descent

All the same, the conical hollows were slowly closing without a trace as soon as they released their red blood cell, which slumped on to the card at the exact center of the same green halo

Camera acted with haste so as to capitalize on the fleeting phenomenon

The red globules lying in sturdy heaps on the *House of God* burned on eight bold echoes of the beautiful green halos whose eternal theme had stimulated Bliss

Finally Camera marked the end of the experiment and abandoned it immediately while Samiya, looking at the tragic story playing out on the canvas revealed by Luke, felt a sudden calm just at the moment she might have suffered from an imminent nervous breakdown

As Bliss suddenly stopped singing, the tarot, distraught, sought unsuccessfully to proceed without any guidance on where to go next

After unsuccessful efforts to pull together its prior thread of musical phraseology, it relapsed into its former noise aesthetic before the green halos went out

Camera started walking toward the river but the group demanded that he not leave the red blood cells on the tarot for other eyes to see

Someone mentioned the issue of "future testimony" and "witnesses"

Then everyone followed Bliss as she carefully held out on the end of her ten fingers the *House of God*, which seemed permanently attached to each and every eye looking at it while they kept walking

Arriving after fifty or so steps to the rocks of the river bank, the group had, at the request of Camera, one by one, while all of the others kept watching the globules, taken a quick look at the absolute vacuity of a small, artificial excavation that, without any explosives, was presented as if it had been blasted open

Leaning the *House of God* just right in the desired direction, Bliss let the red blood cells roll off into the hole below and Camera, after having set a match aflame, asked the group to take caution as he announced an inevitable explosion that would soon take place before them

There, while the tinder smoldered, the artist-guru, to assure collective patience, revealed to the group the following events

* * *

One morning, in one of the beautiful streets of Marseille, the inventive Bliss saw a flat watch whose exposed profile behind the glass of the great watchmaker Frankel revealed the obvious presence of a complex mechanism in a micro thin case

She decided then and there to find a way to enhance its compressor process by creating an infra-thin[94] musical device that would be undetectable when inserted inside certain kinds of tarot cards, which she put to use each day as part of her ongoing prophetic performance-art project

Feeling subordinated to the nature and rhythm of the tunes that would be emitted from the cards, it would be necessary for those who would monitor its strange magical effects in realtime to immerse themselves in its alien power

To maintain this power, then, she decided that the sounds would need to affect a dissonant style of music that exhibited a fortuitous inconsistency, the kind that would never be presented in a normal composition performed by predictable audio mechanisms

Five floors below his garret, housed in a powder store, lived the old bookseller Banks, who was a buyer of countless remaindered titles that he resold at bargain prices

Visiting Banks, whom she was sometimes close with, Bliss asked about a book on insects for her forthcoming art project

94. Duchamp: "The possible, implying the becoming—the passage from one to the other takes place in the infra-thin." If only there were an infra-thin interval that separated Roussel's "original" from my own version, but I suspect that's unreasonable, especially since I am seeking the opposite of "identicality," to use Duchamp's term, and am, in fact, using the writing performance as a *moving away* from a determinable infra-thin difference even if there exists something like the crude conception of the *déja vu* which emerges from a generic grouping (2 scenes, 2 stories, 2 men, 2 novelistic performances triggered by mechanical means).

The old man gave her several well-illustrated treatises on entomology and told her she could browse through them at her leisure

As a result of some of her research, she came upon an illustration of an insect that resembled a natural emerald, one that caught her attention due the extreme flatness of its body

A brief text framing the picture of the drawing spoke of "The Emerald, a parasitic Caledonian wintergreen, native to central Scotland," one that "was gifted at night with an intermittent phosphorescence that when touched at any point would create above itself a kind of individual green halo parallel to its actual shape"

As long as the luminosity endured, the insect, white in its natural state, would, it seems, thanks to the reflection of this halo, exude a rich emerald color that justified its name

Seduced by the idea of this aureole that would shine despite its ultra thin size, Bliss decided that its miraculous appearance in her studies bode well for its inclusion in her mechanical tarot cards and was transfixed by how well they fit into her visionary artwork

Knowing that Banks, as part of his trade, was selling his books in major centers around the world, Bliss, a bit anxious, leaned on him to find some of these insects for her

He wrote to a correspondent in Edinburgh who, after finding a few helpful leads, sent him six earth pots, each one containing a Caledonian pyrrole picked in the Tay valley and loaded with a colony of emeralds

Bliss, who was still quite anxious to put all the pieces of her new-age art collage together, approached the only master technician that she knew who was well-trained in the fine art of micro-mechanics, the watchmaker Frankel, whose enthusiasm about her project led him to offer his services for free as long she agreed to not claim exclusive ownership of the idea she was proposing, since he too wanted to exploit the situation

The deal was agreed upon and Frankel received one of the six earth pots as his compensation

Studying the remaining five plants, one evening Bliss noticed the arrival of the aforementioned halo

An ardent green circle glowed over the body of the insect as part of evolution

Little by little, each emerald emitted a similar halo, whose medium took over its head

It seemed that a single cause must have provoked this consistent illumination

The sorceress, covering all surrounding light, admired the spectacle of the dazzling green rings that, crossing in different directions, produced their own discreet lighting while cleverly shading the insect's white body

A few minutes later, all of the halos went out one by one

Frankel successfully completed his first model of an invaluable, all-metal micro-thin rectangular device that he would use to create a symmetrical square itself composed of eight tiny squares that, set two by two, would have an emerald insect installed at their centers

Each leg movement of each insect would kick a very tiny metal gaiter welded to a connecting rod that would actuate a set of wheels lying flat in the general direction of the object

Finely toothed hubs and edges were lined up in a row, binding each wheel so that they would gain in force what they lost in speed

The first was driven by the crank turning easily by way of the stirrings of a leg in distress

Then things could go slow yet robustly

Another approach would allow for the implementation of a series of quills intentionally stuck in the hub and periodically pushing the end of a tapered blade that, when released, would vibrate and introduce to the environment a pure sound that resembled experimental audio art

Individually equipped with six legs, each giving off its own note, the eight emeralds in their designated squares composing the micro-thin rectangular model were all chromatically covered and included this extended four major sevenths:

In addition to the above, the piece had built into it a well-executed harmonizer, a kind of pre-vocoder, and this function was an integral part of the intricate system as a whole, triggering sounds from the eight areas separately as well from the group as a whole, programmed to oppose any superfluous cacophony while maintaining an open field of possibility for any reasonable combination that could be easily parsed

The instrument was like a miniaturized voice synthesizer before Moog invented such an apparatus

Claimed in advance by Bliss was her interest in preserving the various convergences of sound coming from the tarots standing in their box, and a small sliding weight was produced to paralyze all arts of the mechanism at the slightest drop of the weight

Transformed into a pocket by means of a thin blade that created the perfect thickness, a tarot could lock easily into the metal rectangle without modifying its appearance

Frankel reproduced the model and soon the tarots served as unsuspecting covers for the musical plates enriched by their eight emerald insects, which could be effortlessly attached or unattached to the card

These artistic pursuits resulted in unassailable purity and produced unexpected value-added experiences

For example, being worry-free of any potential obstacles, the halos would shine above the cardboard surface, emphasizing their presence just as the voluptuous music would be emitted from the tarot performers creating some of the best moments of the live audio/visual concert

Under the care of Bliss, all of the insects were requisitioned in turn—and then released into six plants where they found their organic home life

The sorceress had great success with this harmonious tarot performance and she tended to conduct them at night when the halos would turn an especially bright shade of green

Whatever the genre adopted by the emeralds, the old woman could sync her fluency in extracting ingenious corollaries with the readymade predictions she would always make just by looking at the card

When the halos occurred, she eagerly seized on a fertile new theme that she would offer as part of her eloquent prophesy

Having attached the entirely normal aspect of the tarot to the mysterious aspects of these voice and noise symphonies along with the flamboyant green rings would always impress the curious, whose numbers were increasing

During their improvisations, the emeralds, as if under the influence of a hauntological presence[95], often performed in the key of F major

95. You can bet the exact term *hauntological* was not what the auto-translation fed me, but something close enough—like *haunt* or *haunted*—so that I could tweak it for my own ghostwriting purposes. In fact, the reader will not be able to, no matter how hard they may try, retrace the auto-translation / remix operations I have employed here nor will they be able to serve up to themselves the same exact source material that I had at my disposal while rewriting Roussel. But then again, is it really necessary for the reader, any reader, and especially a self-conscious readwrite auto-translator/remixer, to have access to the same source material that I did, or are these apparitions of text conspicuously present enough, conspicuously *transpositioned* to always make an appearance in an exhibition space that Roussel has already mapped out for us?

One of Duchamp's aphorisms reads "A Guest + A Host = A Ghost" and, in the *Green Box*, he also underlines the term "an apparition of an appearance." This relates to Derrida's later use of *hauntology* but in a much more literal and literary-philosophical sense, i.e. a hauntological reading or re-reading of a text, in his case Marx, but a text that presents itself as a kind of apparition, a ghost-text that marks Marx's presence in the practice of everyday life.

Throughout my playful remix of Roussel's *Locus Solus*, I treat the text as first a readymade that I then intentionally recontextualize for my own conceptual practice (and not just lift it *as is* but, rather, sample it and simultaneously filter it through my own metamediumystic apparatus as a work of performance art [writing] or what I sometimes term *pseudo-autobiography*). Throughout the process, I was hyperconscious of the fact that I would be inhabiting the ghost-text as if it were suspended in an oscillating state of presence/absence which is neither being nor non-being. The *spectre*, for me, is always at work in use-value, and for this, I can thank both Marx and Derrida, for they have set me up with enough philosophical heft that I can generate more value-added theoretical currency than my practice-based research would otherwise administer for me. Still, given everything I have read, how could I not think of Derridean hauntology while writing through Roussel's narrative and its cast of endless extras [*figurantes*]? Even Camera, who himself seems incredibly voyeuristic and off to the side most of the time, comes across as an apparition of an appearance. As Derrida writes about the haunted text, "[i]t changes places, one no longer knows exactly where it is, it turns, it invades the stage with its *moves*: there is a step there *and* its allure belongs only to this mutant." What mutant? The one who evolves while mutating, who can no longer resist the urge to ghost-write the apparition of text algorithmically circulating in the networked space of flows? A few sentences later, Derrida starts a list of potential incarnations of the mutant entity: "[. . .] here then is the apparition of a strange creature: at the same time Life, Thing, Beast, Object, Commodity, Automaton—in a word, spectre." Somehow this all reminds me of *GRAMMATRON*.

In endeavoring vainly to continue no matter what, Bliss noticed a certain characteristic of their melody

An English tourist who was part of the usual crowd that would form each night, heard and recognized the melody as soon as the first tarot began to shoot its sound out, and he started singing with it at full volume

The emerald insects, prodded by his voice registering soprano and bass notes over two octaves, started creating bright halos, which appeared with an intense joy they never reached again

Their auras dimmed and Bliss wondered if it had something to do with an anxiety she was not particularly sensitive to

Surprised at being copied in the level of intense output, the Englishman, not silencing himself, leaned up against the sound card to better hear what was coming out of them

When he stood up, Bliss realized she needed to prohibit him and others from getting too close to the eight components of each card

She proceeded to close the demonstration and ignored him, hoping he would leave without a trace

But the crowd began questioning him and he asked them if they had ever heard of the tune "The Blue Bells of Scotland"

Remembering that the emeralds had come from Scotland, Bliss, her curiosity awakened, wrote a note to Banks telling him about the whole adventure

At her request, the bookseller sent a special set of questions to his contact in Edinburgh, from whom he shortly received a copy of the "The Blue Bells of Scotland," along with more detailed information

The plants that had been picked were gathered at the edge of Tay bay, a place full of open pastures near a stone bench where a young shepherd would often sit and play the bagpipe monitoring his herd from a distance

The young man's favorite chorus, "The Blue Bells of Scotland," were played in a traditional key of F major, and he kept repeating this chorus that permeated the environment of the nearby emeralds and that somehow, later, via the musical power of the tarot cards, would trigger a latent memory that they associated with the entire work

The initial joy they had experienced when first hearing the man sing could be attributed to the intoxicating feeling of remembering their life in the colder climate they had come from but that, in their new environment, was too sweet for them to appreciate and probably triggered something like insect nostalgia

Haunted by the impressive details of the event surrounding the singing of the English tourist, Bliss began singing to herself in F major and then sang to the emeralds, over time learning by heart "The Blue Bells of Scotland," which soon produced blinding halos on behalf of the creatures

The original tone, it ends up, favored unanimous agreement among all of the halos, whose splendor was clearly indicated by way of all eight emeralds in each tarot becoming radiant performers

At her events, she would sing the song in the form of an incantation, and for her prophesy-making she used the light force of the green rings as well as the enigmatic and transient appearance of her hands over the circular cavities to conduct what had by now become a ritual

Only halos caused by the execution of "The Bluebells of Scotland," which the insects could never radiate at such intensity without a guide, had the strength to form a kind of therapeutic layer of skin

Intrigued by the very presence of the nimbuses and especially by their secret power punch, Camera vowed to closely examine the insects, which was only briefly mentioned in various books and had up until this point escaped serious research investigation by naturalists

One evening, examining a halo through a sort of magnifying apparatus attached to his watch, while Bliss, with her old voice, was blowing "The Bluebells of Scotland" into the bodies of the eight emeralds stationed in the rectangular music device, he discovered, rapidly rotating in opposite directions, two light cones that were so minuscule as to be almost non-existent and that were joined at their bases, creating a kind of magical equilibrium

One was balanced on the head of an insect and the other was in the air above it

The lower cone was uniformly blue and the one above was all yellow

Without any apparent degradation caused by the two circles grazing each other and forming a rich green shade via the amalgamation of the yellow and blue, the halo, thin and defined, remained fixed in a kind of neutralization of the two movements

This was in contrast to the brilliance of the spinning cones that could not be seen by the naked eye

Taking a dead emerald to dissect it, Camera found in its head, standing base to base, two imperceptible white cones composed of a hard, dry matter that were adhered by their points to the two poles of a tiny spherical recess that he took his scalpel to thus creating an opening in its side

The alchemist, through his continual guesswork, provided a strong electrical current into the desired location and the white cones, as he had projected, swiveled in opposite directions

At the same time, an average halo formed just above the radiant cones that were revealed through the magnifying glass

The puzzle, therefore, was solved

Under the influence of their momentary contentment, the emeralds, by the effect of some subtle innervation coming from the spinning white cones, projected into the air a more radiant image of themselves

It was thanks to an overflowing excess of the brilliant, airy substance that the two factitious bases would pass by the two very real cones that stayed close to their neighbors

For Camera, the appearance of the halos, while serving to express a sensibility not unlike the pull of purring cats, suggested an unspecified well-being that, in theory, was like the phosphorescence of fireflies or glowworms signifying their openness to love and the call for a romantic coupling

The artist later pushed his anatomical investigations further

The tip of each real cone, crossing an opening of the spherical recess, was at the center of a free, small white external disk that ran parallel to the plane of the halo that appeared pregnant with a circular row of nerve filaments—short branches of a single fiber—determined by means of their magnetic influence, creating a whirl that recalled the early invention of electric motors

As soon as the disk turned, it transmitted its momentum to the cone and they became one fluid movement

Probing with intention—the orbit always in full swing—a steel point into the cone below, Camera, as expected, saw shine above the dead insect a photogenic blue stripe that grew in size with another sudden scratch of the probe

Testing it the same way, the higher cone gave its results in exactly the same way, but this time in yellow

Then tracing the ridges in different directions, the artist suddenly produced varying results in the form of thin gleams of colorful space—blue or yellow depending on the cone that was being probed as he reproduced some of his primitive yet still accurate drawings, whose measure increased with his gestural intensity

Confirming his intimate conjectures, these linear appearances showed him how the cones, delivering a full rotation of their entire surface, created a friction in the air that was trapped in the spherical recess and luminously generated their doubles, but were also quick to turn off when it was time to rest

Hoping to assign any material difference to contrast the two colors, Camera, with a fine brush, placed a drop of some preparation on each cone and indeed they had two dissimilar chemical reactions

Each emerald, put right or obliquely, right side up or upside down, always wore their halo, like an aureole adorning the top of its head—the two double cones seeming to move around on a single pivot of ideal length

Relentless experimenter, he sought the cause of the constancy in the relative orientation of the phosphorescent figure and perceived a slight deviation of colors distinguishing the two hemispheres of the spherical recess where he noticed two distinct white substances

He separated them with his scalpel and then tore at the cones and the nerves inside until he saw two finely pierced holes, one of which was the delicate sliver he had made himself during his earlier observations

Shooting two light rays through the cones created, with the sounds of "The Bluebells of Scotland," a glowing insect, and Camera, using his magnifying glass, saw that the emeralds were gifted with a particular transparency that, when their upper hemisphere was disturbed in any way, would not bother the insect, who remained as immutable as an unchanging sun-streak spilling its ray on the glass slide under inspection

On the other hand, the lower hemisphere was in disarray everywhere and becoming an insurmountable obstacle, consisting of pell-mell light atoms that were not only perfectly sealed but full of antipathy and repression

This explained how the insect's head had transformed into a kind of reflector, the lower half of the spherical recess giving the rest of the contraption a specially amplified curvature that was constantly darting away from the brilliant figure as a whole

The disclosures from the magnifying glass put into relief the mysteries sensed by the naked eye, like the appearance of the dermal cavities made by perforating the gyration whereupon the upper air cone thrust its peak into a pore as it distended imperiously

Amazed at first that a simple, impalpable light had the strength to grow a layer of skin, Camera remembered that in America, following some serious evidence that had been presented, a certain wisp of straw, thrown by the force of a hurricane wind and moving with a sharp rotation, had embedded itself in a wooden telephone pole

A quickly spinning object could therefore allow an otherwise frail body to enter something harder than itself and, in his case, it was all the more striking since the side touching the skin, as well as a host of other substances, remained transparent to light

Noting that the cavities never bled due to the inimitable delicacy of the drill method he had employed, Camera felt like he was evoking similar characteristics related to the famous placets of the alchemist Paracelsus whom he looked on with great admiration and, all notes of charlatanism aside, he viewed as one of the most powerful spirits of the 16th century

The theory of the *placets*, so close, in spite of its metaphysical foundation, to the modern scientific theses on vaccines and opotherapy, seemed to him an especially brilliant and prodigious precursory model for what he too was investigating

Paracelsus considered each component of the human body as a thinking being who, having direct observation of the soul better than any outside perspective, knew its malady as well as what remedy would help cure it, and was just waiting to make priceless revelations even as cures were being cleverly proposed by leagues of doctors whose assigned roles were, after all, rather limited

Starting from this basic truth, the alchemist had developed, under the name of *placets*, a number of white powders that came equipped with various defined effects

Each powder, charged with an interrogating mission, would interact with the body and prompt the quick secretion of an unknown substance which, easy to collect, constituted in its properties, an answer, a ready-to-be-claimed remedy

The appellation, taken in the strict sense of "May it please. . .", betrayed the metaphysical essence of its design

It was the humble solicitor Paracelsus who, with conviction, addressed the organs with what he hoped were mysterious powders that he wanted to persuade them with

One such *placet* would influence the liver, which would pour its response into the blood, where he could then get a reading and develop another substance capable of overcoming liver disease, while another would urge the stomach to deliver its response in the same way as the liver, whereupon an effective drug working against dyspepsia would be made, and another one could be targeted at the sovereignty of the heart and its essence . . .

Stimulated by its particular *placet*, each organ located in a healthy subject would manufacture some specific substance that Paracelsus captured and then administered to his patients

Unusually, rather than be swallowed, several *placets* could be directly applied to the skin

Thus the process was extended to the eye and when applied to even a sagacious personality would produce a flow of tears, while another, covering the skin of a clairvoyant entity, would become a radical balm for any epidermal condition

In actuality, this method surely bore no fruit, especially considering the dogmatic speculations of Paracelsus who, in good faith, thought of consulting some great minds and reaping knowledge from their instructions

No virtuous healing phenomenon would accrue as a result of the secretions caused by the famous powders

They were harmless excitations with ineffectual topical effects but whose formulas have still managed to survive

Despite its impotence, the idea behind the various powders created a sustained interest as a kind of avant-garde courier of future information somehow living in an atemporal moment, something that would later catch the fancy of Jenner and Pasteur, who would revolutionize the potential treatments

Paracelsus, according to Comte, had represented an era defined by the theological principle of vaccines, something that continued making its presence felt after an insensitive transition away from metaphysics and into a more positivistic period

For Camera, the studiously acquired insurance that the *placet*, when it first was introduced in the 16th century, was used to designate a request for some kind of response under the spell of a powdery persuasion, was central to the practice and belief system of Paracelsus, as well as the role of free will in relation to each organ's sovereign powers

However, in the *De veto medici mandate*, the voluminous monograph on his *placets*, Paracelsus, in the midst of hundreds of examples, quotes this highlight:

Especially interested in the colloquial point of view of a tribe from West Africa, the explorer Lethem befriended the African alchemist Milne, and brought him back to pursue an intelligent subject he wished to continue as soon as he returned home, namely the idiomatic studies that he had begun on site in West Africa as part of his field research and that he was resigned to pursue under the condition of also bringing Milne's black girlfriend, Doc

For a long time, Milne had been suffering from some endemic dermatosis in his native country

Once he returned to Europe, Lethem led his protégé to Paracelsus for treatment

A slave to his own doctrine, Paracelsus figured that a black skin disease could only be cured with a remedy produced by applying his methods to an African peer

He thus made an application that he put on the arm of Doc, who came from the same tribe as Milne, a dose of the ad hoc *placet*

Soon the suppuration began with an unusual color that he figured was due to his choice of using a black subject that would denote a different reaction than, say, that of the skin of a Caucasian

Feeling moody, Paracelsus noticed for the first time the red blood cells which, when he subjected them to analysis, surprisingly revealed to him "coal, sulfur, and saltpeter"—the elements of gunpowder—as Roger Bacon had invented centuries before

However, softened by the secretion that had brought them in the first place, the tiny grains remained deprived of all potentially explosive power even after various attempts at desiccation

Believing that obtaining a resounding explosion would highlight the illuminating discovery he was now proud of, the alchemist wanted to know if the formation of the gunpowder preceded the arrival of oozing humectant

An affirmative conclusion arose when in a new experiment he collected several white cells while delicately extracting them with various steel instruments after having applied the preparation on Doc's skin, which seemed to resist the devilish pain without any complaints

But this mode of extirpation involved a great deal of bloodshed in spite of Paracelsus' endless precautions, and so he could never guarantee that the cells weren't being contaminated and consequently many were often lost

Meanwhile, the alchemist, using humor as a sedative, cured Milne, or at least his malady had taken care of itself

Meditating on this anecdote, Camera had recomposed the same *placet*, whose formula, taken directly from the monograph, indicated the precise measurements of the fundamental substances: sodium hydrate, arsenious anhydride, ammonium chloride, calcium silicate, and potassium nitrate

Out of curiosity, he extended it on the skin of an African—and, as expected, found that the suppuration, when put under analysis, contained the three substances named by the earlier alchemist

Thinking that the human body contains carbon and sulphur, the artist-guru quickly understood the phenomenon

Elements of the *placet*, rich in potassium nitrate, directly provided saltpeter, sodium hydrate, and arsenious anhydride, identified the greedier carbon and sulfur and began capturing these two properties in the dermis

However, the special pigment that colors black skin, endowed with many chemical affinities, attracts seven various properties, including sodium hydrate, arsenious anhydride, and potassium nitrate

Subjugated by the saltpeter, the sodium hydrate and arsenious oxide had brought to the surface the recent reserves of carbon and sulphur—and these fortuitous interrelationships led to the formation of the globules, thanks to some internal workings of the skin as it prepared to manifest its suppuration

The crucial role of the subject's skin pigment explained the absence, verified by Camera, of the mysterious globules in similar experiments run on Caucasians

Finding, as well, a powerful interest in the explosive potential of the gunpowder, the artist-guru, employing the turn of his fine steel scalpels, like Paracelsus before him, encountered an inability to prematurely dig deep into the skin without soaking everything with blood, due to the inevitable cuts

These sensational blood cells, wet and moody, were always gathering, a corrupt collection of contaminated evidence

Beholding the light of the green insects, the emeralds, by exploring their delicate dermis without breaking the vessels, could allow him to achieve his goal

The black skin, after having received the application of the usual *placet*, would be attacked during the night prior to its inevitable suppuration by eight points of invisible light as well as the sounds of "The Blue Bells of Scotland" performed by a double rectangular music device and the voice of Bliss and, thus conducted at Camera's request, it was the only way to get the insects to perform their intense, irradiating drill

But the artist, his magnifying glass over the glowing orbit, saw the ethereal cones, free of problems, move *through the skin* without opening it, like rays of motion wandering under clear glass

Notoriously less flexible than white-skinned subjects, the black skin was too resistant in its air pores to the scalpel's swivel tip and acted as a transparent material with its element

Other black subjects, men and women, provided the same negative results

Refusing to accept defeat, the artist hoped that by employing a piloerection procedure, goosebumps or small dead pores would emerge that would then become penetrable

But the use of extreme cold in the procedure wasn't enough to get the skin to respond, and so he decided to subject the skin to some kind of grave terror that would produce the goosebumps (but how to do this in a humane way given the law's prohibition of all violence?)

He remembered a deeply felt personal reaction he experienced at a recent exhibition of works by the artist Vollon, one that featured a famous fruit dancer that was considered the great painter's masterpiece

The catalog of the show articulated the work's context, inspired by a Sudenese custom:

"Each year, following quasi-religious tradition, when the nourishing trees full of food are bending the overcrowded branches, the first selection of fruits are made by a dancer who must, at the end of her difficult movement, formally present the offerings at the feet of the king surrounded by his court

If one fruit falls during the dance, the performer is put to death on the spot and another dancer, who can expect a similar fate if she repeats the misstep, restarts the ritual

According to a superstitious belief that explains this rigorous principle, if the first batch is not delivered intact to the sovereign leader, a plague of locusts will all but destroy the remainder of the harvest and possibly ravage the entire culture

The fall of just one fruit signals this huge threat, linking the ceremony to a devastating scourge, and thus mandates that it be avoided at all costs lest the offender be put to immediate death

Given the continuous dread inspired in these countries due to the frequent infestation of locusts, they do not hesitate to sacrifice a few dancers believing they are, in the long run, saving thousands of lives

Necessarily requiring a supreme luxury, the offering to the sovereign leader always includes a huge amount of fruit, set in high pyramids inside three large and quite primitive baskets that the performer, during her complex and aesthetically rendered dance, is threatening to balance on the top of her head as she approaches the thickly fleshed and outstretched hands of the king

These conditions make for a difficult problem, as several victims are often sacrificed in order to successfully achieve the goal

Also, the cruelest sense of fright hangs over the entire scene, creating a sense of dire suspense as they attempt to accomplish their task"

Combining his well-known gifts for rendering fruits and for being an undisputed master of the painterly execution of characters, Vollon had found for himself a wonderful subject

Wise enough to adapt his talents to most subject matter, he rendered the tragic moment when a fruit—not willing to play the role of a stable and attractive red berry staying atop the head of the dancer—had impregnated the scene with a horrific drama for its heroine who, seeing it fall, was already being approached by two executioners ready to strike her dead even as she kept her feet crossed as if still performing her graceful dance in the direction of the king sitting to the right of the other dignitaries

The three unstable fruit baskets, the purple bay in the background, the all-black characters and the amazing truth of the scene being captured in the painting was even compelling to the less knowledgable

Camera had long contemplated the illustrated canvas, surprised to see some superstitions still alive among primitive people

Often, indeed, locusts would infest the area, whether the dancers were successful or not, which one would think would defeat the principle, yet these rituals still remained, just like belief in the immediate powers of rainmakers who had few results, all of it fortuitous

The artist now thought that the sight of such a work, brought forth specifically to hit a barbaric eye unaware of its pictorial artifice, would feel horrified by the depiction of the annual event full of its thousand anxieties and, experiencing a profound fear, would cause a second violent phenomenon, that of *piloerection*

Judging most reproductions insufficient, Camera inquired about the original, on sale at a very successful gallery, and a special arrangement was made for momentary possession of the work until a future date to be determined

An explicit correspondence was exchanged with the French Consulate in Borneo, where he learned about the existence of a dancer named Sumiya who, for five consecutive years, had successfully completed the scary feat, was still in a kind of trance knowing that she would be asked to perform the ritual a sixth time, and so just the thought of it all led her to have convulsions that she wished would disappear forever

Since then, remaining impressionable to an excess, Sumiya avoided the dance by detouring her whereabouts—since she could no doubt even stand the sight, too infested by visions of tortuous memories and imaginings—associated with the place reserved for the dance of the fruit

Provided by Camera with an urgent set of instructions, the consulate, under order to keep things confidential so as to not negatively affect the future intensity of the mental shock sure to await Sumiya, was enticed by the high price Camera was willing to pay, and arranged for her trip to Locus Solus under the aegis of a cotton trafficker ready to leave Borneo for Paris

After Sumiya's arrival, the artist-guru cum practice-based research scientist, before a captivated audience, vowed to illustrate his best experiment which, based on a one-time effect of surprise and illusion, would be totally unique

It was important that the gunpowder make a striking blow upon a fragment of rock right in front of the witnesses, without having dispensed any prior placement of the explosive substance and to, instead, initialize the blast so that it came from the depths of the black skin to the borehole

Banking on everyone's certificates and signatures, Camera, appropriating the edge of a river with rocky banks, prepared everything for the end of the session featuring Bliss who was charged with selecting the time between various tarots that would launch the insects who, by virtue of the enthusiasm of their spontaneous music, would seem well rested and, naked, the musical boxes would not have collected the necessary blood cells

Luke was helping build the momentum and unveiled rather abruptly, on command, Vollon's tableau

* * *

For a while, seeing that the wick was about to end, Camera accelerated its flow

When it stopped, the fire had already gained momentum inside the pit

After some anxious attention, the expected explosion occurred, strong and loud, disrupting the rock, whose fragments, thrown in all directions, confirmed the success of the experiment conclusively

The artist, with a marker provided by Bliss, wrote on a large sheet of paper a concise and fast overview of the event, detailing the irrefutable identity of the blood cells, transported directly in front of everyone's eyes, without substitution or chemical priming, from the bottom of the gaping skin up to the point of the rock's excavation

Everyone signed their names at his request[96]

96. I too will sign my name here, just as a courtesy, but the ghostwriter in me is signaling from the flames, claiming that I have royally botched up what just went on the scene before me, and that I should have quit while I was ahead (but was I ever really ahead?—clearly not, but that's not the point, what matters is that I have one chapter to go and I am going to finish this new work sooner than I ever thought I would). Also, it goes without saying that auto-translating parts of this chapter were especially painful as I could never imagine myself creating such stereotypes although some unpublished manuscripts of mine might belie me.

7

Turning his back on the river, the mischievous artist led the group to the edge of an attractive, thick woodsy area that everyone ducked under and penetrated as a continuation of the exhibition

Soon the group reached a vast, idyllic clearing where a teenager was hanging out, putting some ointments on his complexion, and dressed in a kind of shabby chic outfit meant to capture the attention of his peers whenever he would stroll around town[97]

Camera announced to the group that this was Null, a fortune teller who had recently been touring around the country

Having gotten wind of Bliss's presence at Locus Solus, Null, by emulation, had arrived just the day before to meet with Camera, this strange artist who had encouraged him to practice his black art before tour groups, and who was now, in this enchanting glade, embracing an opportunity he now had been given to showcase his talents in relation to Meta Bliss who was quite different in both age and sex

97. Already, as with Meta Bliss, I am feeling the urge to transpose certain environmental tendencies located in my own home base of Boulder, Colorado, known for being the "New Age Athens" of America and, in the process, am wondering if the young teenager will turn out to be a kind of feral charlatan, one of the post-hippy wanderers who camp out near our town creek during the summer months. Of course, he will turn out to be just that, only this time he will have come from a deeply disturbing, broken family and not, say, the boring suburbs of New Jersey.

A rucksack like the one carried by a soldier was on the back of "Mopsus" (as the adolescent gently called him), a fighting cock that walked beside him, with the personal baggage secured by two straps hugging its neck and tail feathers

The surface of the object whose entire, curved carcass was married to the bird's body, was made of a very fine elastic netting, stuffed with archived newspaper articles and embedded metallic moon reflectors distended over the cock's head

Null put the cock on to a small folding table that, on the group's initial approach, he had installed on the ground and, after removing the bird's netted sack, proposed reading horoscopes to everyone

Hello came forward and was questioned by the teenager, who asked her for her year of birth, exact day, and time

Out of the contents of the daypack still resting on the table and awaiting esoteric actions that he would use as part of his performance, Null consulted a little book, whereupon he acknowledged that the constellation of Hercules had converged with Saturn during her first moments of life

He then handed the book to Mopsus, who took it in its beak, which was already holding a long, smooth, steel rod in it

The cock, owning the middle of the table, laid down on its back without mussing up its feather plume and then, with his right foot, grabbed the thick end of the rod, which he pointed vertically toward the sky

Looking up at where the rod was being pointed, Null was slightly skewing his head toward the small spear, which was now directed at Saturn, a bright star located directly overhead

Therefore, by pointing the magnetic steel communication device right at the planet, the bird became a clairvoyant capable of decrypting the fate of Hello

Strictly immobile, Mopsus, tucking his left foot under himself, leaned toward the middle of his body so that moonbeams would flood it while he securely held tight to the rod

With an obvious and lengthy conviction, the bird filled himself up with the effluvia of auras emanating from the distant star in question

The cock finally lifted himself up after having gripped the rod again with its beak so that he could lay it with the reserve of objects

At the reserve, he grabbed a rosary that he clearly extended to Hello for her consideration

Hearing from Null that Mospus had incited her to ward off her next set of woes by piously reciting a prayer with the rosary, Hello, being superstitious and visibly troubled by the bird's behavior, took the beads in her fingers and murmured the prescribed prayer

In the spoils of the rucksack, near a long glass box containing a supply of straws made of—or so everyone was told—a skillfully prepared sponge material, shined a thin crystal sphere that contained a bright red liquid filled up to its bottleneck

Opening the box, Null took a straw and, without losing sight of the game, sank it into the far end of the tube, replacing a narrow cork stopper which he had just removed

Mopsus, tilting his head so that he could seize the piece in his mandibles, offered the whole to Hello who, at the behest of the the young lad, took hold of the sphere in her entire hand

Bubbling as if placed under heat, the liquid moved inside the tube and eventually entered the straw, which the cock gradually imbibed, drinking the red contents

Having finished his drink, the cock then handed the object back to Null who, expecting it, quickly cooled it down and removed the straw to replace it with the cork

The teenager presented a formal invitation to the group to think about what they just saw, whether it might have been a favorable or harmful series of events, a good way to spend part of the day, or even the effect it might have on the future, perhaps introducing some doubt into Hello's inevitable trajectory

Null kept talking as if in a trance, asking the group if what was being acknowledged here, however uncertain Hello's past and future tenses were or might be, was sufficiently enlightening, that is, did they need some more explanatory context to better understand what Hello's complicity in the scene was actually suggesting?

In a bygone era, Hello could choose for herself how she felt about her role in any scene she was participating in, but now her thoughts were muddled: "What was I thinking? Was there some kind of mutual and sincere love involved in my intervening in what could easily have been a potential accident that may now have been successfully avoided? Have I had, in my fearfulness, opened myself up to some case of unspoken blame that I am robotically attaching to what I imagine to be my heartfelt emotions but are really more like auto-translatable sensations that any literate reader could make their own sense of without me? I have had similar requests to do this or that, to hold on to something, to pray for an imaginary outcome, and in these cases too the future is always offered as the ultimate leisure world composed of limitless opportunities for me to interrogate the experiential forms and conceptual frameworks I continually lose my creativity in."[98]

Having thought about it on her own for a moment, Hello said that his question was too rhetorically obvious and that Null was too caught up in his own head

The boy immediately grabbed two ivory dice which he then tossed

They went whirling up in the air and fell in the middle of the table

The upper face was marked in red and, in addition to the number one that was marked at an angle, there was this short sentence: "Did I ever really have it?" traced in fine characters seemingly formed by veins

Null told Hello that according to the revelation provided by the throw of the dice, it had raised the question regarding an advantageous circumstance in her past

Tilting his face for a sign of affirmation, the young woman, anxious and disappointed, asked in vain for the teenager to answer the question himself since he never seemed to fully reveal nor claim to have the answer to anything

The intimate nature of the matter stirring in her mind suggested something of profound importance that everyone would understand shortly

The goal of the magic dice, according to Null, was to penetrate her thoughts with a playful suspicion without nullifying the field of possibilities, suggesting that his role in this performance was being okayed as if he had just made contact with some direct information that, if one were to drill in deeper, would probably be interpreted as a total lie, used as a teaser to thwart the potential combinations of anyone else who wished to cast the die

While speaking, Null put the dice in his eye sockets

Seen from an angle, the group could read three separate options: "Did I ever really have it? Do I have it now? Will I have it?"

98. This interior monologue Hello shares with us is one I can relate to, perhaps too much, which is why she's thinking it in the first place, no? But then again, I am prone to just giving the game away, not posthumously like Roussel, but as *part of the performance itself*, yes?

The lines were written in both red and black, each occupying the flat space opposite its other

The choice that would result in a fortunate or less fortunate outcome would be revealed by the teenager depending on what side came up: red or black—listing the chronological sequence of the information being subordinated to the tense of the verb

Everywhere the figure followed the hue of the formula

Null opened a long, narrow volume with a luxurious blue binding, old and worn, a sort of cabalistic code that he shared with the group in overdramatized secrecy

The entire book was divided into six sections, each relating to a constellation, composed in short, stand-alone paragraphs, with a few contained in the form of a more or less obscure parable related to human destiny

The equivalent chapters all had their individual pagination

Quickly, the teenager ran through the book made of beautiful vellum but that was now dirty and worn in its binding

All of the sheets were marked in the upper right corner with the name of a constellation in large caps printed with extraordinary finesse

Null, reading these constellation names, stopped on HERCULES, whose stars had, according to his research, converged with SATURN during the birth of Hello as he had declared earlier in regards to the six pages of the chapter in question, including the one crucial question that came up when he rolled the die as part of his initial investigation

A serious review of the book had indeed shown six different kinds of unconscious mediumistic energy dictating respectively the corresponding pages of each chapter, a striking analogy of thought that would carry across all pages marked 1, all pages marked 2, etc., and so on through the entire work with no gaps until all six pages were complete

In preferring the past, both now and in the future, as the location for his secret reading of each individual's unique circumstance, the subject would project an intimate caricature of themselves in a somewhat random light simply based on the teenager's choice of a good or adverse event that had already taken place in the subject's life

Optimism, shyness, hypochondria, defiance, recklessness, scrupulousness, providence . . . all would shine when the time came and the interior core would be revealed as soon as a question was asked and the magic die cast into the infallible world[99]

Impressive in its own right, especially given the survey adopted by the group of six assorted pages, the study of these multiple feelings or states-of-being formed the basis of an alternative cabalistic text

Once a chapter was designated by the stars, then the number on the ivory face of the die that came up determined whose folio would be further scrutinized

Null drew a bisecting line down the middle of page 1 of the HERCULES chapter

Tracing his way over the printed portion, the thin wisp he drew did not encroach the top or bottom margin but started from the first line and ended down in the middle of a paragraph that the boy then touched with his finger

This, where his finger now pointed, was Hello's fate

The processual indicator was, once again, rational

The vitality of the subject and her temperament indeed depended more or less on the bold ascension of the red liquid in the new straw including the climactic moment when it marked the fateful paragraph

However, from the beginning to the end of each page, the wording of the paragraphs included a steady crescendo concerning the artistic, patriotic or romantic exaltations contained within the parabolic tales

99. Both Roussel and I use chance operations to trigger our texts and have foregrounded the role of prophesy in our narratives. The inclusion of figures like Meta Bliss and Null suggests that Roussel, and his alter-ego Camera, are experiential gamblers who enjoy conjuring meaning out of the quantum uncertainty that permeates all of nature's procedural compositions. My own role as the remix artist or author function auto-translating the story is a cross between monkey grammarian, DJ, bachelor apparatus, cyborg-narrator, and/or revolutionary trickster who attempts to apply a rigorous program of determined indeterminacy to whatever subtexts may be nestled in any work. But how does one perform this techno-shamanic, a-teleological function? In my case, I was very opportunistic and capitalized on procedural devices that revealed unintended coincidences, correlations, and atemporal spaces for co-creative postproduction. Whereas John Cage tells us that "I use chance operations instead of operating according to my likes and dislikes," I prefer to use chance operations to discover how my composition wants to itself *become manipulated by me*, and then, intuiting how that sense-data needs to be poetically altered by way of my remixological presence, "manufacture the culture as the event proceeds, as the context sustains." (Tony Conrad)

Using a magnifying glass, Null thus read the group the mysterious passage while Mopsus too appeared to be listening closely:

"In the courtyard of the palace of Byzantium, the courtesan Chrys Mallow is hoisted by his people on Basi, his proud black horse, which neighed impatiently under his royal trappings

Then they went out, radiant, for a free ride through the nearby plains and forests

Toward evening, when it was time to turn back and head home, Basi felt his spurs kick at her flank

Basi darted with a gallop that nothing could stop

When night came, the path lit up with a greenish glow along the Amazon

Seeking the point where the lights shone, Chrys Mallow saw his spur, shining in a murky glow lit up by its surroundings, always leading his foot against the horse, digging in deeper each time he moved and increased the bleeding wound that had started

"The desperate journey lasted years

"The spur, which never ceased to engage the horse, would keep its pallid clarity during the day while at night would once again reveal its fulgurations

"And no one ever saw Chrys Mallow in Byzantine again"

The teenager began to clarify one interpretation of the story

Similar to Chrys Mallow, who started off on a cheerful ride, Hello too would begin her joyful journey, a story whose potential was full of pleasant possibilities

But before long, her love of life would find itself quite frivolous, even superficial, and eventually her disposition could be tagged as outright tyrannical and stubborn, one that was self-absorbed in a tortuous jealousy

The symbol of the love spurs that, despite her best efforts, would always dig into and further victimize her as she proceeded into the fatal unknown, with its murky radiation illuminating the road she was on, she would forever find herself living in the darkest of hours with the occasional appearance of a penetrating, tragic light disseminating its stillborn passion on the black pages of her life

A great deal of madness living in the past, often during resounding idylls, Hello's flighty even loose moralistic manners could have predicted an appropriate singular outcome

Impressed, the young woman, under the control of her burning desires, embraced the intoxicating idea that a powerful, single flame, spurred on by the darting passion for personal self-fulfillment, would drive her mad and create a thousand torments

Null could not help but laugh at the cock who was now insistently offering Hello a sage flower from the erratic movements of its beak, which held the small stem it had taken from the sack

The intended recipient of the flower accepted the gift that, according to the teenager, was being offered to soften the blow of the painful consequences of her now knowing what kind of future she was leaning toward

Clearly articulating for his cock the name Hello, the boy placed on the table a slender metal easel and, as a canvas, a tall, thin sheet of white vellum

Mopsus stood in front of it, short, and making a strange face out of a tic, suddenly began shaking his head several times, twisting and clogging his neck in the process

After a moment of stillness, he opened his beak wide and expectorated a strong and voluntary cough, and with it, a small dose of blood-like liquid from the depths of his throat that hit the top left of the ivory canvas, where there now appeared a little red *H*, capitalized

Quickly coughing again, but aiming lower this time, a second parcel of blood hit the canvas, drawing an *E* just below the *H*

It was as if the letters were already being formed in the depths of his throat and spontaneously printed with each cough

The same procedure was repeated six times, creating other capital letters, one after another, each below the previous one, and eventually, with the addition of a punctuation mark, this name came into view: HELLO! (inscribed, as it were, vertically along the left edge of the ivory sheet)

Null then began to satiate everyone's visibly aroused curiosity

Struck by the intelligence of his learned cock, which he had long been educating, the teenager said that instead of the usual, purely mechanical words that, say, parrots would obtain and routinely speak, Mopsus was able to metamediumystically transmit the thoughts and names of others, to even express their views

But, deprived of certain vested anatomical components native to talking birds, the animal remained rebellious to any demands that he speak publicly and instead used its foot to wield objects like a pencil that, then, Null, at wit's end, thought could be employed in the art of writing

This, though, was not to be

The young man was on the verge of abandoning his project when a fortuitous circumstance indicated to him the means by which he could achieve a singular success

One morning, suspending his usual wanderings, Null, stationed in a villa inn, had breakfast in silence while Mopsus hung out with him

Suddenly two boys, one the son of the inn's host, continually burst out in laughter, as if passionately lost in their child play

The first one, running, violently hit the table Null was sitting at, and knocked over the connected salt-and-pepper-shaker resting at the edge so that it created a kind of cascade of black and white with the pepper more tenuous, forming a small cloud on top of Mopsus's head, whereupon he was soon shaken by a vicious cough

Getting up from his seat, the teenager, worried and coming to take care of the bird, discovered that the cock, in the midst of his spasmodic coughing fit, was releasing small amounts of blood, which dyed the floor a strange array of different geometric designs

Being alert, Null wanted to know what was causing the curious spitting up of blood and so he opened the bird's beak and saw that at the back of the throat, in the membrane, things were very congested, and would thus bleed easily

Heavily innervated, the membrane surface was covered with the stirring movements of microscopic messengers, multiple figures composed in thin lines of relief and injected with a crimson sweat pulsing in visible tremors

Suddenly, the boy, having at first tried to avoid the red phlegm being spat out by the visibly shaken cock, now recognized in the next bloody expectoration the same exact image he had just seen on the surface of the membrane

Having reignited his initial idea, Null, thinking he would use this strange phenomenon to teach writing to the bird, ordered a complete alphabet of twenty-six small stamps as hollowed out upper case letter blocks

Contrary to the way they were supposed to be used, the non-symmetrical letters were implemented in the normal direction, with a view toward reproducing them in the second degree

The metal surface of the first stamp, pressed for a few sensitive moments on the surface of the membrane at the back of the throat, where it would be left for a while and then removed, would leave its trace

Soon, thanks to the ongoing training sessions that maintained a frequent repetition of the experiment, each letter was eventually able to constitute itself strictly by excluding all of the other options, and the nerves, instead of fortuitously moving, casually began obeying Mopsus, who put his mental imprint on the process, deciding whether to create or delete a vowel or consonant—unceasingly emitting them while Null, during these various phases of the writing process, would marry the bird's spirit with a specific sound and form

When after awhile the stamps had all performed their useful function, the cock knew to bring on its membrane any letter commanded by the teenager, who had now taught him to voluntarily cough during the propitious moment

The congestion that accompanied all of the coughing made the gushing blood exceptionally moist and the expectorated letter in question would always stick to the place it was designated to reach

Then Mopsus, through further education, got used to the fact that he would have to time the tic in his neck with the need to facilitate the flow of blood to the membrane

Null, in search of a rigid and washable almost vertical white surface, chose an ivory leaf placed on a small easel, one that offered the perfect receptacle for the red letters

Gradually led to create letters, then syllables, then entire words, Mopsus, in possession of a written language, expressed his hard-won thoughts according to the wishes of the young man who, emboldened, instilled in him many rules of prosody, focusing on the acrostic

From this point on, with each divination session, the cock would construct a poem out of the name of the person who voluntarily occupied the hot seat

Meanwhile, Mopsus worked tirelessly and six Alexandrines, consisting of small red capital letters equal to the first six and projected one by one, were now lined up on the ivory plate

Sometimes he would renew the tic movement to maintain his glottal congestion

The last two lines, due to the same generative frequency of the coughing up of bloody letters, ended the mysterious acrostic by commenting on the strange and dark depths of the parable involving Chrys Mallow . . .

Everyone read the poem at the same time, including Hello, who by this time was lost in a kind of dreamy seizure

As she lost herself in meditation, Null stored away the canvas and easel, and presented to the group a light object consisting of a small rectangular tray made of tulle that had a layer of asbestos on it and that basically consisted of a very loose metal carcass with four feet

Next, he presented a carefully closed, transparent box that contained a cylindrical piece of mica wrapped in on itself with a thick, foil-like lace, designed with a finesse that only a strong microscope could reveal the details of

To the naked eye, one could only guess the air contours of this sculptural work with its tiny cylinder barely occupying one-twentieth of the entire container

The juvenile opened the top of a canvas bag a few inches from where he dropped below the tray, in plain layers, some crushed charcoal and wood fragments

Then, striking a match, whose flame ran under the tray, he set ablaze the transparent box, which did not catch anywhere else

After everyone was advised to check out the assiduously delicate interior roller about to undergo an amazing transformation, the teenager spoke aloud of distant memories

From his early childhood, Null had been learning the nomadic life with an artist named Vascond who, accompanying himself with a guitar, used to sing from the depths of his windpipes the wondrous remains of his tenor vocals

At the end of each session, Null would dance and then beg for money

During brief stops, Vascond would charm the child by talking about his youth, often returning his thoughts to some glorious period of twenty or thirty years ago when he had triumphed at the theater

The peak of his short career was marked by *The Vendetta*, in which he played the lead role in 1839 at the Opera

The author of the play, Count Raoul Montenegro, had previously written a smaller work at the Comedy House, *Wait and Run*, made in collaboration with Frommel Havel

Vascond, just beginning, had taken on a modest role in this lesser work and then, because of his beautiful voice, was chosen by the Count as the protagonist of *The Vendetta*

In his interpretation of this bigger role, Vascond had created a radiant success

His pure and generous body sparked a contagious enthusiasm each and every night

But, suffering from an accident in his larynx just at the height of his career, he had to leave the theater and take on the lesser voice of an educator

In extreme old age, he made arrangements with private students, singing in the streets with his guitar and collecting alms, thanks to his beautiful, persistent notes

One day his nomadic existence led him to the garden gate of a quiet house where began singing the fresh air of *The Vendetta*

After taking a few steps toward the house, an old man appeared at the door, muttering with emotion:

"Oh, that voice! That voice . . . Sir—is it even possible?"

Then advancing, this new face exclaimed as they suddenly joined hands together:

"Vascond! It's him, it's really him!"

Then, Vascond, stopping short, said, trembling:

"Count Raoul Montenegro . . . . "

The two men, crying, fell into the arms of each other, shocked by the sudden memories of youth being aroused in both of their minds

Introduced in the house, Vascond narrated his lamentable history to his friend, who told him about his own life

Pushed toward chemistry by a reversal of fortune, at a time when his musical work was already quite huge, Count Raoul had invented his famous method for melting silver and brown metal

Later he invented the metal phosphide that was eventually used in the manufacturing of French artillery

Recently, Raoul had come to understand, after several years of research, a new discovery that he had kept secret

He decided to give the scoop to his old friend, whose unexpected song, filled with a charm that still intoxicated him, recalled the good old days

Taking him to his laboratory, he spread before him a thin layer of burning embers below a small tray made of fine tulle with four feet that was holding a layer of asbestos—and laid it on the bed of fire, at the bottom of which shone a transparent box that had a small piece of mica inside it, shaped in the form of a tiny roller wrapped with a rigid and intricate lace made of precious metal for the naked eye to only imagine its utmost details

The transparency of the asbestos on the tulle tray was intended to prove to suspicious minds that there was, in fact, no "double bottom"

Under the action of heat, the strange lace grew slowly in all directions, ostensibly widening and thickening while its internal surfaces, due to its new extensions, glided over each other

In addition, the metal eased and magnification made visible every minimal outline of the sculpture

Finally, a long strip of sparkling lace, wrapped tight on itself, occupied the entire available space, covering all sides of the mica

The disconcerting smoothness of the mesh, a kind of finessed drawing, even after their strong amplification, accentuated the magical meticulousness of the original work as revealed in its detail, indicated by Raoul through his use of a powerful microscope, which he now shared with Vascond

But the inherent merit in the performance of such a task was irrelevant to the Count, who was just proud that he had found a sensational metal that expanded when heat was applied to it and became, without changing its basic nature, as flexible as the most supple fabrics

As a flattering ornament known to excite the female lust for its splendid luster, the luxurious lace he had invented would rake in big profits, which Raoul was resolved to pique Vascond's interest with

He gave him, along with the diaphanous box and tray that he promptly emptied of its asbestos, four new metal rollers identical to the first and ready for their own metamorphosis, the only specimens of this kind in existence

Ready to exploit the invaluable mystery contained in the design process, Vascond, profiting from a lucrative early release of the product, could perform an expensive workshop for each of the remaining four transforming experiments, eventually selling the results at a high price

Dazzled by this magnificent gift, Vascond left his benefactor with tears of gratitude

Returning the next day, September 30, 1887, he learned with great personal pain that Count Raoul Montenegro, taking with him forever the secret of his latest invention, died suddenly of an old heart condition

Vascond published a story featuring the interview he conducted with his now deceased friend, and to a selected assembly of like-minded thinkers, he gave a workshop on the expanding metal in the living room of a rich scientist, charging those in attendance an expensive fee for his dazzling execution of the design process, wherein the lacework was created right before their very eyes, using the mica box, the embers, and the tulle tray with its layer of asbestos

To protect his nest egg, which he only used to provide temporary sustenance, the former voice artist continued his life as a nomadic singer, but managed to give his worn-out body more time for resting and general relaxation

Five years later, his money slowly disappearing, he decided to raise more resources by conducting two more workshops with two of the remaining three metal specimens

Several years passed, softened by the extra funds he had been able to procure, although his once abundant reserves were more precarious than ever

He blessed each day with the memory of Raul, without which his old age would have been full of hardship and a torturous living hell

During his wanderings, Vascond had a roommate whose brutal style could be attributed to bouts of alcoholic rage that appeared soon after he became recently widowed and was stuck with his six year old son, Null

Through the thin walls he could hear the monster screaming and hitting the child while accusing him of stealing his food

The kid would often go out and cry in the arms of the old musician, who would tenderly console him

Revolted by this mistreatment, Vascond offered to adopt Null, whose naive grace would help him attract a crowd

Joyfully accepting this offer, the brute, without a tear, separated from the boy, who left the same day with his savior

Marveling at his new life, compared to his past hell, Null began learning things from the old man, whose guitar inspired his rhythmic movements, which he converted into some lively dances that eventually increased their revenue stream

Later, Vascond observed in the child that he tried to steer the song away from the vocals altogether

Pushing in another direction, Null was initiated into the principles of vaticination by a juggler and soon perfected the art form in his own unique way

Eventually, the nest egg Vascond supplemented his income with had depleted yet again and so for the third time he decided to produce his unique workshop experience, which would require him to go on the road

But shortly after taking leave, the old man, whose voice had always kept clear its vocal capabilities, died during the first wintery cold spell after almost a centenary of life, bequeathing to Null, in addition to the recently acquired sum, the last of the four precious metal rollers given to him by Count Raoul Montenegro

Null, dismayed, had lived with the fear of his benefactor and only friend leaving him behind

Shaken by sobs, he followed alone, absolutely alone, the body of the old musician on its way to the cemetery . . .

Then he returned, staggeringly, into the room where his dear friend had passed away

Now Null was his own master

The previous year, while again passing with Vascond through the town where they had first met, he found out about the death of his father due to alcoholism

He continued to ceaselessly wander around telling fortunes and, to enliven his solitude, took on small beasts who, once purchased, became part of his repertoire

In their turn, a dog, a cat, and a monkey, now all dead, amazed the curious with their divination drawings

Finally, Mopsus, ingeniously educated, surpassed the artistic output of his three predecessors

Null was still holding in reserve the last metal specimen of Count Raoul Montenegro

Awaiting the opportunity to benefit greatly from this specimen, the teenager, with his brief personal history, made sure to exhibit in each of his sessions the plate, the box, the embers, etc., as a way to enrich his program

Camera had paid royally for the group to witness the spectacle of the strange molting process as well as the costs for the lace it would produce, and Null had been supplied with a small amount of coal this day to conduct his experiment

During the teenager's presentation, the metal specimen, warmed by the embers, had grown gradually in the box so that it now almost filled the roll up to it contiguous inner slides

Null, finding the developments insufficient, waited until the lace, still developing, touched the six walls of mica

Having put on, to avoid burning himself, some thickly knitted winter gloves, he opened and emptied the box without resorting to nonconductive handles and stretched the lace on the table for faster cooling

An ecstatic cry escaped everyone's mouth as they stood before this wonderful piece of artisan handiwork, comparable with most Valencian relics

Despite the infinite tenuity of the results, the material component remained metal and and was glittered with moonlight

The precious thing that was illuminated before the entire group left them all without fear, in fact astounded them with its perfect flexibility, equal to that of, say, vaporous gases

Camera took the lace object and handed it to Hello who, confused by the magnanimous gesture, put it up to her chest

The point of the object made a nice contrast to the pink bottom of her shirt and all of a sudden everyone wanted to start feeling her up, bringing to mind their opening breakfast scenario and where it might have gone had they not ventured forth on this near psychedelic journey through the art park

Shimmering lace, light flying off her chest, it was completely cool by now and could be touched in such a way as to make a fresh impression

With utmost care, Null began assembling all of the objects he had unveiled at the performance, the session book, the steel rod, the rosary, the box of straws, the crystal sphere, the now reddened straw, the dice, the astrological codes, the magnifying glass, the sage branch, the ivory leaf, the easel, the mica box, the bag of coal and tulle plate with its spent embers—returning it all back into the expandable rucksack, which was then placed on the back of Mopsus, who was placed back on the ground

Folding his table so he could carry it, the teenager took leave, but not without collecting a spontaneous batch of bills and coins and friendly words

As he walked away, followed by the cock, the artist-entrepreneur, who had managed to give the boy some confidence, informed the group about the magic dice whose sagacity seemed inexplicable

By deciphering in his subject's eyes a sense of precision or vagueness, of joy or relative unhappiness, i.e the *double enigma* of the mental interrogation he had put them under, Null knew how to stealthily manipulate the interior weight of the die, forcing it to fall a certain way

Camera, announcing that all of the secrets to his phenomenal exhibition displayed throughout the park were now known, suggested that the group head back to the villa, where they could enjoy a festive dinner, which would give them all a chance to discuss their collective findings[100]

100. As with all such events hosted by artist-provocateurs, this is when the real story starts, the one timed to swerving biological clocks and unchecked urges.